W. Somerset Maugham is the dean of living novelists. *The Razor's Edge, The Moon and Sixpence, The Painted Veil, Cakes and Ale* and many of his other books have given pleasure to millions. OF HUMAN BONDAGE brought Mr. Maugham his first great success and has since become his most widely-read novel, a classic of our time.

Of
Human Bondage

WITH A NEW INTRODUCTION BY THE AUTHOR
ESPECIALLY WRITTEN
FOR THIS ABRIDGED EDITION

W. SOMERSET MAUGHAM

POCKET BOOKS, INC.
New York

This CARDINAL edition has been specially prepared to make it shorter and more easily read. It is printed from brand-new plates made from completely reset, clear, easy-to-read type

OF HUMAN BONDAGE

Doubleday edition published August, 1915

19 PRINTINGS

POCKET BOOK edition published July, 1950

3 PRINTINGS

CARDINAL edition published March, 1952

5th printing .... June, 1955

L

INTRODUCTION

This book was published thirty-five years ago and since then has been offered to the public in a number of different editions and at a variety of prices. But owing to its length it has been impossible to issue it at a price that would put it within the reach of every pocket. Now, the natural desire of an author is to be read by as wide a circle of readers as possible, and when I was given to understand that only by cutting it could my novel be published in this series, I consented without a minute's hesitation. A novel is not like a fugue, for instance, which if you cut, say, twenty bars from it, would be rendered meaningless, nor like a picture in which one element balances another to complete the composition. A novel is a very loose form of art. You can do almost anything with it. It is also a very imperfect form of art. I have explained elsewhere at some length why this is so, and here I need only refer to the matter very briefly.

The novelist, a working man who wants to earn his living, is obliged to conform to the methods of publication common to the time at which he writes. Thus Dickens contracted to write novels which were to be issued in twenty-four numbers of a specified number of sheets, and so sometimes found himself under the necessity of introducing episodes which merely interrupted the course of his narrative and sometimes, to provide the required amount of matter, quite shamelessly padded. Very good critics are agreed that his novels would be more readable if they were reasonably cut. Balzac again, always short of money, was paid so much a line, and he too, though the greatest novelist of them all, was capable of writing pages which had nothing to do with the story he had to tell. On one occasion, for no reason except, I suppose, that he felt like it, he inserted a long disquisition on Italian art. It may be that in those days people, with more time at their disposal, were willing to put up with these digressions; I don't think they are now, perhaps only because the pace of life has increased, but perhaps also because they have come, instinctively, to demand that a novel should have that greater elegance of form which is obtained by a rigid adherence to its theme.

But the author of a piece of fiction is not only subject to the exigences of the publishers and the public, he is influenced by the climate of opinion prevalent at the time he writes. He is influenced by fashion. The romantic era introduced an interest in description for its own sake and novelists wrote long and detailed descriptions of scenery which most of us now are content to skip. It took them a long time to discover that in this matter a line may give the reader a more vivid picture than a page. At the time *Of Human Bondage* was written many novelists, possibly incited by the deep impression made on them by Samuel Butler's *The Way of All Flesh,* were impelled to write semi-autobiographical novels. I say semi-autobiographical because of course they were works of fiction and it was the right of the authors to alter the facts they were dealing with as they chose. Such a book was *Of Human Bondage.* When I made up my mind to write it I was a popular playwright and much in demand; I retired from the theatre for a couple of years because I knew that by writing it I could rid myself of a great number of unhappy recollections that had not ceased to harrow me. This it did.

But obviously there is a danger in writing a novel with this aim in view. The author writes to disembarrass himself of painful memories; he is not concerned with the reader, but only with his own liberation. Any communication he has to make to the reader is adventitious. It may well be that he attaches significance to certain things which are not significant in themselves, but only to him and because they happened to him. It may well be that in *Of Human Bondage* there are passages or episodes which are of too personal a nature to be of general interest or which owing to the passage of time or a change of fashion no longer have much point. I do not know. I am willing to let others judge of that. A writer is a fool if he thinks that every word he wrote is sacrosanct and that his work will be ruined if a comma is omitted or a semi-colon misplaced. A novel is not a scientific work nor a work of edification. So far as the reader is concerned it is a work which purports to offer him intelligent entertainment. If this book, in this shortened version, finds new readers who get just that from it I shall be well satisfied.

W. Somerset Maugham

Of
Human Bondage

The day broke gray and dull. The clouds hung heavily, and there was a rawness in the air that suggested snow. A woman servant came into a room in which a child was sleeping and drew the curtains. She glanced mechanically at the house opposite, a stucco house with a portico, and went to the child's bed.

"Wake up, Philip," she said.

She pulled down the bed-clothes, took him in her arms, and carried him downstairs. He was only half awake.

"Your mother wants you," she said.

She opened the door of a room on the floor below and took the child over to a bed in which a woman was lying. It was his mother. She stretched out her arms, and the child nestled by her side. He did not ask why he had been awakened. The woman kissed his eyes, and with thin, small hands felt the warm body through his white flannel nightgown. She pressed him closer to herself.

"Are you sleepy, darling?" she said.

Her voice was so weak that it seemed to come already from a great distance. The child did not answer, but smiled comfortably. He was very happy in the large, warm bed, with those soft arms about him. He tried to make himself smaller still as he cuddled up against his mother, and he kissed her sleepily. In a moment he closed his eyes and was fast asleep. The doctor came forwards and stood by the bed-side.

"Oh, don't take him away yet," she moaned.

The doctor, without answering, looked at her gravely. Knowing she would not be allowed to keep the child much longer, the woman kissed him again; and she passed her hand down his body till she came to his feet; she held the right foot in her hand and felt the five small toes; and then slowly passed her hand over the left one. She gave a sob.

"What's the matter?" said the doctor. "You're tired."

She shook her head, unable to speak, and the tears rolled down her cheeks. The doctor bent down.

"Let me take him."

She was too weak to resist his wish, and she gave the child up. The doctor handed him back to his nurse.

"You'd better put him back in his own bed."

"Very well, sir."

The little boy, still sleeping, was taken away. His mother sobbed now broken-heartedly.

"What will happen to him, poor child?"

The monthly nurse tried to quiet her, and presently, from exhaustion, the crying ceased. The doctor walked to a table on the other side of the room, upon which, under a towel, lay the body of a still-born child. He lifted the towel and looked. He was hidden from the bed by a screen, but the woman guessed what he was doing.

"Was it a girl or a boy?" she whispered to the nurse.

"Another boy."

The woman did not answer. In a moment the child's nurse came back. She approached the bed.

"Master Philip never woke up," she said.

There was a pause. Then the doctor felt his patient's pulse once more.

"I don't think there's anything I can do just now," he said. "I'll call again after breakfast."

"I'll show you out, sir," said the child's nurse.

They walked downstairs in silence. In the hall the doctor stopped.

"You've sent for Mrs. Carey's brother-in-law, haven't you?"

"Yes, sir."

"D'you know at what time he'll be here?"

"No, sir, I'm expecting a telegram."

"What about the little boy? I should think he'd be better out of the way."

"Miss Watkin said she'd take him, sir."

"Who's she?"

"She's his godmother, sir. D'you think Mrs. Carey will get over it, sir?"

The doctor shook his head.

It was a week later. Philip was sitting on the floor in the drawing-room at Miss Watkin's house in Onslow Gardens. He was an only child and used to amusing himself. The room was filled with massive furniture, and on each of the sofas were three big cushions. There was a cushion too in each arm-chair. All these he had taken and, with the help of the gilt rout chairs, light and easy to move, had made an elaborate cave in which he could hide himself from the Red Indians who were lurking behind the curtains. He put his ear to the floor and listened to the herd of buffaloes that raced across the prairie. Presently, hearing the door open, he held his breath so that he might not be discovered; but a violent hand pulled away a chair and the cushions fell down.

"You naughty boy, Miss Watkin *will* be cross with you."

"Hulloa, Emma!" he said.

The nurse bent down and kissed him, then began to shake out the cushions, and put them back in their places.

"Am I to come home?" he asked.

"Yes, I've come to fetch you."

"You've got a new dress on."

It was in eighteen-eighty-five, and she wore a bustle. Her gown was of black velvet, with tight sleeves and sloping shoulders, and the skirt had three large flounces. She wore a black bonnet with velvet strings. She hesitated. The question she had expected did not come, and so she could not give the answer she had prepared.

"Aren't you going to ask how your mamma is?" she said at length.

"Oh, I forgot. How is mamma?"

Now she was ready.

"Your mamma is quite well and happy."

"Oh, I am glad."

"Your mamma's gone away. You won't ever see her any more."

Philip did not know what she meant.

"Why not?"

"Your mamma's in heaven."

She began to cry, and Philip, though he did not quite understand, cried too. Emma was a tall, big-boned woman, with fair hair and large features. She came from Devonshire and, notwithstanding her many years of service in London, had never lost the breadth of her accent. Her tears increased her emotion, and she pressed the little boy to her heart. She felt vaguely the pity of that child deprived of the only love in the world that is quite unselfish. It seemed dreadful that he must be handed over to strangers. But in a little while she pulled herself together.

"Your Uncle William is waiting in to see you," she said. "Go and say good-bye to Miss Watkin, and we'll go home."

"I don't want to say good-bye," he answered, instinctively anxious to hide his tears.

"Very well, run upstairs and get your hat."

He fetched it, and when he came down Emma was waiting for him in the hall. He heard the sound of voices in the study behind the dining-room. He paused. He knew that Miss Watkin and her sister were talking to friends, and it seemed to him—he was nine years old—that if he went in they would be sorry for him.

"I think I'll go and say good-bye to Miss Watkin."

"I think you'd better," said Emma.

"Go in and tell them I'm coming," he said.

He wished to make the most of his opportunity. Emma

knocked at the door and walked in. He heard her speak.

"Master Philip wants to say good-bye to you, miss."

"There was a sudden hush of the conversation, and Philip limped in. Henrietta Watkin was a stout woman, with a red face and dyed hair. In those days to dye the hair excited comment, and Philip had heard much gossip at home when his godmother's changed colour. She lived with an elder sister, who had resigned herself contentedly to old age. Two ladies, whom Philip did not know, were calling, and they looked at him curiously.

"My poor child," said Miss Watkin, opening her arms.

She began to cry. Philip understood now why she had not been in to luncheon and why she wore a black dress. She could not speak.

"I've got to go home," said Philip, at last.

He disengaged himself from Miss Watkin's arms, and she kissed him again. Then he went to her sister and bade her good-bye too. One of the strange ladies asked if she might kiss him, and he gravely gave her permission. Though crying, he keenly enjoyed the sensation he was causing; he would have been glad to stay a little longer to be made much of, but felt they expected him to go, so he said that Emma was waiting for him. He went out of the room. Emma had gone downstairs to speak with a friend in the basement, and he waited for her on the landing. He heard Henrietta Watkin's voice.

"His mother was my greatest friend. I can't bear to think that she's dead."

"You oughtn't to have gone to the funeral, Henrietta," said her sister. "I knew it would upset you."

Then one of the strangers spoke.

"Poor little boy, it's dreadful to think of him quite alone in the world. I see he limps."

"Yes, he's got a club-foot. It was such a grief to his mother."

Then Emma came back. They called a hansom, and she told the driver where to go.

When they reached the house Mrs. Carey had died in—it was in a dreary, respectable street between Notting Hill Gate and High Street, Kensington—Emma led Philip into the drawing-room. His uncle was writing letters of thanks for the wreaths which had been sent. One of them, which had arrived too late for the funeral, lay in its cardboard box on the hall-table.

"Here's Master Philip," said Emma.

Mr. Carey stood up slowly and shook hands with the little boy. Then on second thoughts he bent down and kissed his forehead. He was a man of somewhat less than average height, inclined to corpulence, with his hair, worn long, arranged over the scalp so as to conceal his baldness. He was clean-shaven. His features were regular, and it was possible to imagine that in his youth he had been good-looking. On his watch-chain he wore a gold cross.

"You're going to live with me now, Philip," said Mr. Carey. "Shall you like that?"

Two years before Philip had been sent down to stay at the vicarage after an attack of chicken-pox; but there remained with him a recollection of an attic and a large garden rather than of his uncle and aunt.

"Yes."

"You must look upon me and your Aunt Louisa as your father and mother."

The child's mouth trembled a little, he reddened, but did not answer.

"Your dear mother left you in my charge."

Mr. Carey had no great ease in expressing himself. When the news came that his sister-in-law was dying, he set off at once for London, but on the way thought of nothing but the disturbance in his life that would be caused if her death forced him to undertake the care of her son. He was well over fifty, and his wife, to whom he had been married for thirty years, was childless; he did not look forward with any pleasure to the presence of a small boy who might be noisy and rough. He had never much liked his sister-in-law.

"I'm going to take you down to Blackstable tomorrow," he said.

"With Emma?"

The child put his hand in hers, and she pressed it.

"I'm afraid Emma must go away," said Mr. Carey.

"But I want Emma to come with me."

Philip began to cry, and the nurse could not help crying too. Mr. Carey looked at them helplessly.

"I think you'd better leave me alone with Master Philip for a moment."

"Very good, sir."

Though Philip clung to her, she released herself gently. Mr. Carey took the boy on his knee and put his arm round him.

"You mustn't cry," he said. "You're too old to have a nurse now. We must see about sending you to school."

"I want Emma to come with me," the child repeated.

"It costs too much money, Philip. Your father didn't leave very much, and I don't know what's become of it. You must look at every penny you spend."

Mr. Carey had called the day before on the family solicitor. Philip's father was a surgeon in good practice, and his hospital appointments suggested an established position; so that it was a surprise on his sudden death from blood-poisoning to find that he had left his widow little more than his life insurance and what could be got for the lease of their house in Bruton Street. This was six months ago; and Mrs. Carey, already in delicate health, finding herself with child, had lost her head and accepted for the lease the first offer that was made. She stored her furniture, and, at a rent which the parson thought outrageous, took a furnished house for a year, so that she might suffer from no inconvenience till her child was born. But she had never been used to the management of money, and was unable to adapt her expenditure to her altered circumstances. The little she had slipped through her fingers in one way and another, so that now, when all expenses were paid, not much more than two thousand pounds remained to support the boy till he was able to earn his own living. It was impossible to explain all this to Philip and he was sobbing still.

"You'd better go to Emma," Mr. Carey said, feeling that she could console the child better than anyone.

Without a word Philip slipped off his uncle's knee, but Mr. Carey stopped him.

"We must go tomorrow, because on Saturday I've got to prepare my sermon, and you must tell Emma to get your things ready today. You can bring all your toys. And if you want anything to remember your father and mother by you can take one thing for each of them. Everything else is going to be sold."

The boy slipped out of the room. Mr. Carey was unused to work, and he turned to his correspondence with resentment. On one side of the desk was a bundle of bills, and these filled him with irritation. One especially seemed preposterous. Immediately after Mrs. Carey's death Emma had ordered from the florist masses of white flowers for the room in which the dead woman lay. It was sheer waste of money. Emma took far too much upon herself. Even if there had been no financial necessity, he would have dismissed her.

But Philip went to her, and hid his face in her bosom, and wept as though his heart would break. And she, feeling that he was almost her own son—she had taken him when he was a month old—consoled him with soft words. She promised that she would come and see him sometimes, and that she would never forget him; and she told him about the country he was going to and about her own home in Devonshire—her father kept a turnpike on the highroad that led to Exeter, and there were pigs in the sty, and there was a cow, and the cow had just had a calf—till Philip forgot his tears and grew excited at the thought of his approaching journey. Presently she put him down, for there was much to be done, and he helped her to lay out his clothes on the bed. She sent him into the nursery to gather up his toys, and in a little while he was playing happily.

But at last he grew tired of being alone and went back to the bed-room, in which Emma was now putting his things into a big tin box; he remembered then that his uncle had said he might take something to remember his father and mother by. He told Emma and asked her what he should take.

"You'd better go into the drawing-room and see what you fancy."

"Uncle William's there."

"Never mind that. They're your own things now."

Philip went downstairs slowly and found the door open. Mr. Carey had left the room. Philip walked slowly round. They had been in the house so short a time that there was little in it that had a particular interest to him. It was a stranger's room, and Philip saw nothing that struck his fancy. But he knew which were his mother's things and which belonged to the landlord, and presently fixed on a little clock that he had once heard his mother say she liked. With this he walked again rather disconsolately upstairs. Outside the door of his mother's bed-room he stopped and listened. Though no one had told him not to go in, he had a feeling that it would be wrong to do so; he was a little frightened, and his heart beat uncomfortably; but at the same time something impelled him to turn the handle. He turned it very gently, as if to prevent anyone within from hearing, and then slowly pushed the door open. He stood on the threshold for a moment before he had the courage to enter. He was not frightened now, but it seemed strange. He closed the door behind him. The blinds were drawn, and the room, in the cold light of a January afternoon, was dark. On the dressing-table were Mrs. Carey's brushes and the hand mirror. In a little tray were hairpins. There was a photograph of himself on the chimney-piece and one of his father. He had often been in the room when his mother was not in it, but now it seemed different. There was something curious in the look of the chairs. The bed was made as though someone were going to sleep in it that night, and in a case on the pillow was a night-dress.

Philip opened a large cupboard filled with dresses and stepping in, took as many of them as he could in his arms and buried his face in them. They smelt of the scent his mother used. Then he pulled open the drawers, filled with his mother's things, and looked at them: there were lavender bags among the linen, and their scent was fresh and pleasant. The strangeness of the room left it, and it seemed to him that his mother had just gone out for a walk. She would be in presently and would come upstairs to have nursery tea with him. And he seemed to feel her kiss on his lips.

It was not true that he would never see her again. It was not true simply because it was impossible. He climbed up on the bed and put his head on the pillow. He lay there quite still.

Philip parted from Emma with tears, but the journey to Blackstable amused him, and, when they arrived, he was resigned and cheerful. Blackstable was sixty miles from London. Giving their luggage to a porter, Mr. Carey set out to walk with Philip to the vicarage; it took them little more than five minutes, and, when they reached it, Philip suddenly remembered the gate. It was red and five-barred: it swung both ways on easy hinges; and it was possible, though forbidden, to swing backwards and forwards on it. They walked through the garden to the front-door. This was only used by visitors and on Sundays, and on special occasions, as when the Vicar went up to London or came back. The traffic of the house took place through a side-door, and there was a back door as well for the gardener and for beggars and tramps. It was a fairly large house of yellow brick, with a red roof, built about five and twenty years before in an ecclesiastical style. The front-door was like a church porch, and the drawing-room windows were gothic.

Mrs. Carey, knowing by what train they were coming, waited in the drawing-room and listened for the click of the gate. When she heard it she went to the door.

"There's Aunt Louisa," said Mr. Carey, when he saw her. "Run and give her a kiss."

Philip started to run, awkwardly, trailing his club-foot, and then stopped. Mrs. Carey was a little, shrivelled woman of the same age as her husband, with a face extraordinarily filled with deep wrinkles, and pale blue eyes. Her gray hair was arranged in ringlets according to the fashion of her youth. She wore a black dress, and her only ornament was a gold chain, from which hung a cross. She had a shy manner and a gentle voice.

"Did you walk, William?" she said, almost reproachfully, as she kissed her husband.

"I didn't think of it," he answered, with a glance at his nephew.

"It didn't hurt you to walk, Philip, did it?" she asked the child.

"No. I always walk."

He was a little surprised at their conversation. Aunt Louisa told him to come in, and they entered the hall. It was paved with red and yellow tiles, on which alternately were a Greek Cross and the Lamb of God. An imposing staircase led out of the hall. It was of polished pine, with a peculiar smell, and had been put in because fortunately, when the church was reseated, enough wood remained over.

The balusters were decorated with emblems of the Four Evangelists.

"I've had the stove lighted as I thought you'd be cold after your journey," said Mrs. Carey.

It was a large black stove that stood in the hall and was only lighted if the weather was very bad and the Vicar had a cold. It was not lighted if Mrs. Carey had a cold. Coal was expensive. Besides, Mary Ann, the maid, didn't like fires all over the place. If they wanted all them fires they must keep a second girl. In the winter Mr. and Mrs. Carey lived in the dining-room so that one fire should do, and in the summer they could not get out of the habit, so the drawing-room was used only by Mr. Carey on Sunday afternoons for his nap. But every Saturday he had a fire in the study so that he could write his sermon.

Aunt Louisa took Philip upstairs and showed him into a tiny bed-room that looked out on the drive. Immediately in front of the window was a large tree, which Philip remembered now because the branches were so low that it was possible to climb quite high up it.

"A small room for a small boy," said Mrs. Carey. "You won't be frightened at sleeping alone?"

"Oh, no."

On his first visit to the vicarage he had come with his nurse, and Mrs. Carey had had little to do with him. She looked at him now with some uncertainty.

"Can you wash your own hands, or shall I wash them for you?"

"I can wash myself," he answered firmly.

"Well, I shall look at them when you come down to tea," said Mrs. Carey.

She knew nothing about children. After it was settled that Philip should come down to Blackstable, Mrs. Carey had thought much how she should treat him; she was anxious to do her duty; but now he was there she found herself just as shy of him as he was of her. She hoped he would not be noisy and rough, because her husband did not like rough and noisy boys. Mrs. Carey made an excuse to leave Philip alone, but in a moment came back and knocked at the door; she asked him, without coming in, if he could pour out the water himself. Then she went downstairs and rang the bell for tea.

The dining-room, large and well-proportioned, had windows on two sides of it, with heavy curtains of red rep; there was a big table in the middle; and at one end an imposing mahogany sideboard with a looking-glass in it. In one corner stood a harmonium. On each side of the fireplace were chairs covered in stamped leather, each with an antimacassar; one had arms and was called the husband, and the other had none and was called the wife. Mrs. Carey never sat in the arm-chair: she said she preferred a chair that was not too comfortable; there was always a lot to do, and if her chair had had arms she might not be so ready to leave it.

Mr. Carey was making up the fire when Philip came in, and he pointed out to his nephew that there were two pokers. One was large and bright and polished and unused, and was called the Vicar; and the other, which was much smaller and had evidently passed through many fires, was called the Curate.

"What are we waiting for?" said Mr. Carey.

"I told Mary Ann to make you an egg. I thought you'd be hungry after your journey."

Mrs. Carey thought the journey from London to Blackstable very tiring. She seldom travelled herself, for the living was only three hundred a year, and, when her husband wanted a holiday, since there was not money for two, he went by himself. He was very fond of Church Congresses and usually managed to go up to London once a year; and once he had been to Paris for the exhibition, and two or three times to Switzerland. Mary Ann brought in the egg, and they sat down. The chair was much too low for

Philip, and for a moment neither Mr. Carey nor his wife knew what to do.

"I'll put some books under him," said Mary Ann.

She took from the top of the harmonium the large Bible and the prayer-book from which the Vicar was accustomed to read prayers, and put them on Philip's chair.

"Oh, William, he can't sit on the Bible," said Mrs. Carey, in a shocked tone. "Couldn't you get him some books out of the study?"

Mr. Carey considered the question for an instant.

"I don't think it matters this once if you put the prayer-book on the top, Mary Ann," he said. "The book of Common Prayer is the composition of men like ourselves. It has no claim to divine authorship."

"I hadn't thought of that, William," said Aunt Louisa.

Philip perched himself on the books, and the Vicar, having said grace, cut the top off his egg.

"There," he said, handing it to Philip, "you can eat my top if you like."

Philip would have liked an egg to himself, but he was not offered one, so took what he could.

"How have the chickens been laying since I went away?" asked the Vicar.

"Oh, they've been dreadful, only one or two a day."

"How did you like that top, Philip?" asked his uncle.

"Very much, thank you."

"You shall have another one on Sunday afternoon."

Mr. Carey always had a boiled egg at tea on Sunday, so that he might be fortified for the evening service.

Philip had led always the solitary life of an only child, and his loneliness at the vicarage was no greater than it had been when his mother lived. He made friends with Mary Ann. She was a chubby little person of thirty-five, the daughter of a fisherman, and had come to the vicarage at eighteen; it was her first place and she had no intention of leaving it;

but she held a possible marriage as a rod over the timid heads of her master and mistress. Her father and mother lived in a little house off Harbour Street, and she went to see them on her evenings out. Her stories of the sea touched Philip's imagination, and the narrow alleys round the harbour grew rich with the romance which his young fancy lent them. One evening he asked whether he might go home with her; but his aunt was afraid that he might catch something, and his uncle said that evil communications corrupted good manners. He disliked the fisher folk, who were rough, uncouth, and went to chapel. But Philip was more comfortable in the kitchen than in the dining-room, and, whenever he could, he took his toys and played there. His aunt was not sorry. She did not like disorder, and though she recognised that boys must be expected to be untidy she preferred that he should make a mess in the kitchen. If he fidgetted his uncle was apt to grow restless and say it was high time he went to school. Mrs. Carey thought Philip very young for this, and her heart went out to the motherless child; but her attempts to gain his affection were awkward, and the boy, feeling shy, received her demonstrations with so much sullenness that she was mortified. Sometimes she heard his shrill voice raised in laughter in the kitchen, but when she went in, he grew suddenly silent, and he flushed darkly when Mary Ann explained the joke. Mrs. Carey could not see anything amusing in what she heard, and she smiled with constraint.

"He seems happier with Mary Ann than with us, William," she said, when she returned to her sewing.

"One can see he's been very badly brought up. He wants licking into shape."

On the second Sunday after Philip arrived an unlucky incident occurred. Mr. Carey had retired as usual after dinner for a little snooze in the drawing-room, but he was in an irritable mood and could not sleep. Josiah Graves that morning had objected strongly to some candlesticks with

which the Vicar had adorned the altar. He had bought them
second-hand in Tercanbury, and he thought they looked
very well. But Josiah Graves said they were popish. This
was a taunt that always aroused the Vicar. He had been at
Oxford during the movement which ended in the secession
from the Established Church of Edward Manning, and he
felt a certain sympathy for the Church of Rome. He would
willingly have made the service more ornate than had been
usual in the low-church parish of Blackstable, and in his
secret soul he yearned for processions and lighted candles.
He drew the line at incense. He hated the word protestant.
He called himself a Catholic. He was accustomed to say that
Papists required an epithet, they were Roman Catholic; but
the Church of England was Catholic in the best, the fullest,
and the noblest sense of the term. He was pleased to think
that his shaven face gave him the look of a priest, and in his
youth he had possessed an ascetic air which added to the
impression. He often related that on one of his holidays in
Boulogne, one of those holidays upon which his wife for
economy's sake did not accompany him, when he was sitting
in a church, the *curé* had come up to him and invited him
to preach a sermon. He dismissed his curates when they married, having decided views on the celibacy of the unbeneficed
clergy. But when at an election the Liberals had written
on his garden fence in large blue letters: This way to Rome,
he had been very angry, and threatened to prosecute the
leaders of the Liberal party in Blackstable. He made up his
mind now that nothing Josiah Graves said would induce
him to remove the candlesticks from the altar, and he muttered Bismarck to himself once or twice irritably.

Suddenly he heard an unexpected noise. He pulled the
handkerchief off his face, got up from the sofa on which he
was lying, and went into the dining-room. Philip was seated
on the table with all his bricks around him. He had built a
monstrous castle, and some defect in the foundation had
just brought the structure down in noisy ruin.

"What are you doing with those bricks, Philip? You know you're not allowed to play games on Sunday."

Philip stared at him for a moment with frightened eyes, and, as his habit was, flushed deeply.

"I always used to play at home," he answered.

"I'm sure your dear mamma never allowed you to do such a wicked thing as that."

Philip did not know it was wicked; but if it was, he did not wish it to be supposed that his mother had consented to it. He hung his head and did not answer.

"Don't you know it's very, very wicked to play on Sunday? What d'you suppose it's called the day of rest for? You're going to church tonight, and how can you face your Maker when you've been breaking one of His laws in the afternoon?"

Mr. Carey told him to put the bricks away at once, and stood over him while Philip did so.

"You're a very naughty boy," he repeated. "Think of the grief you're causing your poor mother in heaven."

Philip felt inclined to cry, but he had an instinctive disinclination to letting other people see his tears, and he clenched his teeth to prevent the sobs from escaping. Mr. Carey sat down in his arm-chair and began to turn over the pages of a book. Philip stood at the window. The vicarage was set back from the highroad to Tercanbury, and from the dining-room one saw a semicircular strip of lawn and then as far as the horizon green fields. Sheep were grazing in them. The sky was forlorn and gray. Philip felt infinitely unhappy.

Presently Mary Ann came in to lay the tea, and Aunt Louisa descended the stairs.

"Have you had a nice little nap, William?" she asked.

"No," he answered. "Philip made so much noise that I couldn't sleep a wink."

This was not quite accurate, for he had been kept awake by his own thoughts; and Philip, listening sullenly, reflected that he had only made a noise once, and there was no reason why his uncle should not have slept before or after. When Mrs. Carey asked for an explanation the Vicar narrated the facts.

"He hasn't even said he was sorry," he finished.

"Oh, Philip, I'm sure you're sorry," said Mrs. Carey, anxious that the child should not seem wickeder to his uncle than need be.

Philip did not reply. He went on munching his bread and butter. He did not know what power it was in him that prevented him from making any expression to regret. He felt his ears tingling, he was a little inclined to cry, but no word would issue from his lips.

"You needn't make it worse by sulking," said Mr. Carey.

Tea was finished in silence. Mrs. Carey looked at Philip surreptitiously now and then, but the Vicar elaborately ignored him. When Philip saw his uncle go upstairs to get ready for church he went into the hall and got his hat and coat, but when the Vicar came downstairs and saw him, he said:

"I don't wish you to go to church tonight, Philip. I don't think you're in a proper frame of mind to enter the House of God."

Philip did not say a word. He felt it was a deep humiliation that was placed upon him, and his cheeks reddened. He stood silently watching his uncle put on his broad hat and his voluminous cloak. Mrs. Carey as usual went to the door to see him off. Then she turned to Philip.

"Never mind, Philip, you won't be a naughty boy next Sunday, will you, and then your uncle will take you to church with him in the evening."

She took off his hat and coat, and led him into the dining-room.

"Shall you and I read the service together, Philip, and we'll sing the hymns at the harmonium. Would you like that?"

Philip shook his head decidedly. Mrs. Carey was taken

aback. If he would not read the evening service with her she did not know what to do with him.

"Then what would you like to do until your uncle comes back?" she asked helplessly.

Philip broke his silence at last.

"I want to be left alone," he said.

"Philip, how can you say anything so unkind? Don't you know that your uncle and I only want your good? Don't you love me at all?"

"I hate you. I wish you was dead."

Mrs. Carey gasped. He said the words so savagely that it gave her quite a start. She had nothing to say. She sat down in her husband's chair; and as she thought of her desire to love the friendless, crippled boy and her eager wish that he should love her—she was a barren woman and, even though it was clearly God's will that she should be childless, she could scarcely bear to look at little children sometimes, her heart ached so—the tears rose to her eyes and one by one, slowly, rolled down her cheeks. Philip watched her in amazement. She took out her handkerchief, and now she cried without restraint. Suddenly Philip realised that she was crying because of what he had said, and he was sorry. He went up to her silently and kissed her. It was the first kiss he had ever given her without being asked. And the poor lady, so small in her black satin, shrivelled up and sallow, with her funny corkscrew curls, took the little boy on her lap and put her arms around him and wept as though her heart would break. But her tears were partly tears of happiness, for she felt that the strangeness between them was gone. She loved him now with a new love because he had made her suffer.

The Careys made up their minds to send Philip to King's School at Tercanbury. The neighbouring clergy sent their sons there. It was united by long tradition to the Cathedral: its headmaster was an honorary Canon, and a past headmaster was the Archdeacon. Boys were encouraged there to aspire to Holy Orders, and the education was such as might prepare an honest lad to spend his life in God's service. A preparatory school was attached to it, and to this it was arranged that Philip should go. Mr. Carey took him into Tercanbury one Thursday afternoon towards the end of September. All day Philip had been excited and rather frightened. He knew little of school life but what he had read in the stories of *The Boy's Own Paper*. He had also read *Eric, or Little by Little*.

When they got out of the train at Tercanbury, Philip felt sick with apprehension, and during the drive in to the town sat pale and silent. The high brick wall in front of the school gave it the look of a prison. There was a little door in it, which opened on their ringing; and a clumsy, untidy man came out and fetched Philip's tin trunk and his play-box. They were shown into the drawing-room; it was filled with massive, ugly furniture, and the chairs of the suite were placed round the walls with a forbidding rigidity. They waited for the headmaster.

"What's Mr. Watson like?" asked Philip, after a while.

"You'll see for yourself."

There was another pause. Mr. Carey wondered why the headmaster did not come. Presently Philip made an effort and spoke again.

"Tell him I've got a club-foot," he said.

Before Mr. Carey could speak the door burst open and Mr. Watson swept into the room. To Philip he seemed gigantic. He was a man of over six feet high, and broad, with enormous hands and a great red beard; he talked loudly in a jovial manner; but his aggressive cheerfulness struck terror in Philip's heart. He shook hands with Mr. Carey, and then took Philip's small hand in his.

"Well, young fellow, are you glad to come to school?" he shouted.

Philip reddened and found no word to answer.

"How old are you?"

"Nine," said Philip.

"You must say sir," said his uncle.

"I expect you've got a good lot to learn," the head-master bellowed cheerily.

To give the boy confidence he began to tickle him with rough fingers. Philip, feeling shy and uncomfortable, squirmed under his touch.

"I've put him in the small dormitory for the present. . . . You'll like that, won't you?" he added to Philip. "Only eight of you in there. You won't feel so strange."

Then the door opened, and Mrs. Watson came in. She was a dark woman with black hair, neatly parted in the middle. She had curiously thick lips and a small round nose. Her eyes were large and black. There was a singular coldness in her appearance. She seldom spoke and smiled more seldom still. Her husband introduced Mr. Carey to her, and then gave Philip a friendly push towards her.

"This is a new boy, Helen. His name's Carey."

Without a word she shook hands with Philip and then sat down, not speaking, while the headmaster asked Mr. Carey how much Philip knew and what books he had been working with. The Vicar of Blackstable was a little embarrassed by Mr. Watson's boisterous heartiness, and in a moment or two got up.

"I think I'd better leave Philip with you now."

"That's all right," said Mr. Watson. "He'll be safe with me. He'll get on like a house on fire. Won't you, young fellow?"

Without waiting for an answer from Philip the big man burst into a great bellow of laughter. Mr. Carey kissed Philip on the forehead and went away.

"Come along, young fellow," shouted Mr. Watson. "I'll show you the school-room."

He swept out of the drawing-room with giant strides, and Philip hurriedly limped behind him. He was taken into a long, bare room with two tables that ran along its whole length; on each side of them were wooden forms.

"Nobody much here yet," said Mr. Watson. "I'll just show you the playground, and then I'll leave you to shift for yourself."

Mr. Watson led the way. Philip found himself in a large playground with high brick walls on three sides of it. On the fourth side was an iron railing through which you saw a vast lawn and beyond this some of the buildings of King's School. One small boy was wandering disconsolately, kicking up the gravel as he walked.

"Hulloa, Venning," shouted Mr. Watson. "When did you turn up?"

The small boy came forward and shook hands.

"Here's a new boy. He's older and bigger than you, so don't you bully him."

The headmaster glared amicably at the two children, filling them with fear by the roar of his voice, and then with a guffaw left them.

"What's your name?"

"Carey."

"What's your father?"

"He's dead."

"Oh! Does your mother wash?"

"My mother's dead too."

Philip thought this answer would cause the boy a certain awkwardness, but Venning was not to be turned from his facetiousness for so little.

"Well, did she wash?" he went on.

"Yes," said Philip indignantly.

"She was a washerwoman then?"

"No, she wasn't."

"Then she didn't wash."

The little boy crowed with delight at the success of his dialectic. Then he caught sight of Philip's feet.

"What's the matter with your foot?"

Philip instinctively tried to withdraw it from sight. He hid it behind the one which was whole.

"I've got a club-foot," he answered.

"How did you get it?"

"I've always had it."

"Let's have a look."

"No."

"Don't then."

The little boy accompanied the words with a sharp kick on Philip's shin, which Philip did not expect and thus could not guard against. The pain was so great that it made him gasp, but greater than the pain was the surprise. He did not know why Venning kicked him. He had not the presence of mind to give him a black eye. Besides, the boy was smaller than he, and he had read in *The Boy's Own Paper* that it was a mean thing to hit anyone smaller than yourself. While Philip was nursing his shin a third boy appeared, and his tormentor left him. In a little while he noticed that the pair were talking about him, and he felt they were looking at his feet. He grew hot and uncomfortable.

But others arrived, a dozen together, and then more, and they began to talk about their doings during the holidays, where they had been, and what wonderful cricket they had played. A few new boys appeared, and with these presently Philip found himself talking. He was shy and nervous. He was anxious to make himself pleasant, but he could not think of anything to say. He was asked a great many questions and answered them all quite willingly. One boy asked him whether he could play cricket.

"No," answered Philip. "I've got a club-foot."

The boy looked down quickly and reddened. Philip saw that he felt he had asked an unseemly question. He was too shy to apologise and looked at Philip awkwardly.

As time went on Philip's deformity ceased to interest. It was accepted like one boy's red hair and another's unreasonable corpulence. But meanwhile he had grown horribly sensitive. He never ran if he could help it, because he knew it made his limp more conspicuous, and he adopted a peculiar walk. He stood still as much as he could, with his club-foot behind the other, so that it should not attract notice, and he was constantly on the look out for any reference to it. Because he could not join in the games which other boys played, their life remained strange to him; he only interested himself from the outside in their doings; and it seemed to him that there was a barrier between them and him. Sometimes they seemed to think that it was his fault if he could not play football, and he was unable to make them understand. He was left a good deal to himself. He had been inclined to talkativeness, but gradually he became silent. He began to think of the difference between himself and others.

Two years passed, and Philip was nearly twelve. He was in the first form, within two or three places of the top, and after Christmas when several boys would be leaving for the senior school he would be head boy. He had already quite a collection of prizes, worthless books on bad paper, but in gorgeous bindings decorated with the arms of the school: his position had freed him from bullying, and he was not unhappy. His fellows forgave him his success because of his deformity.

"After all, it's jolly easy for him to get prizes," they said, "there's nothing he *can* do but swat."

He had lost his early terror of Mr. Watson. He had grown used to the loud voice, and when the headmaster's heavy hand was laid on his shoulder Philip discerned vaguely the intention of a caress. He had the good memory which is more useful for scholastic achievements than mental power, and he knew Mr. Watson expected him to leave the preparatory school with a scholarship.

But he had grown very self-conscious. The new-born child does not realise that his body is more a part of himself than surrounding objects, and will play with his toes without any feeling that they belong to him more than the rattle by his side; and it is only by degrees, through pain, that he understands the fact of the body. And experiences of the same kind are necessary for the individual to become conscious of himself; but here there is the difference that, although everyone becomes equally conscious of his body as a separate and complete organism, everyone does not become equally consicous of himself as a complete and separate personality. The feeling of apartness from others comes to most with puberty, but it is not always developed to such a degree as to make the difference between the individual and his fellows noticeable to the individual. It is such as he, as little conscious of himself as the bee in a hive, who are the lucky in life, for they have the best chance of happiness: their activities are shared by all, and their pleasures are only pleasures because they are enjoyed in common; you will see them on Whit-Monday dancing on Hampstead Heath, shouting at a football match, or from club windows in Pall Mall cheering a royal procession. It is because of them that man has been called a social animal.

Philip passed from the innocence of childhood to bitter consciousness of himself by the ridicule which his club-foot had excited. The circumstances of his case were so peculiar that he could not apply to them the ready-made rules which acted well enough in ordinary affairs, and he was forced to think for himself. The many books he had read filled his mind with ideas which, because he only half understood them, gave more scope to his imagination. Beneath his painful shyness something was growing up within him, and obscurely he realised his personality. But at times it gave him odd surprises; he did things, he knew not why, and afterwards when he thought of them found himself all at sea.

Then a wave of religiosity passed through the school. Bad

language was no longer heard, and the little nastinesses of small boys were looked upon with hostility; the bigger boys, like the lords temporal of the Middle Ages, used the strength of their arms to persuade those weaker than themselves to virtuous courses.

Philip, his restless mind avid for new things, became very devout. He heard soon that it was possible to join a Bible League, and wrote to London for particulars. These consisted in a form to be filled up with applicant's name, age, and school; a solemn declaration to be signed that he would read a set portion of Holy Scripture every night for a year; and a request for half a crown; this, is was explained, was demanded partly to prove the earnestness of the applicant's desire to become a member of the League, and partly to cover clerical expenses. Phillip duly sent the papers and the money, and in return received a calendar worth about a penny, on which was set down the appointed passage to be read each day, and a sheet of paper on one side of which was a picture of the Good Shepherd and a lamb, and on the other, decoratively framed in red lines, a short prayer which had to be said before beginning to read.

Every evening he undressed as quickly as possible in order to have time for his task before the gas was put out. He read industriously, as he read always, without criticism, stories of cruelty, deceit, ingratitude, dishonesty, and low cunning. Actions which would have excited his horror in the life about him, in the reading passed through his mind without comment, because they were committed under direct inspiration of God. The method of the League was to alternate a book of the Old Testament with a book of the New, and one night Philip came across these words of Jesus Christ:

If ye have faith, and doubt not, ye shall not only do this which is done to the fig-tree, but also if ye shall say unto this mountain, Be thou removed, and be thou cast into the sea; it shall be done.

*And all this, whatsoever ye shall ask in prayer, believing,
ye shall receive.*

They made no particular impression on him, but it happened that two or three days later, being Sunday, the Canon
in residence chose them for the text of his sermon. Even if
Philip had wanted to hear this it would have been impossible, for the boys of King's School sit in the choir, and the
pulpit stands at the cornor of the transept so that the preach-
er's back is almost turned to them. The distance also is so
great that it needs a man with a fine voice and a knowledge
of elocution to make himself heard in the choir; and according to long usage the Canons of Tercanbury are chosen for
their learning rather than for any qualities which might be
of use in a cathedral church. But the words of the text, perhaps because he had read them so short a while before, came
clearly enough to Philip's ears, and they seemed on a sudden
to have a personal application. He thought about them
through most of the sermon, and that night, on getting into
bed, he turned over the pages of the Gospel and found once
more the passage. Though he believed implicitly everything
he saw in print, he had learned already that in the Bible
things that said one thing quite clearly often mysteriously
meant another. There was no one he liked to ask at school,
so he kept the question he had in mind till the Christmas
holidays, and then one day he made an opportunity. It was
after supper and prayers were just finished. Mrs. Carey was
counting the eggs that Mary Ann had brought in as usual
and writing on each one the date. Philip stood at the table
and pretended to turn listlessly the pages of the Bible.

"I say, Uncle William, this passage here, does it really
mean that?"

He put his finger against it as though he had come across
it accidentally.

Mr. Carey looked up over his spectacles. He was holding
The Blackstable Times in front of the fire. It had come in

that evening damp from the press, and the Vicar always aired it for ten minutes before he began to read.

"What passage is that?" he asked.

"Why, this about if you have faith you can remove mountains."

"If it says so in the Bible it is so, Philip," said Mrs. Carey gently, taking up the plate-basket.

Philip looked at his uncle for an answer.

"It's a matter of faith."

"D'you mean to say that if you really believed you could move mountains you could?"

"By the grace of God," said the Vicar.

"Now, say good-night to your uncle, Philip," said Aunt Louisa. "You're not wanting to move a mountain tonight, are you?"

Philip allowed himself to be kissed on the forehead by his uncle and preceded Mrs. Carey upstairs. He had got the information he wanted. His little room was icy, and he shivered when he put on his nightgown. But he always felt that his prayers were more pleasing to God when he said them under conditions of discomfort. The coldness of his hands and feet were an offering to the Almighty. And tonight he sank on his knees, buried his face in his hands, and prayed to God with all his might that He would make his club-foot whole. It was a very small thing beside the moving of mountains. He knew that God could do it if He wished, and his own faith was complete. Next morning, finishing his prayers with the same request, he fixed a date for the miracle.

"Oh, God, in Thy loving mercy and goodness, if it be Thy will, please make my foot all right on the night before I go back to school."

He was glad to get his petition into a formula, and he repeated it later in the dining-room during the short pause which the Vicar always made after prayers, before he rose from his knees. He said it again in the evening and again,

shivering in his nightshirt, before he got into bed. And he
believed. For once he looked forward with eagerness to the
end of the holidays. He laughed to himself as he thought of
his uncle's astonishment when he ran down the stairs three
at a time; and after breakfast he and Aunt Louisa would
have to hurry out and buy a new pair of boots. At school
they would be astounded.

"Hulloa, Carey, what have you done with your foot?"

"Oh, it's all right now," he would answer casually, as
though it were the most natural thing in the world.

He would be able to play football. His heart leaped as he
saw himself running, running, faster than any of the other
boys. At the end of the Easter term there were the sports,
and he would be able to go in for the races; he rather fancied
himself over the hurdles. It would be splendid to be like
everyone else, not to be stared at curiously by new boys who
did not know about his deformity, nor at the baths in summer to need incredible precautions, while he was undressing,
before he could hide his foot in the water.

He prayed with all the power of his soul. No doubts assailed him. He was confident in the word of God. And the
night before he was to go back to school he went up to bed
tremulous with excitement. There was snow on the ground,
and Aunt Louisa had allowed herself the unaccustomed
luxury of a fire in her bed-room; but in Philip's little room
it was so cold that his fingers were numb, and he had great
difficulty in undoing his collar. His teeth chattered. The idea
came to him that he must do something more than usual to
attract the attention of God, and he turned back the rug
which was in front of his bed so that he could kneel on the
bare boards; and then it struck him that his nightshirt was a
softness that might displease his Maker, so he took it off and
said his prayers naked. When he got into bed he was so
cold that for some time he could not sleep, but when he did,
it was so soundly that Mary Ann had to shake him when she
brought in his hot water next morning. She talked to him

while she drew the curtains, but he did not answer; he had remembered at once that this was the morning for the miracle. His heart was filled with joy and gratitude. His first instinct was to put down his hand and feel the foot which was whole now, but to do this seemed to doubt the goodness of God. He knew that his foot was well. But at last he made up his mind, and with the toes of his right foot he just touched his left. Then he passed his hand over it.

He limped downstairs just as Mary Ann was going into the dining-room for prayers, and then he sat down to breakfast.

"You're very quiet this morning, Philip," said Aunt Louisa presently.

"He's thinking of the good breakfast he'll have at school tomorrow," said the Vicar.

When Philip answered, it was in a way that always irritated his uncle, with something that had nothing to do with the matter in hand. He called it a bad habit of wool-gathering.

"Supposing you'd asked God to do something," said Philip, "and really believed it was going to happen, like moving a mountain, I mean, and you had faith, and it didn't happen, What would it mean?"

"What a funny boy you are!" said Aunt Louisa. "You asked about moving mountains two or three weeks ago."

"It would just mean that you hadn't got faith," answered Uncle William.

Philip accepted the explanation. If God had not cured him, it was because he did not really believe. And yet he did not see how he could believe more than he did. But perhaps he had not given God enough time. He had only asked Him for nineteen days. In a day or two he began his prayer again, and this time he fixed upon Easter. That was the day of His Son's glorious resurrection, and God in His happiness might be mercifully inclined. But now Philip added other means of attaining his desire: he began to wish, when he saw a new moon or a dappled horse, and he looked out for shooting stars; during exeat they had a chicken at the vicarage, and he broke the lucky bone with Aunt Louisa and wished again, each time that his foot might be made whole. He was appealing unconsciously to gods older to his race than the God of Israel. And he bombarded the Almighty with his prayer, at odd times of the day, whenever it occurred to him, in identical words always, for it seemed to him important to make his request in the same terms. But presently the feeling came to him that this time also his faith would not be great enough. He could not resist the doubt that assailed him. He made his own experience into a general rule.

"I suppose no one ever has faith enough," he said.

It was like the salt which his nurse used to tell him about: you could catch any bird by putting salt on his tail; and once he had taken a little bag of it into Kensington Gardens. But he could never get near enough to put the salt on a bird's tail. Before Easter he had given up the struggle. He felt a dull resentment against his uncle for taking him in. The text which spoke of the moving of mountains was just one of those that said one thing and meant another. He thought his uncle had been playing a practical joke on him.

The King's School at Tercanbury, to which Philip went when he was thirteen, prided itself on its antiquity. The masters had no patience with modern ideas of education, which they read of sometimes in *The Times* or *The Guardian,* and hoped fervently that King's School would remain true to its old traditions. The dead languages were taught with such thoroughness that an old boy seldom thought of Homer or Virgil in after life without a qualm of boredom; and though in the common room at dinner one or two bolder spirits suggested that mathematics were of increasing importance, the general feeling was that they were a less noble study than the classics. Neither German nor chemistry was taught, and French only by the form-masters; they could keep order better than a foreigner, and, since they knew the grammar as well as any Frenchman, it seemed unimportant that none of them could have got a cup of coffee in the restaurant at Boulogne unless the waiter had known a little English. Geography was taught chiefly by making boys draw maps, and this was a favourite occupation, especially when the country dealt with was mountainous: it was possible to waste a great deal of time in drawing the Andes or the Apennines.

But a year before Philip entered the school a great change had come over it. It had been obvious for some time that Dr. Fleming, who had been headmaster for the quarter of a century, was become too deaf to continue his work to the greater glory of God.

It became necessary to find a successor. It was contrary to the traditions of the school that one of the lower-masters should be chosen. The common-room was unanimous in desiring the election of Mr. Watson, headmaster of the preparatory school; he could hardly be described as already a master of King's School, they had all known him for twenty years, and there was no danger that he would make a nuisance of himself. But the Chapter sprang a surprise on them. It chose a man called Perkins. At first nobody knew who Perkins was, and the name favourably impressed no one; but before the shock of it had passed away, it was realised that Perkins was the son of Perkins the linendraper. Dr. Fleming informed the masters just before dinner, and his manner showed his consternation. Such of them as were dining in, ate their meal almost in silence, and no reference was made to the matter till the servants had left the room. Then they set to. The names of those present on this occasion are unimportant, but they had been known to generations of school-boys as Sighs, Tar, Winks, Squirts, and Pat.

They all knew Tom Perkins. The first thing about him was that he was not a gentleman. They remembered him quite well. He was a small, dark boy, with untidy black hair and large eyes. He looked like a gipsy. He had come to the school as a day-boy, with the best scholarship on their endowment, so that his education had cost him nothing. Of course he was brilliant. At every Speech-Day he was loaded with prizes. He was their show-boy, and they remembered now bitterly their fear that he would try to get some scholarship at one of the larger public schools and so pass out of their hands. Dr. Fleming had gone to the linendraper his father—they all remembered the shop, Perkins and Cooper, in St. Catherine's Street—and said he hoped Tom would remain with them till he went to Oxford. The school was Perkins and Cooper's best customer, and Mr. Perkins was only too glad to give the required assurance. Tom Perkins continued to triumph, he was the finest classical scholar that Dr. Fleming remembered, and on leaving the school took with him the most valuable scholarship they had to offer. He got another at Magdalen and settled down to a brilliant career at the University.

The school magazine recorded the distinctions he achieved year after year, and when he got his double first Dr. Fleming himself wrote a few words of eulogy on the front page. It was with greater satisfaction that they welcomed his success, since Perkins and Cooper had fallen upon evil days: Cooper drank like a fish, and just before Tom Perkins took his degree the linendrapers filed their petition in bankruptcy.

In due course Tom Perkins took Holy Orders and entered upon the profession for which he was so admirably suited. He had been an assistant master at Wellington and then at Rugby.

But there was quite a difference between welcoming his success at other schools and serving under his leadership in their own. Tar had frequently given him lines, and Squirts had boxed his ears. They could not imagine how the Chapter had made such a mistake. No one could be expected to forget that he was the son of a bankrupt linendraper, and the alcoholism of Cooper seemed to increase the disgrace. It was understood that the Dean had supported his candidature with zeal, so the Dean would probably ask him to dinner; but would the pleasant little dinners in the precincts ever be the same when Tom Perkins sat at the table? And what about the dépôt? He really could not expect officers and gentlemen to receive him as one of themselves. It would do the school incalculable harm. Parents would be dissatisfied, and no one could be surprised if there were wholesale withdrawals. And then the indignity of calling him Mr. Perkins! The masters thought by way of protest of sending in their resignations in a body, but the uneasy fear that they would be accepted with equanimity restrained them.

"The only thing is to prepare ourselves for changes," said Sighs, who had conducted the fifth form for five and twenty years with unparalleled incompetence.

A year passed, and when Philip came to the school the old masters were all in their places; but a good many changes had taken place notwithstanding their stubborn resistance, none the less formidable because it was concealed under an apparent desire to fall in with the new head's ideas. Though the form-masters still taught French to the lower school, another master had come, with a degree of doctor of philology from the University of Heidelberg and a record of three years spent in a French lycée, to teach French to the upper forms and German to anyone who cared to take it up instead of Greek. Another master was engaged to teach mathematics more systematically than had been found necessary hitherto. Neither of these was ordained. This was a real revolution, and when the pair arrived the older masters received them with distrust. A laboratory had been fitted up, army classes were instituted; they all said the character of the school was changing. And heaven only knew what further projects Mr. Perkins turned in that untidy head of his. The school was small as public schools go, there were not more than two hundred boarders; and it was difficult for it to grow larger, for it was huddled up against the Cathedral; the precincts, with the exception of a house in which some of the masters lodged, were occupied by the cathedral clergy; and there was no more room for building. But Mr. Perkins devised an elaborate scheme by which he might obtain sufficient space to make the school double its present size. He wanted to attract boys from London. He thought it would be good for them to be thrown in contact with the Kentish lads, and it would sharpen the country wits of these.

"It's against all our traditions," said Sighs, when Mr. Perkins made the suggestion to him. "We've rather gone out of our way to avoid the contamination of boys from London."

"Oh, what nonsense!" said Mr. Perkins.

But Mr. Perkins' most unpopular innovation was his system of taking occasionally another man's form. He asked it as a favour, but after all it was a favour which could not be refused, and as Tar, otherwise Mr. Turner, said, it was undignified for all parties. He gave no warning, but after morning prayers would say to one of the masters:

"I wonder if you'd mind taking the Sixth today at eleven. We'll change over, shall we?"

They did not know whether this was usual at other schools, but certainly it had never been done at Tercanbury. The results were curious. Mr. Turner, who was the first victim, broke the news to his form that the headmaster would take them for Latin that day, and on the pretence that they might like to ask him a question or two so that they should not make perfect fools of themselves, spent the last quarter of an hour of the history lesson in construing for them the passage of Livy which had been set for the day; but when he rejoined his class and looked at the paper on which Mr. Perkins had written the marks, a surprise awaited him; for

the two boys at the top of the form seemed to have done
very ill, while others who had never distinguished themselves before were given full marks. When he asked Eldridge, his cleverest boy, what was the meaning of this the
answer came sullenly:

"Mr. Perkins never gave us any construing to do. He
asked me what I knew about General Gordon."

Mr. Turner looked at him in astonishment. The boys
evidently felt they had been hardly used, and he could not
help agreeing with their silent dissatisfaction. He could not
see either what General Gordon had to do with Livy. He
hazarded an enquiry afterwards.

"Eldridge was dreadfully put out because you asked him
what he knew about General Gordon," he said to the headmaster, with an attempt at a chuckle.

Mr. Perkins laughed.

"I saw they'd got to the agrarian laws of Caius Gracchus,
and I wondered if they knew anything about the agrarian
troubles in Ireland. But all they knew about Ireland was
that Dublin was on the Liffey. So I wondered if they'd ever
heard of General Gordon."

Then the horrid fact was disclosed that the new head had
a mania for general information. He had doubts about the
utility of examinations on subjects which had been crammed
for the occasion. He wanted common sense.

Sighs grew more worried every month; and he hated the
attitude the head adopted towards classical literature. And
Squirts, the master of the middle-third, grew more ill-tempered every day.

It was in his form that Philip was put on entering the
school. The Rev. B. B. Gordon was a man by nature ill-
suited to be a schoolmaster: he was impatient and choleric.
No master could have been more unfitted to teach things
to so shy a boy as Philip. He had come to the school with
fewer terrors than he had when first he went to Mr. Watson's. He knew a good many boys who had been with him

at the preparatory school. He felt more grown-up, and instinctively realised that among the larger numbers his deformity would be less noticeable. But from the first day Mr. Gordon struck terror in his heart; and the master, quick to discern the boys who were frightened of him, seemed on that account to take a peculiar dislike to him. Philip had enjoyed his work, but now he began to look upon the hours passed in school with horror. Rather than risk an answer which might be wrong and excite a storm of abuse from the master, he would sit stupidly silent, and when it came towards his turn to stand up and construe he grew sick and white with apprehension. His happy moments were those when Mr. Perkins took the form. He was able to gratify the passion for general knowledge which beset the headmaster; he had read all sorts of strange books beyond his years, and often Mr. Perkins, when a question was going round the room, would stop at Philip with a smile that filled the boy with rapture, and say:

"Now, Carey, you tell them."

The good marks he got on these occasions increased Mr. Gordon's indignation. One day it came to Philip's turn to translate, and the master sat there glaring at him and furiously biting his thumb. He was in a ferocious mood. Philip began to speak in a low voice.

"Don't mumble," shouted the master.

Something seemed to stick in Philip's throat.

"Go on. Go on. Go on."

Each time the words were screamed more loudly. The effect was to drive all he knew out of Philip's head, and he looked at the printed page vacantly. Mr. Gordon began to breathe heavily.

"If you don't know why don't you say so? Do you know it or not? Did you hear all this construed last time or not? Why don't you speak? Speak, you blockhead, speak!"

The master seized the arms of his chair and grasped them as though to prevent himself from falling upon Philip. They knew that in past days he often used to seize boys by the throat till they almost choked. The veins in his forehead stood out and his face grew dark and threatening. He was a man insane.

Philip had known the passage perfectly the day before, but now he could remember nothing.

"I don't know it," he gasped.

"Why don't you know it? Let's take the words one by one. We'll soon see if you don't know it."

Philip stood silent, very white, trembling a little, with his head bent down on the book. The master's breathing grew almost stertorous.

"The headmaster says you're clever. I don't know how he sees it. General information." He laughed savagely. "I don't know what they put you in his form for. Blockhead."

He was pleased with the word, and he repeated it at the top of his voice.

"Blockhead! Blockhead! Club-footed blockhead!"

That relieved him a little. He saw Philip redden suddenly. He told him to fetch the Black Book. Philip put down his Cæsar and went silently out. The Black Book was a sombre volume in which the names of boys were written with their misdeeds, and when a name was down three times it meant a caning. Philip went to the headmaster's house and knocked at his study-door. Mr. Perkins was seated at his table.

"May I have the Black Book, please, sir?"

"There it is," answered Mr. Perkins, indicating its place by a nod of his head. "What have you been doing that you shouldn't?"

"I don't know, sir."

Mr. Perkins gave him a quick look, but without answering went on with his work. Philip took the book and went out. When the hour was up, a few minutes later, he brought it back.

"Let me have a look at it," said the headmaster. "I see

Mr. Gordon has black-booked you for 'gross impertinence.' What was it?"

"I don't know, sir. Mr. Gordon said I was a club-footed blockhead."

Mr. Perkins looked at him again. He wondered whether there was sarcasm behind the boy's reply, but he was still much too shaken. His face was white and his eyes had a look of terrified distress. Mr. Perkins got up and put the book down. As he did so he took up some photographs.

"A friend of mine sent me some pictures of Athens this morning," he said casually. "Look here, there's the Akropolis."

He began explaining to Philip what he saw. The ruin grew vivid with his words. He showed him the theatre of Dionysus and explained in what order the people sat, and how beyond they could see the blue Aegean. And then suddenly he said:

"I remember Mr. Gordon used to call me a gipsy counter-jumper when I was in his form."

And before Philip, his mind fixed on the photographs, had time to gather the meaning of the remark, Mr. Perkins was showing him a picture of Salamis, and with his finger, a finger of which the nail had a little black edge to it, was pointing out how the Greek ships were placed and how the Persian.

Philip passed the next two years with comfortable monotony. He was not bullied more than other boys of his size; and his deformity, withdrawing him from games, acquired for him an insignificance for which he was grateful. He was not popular, and he was very lonely.

Then he began to go to the classes which were held in the headmaster's study, immediately after tea, to prepare boys for confirmation. Mr. Perkins took this part of his work with great seriousness. There was never here any of that flashing humour which made the other masters suspect him of flippancy. Finding time for everything in his busy day, he was able at certain intervals to take separately for a quarter of an hour or twenty minutes the boys whom he was preparing for confirmation. He wanted to make them feel that this was the first consciously serious step in their lives; he tried to grope into the depths of their souls; he wanted to instil in them his own vehement devotion. In Philip, notwithstanding his shyness, he felt the possibility of a passion equal to his own. The boy's temperament seemed to him essentially religious. One day he broke off suddenly from the subject on which he had been talking.

"Have you thought at all what you're going to be when you grow up?" he asked.

"My uncle wants me to be ordained," said Philip.

"And you?"

Philip looked away. He was ashamed to answer that he felt himself unworthy.

"I don't know any life that's so full of happiness as ours. I wish I could make you feel what a wonderful privilege it is. One can serve God in every walk, but we stand nearer to Him. I don't want to influence you, but if you made up your mind—oh, at once—you couldn't help feeling that joy and relief which never desert one again."

Philip did not answer, but the headmaster read in his eyes that he realised already something of what he tried to indicate.

"If you go on as you are now you'll find yourself head of the school one of these days, and you ought to be pretty safe for a scholarship when you leave. Have you got anything of your own?"

"My uncle says I shall have a hundred a year when I'm twenty-one."

"You'll be rich. I had nothing."

The headmaster hesitated a moment, and then, idly drawing lines with a pencil on the blotting paper in front of him, went on.

"I'm afraid your choice of professions will be rather limited. You naturally couldn't go in for anything that required physical activity."

Philip reddened to the roots of his hair, as he always did when any reference was made to his club-foot. Mr. Perkins looked at him gravely.

"I wonder if you're not oversensitive about your misfortune. Has it ever struck you to thank God for it?"

Philip looked up quickly. His lips tightened. He remembered how for months, trusting in what they told him, he had implored God to heal him as He had healed the Leper and made the Blind to see.

"As long as you accept it rebelliously it can only cause you shame. But if you looked upon it as a cross that was given you to bear only because your shoulders were strong enough to bear it, a sign of God's favour, then it would be a source of happiness to you instead of misery."

He saw that the boy hated to discuss the matter and he let him go.

But Philip thought over all that the headmaster had said, and presently, his mind taken up entirely with the ceremony that was before him, a mystical rapture seized him. His spirit seemed to free itself from the bonds of the flesh and he seemed to be living a new life. He aspired to perfection with all the passion that was in him. He wanted to surrender himself entirely to the service of God, and he made up his mind definitely that he would be ordained. When the great day arrived, his soul deeply moved by all the preparation, by the books he had studied and above all by the overwhelming influence of the head, he could hardly contain himself for fear and joy. One thought had tormented him. He knew that he would have to walk alone through the chancel, and he dreaded showing his limp thus obviously, not only to the whole school, who were attending the service, but also to the strangers, people from the city or parents who had come to see their sons confirmed. But when the time came he felt suddenly that he could accept the humiliation joyfully; and as he limped up the chancel, very small and insignificant beneath the lofty vaulting of the Cathedral, he offered consciously his deformity as a sacrifice to the God who loved him.

But Philip could not live long in the rarefied air of the hilltops. What had happened to him when first he was seized by the religious emotion happened to him now. Because he felt so keenly the beauty of faith, because the desire for self-sacrifice burned in his heart with such a gem-like glow, his strength seemed inadequate to his ambition. He was tired out by the violence of his passion. His soul was filled on a sudden with a singular aridity. He began to forget the presence of God which had seemed so surrounding; and his religious exercises, still very punctually performed, grew merely formal. At first he blamed himself for this falling away, and the fear of hell-fire urged him to renewed vehemence; but the passion was dead, and gradually other interests distracted his thoughts.

Philip had few friends. His habit of reading isolated him: it became such a need that after being in company for some time he grew tired and restless; he was vain of the wider knowledge he had acquired from the perusal of so many books, his mind was alert, and he had not the skill to hide his contempt for his companions' stupidity. They complained that he was conceited; and, since he excelled only in matters which to them were unimportant, they asked satirically what he had to be conceited about. He was developing a sense of humour, and found that he had a knack of saying bitter things, which caught people on the raw; he said them because they amused him, hardly realising how much they hurt, and was much offended when he found that his victims regarded him with active dislike. The humiliations he suffered when first he went to school had caused in him a shrinking from his fellows which he could never entirely overcome; he remained shy and silent. But though he did everything to alienate the sympathy of other boys he longed with all his heart for the popularity which to some was so easily accorded. These from his distance he admired extravagantly; and though he was inclined to be more sarcastic with them than with others, though he made little jokes at their expense, he would have given anything to change places with them. Indeed he would gladly have changed places with the dullest boy in the school who was whole of limb.

Philip was moved into the Sixth, but he hated school now with all his heart, and, having lost his ambition, cared nothing whether he did ill or well. He awoke in the morning with a sinking heart because he must go through another day of drudgery. He was tired of having to do things because he was told; and the restrictions irked him, not because they were unreasonable, but because they were restrictions. He yearned for freedom. He was weary of repeating things that he knew already and of the hammering away, for the sake of a thick-witted fellow, at something that he understood from the beginning.

With Mr. Perkins you could work or not as you chose. He was at once eager and abstracted. The Sixth Form room was in a part of the old abbey which had been restored, and it had a gothic window: Philip tried to cheat his boredom by drawing this over and over again; and sometimes out of his head he drew the great tower of the Cathedral or the gateway that led into the precincts. He had a knack for drawing. Aunt Louisa during her youth had painted in water colours, and she had several albums filled with sketches of churches, old bridges, and picturesque cottages. They were often shown at the vicarage tea-parties. She had once given Philip a paint-box as a Christmas present, and he had started by copying her pictures. He copied them better than anyone could have expected, and presently he did little pictures of his own. Mrs. Carey encouraged him. It was a good way to keep him out of mischief, and later on his sketches would be useful for bazaars. Two or three of them had been framed and hung in his bed-room.

But one day, at the end of the morning's work, Mr. Perkins stopped him as he was lounging out of the form-room.

"I want to speak to you, Carey."

Philip waited. Mr. Perkins ran his lean fingers through his beard and looked at Philip. He seemed to be thinking over what he wanted to say.

"What's the matter with you, Carey?" he said abruptly.

Philip, flushing, looked at him quickly. But knowing him well by now, without answering, he waited for him to go on.

"I've been dissatisfied with you lately. You've been slack and inattentive. You seem to take no interest in your work. It's been slovenly and bad."

"I'm very sorry, sir," said Philip.

"Is that all you have to say for yourself?"

Philip looked down sulkily. How could he answer that he was bored to death?

"You know, this term you'll go down instead of up. I shan't give you a very good report."

Philip wondered what he would say if he knew how the report was treated. It arrived at breakfast, Mr. Carey glanced at it indifferently, and passed it over to Philip.

"There's your report. You'd better see what it says," he remarked, as he ran his fingers through the wrapper of a catalogue of second-hand books.

Philip read it.

"Is it good?" asked Aunt Louisa.

"Not so good as I deserve," answered Philip, with a smile, giving it to her.

"I'll read it afterwards when I've got my spectacles," she said.

But after breakfast Mary Ann came in to say the butcher was there, and she generally forgot.

Mr. Perkins went on.

"I'm disappointed with you. And I can't understand. I know you *can* do things if you want to, but you don't seem to want to any more. I was going to make you a monitor next term, but I think I'd better wait a bit."

Philip flushed. He did not like the thought of being passed over. He tightened his lips.

"And there's something else. You must begin thinking of your scholarship now. You won't get anything unless you start working very seriously."

Philip was irritated by the lecture. He was angry with the headmaster, and angry with himself.

"I don't think I'm going up to Oxford," he said.

"Why not? I thought your idea was to be ordained."

"I've changed my mind."

"Why?"

Philip did not answer. Mr. Perkins, holding himself oddly as he always did, like a figure in one of Perugino's pictures, drew his fingers thoughtfully through his beard. He looked at Philip as though he were trying to understand and then abruptly told him he might go.

Apparently he was not satisfied, for one evening, a week later, when Philip had to go into his study with some papers, he resumed the conversation; but this time he adopted a different method: he spoke to Philip not as a schoolmaster with a boy but as one human being with another. He did not seem to care now that Philip's work was poor, that he ran small chance against keen rivals of carrying off the scholarship necessary for him to go to Oxford: the important matter was his changed intention about his life afterwards. Mr. Perkins set himself to revive his eagerness to be ordained. With infinite skill he worked on his feelings, and this was easier since he was himself genuinely moved. Philip's change of mind caused him bitter distress, and he really thought he was throwing away his chance of happiness in life for he knew not what. His voice was very persuasive. And Philip, easily moved by the emotion of others, very emotional himself notwithstanding a placid exterior—his face, partly by nature but also from the habit of all these years at school, seldom except by his quick flushing showed what he felt—Philip was deeply touched by what the master said. He was very grateful to him for the interest he showed, and he was conscience-stricken by the grief which he felt his behaviour caused him. It was subtly flattering to know that with the whole school to think about Mr. Perkins should trouble with him, but at the same time something else in him, like another person standing at his elbow, clung desperately to two words.

"I won't. I won't. I won't."

He felt himself slipping. He was powerless against the weakness that seemed to well up in him; it was like the water that rises up in an empty bottle held over a full basin; and he set his teeth, saying the words over and over to himself.

"I won't. I won't. I won't."

At last Mr. Perkins put his hand on Philip's shoulder.

"I don't want to influence you," he said. "You must decide for yourself. Pray to Almighty God for help and guidance."

When Philip came out of the headmaster's house there was a light rain falling. He went under the archway that led to the precincts, there was not a soul there, and the rooks were silent in the elms. He walked round slowly. He felt hot, and the rain did him good. He thought over all that Mr. Perkins had said, calmly now that he was withdrawn from the fervour of his personality, and he was thankful he had not given way.

In the darkness he could but vaguely see the great mass of the Cathedral: he hated it now because of the irksomeness of the long services which he was forced to attend. The anthem was interminable, and you had to stand drearily while it was being sung; you could not hear the droning sermon, and your body twitched because you had to sit still when you wanted to move about. Then Philip thought of the two services every Sunday at Blackstable. The church was bare and cold, and there was a smell all about one of pomade and starched clothes. The curate preached once and his uncle preached once. As he grew up he had learned to know his uncle; Philip was downright and intolerant, and he could not understand that a man might sincerely say things as a clergyman which he never acted up to as a man. The deception outraged him. His uncle was a weak and selfish man, whose chief desire it was to be saved trouble.

Mr. Perkins had spoken to him of the beauty of a life dedicated to the service of God. Philip knew what sort of lives the clergy led in the corner of East Anglia which was his home. There was the Vicar of Whitestone, a parish a little way from Blackstable: he was a bachelor and to give himself something to do had lately taken up farming: the local paper constantly reported the cases he had in the county court against this one and that, labourers he would not pay their wages to or tradesmen whom he accused of cheating him; scandal said he starved his cows, and there was much talk about some general action which should be taken against him. Then there was the Vicar of Ferne, a bearded, fine figure of a man: his wife had been forced to leave him because of his cruelty, and she had filled the neighbourhood with stories of his immorality. The Vicar of Surle, a tiny hamlet by the sea, was to be seen every evening in the public house a stone's throw from his vicarage; and the church-wardens had been to Mr. Carey to ask his advice. There was not a soul for any of them to talk to except small farmers or fishermen; there were long winter evenings when the wind blew, whistling drearily through the leafless trees, and all around they saw nothing but the bare monotony of ploughed fields; and there was poverty, and there was lack of any work that seemed to matter; every kink in their characters had free play; there was nothing to restrain them; they grew narrow and eccentric: Philip knew all this, but in his young intolerance he did not offer it as an excuse. He shivered at the thought of leading such a life; he wanted to get out into the world.

Mr. Perkins soon saw that his words had had no effect on Philip, and for the rest of the term ignored him. He wrote a report which was vitriolic. When it arrived and Aunt Louisa asked Philip what it was like, he answered cheerfully:

"Rotten."

"Is it?" said the Vicar. "I must look at it again."

"Do you think there's any use in my staying on at Tercanbury? I should have thought it would be better if I went to Germany for a bit."

"What has put that in your head?" said Aunt Louisa.

"Don't you think it's rather a good idea?"

"But then you wouldn't get a scholarship."

"I haven't a chance of getting one anyhow. And besides, I don't know that I particularly want to go to Oxford."

"But if you're going to be ordained, Philip?" Aunt Louisa exclaimed in dismay.

"I've given up that idea long ago."

Mrs. Carey looked at him with startled eyes, and then, used to self-restraint, she poured out another cup of tea for his uncle. They did not speak. In a moment Philip saw tears slowly falling down her cheeks. His heart was suddenly wrung because he caused her pain. In her tight black dress, made by the dressmaker down the street, with her wrinkled face and pale tired eyes, her gray hair still done in the frivolous ringlets of her youth, she was a ridiculous but strangely pathetic figure. Philip saw it for the first time.

Afterwards, when the Vicar was shut up in his study with the curate, he put his arms round her waist.

"I say, I'm sorry you're upset, Aunt Louisa," he said. "But it's no good my being ordained if I haven't a real vocation, is it?"

"I'm so disappointed, Philip," she moaned. "I'd set my heart on it. I thought you could be your uncle's curate, and then when our time came—after all, we can't last for ever, can we?—you might have taken his place."

Philip shivered. He was seized with panic. His heart beat like a pigeon in a trap beating with its wings. His aunt wept softly, her head upon his shoulder.

"I wish you'd persuade Uncle William to let me leave Tercanbury. I'm so sick of it."

But the Vicar of Blackstable did not easily alter any arrangements he had made, and it had always been intended that Philip should stay at King's School till he was eighteen, and should then go to Oxford. At all events he would not hear of Philip leaving then, for no notice had been given and the term's fee would have to be paid in any case.

"Then will you give notice for me to leave at Christmas?" said Philip, at the end of a long and often bitter conversation.

"I'll write to Mr. Perkins about it and see what he says."

"Oh, I wish to goodness I were twenty-one. It is awful to be at somebody else's beck and call."

"Philip, you shouldn't speak to your uncle like that," said Mrs. Carey gently.

"But don't you see that Perkins will want me to stay? He gets so much a head for every chap in the school."

"Why don't you want to go to Oxford?"

"What's the good if I'm not going into the Church?"

"You can't go into the Church; you're in the Church already," said the Vicar.

"Ordained then," replied Philip impatiently.

"What are you going to be, Philip?" asked Mrs. Carey.

"I don't know. I've not made up my mind. But whatever I am, it'll be useful to know foreign languages. I shall get far more out of a year in Germany than by staying on at that hole."

He would not say that he felt Oxford would be little

better than a continuation of his life at school. He wished immensely to be his own master. Besides he would be known to a certain extent among old schoolfellows, and he wanted to get away from them all. He felt that his life at school had been a failure. He wanted to start fresh.

It happened that his desire to go to Germany fell in with certain ideas which had been of late discussed at Blackstable. Sometimes friends came to stay with the doctor and brought news of the world outside; and the visitors spending August by the sea had their own way of looking at things. The Vicar had heard that there were people who did not think the old-fashioned education so useful nowadays as it had been in the past, and modern languages were gaining an importance which they had not had in his own youth. His own mind was divided, for a younger brother of his had been sent to Germany when he failed in some examination, thus creating a precedent, but since he had there died of typhoid it was impossible to look upon the experiment as other than dangerous. The result of innumerable conversations was that Philip should go back to Tercanbury for another term, and then should leave. With this agreement Philip was not dissatisfied. But when he had been back a few days the headmaster spoke to him.

"I've had a letter from your uncle. It appears you want to go to Germany, and he asks me what I think about it."

Philip was astounded. He was furious with his guardian for going back on his word.

"I thought it was settled, sir," he said.

"Far from it. I've written to say I think it the greatest mistake to take you away."

Philip immediately sat down and wrote a violent letter to his uncle. He did not measure his language. He was so angry that he could not get to sleep till quite late that night, and he awoke in the early morning and began brooding over the way they had treated him. He waited impatiently for an answer. In two or three days it came. It was a mild, pained letter from Aunt Louisa, saying that he should not write such things to his uncle, who was very much distressed. He was unkind and unchristian. He must know they were only trying to do their best for him, and they were so much older than he that they must be better judges of what was good for him. Philip clenched his hands. He had heard that statement so often, and he could not see why it was true; they did not know the conditions as he did, why should they accept it as self-evident that their greater age gave them greater wisdom? The letter ended with the information that Mr. Carey had withdrawn the notice he had given.

Philip nursed his wrath till the next half-holiday. They had them on Tuesdays and Thursdays, since on Saturday afternoons they had to go to a service in the Cathedral. He stopped behind when the rest of the Sixth went out.

"May I go to Blackstable this afternoon, please, sir?" he asked.

"No," said the headmaster briefly.

"I wanted to see my uncle about something very important."

"Didn't you hear me say no?"

Philip did not answer. He went out. He felt almost sick with humiliation, the humiliation of having to ask and the humiliation of the curt refusal. He hated the headmaster now. Philip writhed under that despotism which never vouchsafed a reason for the most tyrannous act. He was too angry to care what he did, and after dinner walked down to the station, by the back ways he knew so well, just in time to catch the train to Blackstable. He walked into the vicarage and found his uncle and aunt sitting in the dining-room.

"Hulloa, where have you sprung from?" said the Vicar.

It was very clear that he was not pleased to see him. He looked a little uneasy.

"I thought I'd come and see you about my leaving. I want to know what you mean by promising me one thing when

I was here, and doing something different a week after."

He was a little frightened at his own boldness, but he had made up his mind exactly what words to use, and, though his heart beat violently, he forced himself to say them.

"Have you got leave to come here this afternoon?"

"No. I asked Perkins and he refused. If you like to write and tell him I've been here you can get me into a really fine old row."

Mrs. Carey sat knitting with trembling hands. She was unused to scenes and they agitated her extremely.

"It would serve you right if I told him," said Mr. Carey.

"If you like to be a perfect sneak you can. After writing to Perkins as you did you're quite capable of it."

It was foolish of Philip to say that, because it gave the Vicar exactly the opportunity he wanted.

"I'm not going to sit still while you say impertinent things to me," he said with dignity.

He got up and walked quickly out of the room into his study. Philip heard him shut the door and lock it.

"Oh, I wish to God I were twenty-one. It is awful to be tied down like this."

Aunt Louisa began to cry quietly.

"Oh, Philip, you oughtn't to have spoken to your uncle like that. Do please go and tell him you're sorry."

"I'm not in the least sorry. He's taking a mean advantage. Of course it's just waste of money keeping me on at school, but what does he care? It's not his money. It was cruel to put me under the guardianship of people who know nothing about things."

"Philip."

Philip in his voluble anger stopped suddenly at the sound of her voice. It was heart-broken. He had not realised what bitter things he was saying.

"Philip, how can you be so unkind? You know we are only trying to do our best for you, and we know that we have no experience; it isn't as if we'd had any children of our own: that's why we consulted Mr. Perkins." Her voice broke. "I've tried to be like a mother to you. I've loved you as if you were my own son."

She was so small and frail, there was something so pathetic in her old-maidish air, that Philip was touched. A great lump came suddenly in his throat and his eyes filled with tears.

"I'm so sorry," he said. "I didn't mean to be beastly."

He knelt down beside her and took her in his arms, and kissed her wet, withered cheeks. She sobbed bitterly, and he seemed to feel on a sudden the pity of that wasted life. She had never surrendered herself before to such a display of emotion.

"I know I've not been what I wanted to be to you, Philip, but I didn't know how. It's been just as dreadful for me to have no children as for you to have no mother."

Philip forgot his anger and his own concerns, but thought only of consoling her, with broken words and clumsy little caresses. Then the clock struck, and he had to bolt off at once to catch the only train that would get him back to Tercanbury in time for call-over. As he sat in the corner of the railway carriage he saw that he had done nothing. He was angry with himself for his weakness. It was despicable to have allowed himself to be turned from his purpose by the pompous airs of the Vicar and the tears of his aunt. But as the result of he knew not what conversations between the couple another letter was written to the headmaster. Mr. Perkins read it with an impatient shrug of the shoulders. He showed it to Philip. It ran:

Dear Mr. Perkins,

Forgive me for troubling you again about my ward, but both his Aunt and I have been uneasy about him. He seems very anxious to leave school, and his Aunt thinks he is unhappy. It is very difficult for us to know what to do as we are not his parents. He does not seem to think he is doing very well and he feels it is wasting his money to stay on. I should be very much obliged if you would have a talk to him, and if he is still of the same mind perhaps it would be better if he left at Christmas as I originally intended.

Yours very truly,
William Carey.

Philip gave him back the letter. He felt a thrill of pride in his triumph. He had got his own way, and he was satisfied. His will had gained a victory over the wills of others.

"It's not much good my spending half an hour writing to your uncle if he changes his mind the next letter he gets from you," said the headmaster irritably.

Philip said nothing, and his face was perfectly placid; but he could not prevent the twinkle in his eyes. Mr. Perkins noticed it and broke into a little laugh.

"You've rather scored, haven't you?" he said.

Then Philip smiled outright. He could not conceal his exultation.

"Is it true that you're very anxious to leave?"

"Yes, sir."

"Are you unhappy here?"

Philip blushed. He hated instinctively any attempt to get into the depths of his feelings.

"Oh, I don't know, sir."

Mr. Perkins, slowly dragging his fingers through his beard, looked at him thoughtfully. He seemed to speak almost to himself.

"Of course schools are made for the average. The holes are all round, and whatever shape the pegs are they must wedge in somehow. One hasn't time to bother about anything but the average." Then suddenly he addressed himself to Philip: "Look here, I've got a suggestion to make to you. It's getting on towards the end of the term now. Another term won't kill you, and if you want to go to Germany you'd better go after Easter than after Christmas. It'll be much pleasanter in the spring than in midwinter. If at the end of the next term you still want to go I'll make no objection. What d'you say to that?"

"Thank you very much, sir."

Philip was so glad to have gained the last three months that he did not mind the extra term. The school seemed less of a prison when he knew that before Easter he would be free from it for ever. His heart danced within him.

Philip had learned not to express his emotions by outward signs, and shyness still tormented him, but he had often very high spirits; and then, though he limped about demurely, silent and reserved, it seemed to be hallooing in his heart. He seemed to himself to walk more lightly. All sorts of ideas danced through his head, fancies chased one another so furiously that he could not catch them; but their coming and their going filled him with exhilaration. Now, being happy, he was able to work, and during the remaining weeks of the term set himself to make up for his long neglect. His brain worked easily, and he took a keen pleasure in the activity of his intellect. He did very well in the examinations that closed the term. Mr. Perkins made only one remark: he was talking to him about an essay he had written, and, after the usual criticisms, said:

"So you've made up your mind to stop playing the fool for a bit, have you?"

He smiled at him with his shining teeth, and Philip, looking down, gave an embarrassed smile.

The half dozen boys who expected to divide between them the various prizes which were given at the end of the summer term had ceased to look upon Philip as a serious rival, but now they began to regard him with some uneasiness. He told no one that he was leaving at Easter and so was in no sense a competitor, but left them to their anxieties.

It entertained him to think that he held someone else's future in his hand. There was something romantic in getting these various rewards actually in his grasp, and then

leaving them to others because he disdained them. At last
the breaking-up day came, and he went to Mr. Perkins to
bid him good-bye.

"You don't mean to say you really want to leave?"

Philip's face fell at the headmaster's evident surprise.

"You said you wouldn't put any objection in the way,
sir," he answered.

"I thought it was only a whim that I'd better humour.
I know you're obstinate and headstrong. What on earth
d'you want to leave for now? You've only got another term
in any case. You can get the Magdalen scholarship easily;
you'll get half the prizes we've got to give."

Philip looked at him sullenly. He felt that he had been
tricked; but he had the promise, and Perkins would have
to stand by it.

"You'll have a very pleasant time at Oxford. You needn't
decide at once what you're going to do afterwards. I wonder if you realise how delightful the life is up there for anyone who has brains."

"I've made all my arrangements now to go to Germany,
sir," said Philip.

"Are they arrangements that couldn't possibly be altered?" asked Mr. Perkins, with his quizzical smile. "I shall
be very sorry to lose you. In schools the rather stupid boys
who work always do better than the clever boy who's idle,
but when the clever boy works—why then, he does what
you've done this term."

Philip flushed darkly. He was unused to compliments,
and no one had ever told him he was clever. The headmaster put his hand on Philip's shoulder.

"You know, driving things into the heads of thick-witted
boys is dull work, but when now and then you have the
chance of teaching a boy who comes half-way towards you,
who understands almost before you've got the words out of
your mouth, why, then teaching is the most exhilarating
thing in the world."

Philip was melted by kindness; it had never occurred to him that it mattered really to Mr. Perkins whether he went or stayed. He was touched and immensely flattered. It would be pleasant to end up his school-days with glory and then go to Oxford: in a flash there appeared before him the life which he had heard described from boys who came back to play in the O.K.S. match or in letters from the University read out in one of the studies. But he was ashamed; he would look such a fool in his own eyes if he gave in now; his uncle would chuckle at the success of the headmaster's ruse. It was rather a come-down from the dramatic surrender of all these prizes which were in his reach, because he disdained to take them, to the plain, ordinary winning of them. It only required a little more persuasion, just enough to save his self-respect, and Philip would have done anything that Mr. Perkins wished; but his face showed nothing of his conflicting emotions. It was placid and sullen.

"I think I'd rather go, sir," he said.

Mr. Perkins, like many men who manage things by their personal influence, grew a little impatient when his power was not immediately manifest. He had a great deal of work to do, and could not waste more time on a boy who seemed to him insanely obstinate.

"Very well, I promised to let you if you really wanted it, and I keep my promise. When do you go to Germany?"

Philip's heart beat violently. The battle was won, and he did not know whether he had not rather lost it.

"At the beginning of May, sir," he answered.

"Well, you must come and see us when you get back."

He held out his hand. If he had given him one more chance Philip would have changed his mind, but he seemed to look upon the matter as settled. Philip walked out of the house. His school-days were over, and he was free; but the wild exultation to which he had looked forward at that moment was not there. He walked round the precincts slowly, and a profound depression seized him. He wished now that he had not been foolish. He did not want to go, but he knew he could never bring himself to go to the headmaster and tell him he would stay. That was a humiliation he could never put upon himself. He wondered whether he had done right. He was dissatisfied with himself and with all his circumstances. He asked himself dully whether whenever you got your way you wished afterwards that you hadn't.

Philip's uncle had an old friend, called Miss Wilkinson, who lived in Berlin. She was the daughter of a clergyman, and it was with her father, the rector of a village in Lincolnshire, that Mr. Carey had spent his last curacy; on his death, forced to earn her living, she had taken various situations as a governess in France and Germany. She had kept up a correspondence with Mrs. Carey, and two or three times had spent her holidays at Blackstable Vicarage, paying as was usual with the Careys' unfrequent guests a small sum for her keep. When it became clear that it was less trouble to yield to Philip's wishes than to resist them, Mrs. Carey wrote to ask her for advice. Miss Wilkinson recommended Heidelberg as an excellent place to learn German in and the house of Frau Professor Erlin as a comfortable home. Philip might live there for thirty marks a week, and the Professor himself, a teacher at the local high school, would instruct him. Philip arrived in Heidelberg one morning in May. His things were put on a barrow and he followed the porter out of the station. The sky was bright blue, and the trees in the avenue through which they passed were thick with leaves; there was something in the air fresh to Philip, and mingled with the timidity he felt at entering on a new life, among strangers, was a great exhilaration. He was a little disconsolate that no one had come to meet him, and felt very shy when the porter left him at the front door of a big white house. An untidy lad let him in and took him into a drawing-room. It was filled with a large suite covered in green velvet, and in the middle was a round table. On this in water stood a bouquet of flowers tightly packed together in a paper frill like the bone of a mutton chop, and carefully spaced round it were books in leather bindings. There was a musty smell.

Presently, with an odour of cooking, the Frau Professor came in, a short, very stout woman with tightly dressed hair and a red face; she had little eyes, sparkling like beads, and an effusive manner. She took both Philip's hands and asked him about Miss Wilkinson, who had twice spent a few weeks with her. She spoke in German and in broken English. Philip could not make her understand that he did not know Miss Wilkinson. Then her two daughters appeared. They seemed hardly young to Philip, but perhaps they were not more than twenty-five: the elder, Thekla, was as short as her mother, with the same, rather shifty air, but with a pretty face and abundant dark hair; Anna, her younger sister, was tall and plain, but since she had a pleasant smile Philip immediately preferred her. After a few minutes of polite conversation the Frau Professor took Philip to his room and left him. It was in a turret, looking over the tops of the trees in the Anlage; and the bed was in an alcove, so that when you sat at the desk it had not the look of a bedroom at all. Philip unpacked his things and set out all his books. He was his own master at last.

A bell summoned him to dinner at one o'clock, and he found the Frau Professor's guests assembled in the drawing-room. He was introduced to her husband, a tall man of middle age with a large fair head, turning now to gray, and mild blue eyes. He spoke to Philip in correct, rather archaic English, having learned it from a study of the English classics, not from conversation; and it was odd to hear him use words colloquially which Philip had only met in the plays of Shakespeare. Frau Professor Erlin called her establishment a family and not a pension; but it would have required the subtlety of a metaphysician to find out exactly where the difference lay. When they sat down to dinner in

a long dark apartment that led out of the drawing-room,
Philip, feeling very shy, saw that there were sixteen people.
The Frau Professor sat at one end and carved. The service
was conducted, with a great clattering of plates, by the
same clumsy lout who had opened the door for him; and
though he was quick, it happened that the first persons to
be served had finished before the last had received their appointed portions. The Frau Professor insisted that nothing
but German should be spoken, so that Philip, even if his
bashfulness had permitted him to be talkative, was forced
to hold his tongue. He looked at the people among whom
he was to live. By the Frau Professor sat several old ladies,
but Philip did not give them much of his attention. There
were two young girls, both fair and one of them very
pretty, whom Philip heard addressed as Fräulein Hedwig and Fräulein Cäcilie. Fräulein Cäcilie had a long pigtail hanging down her back. They sat side by side and
chattered to one another, with smothered laughter: now and
then they glanced at Philip and one of them said something
in an undertone; they both giggled, and Philip blushed
awkwardly, feeling that they were making fun of him. Near
them sat a Chinaman, with a yellow face and an expansive
smile, who was studying Western conditions at the University. He spoke so quickly, with a queer accent, that the
girls could not always understand him, and then they burst
out laughing. He laughed too, good-humouredly, and his
almond eyes almost closed as he did so. There were two or
three American men, in black coats, rather yellow and dry
of skin: they were theological students; Philip heard the
twang of their New England accent through their bad German, and he glanced at them with suspicion; for he had
been taught to look upon Americans as wild and desperate
barbarians.

Afterwards, when they had sat for a little on the stiff
green velvet chairs of the drawing-room, Fräulein Anna
asked Philip if he would like to go for a walk with them.

Philip accepted the invitation. They were quite a party.
There were the two daughters of the Frau Professor, the two
other girls, one of the American students, and Philip.
Philip walked by the side of Anna and Fräulein Hedwig.
He was a little fluttered. He had never known any girls.
At Blackstable there were only the farmers' daughters and
the girls of the local tradesmen. He knew them by name
and by sight, but he was timid, and he thought they laughed
at his deformity. He accepted willingly the difference which
the Vicar and Mrs. Carey put between their own exalted
rank and that of the farmers. The doctor had two daughters,
but they were both much older than Philip and had been
married to successive assistants while Philip was still a small
boy. At school there had been two or three girls of more
boldness than modesty whom some of the boys knew; and
desperate stories, due in all probability to the masculine
imagination, were told of intrigues with them; but Philip
had always concealed under a lofty contempt the terror
with which they filled him. His imagination and the books
he had read had inspired in him a desire for the Byronic
attitude; and he was torn between a morbid self-consciousness and a conviction that he owed it to himself to be gallant. He felt now that he should be bright and amusing,
but his brain seemed empty and he could not for the life of
him think of anything to say. Fräulein Anna, the Frau
Professor's daughter, addressed herself to him frequently
from a sense of duty, but the other said little: she looked
at him now and then with sparkling eyes, and sometimes to
his confusion laughed outright. Philip felt that she thought
him perfectly ridiculous. They walked along the side of
a hill among pine-trees, and their pleasant odour caused
Philip a keen delight. The day was warm and cloudless.
At last they came to an eminence from which they saw
the valley of the Rhine spread out before them under the
sun. It was a vast stretch of country, sparkling with golden
light, with cities in the distance; and through it meandered

the silver ribband of the river. Wide spaces are rare in the corner of Kent which Philip knew, the sea offers the only broad horizon, and the immense distance he saw now gave him a peculiar, an indescribable thrill. He felt suddenly elated. Though he did not know it, it was the first time that he had experienced, quite undiluted with foreign emotions, the sense of beauty. They sat on a bench, the three of them, for the others had gone on, and while the girls talked in rapid German, Philip, indifferent to their proximity, feasted his eyes.

"By Jove, I am happy," he said to himself unconsciously.

Philip had spent three months in Heidelberg when one morning the Frau Professor told him that an Englishman named Hayward was coming to stay in the house, and the same evening at supper he saw a new face. For some days the family had lived in a state of excitement. First, as the result of heaven knows what scheming, by dint of humble prayers and veiled threats, the parents of the young Englishman to whom Fräulein Thekla was engaged had invited her to visit them in England, and she had set off with an album of water colours to show how accomplished she was and a bundle of letters to prove how deeply the young man had compromised himself. A week later Fräulein Hedwig with radiant smiles announced that the lieutenant of her affections was coming to Heidelberg with his father and mother. Exhausted by the importunity of their son and touched by the dowry which Fräulein Hedwig's father offered, the lieutenant's parents had consented to pass through Heidelberg to make the young woman's acquaintance. The interview was satisfactory and Fräulein Hedwig had the satisfaction of showing her lover in the Stadtgarten to the whole of Frau Professor Erlin's household. The silent old ladies who sat at the top of the table near the Frau Professor were in a flutter, and when Fräulein Hedwig said she was to go home at once for the formal engagement to take place, the Frau Professor, regardless of expense, said she would give a *Maibowle*. Professor Erlin prided himself on his skill in preparing this mild intoxicant, and after supper the large bowl of hock and soda, with scented herbs floating in it and wild strawberries, was placed with solemnity on the round table in the drawing-room. Fräulein Anna teased Philip about the departure of his lady-love, and he felt very uncomfortable and rather melancholy. Fräulein Hedwig sang several songs, Fräulein Anna played the Wedding March, and the Professor sang *Die Wacht am Rhein*. Amid all this jollification Philip paid little attention to the new arrival. They had sat opposite one another at supper, but Philip was chattering busily with Fräulein Hedwig, and the stranger, knowing no German, had eaten his food in silence. Philip, observing that he wore a pale blue tie, had on that account taken a sudden dislike to him. He was a man of twenty-six, very fair, with long, wavy hair through which he passed his hand frequently with a careless gesture. His eyes were large and blue, but the blue was very pale, and they looked rather tired already. He was clean-shaven, and his mouth, notwithstanding its thin lips, was well-shaped. Fräulein Anna took an interest in physiognomy, and she made Philip notice afterwards how finely shaped was his skull, and how weak was the lower part of his face. The head, she remarked, was the head of a thinker, but the jaw lacked character. Fräulein Anna, foredoomed to a spinster's life, with her high cheekbones and large misshapen nose, laid great stress upon character. While they talked of him he stood a little apart from the others, watching the noisy party with a good-humoured but faintly supercilious expression. He was tall and slim. He held himself with a deliberate grace. Weeks, one of the American students, seeing him alone, went up and began to talk to him. The pair were oddly contrasted: the American very neat in his black coat and pepper-and-salt trousers, thin and dried-up, with something of ecclesiastical unction already in his manner; and the Englishman in his loose tweed suit, large-limbed and slow of gesture.

Philip did not speak to the new-comer till next day. They found themselves alone on the balcony of the drawing-room before dinner. Hayward addressed him.

"You're English, aren't you?"

"Yes."

"Is the food always as bad as it was last night?"

"It's always about the same."

"Beastly, isn't it?"

"Beastly."

Philip had found nothing wrong with the food at all, and in fact had eaten it in large quantities with appetite and enjoyment, but he did not want to show himself a person of so little discrimination as to think a dinner good which another thought execrable.

Fräulein Thekla's visit to England made it necessary for her sister to do more in the house, and she could not often spare the time for long walks; and Fräulein Cäcilie, with her long plait of fair hair and her little snub-nosed face, had of late shown a certain disinclination for society. Fräulein Hedwig was gone, and Weeks, the American who generally accompanied them on their rambles, had set out for a tour of South Germany. Philip was left a good deal to himself. Hayward sought his acquaintance; but Philip had an unfortunate trait: from shyness or from some atavistic inheritance of the cave-dweller, he always disliked people on first acquaintance; and it was not till he became used to them that he got over his first impression. It made him difficult of access. He received Hayward's advances very shyly, and when Hayward asked him one day to go for a walk he accepted only because he could not think of a civil excuse. He made his usual apology, angry with himself for the flushing cheeks he could not control, and trying to carry it off with a laugh.

"I'm afraid I can't walk very fast."

"Good heavens, I don't walk for a wager. I prefer to stroll. Don't you remember the chapter in *Marius* where Pater talks of the gentle exercise of walking as the best incentive to conversation?"

Philip was a good listener; though he often thought of clever things to say, it was seldom till after the opportunity to say them had passed; but Hayward was communicative; anyone more experienced than Philip might have thought he liked to hear himself talk. His supercilious attitude impressed Philip. He could not help admiring, and yet being awed by, a man who faintly despised so many things which Philip had looked upon as almost sacred. He cast down the fetish of exercise, damning with the contemptuous word pot-hunters all those who devoted themselves to its various forms; and Philip did not realise that he was merely putting up in its stead the other fetish culture.

They wandered up to the castle, and sat on the terrace that overlooked the town. It nestled in the valley along the pleasant Neckar with a comfortable friendliness. The smoke from the chimneys hung over it, a pale blue haze; and the tall roofs, the spires of the churches, gave it a pleasantly mediæval air. There was a homeliness in it which warmed the heart. Hayward talked of *Richard Feverel* and *Madame Bovary,* of Verlaine, Dante, and Matthew Arnold. In those days Fitzgerald's translation of Omar Khayam was known only to the elect, and Hayward repeated it to Philip. He was very fond of reciting poetry, his own and that of others, which he did in a monotonous sing-song. By the time they reached home Philip's distrust of Hayward was changed to enthusiastic admiration.

They made a practice of walking together every afternoon, and Philip learned presently something of Hayward's circumstances. He was the son of a country judge, on whose death some time before he had inherited three hundred a year. His record at Charterhouse was so brilliant that when he went to Cambridge the Master of Trinity Hall went out of his way to express his satisfaction that he was going to that college. He prepared himself for a distinguished career. He moved in the most intellectual circles: he read Browning with enthusiasm and turned up his well-shaped nose at Tennyson; he knew all the details of Shelley's treatment of Harriet; he dabbled in the history of art (on the walls of his rooms were reproductions of pictures by G. F. Watts, Burne-Jones, and Botticelli); and he wrote not without distinction verses of a pessimistic character. His friends told one another that he was a man of excellent gifts, and he listened to them willingly when they prophesied his future eminence. In course of time he became an authority on art and literature. He came under the influence of Newman's *Apologia;* the picturesqueness of the Roman Catholic faith appealed to his æsthetic sensibility; and it was only the fear of his father's wrath (a plain, blunt man of narrow ideas, who read Macaulay) which prevented him from 'going over.' When he only got a pass degree his friends were astonished; but he shrugged his shoulders and delicately insinuated that he was not the dupe of examiners. He made one feel that a first class was ever so slightly vulgar. He described one of the vivas with tolerant humour; some fellow in an outrageous collar was asking him questions in logic; it was infinitely tedious, and suddenly he noticed that he wore elastic-sided boots: it was grotesque and ridiculous; so he withdrew his mind and thought of the gothic beauty of the Chapel at King's. But he had spent some delightful days at Cambridge; he had given better dinners than anyone he knew; and the conversation in his rooms had been often memorable. He quoted to Philip the exquisite epigram:

"They told me, Herakleitus, they told me you were dead."

And now, when he related again the picturesque little anecdote about the examiner and his boots, he laughed.

"Of course it was folly," he said, "but it was a folly in which there was something fine."

Philip, with a little thrill, thought it magnificent.

Then Hayward went to London to read for the bar. He had charming rooms in Clement's Inn, with panelled walls, and he tried to make them look like his old rooms at the Hall. He had ambitions that were vaguely political, he described himself as a Whig, and he was put up for a club which was of Liberal but gentlemanly flavour. His idea was to practise at the Bar (he chose the Chancery side as less brutal), and get a seat for some pleasant constituency as soon as the various promises made him were carried out; meanwhile he went a great deal to the opera, and made acquaintance with a small number of charming people who admired the things that he admired. He joined a dining-club of which the motto was, The Whole, The Good, and The Beautiful. He formed a platonic friendship with a lady some years older than himself, who lived in Kensington Square; and nearly every afternoon he drank tea with her by the light of shaded candles, and talked of George Meredith and Walter Pater. It was notorious that any fool could pass the examinations of the Bar Council, and he pursued his studies in a dilatory fashion. When he was ploughed for his final he looked upon it as a personal affront. At the same time the lady in Kensington Square told him that her husband was coming home from India on leave, and was a man, though worthy in every way, of a commonplace mind, who would not understand a young man's frequent visits. Hayward felt that life was full of ugliness, his soul revolted from the thought of affronting again the cynicism of examiners, and he saw something rather splendid in kicking away the ball which lay at his feet. He was also a good deal in debt: it was difficult to live in London like a gentleman on three hundred a year; and his heart yearned for the Venice and Florence which John Ruskin had so magically described. He felt that he was unsuited to the vulgar bustle of the Bar, for he had discovered that it was not sufficient to put your name on a door to get briefs; and modern politics seemed to lack nobility. He felt himself a poet. He disposed of his rooms in Clement's Inn and went to Italy. He had spent a winter in Florence and a winter in Rome, and now was passing his second summer abroad in Germany so that he might read Goethe in the original.

Hayward had one gift which was very precious. He had a real feeling for literature, and he could impart his own passion with an admirable fluency. He could throw himself into sympathy with a writer and see all that was best in him, and then he could talk about him with understanding. Philip had read a great deal, but he had read without discrimination everything that he happened to come across, and it was very good for him now to meet someone who could guide his taste. He borrowed books from the small lending library which the town possessed and began reading all the wonderful things that Hayward spoke of. He did not read always with enjoyment but invariably with perseverance. He was eager for self-improvement. He felt himself very ignorant and very humble. By the end of August, when Weeks returned from South Germany, Philip was completely under Hayward's influence. Hayward did not like Weeks. He deplored the American's black coat and pepper-and-salt trousers, and spoke with a scornful shrug of his New England conscience. Philip listened complacently to the abuse of a man who had gone out of his way to be kind to him, but when Weeks in his turn made disagreeable remarks about Hayward he lost his temper.

"Your new friend looks like a poet," said Weeks, with a thin smile on his careworn, bitter mouth.

"He is a poet."

"Did he tell you so? In America we should call him a pretty fair specimen of a waster."

"Well, we're not in America," said Philip frigidly.

"How old is he? Twenty-five? And he does nothing but stay in pensions and write poetry."

"You don't know him," said Philip hotly.

"Oh yes, I do: I've met a hundred and forty-seven of him."

Weeks' eyes twinkled, but Philip, who did not understand American humour, pursed his lips and looked severe. Weeks to Philip seemed a man of middle-age, but he was in point of fact little more than thirty. He had a long, thin body and the scholar's stoop; his head was large and ugly; he had pale scanty hair and an earthy skin; his thin mouth and thin, long nose, and the great protuberance of his frontal bones, gave him an uncouth look. He was cold and precise in his manner, a bloodless man, without passion; but he had a curious vein of frivolity which disconcerted the serious-minded among whom his instincts naturally threw him. He was studying theology in Heidelberg, but the other theological students of his own nationality looked upon him with suspicion. He was very unorthodox, which frightened them; and his freakish humour excited their disapproval.

"How can you have known a hundred and forty-seven of him?" asked Philip seriously.

"I've met him in the Latin Quarter in Paris, and I've met him in pensions in Berlin and Munich. He lives in small hotels in Perugia and Assisi. He stands by the dozen before the Botticellis in Florence, and he sits on all the benches of the Sistine Chapel in Rome. In Italy he drinks a little too much wine, and in Germany he drinks a great deal too much beer. He always admires the right thing whatever the right thing is, and one of these days he's going to write a great work. Think of it, there are a hundred and forty-seven great works reposing in the bosoms of a hundred and forty-seven great men, and the tragic thing is that not one of those hundred and forty-seven great works will ever be written. And yet the world goes on."

Weeks spoke seriously, but his gray eyes twinkled a little at the end of his long speech, and Philip flushed when he saw that the American was making fun of him.

"You do talk rot," he said crossly.

Hayward, after saying for a month that he was going South next day and delaying from week to week out of inability to make up his mind to the bother of packing and the tedium of a journey, had at last been driven off just before Christmas by the preparations for that festival. He could not support the thought of a Teutonic merry-making. It gave him goose-flesh to think of the season's aggressive cheerfulness, and in his desire to avoid the obvious he determined to travel on Christmas Eve.

Philip was not sorry to see him off, for he was a downright person and it irritated him that anybody should not know his own mind. Though much under Hayward's influence, he would not grant that indecision pointed to a charming sensitiveness; and he resented the shadow of a sneer with which Hayward looked upon his straight ways. They corresponded. Hayward was an admirable letter-writer, and knowing his talent took pains with his letters. His temperament was receptive to the beautiful influences with which he came in contact, and he was able in his letters from Rome to put a subtle fragrance of Italy. He thought the city of the ancient Romans a little vulgar, finding distinction only in the decadence of the Empire; but the Rome of the Popes appealed to his sympathy, and in his chosen words, quite exquisitely, there appeared a Rococo beauty. He wrote of old church music and the Alban Hills, and of the languor of incense and the charm of the streets by night, in the rain, when the pavements shone and the light of the street lamps was mysterious. Perhaps he repeated these admirable letters to various friends. He did not know what a troubling effect they had upon Philip; they seemed to make his life very hum-drum. With the spring Hayward grew dithyrambic. He proposed that Philip should come down to Italy. He was wasting his time at Heidelberg. The Germans were gross and life there was common; how could the soul come to her own in that prim landscape? In Tuscany the spring was scattering flowers

through the land, and Philip was nineteen; let him come
and they could wander through the mountain towns of
Umbria. Their names sang in Philip's heart. And Cäcilie
too, with her lover, had gone to Italy. When he thought
of them Philip was seized with a restlessness he could not
account for. He cursed his fate because he had no money
to travel, and he knew his uncle would not send him more
than the fifteen pounds a month which had been agreed
upon. He had not managed his allowance very well. His
pension and the price of his lessons left him very little over,
and he had found going about with Hayward expensive.
Hayward had often suggested excursions, a visit to the
play, or a bottle of wine, when Philip had come to the end
of his month's money; and with the folly of his age he had
been unwilling to confess he could not afford an extravagance.

Luckily Hayward's letters came seldom, and in the intervals Philip settled down again to his industrious life.
He had matriculated at the university and attended one or
two courses of lectures. Kuno Fischer was then at the height
of his fame and during the winter had been lecturing bril-
liantly on Schopenhauer. It was Philip's introduction to
philosophy. He had a practical mind and moved uneasily
amid the abstract; but he found an unexpected fascination
in listening to metaphysical disquisitions; they made him
breathless; it was a little like watching a tight-rope dancer
doing perilous feats over an abyss; but it was very exciting.
The pessimism of the subject attracted his youth; and he
believed that the world he was about to enter was a place
of pitiless woe and darkness. That made him none the less
eager to enter it; and when, in due course, Mrs. Carey, acting as the correspondent for his guardian's views, suggested
that it was time for him to come back to England, he
agreed with enthusiasm. He must make up his mind now
what he meant to do. If he left Heidelberg at the end of

July they could talk things over during August, and it would be a good time to make arrangements.

The date of his departure was settled, and Mrs. Carey wrote to him again. She reminded him of Miss Wilkinson, through whose kindness he had gone to Frau Erlin's house at Heidelberg, and told him that she had arranged to spend a few weeks with them at Blackstable. She would be crossing from Flushing on such and such a day, and if he travelled at the same time he could look after her and come on to Blackstable in her company. Philip's shyness immediately made him write to say that he could not leave till a day or two afterwards. He pictured himself looking out for Miss Wilkinson, the embarrassment of going up to her and asking if it were she (and he might so easily address the wrong person and be snubbed), and then the difficulty of knowing whether in the train he ought to talk to her or whether he could ignore her and read his book.

At last he left Heidelberg. For three months he had been thinking of nothing but the future; and he went without regret. He never knew that he had been happy there. Fräulein Anna gave him a copy of *Der Trompeter von Säckingen* and in return he presented her with a volume of William Morris. Very wisely neither of them ever read the other's present.

Philip was surprised when he saw his uncle and aunt. He had never noticed before that they were quite old people. The Vicar received him with his usual, not unamiable indifference. He was a little stouter, a little balder, a little grayer. Philip saw how insignificant he was. His face was weak and self-indulgent. Aunt Louisa took him in her arms and kissed him; and tears of happiness flowed down her cheeks. Philip was touched and embarrassed; he had not known with what a hungry love she cared for him.

"Oh, the time has seemed long since you've been away, Philip," she cried.

She stroked his hands and looked into his face with glad eyes.

"You've grown. You're quite a man now."

There was a very small moustache on his upper lip. He had bought a razor and now and then with infinite care shaved the down off his smooth chin.

"We've been so lonely without you." And then shyly, with a little break in her voice, she asked: "You are glad to come back to your home, aren't you?"

"Yes, rather."

She was so thin that she seemed almost transparent, the arms she put round his neck were frail bones that reminded you of chicken bones, and her faded face was oh! so wrinkled. The gray curls which she still wore in the fashion of her youth gave her a queer, pathetic look; and her little withered body was like an autumn leaf, you felt it might be blown away by the first sharp wind. Philip realised that they had done with life, these two quiet little people: they belonged to a past generation, and they were waiting there patiently, rather stupidly, for death; and he, in his vigour and his youth, thirsting for excitement and adventure, was appalled at the waste. They had done nothing, and when they went it would be just as if they had never been. He felt a great pity for Aunt Louisa, and he loved her suddenly because she loved him.

Then Miss Wilkinson, who had kept discreetly out of the way till the Careys had had a chance of welcoming their nephew, came into the room.

"This is Miss Wilkinson, Philip," said Mrs. Carey.

"The prodigal has returned," she said, holding out her hand. "I have brought a rose for the prodigal's button-hole."

With a gay smile she pinned to Philip's coat the flower she had just picked in the garden. He blushed and felt foolish. He knew that Miss Wilkinson was the daughter of his Uncle William's last rector, and he had a wide acquaintance with the daughters of clergymen. They wore ill-cut clothes and stout boots. They were generally dressed in black, for in Philip's early years at Blackstable homespuns had not reached East Anglia, and the ladies of the clergy did not favour colours. Their hair was done very untidily, and they smelt aggressively of starched linen. They considered the feminine graces unbecoming and looked the same whether they were old or young. They bore their religion arrogantly. The closeness of their connection with the church made them adopt a slightly dictatorial attitude to the rest of mankind.

Miss Wilkinson was very different. She wore a white muslin gown stamped with gray little bunches of flowers, and pointed, high-heeled shoes, with open-work stockings. To Philip's inexperience it seemed that she was wonderfully dressed; he did not see that her frock was cheap and showy. Her hair was elaborately dressed, with a neat curl in the middle of the forehead: it was very black, shiny and hard, and it looked as though it could never be in the least disarranged. She had large black eyes and her nose was slightly aquiline; in profile she had somewhat the look of a bird of prey, but full face she was prepossessing. She smiled a great deal, but her mouth was large and when she smiled she tried to hide her teeth, which were big and rather yellow. But what embarrassed Philip most was that she was heavily powdered: he had very strict views on feminine behaviour and did not think a lady ever powdered; but of course Miss Wilkinson was a lady because she was a clergyman's daughter, and a clergyman was a gentleman.

Philip made up his mind to dislike her thoroughly. She spoke with a slight French accent; and he did not know why she should, since she had been born and bred in the heart of England. He thought her smile affected, and the coy sprightliness of her manner irritated him. For two or three days he remained silent and hostile, but Miss Wilkinson apparently did not notice it. She was very affable. She

addressed her conversation almost exclusively to him, and
there was something flattering in the way she appealed constantly to his sane judgment. She made him laugh too,
and Philip could never resist people who amused him: he
had a gift now and then of saying neat things; and it was
pleasant to have an appreciative listener. Neither the Vicar
nor Mrs. Carey had a sense of humour, and they never
laughed at anything he said. As he grew used to Miss
Wilkinson, and his shyness left him, he began to like
her better; he found the French accent picturesque; and at
a garden party which the doctor gave she was very much
better dressed than anyone else. She wore a blue foulard
with large white spots, and Philip was tickled at the sensation it caused.

"I'm certain they think you're no better than you should
be," he told her, laughing.

"It's the dream of my life to be taken for an abandoned
hussy," she answered.

One day when Miss Wilkinson was in her room he asked
Aunt Louisa how old she was.

"Oh, my dear, you should never ask a lady's age; but
she's certainly too old for you to marry."

The Vicar gave his slow, obese smile.

"She's no chicken, Louisa," he said. "She was nearly
grown up when we were in Lincolnshire, and that was
twenty years ago. She wore a pigtail hanging down her
back."

"She may not have been more than ten," said Philip.

"She was older than that," said Aunt Louisa.

"I think she was near twenty," said the Vicar.

"Oh no, William. Sixteen or seventeen at the outside."

"That would make her well over thirty," said Philip.

At that moment Miss Wilkinson tripped downstairs, singing a song by Benjamin Goddard. She had put her hat on,
for she and Philip were going for a walk, and she held out
her hand for him to button her glove. He did it awkwardly.

He felt embarrassed but gallant. Conversation went easily between them now, and as they strolled along they talked of all manner of things. She told Philip about Berlin, and he told her of his year in Heidelberg. As he spoke, things which had appeared of no importance gained a new interest: he described the people at Frau Erlin's house; and to the conversations between Hayward and Weeks, which at the time seemed so significant, he gave a little twist, so that they looked absurd. He was flattered at Miss Wilkinson's laughter.

"I'm quite frightened of you," she said. "You're so sarcastic."

Then she asked him playfully whether he had not had any love affairs at Heidelberg. Without thinking, he frankly answered that he had not; but she refused to believe him.

"How secretive you are!" she said. "At your age is it likely?"

He blushed and laughed.

"You want to know too much," he said.

"Ah, I thought so," she laughed triumphantly. "Look at him blushing."

During the fortnight he had been back from Germany there had been much discussion between himself and his uncle about his future. He had refused definitely to go to Oxford, and now that there was no chance of his getting scholarships even Mr. Carey came to the conclusion that he could not afford it. His entire fortune had consisted of only two thousand pounds, and though it had been invested in mortgages at five per cent, he had not been able to live on the interest. It was now a little reduced. It would be absurd to spend two hundred a year, the least he could live on at a university, for three years at Oxford which would lead him no nearer to earning his living. He was anxious to go straight to London. Mrs. Carey thought there were only four professions for a gentleman, the Army, the Navy, the Law, and the Church. She had added medicine because her brother-in-law practised it, but did not forget that in her young days no one ever considered the doctor a gentleman. The first two were out of the question, and Philip was firm in his refusal to be ordained. Only the law remained. The local doctor had suggested that many gentlemen now went in for engineering, but Mrs. Carey opposed the idea at once.

"I shouldn't like Philip to go into trade," she said.

"No, he must have a profession," answered the Vicar.

"Why not make him a doctor like his father?"

"I should hate it," said Philip.

Mrs. Carey was not sorry. The Bar seemed out of the question, since he was not going to Oxford, for the Careys were under the impression that a degree was still necessary for success in that calling; and finally it was suggested that he should become articled to a solicitor. They wrote to the family lawyer, Albert Nixon, who was co-executor with the Vicar of Blackstable for the late Henry Carey's estate, and asked him whether he would take Philip. In a day or two the answer came back that he had not a vacancy, and was very much opposed to the whole scheme; the profession was greatly overcrowded, and without capital or connections a man had small chance of becoming more than a managing clerk; he suggested, however, that Philip should become a chartered accountant. Neither the Vicar nor his wife knew in the least what this was, and Philip had never heard of anyone being a chartered accountant; but another letter from the solicitor explained that the growth of modern businesses and the increase of companies had led to the formation of many firms of accountants to examine the books and put into the financial affairs of their clients an order which old-fashioned methods had lacked. Some years before a Royal Charter had been obtained, and the profession was becoming every year more respectable, lucrative,

and important. The chartered accountants whom Albert
Nixon had employed for thirty years happened to have a
vacancy for an articled pupil, and would take Philip for a
fee of three hundred pounds. Half of this would be returned
during the five years the articles lasted in the form of salary.
The prospect was not exciting, but Philip felt that he must
decide on something, and the thought of living in London
over-balanced the slight shrinking he felt. The Vicar of
Blackstable wrote to ask Mr. Nixon whether it was a profession suited to a gentleman; and Mr. Nixon replied that,
since the Charter, men were going into it who had been
to public schools and a university; moreover, if Philip disliked the work and after a year wished to leave, Herbert
Carter, for that was the accountant's name, would return
half the money paid for the articles. This settled it, and it
was arranged that Philip should start work on the fifteenth
of September.

"I have a full month before me," said Philip.

"And then you go to freedom and I to bondage," returned
Miss Wilkinson.

Her holidays were to last six weeks, and she would be
leaving Blackstable only a day or two before Philip.

"I wonder if we shall ever meet again," she said.

"I don't know why not."

"Oh, don't speak in that practical way. I never knew anyone so unsentimental."

Philip reddened. He was afraid that Miss Wilkinson
would think him a milksop: after all she was a young woman, sometimes quite pretty, and he was getting on for
twenty; it was absurd that they should talk of nothing but
art and literature. He ought to make love to her. They had
talked a good deal of love. There was the painter in whose
family she had lived so long in Paris: he had asked her to
sit for him, and had started to make love to her so violently
that she was forced to invent excuses not to sit to him again.
It was clear enough that Miss Wilkinson was used to atten-

tions of that sort. She looked very nice now in a large straw hat: it was hot that afternoon, the hottest day they had had, and beads of sweat stood in a line on her upper lip. He had a chance of romance. Miss Wilkinson was practically French, and that added zest to a possible adventure. When he thought of it at night in bed, or when he sat by himself in the garden reading a book, he was thrilled by it; but when he saw Miss Wilkinson it seemed less picturesque.

At all events, after what she had told him, she would not be surprised if he made love to her. He had a feeling that she must think it odd of him to make no sign: perhaps it was only his fancy, but once or twice in the last day or two he had imagined that there was a suspicion of contempt in her eyes.

"A penny for your thoughts," said Miss Wilkinson, looking at him with a smile.

"I'm not going to tell you," he answered.

He was thinking that he ought to kiss her there and then. He wondered if she expected him to do it; but after all he didn't see how he could without any preliminary business at all. She would just think him mad, or she might slap his face; and perhaps she would complain to his uncle. It would be beastly if she told his uncle: he knew what his uncle was, he would tell the doctor and Josiah Graves; and he would look a perfect fool. Aunt Louisa kept on saying that Miss Wilkinson was thirty-seven if she was a day; he shuddered at the thought of the ridicule he would be exposed to; they would say she was old enough to be his mother.

"Twopence for your thoughts," smiled Miss Wilkinson.

"I was thinking about you," he answered boldly.

That at all events committed him to nothing.

"What were you thinking?"

"Ah, now you want to know too much."

"Naughty boy!" said Miss Wilkinson.

There it was again! Whenever he had succeeded in working himself up she said something which reminded him of the governess. She called him playfully a naughty boy when he did not sing his exercises to her satisfaction. This time he grew quite sulky.

"I wish you wouldn't treat me as if I were a child."

"Are you cross?"

"Very."

"I didn't mean to."

She put out her hand and he took it. Once or twice lately when they shook hands at night he had fancied she slightly pressed his hand, but this time there was no doubt about it.

The following day there was not a cloud in the sky, and the garden was sweet and fresh after the rain. Philip went down to the beach to bathe and when he came home ate a magnificent dinner. They were having a tennis party at the vicarage in the afternoon and Miss Wilkinson put on her best dress. She certainly knew how to wear her clothes, and Philip could not help noticing how elegant she looked beside the curate's wife and the doctor's married daughter. There were two roses in her waistband. She sat in a garden chair by the side of the lawn, holding a red parasol over herself, and the light on her face was very becoming. Philip was fond of tennis. He served well and as he ran clumsily played close to the net: notwithstanding his club-foot he was quick, and it was difficult to get a ball past him. He was pleased because he won all his sets. At tea he lay down at Miss Wilkinson's feet, hot and panting.

"Flannels suit you," she said. "You look very nice this afternoon."

He blushed with delight.

"I can honestly return the compliment. You look perfectly ravishing."

She smiled and gave him a long look with her black eyes.

After supper he insisted that she should come out.

"Haven't you had enough exercise for one day?"

"It'll be lovely in the garden tonight. The stars are all out."

He was in high spirits.

"D'you know, Mrs. Carey has been scolding me on your account?" said Miss Wilkinson, when they were sauntering through the kitchen garden. "She says I mustn't flirt with you."

"Have you been flirting with me? I hadn't noticed it."

"She was only joking."

Philip put his arm round her waist and kissed her lips. She only laughed a little and made no attempt to withdraw. It had come quite naturally. Philip was very proud of himself. He said he would, and he had. It was the easiest thing in the world. He wished he had done it before. He did it again.

"Oh, you mustn't," she said.

"Why not?"

"Because I like it," she laughed.

After that things were different between them. The next day and the day after Philip showed himself an eager lover. He was deliciously flattered to discover that Miss Wilkinson was in love with him: she told him so in English, and she told him so in French. She paid him compliments. No one had ever informed him before that his eyes were charming and that he had a sensual mouth. He had never bothered much about his personal appearance, but now, when occasion presented, he looked at himself in the glass with satisfaction. When he kissed her it was wonderful to feel the passion that seemed to thrill her soul. He kissed her a good deal, for he found it easier to do that than to say the things he instinctively felt she expected of him. It still made him feel a fool to say he worshipped her. He wished there were someone to whom he could boast a little, and he would willingly have discussed minute points of his conduct. Sometimes she said things that were enigmatic, and he was puzzled. He wished Hayward had been there so that he could ask him what he thought she meant, and what he had better do next. He could not make up his mind whether he ought to rush things or let them take their time. There were only three weeks more.

"I can't bear to think of that," she said. "It breaks my heart. And then perhaps we shall never see one another again."

"If you cared for me at all, you wouldn't be so unkind to me," he whispered.

"Oh, why can't you be content to let it go on as it is? Men are always the same. They're never satisfied."

And when he pressed her, she said:

"But don't you see it's impossible. How can we here?"

He proposed all sorts of schemes, but she would not have anything to do with them.

"I daren't take the risk. It would be too dreadful if your aunt found out."

A day or two later he had an idea which seemed brilliant.

"Look here, if you had a headache on Sunday evening and offered to stay at home and look after the house, Aunt Louisa would go to church."

Generally Mrs. Carey remained in on Sunday evening in order to allow Mary Ann to go to church, but she would welcome the opportunity of attending evensong.

Philip had not found it necessary to impart to his relations the change in his views on Christianity which had occurred in Germany; they could not be expected to understand; and it seemed less trouble to go to church quietly. But he only went in the morning. He regarded this as a graceful concession to the prejudices of society and his refusal to go a second time as an adequate assertion of free thought.

When he made the suggestion, Miss Wilkinson did not speak for a moment, then shook her head.

"No, I won't," she said.

But on Sunday at tea-time she surprised Philip.

"I don't think I'll come to church this evening," she said suddenly. "I've really got a dreadful headache."

Mrs. Carey, much concerned, insisted on giving her some

"drops" which she was herself in the habit of using. Miss Wilkinson thanked her, and immediately after tea announced that she would go to her room and lie down.

"Are you sure there's nothing you'll want?" asked Mrs. Carey anxiously.

"Quite sure, thank you."

"Because, if there isn't, I think I'll go to church. I don't often have the chance of going in the evening."

"Oh yes, do go."

"I shall be in," said Philip. "If Miss Wilkinson wants anything, she can always call me."

"You'd better leave the drawing-room door open, Philip, so that if Miss Wilkinson rings, you'll hear."

"Certainly," said Philip.

So after six o'clock Philip was left alone in the house with Miss Wilkinson. He felt sick with apprehension. He wished with all his heart that he had not suggested the plan; but it was too late now; he must take the opportunity which he had made. What would Miss Wilkinson think of him if he did not! He went into the hall and listened. There was not a sound. He wondered if Miss Wilkinson really had a headache. Perhaps she had forgotten his suggestion. His heart beat painfully. He crept up the stairs as softly as he could, and he stopped with a start when they creaked. He stood outside Miss Wilkinson's room and listened; he put his hand on the knob of the door-handle. He waited. It seemed to him that he waited for at least five minutes, trying to make up his mind; and his hand trembled. He would willingly have bolted, but he was afraid of the remorse which he knew would seize him. It was like getting on the highest diving-board in a swimming-bath; it looked nothing from below, but when you got up there and stared down at the water your heart sank; and the only thing that forced you to dive was the shame of coming down meekly by the steps you had climbed up. Philip screwed up his courage. He turned the handle softly and walked in. He seemed to himself to be trembling like a leaf.

Miss Wilkinson was standing at the dressing-table with her back to the door, and she turned round quickly when she heard it open.

"Oh, it's you. What d'you want?"

She had taken off her skirt and blouse, and was standing in her petticoat. It was short and only came down to the top of her boots; the upper part of it was black, of some shiny material, and there was a red flounce. She wore a camisole of white calico with short arms. She looked grotesque. Philip's heart sank as he stared at her; she had never seemed so unattractive; but it was too late now. He closed the door behind him and locked it.

Philip woke early next morning. His sleep had been restless; but when he stretched his legs and looked at the sunshine that slid through the Venetian blinds, making patterns on the floor, he sighed with satisfaction. He was delighted with himself. He began to think of Miss Wilkinson. She had asked him to call her Emily, but, he knew not why, he could not; he always thought of her as Miss Wilkinson. Since she chid him for so addressing her, he avoided using her name at all. During his childhood he had often heard a sister of Aunt Louisa, the widow of a naval officer, spoken of as Aunt Emily. It made him uncomfortable to call Miss Wilkinson by that name, nor could he think of any that would have suited her better. She had begun as Miss Wilkinson, and it seemed inseparable from his impression of her. He frowned a little: somehow or other he saw her now at her worst; he could not forget his dismay when she turned round and he saw her in her camisole and the short petticoat; he remembered the slight roughness of her skin and the sharp, long lines on the side of the neck. His triumph was short-lived. He reckoned out her age again, and he did not see how she could be less than forty. It made the affair ridiculous. She was plain and old. His quick fancy showed her to him, wrinkled, haggard, made-up, in those frocks which were too showy for her position and too young for her years. He shuddered; he felt suddenly that he never wanted to see her again; he could not bear the thought of kissing her. He was horrified with himself. Was that love?

He took as long as he could over dressing in order to put back the moment of seeing her, and when at last he went into the dining-room it was with a sinking heart. Prayers were over, and they were sitting down at breakfast.

"Lazy bones," Miss Wilkinson cried gaily.

He looked at her and gave a little gasp of relief. She was sitting with her back to the window. She was really quite nice. He wondered why he had thought such things about her. His self-satisfaction returned to him.

He was taken aback by the change in her. She told him in a voice thrilling with emotion immediately after breakfast that she loved him; and when a little later they went into the drawing-room for his singing lesson and she sat down on the music-stool she put up her face in the middle of a scale and said:

"*Embrasse-moi.*"

When he bent down she flung her arms round his neck. It was slightly uncomfortable, for she held him in such a position that he felt rather choked.

"*Ah, je t'aime. Je t'aime. Je t'aime,*" she cried, with her extravagantly French accent.

Philip wished she would speak English.

"I say, I don't know if it's struck you that the gardener's quite likely to pass the window any minute."

"*Ah, je m'en fiche du jardinier. Je m'en refiche, et je m'en contrefiche.*"

Philip thought it was very like a French novel, and he did not know why it slightly irritated him.

At last he said:

"Well, I think I'll tootle along to the beach and have a dip."

"Oh, you're not going to leave me this morning—of all mornings?"

Philip did not quite know why he should not, but it did not matter.

"Would you like me to stay?" he smiled.

"Oh, you darling! But no, go. Go. I want to think of you mastering the salt sea waves, bathing your limbs in the broad ocean."

He got his hat and sauntered off.

"What rot women talk!" he thought to himself.

But he was pleased and happy and flattered. She was evidently frightfully gone on him.

The fortnight that remained passed quickly, and though each evening, when they went into the garden after supper, Miss Wilkinson remarked that one day more had gone, Philip was in too cheerful spirits to let the thought depress him. One night Miss Wilkinson suggested that it would be delightful if she could exchange her situation in Berlin for one in London. Then they could see one another constantly. Philip said it would be very jolly, but the prospect aroused no enthusiasm in him; he was looking forward to a wonderful life in London, and he preferred not to be hampered. He spoke a little too freely of all he meant to do, and allowed Miss Wilkinson to see that already he was longing to be off.

At length the day came on which Miss Wilkinson was to go, and she came down to breakfast, pale and subdued, in a serviceable travelling dress of black and white check. She looked a very competent governess. Philip was silent too, for he did not quite know what to say that would fit the circumstance; and he was terribly afraid that, if he said something flippant, Miss Wilkinson would break down before his uncle and make a scene. They had said their last good-bye to one another in the garden the night before, and Philip was relieved that there was now no opportunity for them to

be alone. He remained in the dining-room after breakfast in
case Miss Wilkinson should insist on kissing him on the
stairs. He did not want Mary Ann, now a woman hard upon
middle age with a sharp tongue, to catch them in a com-
promising position. Mary Ann did not like Miss Wilkinson
and called her an old cat. Aunt Louisa was not very well
and could not come to the station, but the Vicar and Philip
saw her off. Just as the train was leaving she leaned out and
kissed Mr. Carey.

"I must kiss you too, Philip," she said.

"All right," he said, blushing.

He stood up on the step and she kissed him quickly. The
train started, and Miss Wilkinson sank into the corner of her
carriage and wept disconsolately. Philip as he walked back
to the vicarage felt a distinct sensation of relief.

"Well, did you see her safely off?" asked Aunt Louisa,
when they got in.

"Yes, she seemed rather weepy. She insisted on kissing me
and Philip."

"Oh, well, at her age it's not dangerous," said Mrs. Carey.

A few days later Philip went to London. The curate
had recommended rooms in Barnes, and these Philip
engaged by letter at fourteen shillings a week. He reached
them in the evening; and the landlady, a funny little old
woman with a shrivelled body and a deeply wrinkled face,
had prepared high tea for him. Most of the sitting-room was
taken up by the sideboard and a square table; against one
wall was a sofa covered with horsehair, and by the fireplace
an arm-chair to match: there was a white antimacassar over
the back of it, and on the seat, because the springs were
broken, a hard cushion.

After having his tea he unpacked and arranged his books,
then he sat down and tried to read; but he was depressed.

The silence in the street made him slightly uncomfortable, and he felt very much alone.

Next day he got up early. He put on his tail-coat and the tall hat which he had worn at school; but it was very shabby, and he made up his mind to stop at the Stores on his way to the office and buy a new one. When he had done this he found himself in plenty of time and so walked along the Strand. The office of Messrs. Herbert Carter & Co. was in a little street off Chancery Lane, and he had to ask his way two or three times. He felt that people were staring at him a great deal, and once he took off his hat to see whether by chance the label had been left on. When he arrived he knocked at the door; but no one answered, and looking at his watch he found it was barely half past nine; he supposed he was too early. He went away and ten minutes later returned to find an office-boy, with a long nose, pimply face, and a Scotch accent, opening the door. Philip asked for Mr. Herbert Carter. He had not come yet.

"When will he be here?"

"Between ten and half past."

"I'd better wait," said Philip.

"What are you wanting?" asked the office-boy.

Philip was nervous, but tried to hide the fact by a jocose manner.

"Well, I'm going to work here if you have no objection."

"Oh, you're the new articled clerk? You'd better come in. Mr. Goodworthy'll be here in a while."

Philip walked in, and as he did so saw the office-boy—he was about the same age as Philip and called himself a junior clerk—look at his foot. He flushed and, sitting down, hid it behind the other. He looked round the room. It was dark and very dingy. It was lit by a skylight. There were three rows of desks in it and against them high stools. Over the chimney-piece was a dirty engraving of a prize-fight. Presently a clerk came in and then another; they glanced at Philip and in an undertone asked the office-boy (Philip found his name was Macdougal) who he was. A whistle blew, and Macdougal got up.

"Mr. Goodworthy's come. He's the managing clerk. Shall I tell him you're here?"

"Yes, please," said Philip.

The office-boy went out and in a moment returned.

"Will you come this way?"

Philip followed him across the passage and was shown into a room, small and barely furnished, in which a little, thin man was standing with his back to the fireplace. He was much below the middle height, but his large head, which seemed to hang loosely on his body, gave him an odd ungainliness. His features were wide and flattened, and he had prominent, pale eyes; his thin hair was sandy; he wore whiskers that grew unevenly on his face, and in places where you would have expected the hair to grow thickly there was no hair at all. His skin was pasty and yellow. He held out his hand to Philip, and when he smiled showed badly decayed teeth. He spoke with a patronising and at the same time a timid air, as though he sought to assume an importance which he did not feel. He said he hoped Philip would like the work; there was a good deal of drudgery about it, but when you got used to it, it was interesting; and one made money, that was the chief thing, wasn't it? He laughed with his odd mixture of superiority and shyness.

"Mr. Carter will be here presently," he said. "He's a little late on Monday mornings sometimes. I'll call you when he comes. In the meantime I must give you something to do. Do you know anything about book-keeping or accounts?"

"I'm afraid not," answered Philip.

"I didn't suppose you would. They don't teach you things at school that are much use in business, I'm afraid." He considered for a moment. "I think I can find you something to do."

He went into the next room and after a little while came out with a large cardboard box. It contained a vast number of letters in great disorder, and he told Philip to sort them out and arrange them alphabetically according to the names of the writers.

"I'll take you to the room in which the articled clerk generally sits. There's a very nice fellow in it. His name is Watson. He's a son of Watson, Crag, and Thompson—you know—the brewers. He's spending a year with us to learn business."

Mr. Goodworthy led Philip through the dingy office, where now six or eight clerks were working, into a narrow room behind. It had been made into a separate apartment by a glass partition, and here they found Watson sitting back in a chair, reading *The Sportsman*. He was a large, stout young man, elegantly dressed, and he looked up as Mr. Goodworthy entered. He asserted his position by calling the managing clerk Goodworthy. The managing clerk objected to the familiarity, and pointedly called him Mr. Watson, but Watson, instead of seeing that it was a rebuke, accepted the title as a tribute to his gentlemanliness.

"I see they've scratched Rigoletto," he said to Philip, as soon as they were left alone.

"Have they?" said Philip, who knew nothing about horse-racing.

He looked with awe upon Watson's beautiful clothes. His tail-coat fitted him perfectly, and there was a valuable pin artfully stuck in the middle of an enormous tie. On the chimney-piece rested his tall hat; it was saucy and bell-shaped and shiny. Philip felt himself very shabby. Watson began to talk of hunting—it was such an infernal bore having to waste one's time in an infernal office, he would only be able to hunt on Saturdays—and shooting: he had ripping invitations all over the country and of course he had to refuse them. It was infernal luck, but he wasn't going to put up with it long; he was only in this infernal hole for a year, and then he was going into the business, and he would hunt four days a week and get all the shooting there was.

"You've got five years of it, haven't you?" he said, waving his arm round the tiny room.

"I suppose so," said Philip.

"I daresay I shall see something of you. Carter does our accounts, you know."

Philip was somewhat overpowered by the young gentleman's condescension. At Blackstable they had always looked upon brewing with civil contempt, the Vicar made little jokes about the beerage, and it was a surprising experience for Philip to discover that Watson was such an important and magnificent fellow. He had been to Winchester and to Oxford, and his conversation impressed the fact upon one with frequency. When he discovered the details of Philip's education his manner became more patronising still.

"Of course, if one doesn't go to a public school those sort of schools are the next best thing, aren't they?"

Philip asked about the other men in the office.

"Oh, I don't bother about them much, you know," said Watson. "Carter's not a bad sort. We have him to dine now and then. All the rest are awful bounders."

Presently Watson applied himself to some work he had in hand, and Philip set about sorting his letters. Then Mr. Goodworthy came in to say that Mr. Carter had arrived. He took Philip into a large room next door to his own. There was a big desk in it, and a couple of big armchairs; a turkey carpet adorned the floor, and the walls were decorated with sporting prints. Mr. Carter was sitting at the desk and got up to shake hands with Philip. He was dressed in a long frock coat. He looked like a military man; his moustache was waxed, his gray hair was short and neat, he held himself upright, he talked in a breezy way, he lived at Enfield. He was very keen on games and the good of the country. He was an officer in the Hertfordshire Yeomanry and chairman of the Conservative Association. When he was told that a local magnate had said no one would take him for a City man, he felt that he had not lived in vain. He talked to

Philip in a pleasant, off-hand fashion. Mr. Goodworthy would look after him. Watson was a nice fellow, perfect gentleman, good sportsman—did Philip hunt? Pity, *the* sport for gentlemen. Didn't have much chance of hunting now, had to leave that to his son. His son was at Cambridge, he'd sent him to Rugby, fine school Rugby, nice class of boys there, in a couple of years his son would be articled, that would be nice for Philip, he'd like his son, thorough sportsman. He hoped Philip would get on well and like the work, he mustn't miss his lectures, they were getting up the tone of the profession, they wanted gentlemen in it. Well, well, Mr. Goodworthy was there. If he wanted to know anything Mr. Goodworthy would tell him. What was his handwriting like? Ah well, Mr. Goodworthy would see about that.

Philip was overwhelmed by so much gentlemanliness: in East Anglia they knew who were gentlemen and who weren't, but the gentlemen didn't talk about it.

At the end of the year there was a great deal to do. Philip went to various places with a clerk named Thompson and spent the day monotonously calling out items of expenditure, which the other checked; and sometimes he was given long pages of figures to add up. He had never had a head for figures, and he could only do this slowly. Thompson grew irritated at his mistakes. His fellow-clerk was a long, lean man of forty, sallow, with black hair and a ragged moustache; he had hollow cheeks and deep lines on each side of his nose. He took a dislike to Philip because he was an articled clerk. Because he could put down three hundred guineas and keep himself for five years Philip had the chance of a career; while he, with his experience and ability, had no possibility of ever being more than a clerk at thirty-five shillings a week. He was a cross-grained man, oppressed by a large family, and he resented the superciliousness which he fancied he saw in Philip. He sneered at Philip because he was better educated than himself, and he mocked at Philip's pronunciation; he could not forgive him because he spoke without a cockney accent, and when he talked to him sarcastically exaggerated his aitches. At first his manner was merely gruff and repellent, but as he discovered that Philip had no gift for accountancy he took pleasure in humiliating him; his attacks were gross and silly, but they wounded Philip, and in self-defence he assumed an attitude of superiority which he did not feel.

"Had a bath this morning?" Thompson said when Philip came to the office late, for his early punctuality had not lasted.

"Yes, haven't you?"

"No, I'm not gentleman, I'm only a clerk. I have a bath on Saturday night."

"I suppose that's why you're more than usually disagreeable on Monday."

"Will you condescend to do a few sums in simple addition today? I'm afraid it's asking a great deal from a gentleman who knows Latin and Greek."

"Your attempts at sarcasm are not very happy."

But Philip could not conceal from himself that the other clerks, ill-paid and uncouth, were more useful than himself. Once or twice Mr. Goodworthy grew impatient with him.

"You really ought to be able to do better than this by now," he said. "You're not even as smart as the office-boy."

Philip listened sulkily. He did not like being blamed, and it humiliated him, when, having been given accounts to make fair copies of, Mr. Goodworthy was not satisfied and gave them to another clerk to do. At first the work had been tolerable from its novelty, but now it grew irksome; and when he discovered that he had no aptitude for it, he began to hate it. Often, when he should have been doing something that was given him, he wasted his time drawing little pictures on the office note-paper. He made sketches of Watson in every conceivable attitude, and Watson was impressed by his talent. It occurred to him to take the drawings home, and he came back next day with the praises of his family.

"I wonder you didn't become a painter," he said. "Only of course there's no money in it."

It chanced that Mr. Carter two or three days later was dining with the Watsons, and the sketches were shown him. The following morning he sent for Philip. Philip saw him seldom and stood in some awe of him.

"Look here, young fellow, I don't care what you do out of office-hours, but I've seen those sketches of yours and they're on office-paper, and Mr. Goodworthy tells me you're slack. You won't do any good as a chartered accountant unless you look alive. It's a fine profession, and we're getting a very good class of men in it, but it's a profession in which you have to . . ." he looked for the termination of his phrase, but could not find exactly what he wanted, so finished rather tamely, "in which you have to look alive."

Perhaps Philip would have settled down but for the agreement that if he did not like the work he could leave after a year, and get back half the money paid for his articles. He felt that he was fit for something better than to add up accounts, and it was humiliating that he did so ill something which seemed contemptible. The vulgar scenes with Thompson got on his nerves. In March Watson ended his year at the office and Philip, though he did not care for him, saw him go with regret. The fact that the other clerks disliked them equally, because they belonged to a class a little higher than their own, was a bond of union. When Philip thought that he must spend over four years more with that dreary set of fellows his heart sank. He had expected wonderful things from London and it had given him nothing. He hated it now. He did not know a soul, and he had no idea how he was to get to know anyone. He was tired of going everywhere by himself. He began to feel that he could not stand much more of such a life. He would lie in bed at night and think of the joy of never seeing again that dingy office or any of the men in it, and of getting away from those drab lodgings.

A great disappointment befell him in the spring. Hayward had announced his intention of coming to London for the season, and Philip had looked forward very much to seeing him again. He had read so much lately and thought so much that his mind was full of ideas which he wanted to discuss, and he knew nobody who was willing to interest himself in abstract things. He was quite excited at the thought of talking his fill with someone, and he was wretched when Hayward wrote to say that the spring was lovelier than ever he had known it in Italy, and he could not bear to tear himself away. He went on to ask why Philip did not come. What was the use of squandering the days of his youth in an office when the world was beautiful? The letter proceeded.

I wonder you can bear it. I think of Fleet Street and Lincoln's Inn now with a shudder of disgust. There are only two things in the world that make life worth living, love and art. I cannot imagine you sitting in an office over a ledger, and do you wear a tall hat and an umbrella and a little black bag? My feeling is that one should look upon life as an adventure, one should burn with the hard, gemlike flame, and one should take risks, one should expose oneself to danger. Why do you not go to Paris and study art? I always thought you had talent.

The suggestion fell in with the possibility that Philip for some time had been vaguely turning over in his mind. It startled him at first, but he could not help thinking of it, and in the constant rumination over it he found his only escape from the wretchedness of his present state. They all thought he had talent; at Heidelberg they had admired his water colours, Miss Wilkinson had told him over and over again that they were charming; even strangers like the

Watsons had been struck by his sketches. *La Vie de Bohème* had made a deep impression on him. He had brought it to London and when he was most depressed he had only to read a few pages to be transported into those charming attics where Rodolphe and the rest of them danced and loved and sang. He began to think of Paris as before he had thought of London, but he had no fear of a second disillusion; he yearned for romance and beauty and love, and Paris seemed to offer them all. He had a passion for pictures, and why should he not be able to paint as well as anybody else? He wrote to Miss Wilkinson and asked her how much she thought he could live on in Paris. She told him that he could manage easily on eighty pounds a year, and she enthusiastically approved of his project. She told him he was too good to be wasted in an office. Who would be a clerk when he might be a great artist, she asked dramatically, and she besought Philip to believe in himself: that was the great thing. But Philip had a cautious nature. It was all very well for Hayward to talk of taking risks, he had three hundred a year in gilt-edged securities; Philip's entire fortune amounted to no more than eighteen-hundred pounds. He hesitated.

Then it chanced that one day Mr. Goodworthy asked him suddenly if he would like to go to Paris. The firm did the accounts for a hotel in the Faubourg St. Honoré, which was owned by an English company, and twice a year Mr. Goodworthy and a clerk went over. The clerk who generally went happened to be ill, and a press of work prevented any of the others from getting away. Mr. Goodworthy thought of Philip because he could best be spared, and his articles gave him some claim upon a job which was one of the pleasures of the business. Philip was delighted.

"You'll 'ave to work all day," said Mr. Goodworthy, "but we get our evenings to ourselves, and Paris is Paris." He smiled in a knowing way. "They do us very well at the hotel, and they give us all our meals, so it don't cost one anything.

That's the way I like going to Paris, at other people's expense."

When they arrived at Calais and Philip saw the crowd of gesticulating porters his heart leaped.

"This is the real thing," he said to himself.

He was all eyes as the train sped through the country; he adored the sand dunes, their colour seemed to him more lovely than anything he had ever seen; and he was enchanted with the canals and the long lines of poplars. When they got out of the Gare du Nord, and trundled along the cobbled streets in a ramshackle, noisy cab, it seemed to him that he was breathing a new air so intoxicating that he could hardly restrain himself from shouting aloud. They were met at the door of the hotel by the manager, a stout, pleasant man, who spoke tolerable English; Mr. Goodworthy was an old friend and he greeted them effusively; they dined in his private room with his wife, and to Philip it seemed that he had never eaten anything so delicious as the *beefsteak aux pommes,* nor drunk such nectar as the vin ordinaire, which were set before them.

To Mr. Goodworthy, a respectable householder with excellent principles, the capital of France was a paradise of the joyously obscene. He asked the manager next morning what there was to be seen that was 'thick.' He thoroughly enjoyed these visits of his to Paris; he said they kept you from growing rusty. In the evenings, after their work was over and they had dined, he took Philip to the Moulin Rouge and the Folies Bergères. His little eyes twinkled and his face wore a sly, sensual smile as he sought out the pornographic. He went into all the haunts which were specially arranged for the foreigner, and afterwards said that a nation could come to no good which permitted that sort of thing. He nudged Philip when at some revue a woman appeared with practically nothing on, and pointed out to him the most strapping of the courtesans who walked about the hall. It was a vulgar Paris that he showed Philip, but Philip saw it with eyes blinded with illusion. In the early morning he would rush out of the hotel and go to the Champs Elysées, and stand at the Place de la Concorde. It was June, and Paris was silvery with the delicacy of the air. Philip felt his heart go out to the people. Here he thought at last was romance.

They spent the inside of a week there, leaving on Sunday, and when Philip late at night reached his dingy rooms in Barnes his mind was made up; he would surrender his articles, and go to Paris to study art; but so that no one should think him unreasonable he determined to stay at the office till his year was up. He was to have his holiday during the last fortnight in August, and when he went away he would tell Herbert Carter that he had no intention of returning. But though Philip could force himself to go to the office every day he could not even pretend to show any interest in the work. His mind was occupied with the future. After the middle of July there was nothing much to do and he escaped a good deal by pretending he had to go to lectures for his first examination. The time he got in this way he spent in the National Gallery. He read books about Paris and books about painting. He was steeped in Ruskin. He read many of Vasari's lives of the painters. He liked that story of Correggio, and he fancied himself standing before some great masterpiece and crying: *Anch' io son' pittore*. His hesitation had left him now, and he was convinced that he had in him the makings of a great painter.

"After all, I can only try," he said to himself. "The great thing in life is to take risks."

At last came the middle of August. Mr. Carter was spending the month in Scotland, and the managing clerk was in charge of the office. Mr. Goodworthy had seemed pleasantly disposed to Philip since their trip to Paris, and now that Philip knew he was so soon to be free, he could look upon the funny little man with tolerance.

"You're going for your holiday tomorrow, Carey?" he said to him in the evening.

All day Philip had been telling himself that this was the last time he would ever sit in that hateful office.

"Yes, this is the end of my year."

"I'm afraid you've not done very well. Mr. Carter's very dissatisfied with you."

"Not nearly so dissatisfied as I am with Mr. Carter," returned Philip cheerfully.

"I don't think you should speak like that, Carey."

"I'm not coming back. I made the arrangement that if I didn't like accountancy Mr. Carter would return me half the money I paid for my articles and I could chuck it at the end of a year."

"You shouldn't come to such a decision hastily."

"For ten months I've loathed it all, I've loathed the work, I've loathed the office, I loathe London. I'd rather sweep a crossing than spend my days here."

"Well, I must say, I don't think you're very fitted for accountancy."

"Good-bye," said Philip, holding out his hand. "I want to thank you for your kindness to me. I'm sorry if I've been troublesome. I knew almost from the beginning I was no good."

"Well, if you really do make up your mind it is good-bye. I don't know what you're going to do, but if you're in the neighbourhood at any time come in and see us."

Philip gave a little laugh.

"I'm afraid it sounds very rude, but I hope from the bottom of my heart that I shall never set eyes on any of you again."

*T*he Vicar of Blackstable would have nothing to do with with the scheme which Philip laid before him. He had a great idea that one should stick to whatever one had begun. Like all weak men he laid an exaggerated stress on not changing one's mind.

"You chose to be an accountant of your own free will," he said.

"I just took that because it was the only chance I saw of getting up to town. I hate London, I hate the work, and nothing will induce me to go back to it."

Mr. and Mrs. Carey were frankly shocked at Philip's idea of being an artist. He should not forget, they said, that his father and mother were gentlefolk, and painting wasn't a serious profession; it was Bohemian, disreputable, immoral. And then Paris!

"So long as I have anything to say in the matter, I shall not allow you to live in Paris," said the Vicar firmly.

It was a sink of iniquity. The scarlet woman and she of Babylon flaunted their vileness there; the cities of the plain were not more wicked.

"You've been brought up like a gentleman and Christian, and I should be false to the trust laid upon me by your dead father and mother if I allowed you to expose yourself to such temptation."

"Well, I know I'm not a Christian and I'm beginning to doubt whether I'm a gentleman," said Philip.

The dispute grew more violent. There was another year before Philip took possession of his small inheritance, and during that time Mr. Carey proposed only to give him an allowance if he remained at the office. It was clear to Philip that if he meant not to continue with accountancy he must leave it while he could still get back half the money that he had been paid for his articles. The Vicar would not listen. Philip, losing all reserve, said things to wound and irritate.

"You've got no right to waste my money," he said at last. "After all it's my money, isn't it? I'm not a child. You can't prevent me from going to Paris if I make up my mind to. You can't force me to go back to London."

"All I can do is to refuse you money unless you do what I think fit."

"Well, I don't care. I've made up my mind to go to Paris.

I shall sell my clothes, and my books, and my father's jewellery."

Aunt Louisa sat by in silence, anxious and unhappy: she saw that Philip was beside himself, and anything she said then would but increase his anger. Finally the Vicar announced that he wished to hear nothing more about it and with dignity left the room. For the next three days neither Philip nor he spoke to one another. Philip wrote to Hayward for information about Paris, and made up his mind to set out as soon as he got a reply. Mrs. Carey turned the matter over in her mind incessantly; she felt that Philip included her in the hatred he bore her husband, and the thought tortured her. She loved him with all her heart. At length she spoke to him; she listened attentively while he poured out all his disillusionment of London and his eager ambition for the future.

"I may be no good, but at least let me have a try. I can't be a worse failure than I was in that beastly office. And I feel that I *can* paint. I know I've got it in me."

She was not so sure as her husband that they did right in thwarting so strong an inclination. She had read of great painters whose parents had opposed their wish to study, the event had shown with what folly; and after all it was just as possible for a painter to lead a virtuous life to the glory of God as for a chartered accountant.

"I'm so afraid of your going to Paris," she said piteously. "It wouldn't be so bad if you studied in London."

"If I'm going in for painting I must do it thoroughly, and it's only in Paris that you can get the real thing."

At his suggestion Mrs. Carey wrote to the solicitor, saying that Philip was discontented with his work in London, and asking what he thought of a change. Mr. Nixon answered as follows:

Dear Mrs. Carey,
I have seen Mr. Herbert Carter, and I am afraid I must

tell you that Philip has not done so well as one could have wished. If he is very strongly set against the work, perhaps it is better that he should take the opportunity there is now to break his articles. I am naturally very disappointed, but as you know you can take a horse to the water, but you can't make him drink.

> *Yours very sincerely,*
> *Albert Nixon.*

The letter was shown to the Vicar, but served only to increase his obstinacy. He was willing enough that Philip should take up some other profession, he suggested his father's calling, medicine, but nothing would induce him to pay an allowance if Philip went to Paris.

"It's a mere excuse for self-indulgence and sensuality," he said.

"I'm interested to hear you blame self-indulgence in others," retorted Philip acidly.

But by this time an answer had come from Hayward, giving the name of a hotel where Philip could get a room for thirty francs a month and enclosing a note of introduction to the *massière* of a school. Philip read the letter to Mrs. Carey and told her he proposed to start on the first of September.

"But you haven't got any money?" she said.

"I'm going into Tercanbury this afternoon to sell the jewellery."

He had inherited from his father a gold watch and chain, two or three rings, some links, and two pins. One of them was a pearl and might fetch a considerable sum.

"It's a very different thing, what a thing's worth and what it'll fetch," said Aunt Louisa.

Philip smiled, for this was one of his uncle's stock phrases.

"I know, but at the worst I think I can get a hundred pounds on the lot, and that'll keep me till I'm twenty-one."

Mrs. Carey did not answer, but she went upstairs, put on

her little black bonnet, and went to the bank. In an hour she came back. She went to Philip, who was reading in the drawing-room, and handed him an envelope.

"What's this?" he asked.

"It's a little present for you," she answered, smiling shyly.

He opened it and found eleven five-pound notes and a little paper sack bulging with sovereigns.

"I couldn't bear to let you sell your father's jewellery. It's the money I had in the bank. It comes to very nearly a hundred pounds."

Philip blushed, and, he knew not why, tears suddenly filled his eyes.

"Oh, my dear, I can't take it," he said. "It's most awfully good of you, but I couldn't bear to take it."

When Mrs. Carey was married she had three hundred pounds, and this money, carefully watched, had been used by her to meet any unforseen expense, any urgent charity, or to buy Christmas and birthday presents for her husband and for Philip. In the course of years it had diminished sadly, but it was still with the Vicar a subject for jesting. He talked of his wife as a rich woman and he constantly spoke of the 'nest egg.'

"Oh, please take it, Philip. I'm so sorry I've been extravagant, and there's only that left. But it'll make me so happy if you'll accept it."

"But you'll want it," said Philip.

"No, I don't think I shall. I was keeping it in case your uncle died before me. I thought it would be useful to have a little something I could get at immediately if I wanted it, but I don't think I shall live very much longer now."

"Oh, my dear, don't say that. Why, of course you're going to live for ever. I can't possibly spare you."

"Oh, I'm not sorry." Her voice broke and she hid her eyes, but in a moment, drying them, she smiled bravely.

"At first, I used to pray to God that He might not take me first, because I didn't want your uncle to be left alone, I didn't want him to have all the suffering, but now I know that it wouldn't mean so much to your uncle as it would mean to me. He wants to live more than I do, I've never been the wife he wanted, and I daresay he'd marry again if anything happened to me. So I should like to go first. You don't think it's selfish of me, Philip, do you? But I couldn't bear it if he went."

Philip kissed her wrinkled, thin cheek. He did not know why the sight he had of that overwhelming love made him feel strangely ashamed. It was incomprehensible that she should care so much for a man who was so indifferent, so selfish, so grossly self-indulgent; and he divined dimly that in her heart she knew his indifference and his selfishness, knew them and loved him humbly all the same.

"You will take the money, Philip?" she said, gently stroking his hand. "I know you can do without it, but it'll give me so much happiness. I've always wanted to do something for you. You see, I never had a child of my own, and I've loved you as if you were my son. When you were a little boy, though I knew it was wicked, I used to wish almost that you might be ill, so that I could nurse you day and night. But you were only ill once and then it was at school. I should so like to help you. It's the only chance I shall ever have. And perhaps some day when you're a great artist you won't forget me, but you'll remember that I gave you your start."

"It's very good of you," said Philip. "I'm very grateful."

A smile came into her tired eyes, a smile of pure happiness. "Oh, I'm so glad."

A *few days* later Mrs. Carey went to the station to see Philip off. She stood at the door of the carriage, trying to keep back her tears. Philip was restless and eager. He wanted to be gone.

"Kiss me once more," she said.

He leaned out of the window and kissed her. The train started, and she stood on the wooden platform of the little station, waving her handkerchief till it was out of sight. Her heart was dreadfully heavy, and the few hundred yards to the vicarage seemed very, very long. It was natural enough that he should be eager to go, she thought, he was a boy and the future beckoned to him; but she—she clenched her teeth so that she should not cry. She uttered a little inward prayer that God would guard him, and keep him out of temptation, and give him happiness and good fortune.

But Philip ceased to think of her a moment after he had settled down in his carriage. He thought only of the future. He had written to Mrs. Otter, the *massière* to whom Hayward had given him an introduction, and had in his pocket an invitation to tea on the following day. When he arrived in Paris he had his luggage put on a cab and trundled off slowly through the gay streets, over the bridge, and along the narrow ways of the Latin Quarter. He had taken a room at the Hôtel des Deux Ecoles, which was in a shabby street off the Boulevard du Montparnasse; it was convenient for Amitrano's School at which he was going to work. A waiter took his box up five flights of stairs, and Philip was shown into a tiny room, fusty from unopened windows, the greater part of which was taken up by a large wooden bed with a canopy over it of red rep; there were heavy curtains on the windows of the same dingy material; the chest of drawers served also as a washing-stand; and there was a massive wardrobe of the style which is connected with the good King Louis Philippe. The wall-paper was discoloured with age; it was dark gray, and there could be vaguely seen on it garlands of brown leaves. To Philip the room seemed quaint and charming.

Though it was late he felt too excited to sleep and, going out, made his way into the boulevard and walked towards the light. This led him to the station; and the square in front of it, vivid with arc-lamps, noisy with the yellow trams that seemed to cross it in all directions, made him laugh aloud with joy. There were cafés all round, and by chance, thirsty and eager to get a nearer sight of the crowd, Philip installed himself at a little table outside the Café de Versailles. Every other table was taken, for it was a fine night; and Philip looked curiously at the people, here little family groups, there a knot of men with odd-shaped hats and beards talking loudly and gesticulating; next to him were two men who looked like painters with women who Philip hoped were not their lawful wives; behind him he heard Americans loudly arguing on art. His soul was thrilled. He sat till very late, tired out but too happy to move, and when at last he went to bed he was wide awake; he listened to the manifold noise of Paris.

Next day about tea-time he made his way to the Lion de Belfort, and in a new street that led out of the Boulevard Raspail found Mrs. Otter. She was an insignificant woman of thirty, with a provincial air and a deliberately lady-like manner; she introduced him to her mother. He discovered presently that she had been studying in Paris for three years and later that she was separated from her husband. She had in her small drawing-room one or two portraits which she had painted, and to Philip's inexperience they seemed extremely accomplished.

"I wonder if I shall ever be able to paint as well as that," he said to her.

"Oh, I expect so," she replied, not without self-satisfaction. "You can't expect to do everything all at once, of course."

She was very kind. She gave him the address of a shop where he could get a portfolio, drawing-paper, and charcoal.

"I shall be going to Amitrano's about nine tomorrow, and if you'll be there then I'll see that you get a good place and all that sort of thing."

When he left Mrs. Otter Philip went to buy drawing materials; and next morning at the stroke of nine, trying to seem self-assured, he presented himself at the school. Mrs.

Otter was already there, and she came forward with a friendly smile. He had been anxious about the reception he would
have as a *nouveau,* for he had read a good deal of the rough
joking to which a newcomer was exposed at some of the
studios; but Mrs. Otter had reassured him.

"Oh, there's nothing like that here," she said. "You see,
about half our students are ladies, and they set a tone to the
place."

The studio was large and bare, with gray walls, on which
were pinned the studies that had received prizes. A model
was sitting in a chair with a loose wrap thrown over her, and
about a dozen men and women were standing about,
some talking and others still working on their sketch. It was
the first rest of the model.

"You'd better not try anything too difficult at first," said
Mrs. Otter. "Put your easel here. You'll find that's the easiest
pose."

Philip placed an easel where she indicated, and Mrs. Otter
introduced him to a young woman who sat next to him.

"Mr. Carey—Miss Price. Mr. Carey's never studied before,
you won't mind helping him a little just at first, will you?"
Then she turned to the model. *"La Pose."*

The model threw aside the paper she had been reading,
La Petite République, and sulkily, throwing off her gown,
got on to the stand. She stood, squarely on both feet, with
her hands clasped behind her head.

"It's a stupid pose," said Miss Price. "I can't imagine why
they chose it."

When Philip entered, the people in the studio had looked
at him curiously, and the model gave him an indifferent
glance, but now they ceased to pay attention to him. Philip,
with his beautiful sheet of paper in front of him, stared
awkwardly at the model. He did not know how to begin.
He had never seen a naked woman before. She was not
young and her breasts were shrivelled. She had colourless,
fair hair that fell over her forehead untidily, and her face was

covered with large freckles. He glanced at Miss Price's work. She had only been working on it two days, and it looked as though she had had trouble; her paper was in a mess from constant rubbing out, and to Philip's eyes the figure looked strangely distorted.

"I should have thought I could do as well as that," he said to himself.

He began on the head, thinking that he would work slowly downwards, but, he could not understand why, he found it infinitely more difficult to draw a head from the model than to draw one from his imagination. He got into difficulties. He glanced at Miss Price. She was working with vehement gravity. Her brow was wrinkled with eagerness, and there was an anxious look in her eyes. It was hot in the studio, and drops of sweat stood on her forehead. She was a girl of twenty-six, with a great deal of dull gold hair; it was handsome hair, but it was carelessly done, dragged back from her forehead and tied in a hurried knot. She had a large face, with broad, flat features and small eyes; her skin was pasty, with a singular unhealthiness of tone, and there was no colour in the cheeks. She had an unwashed air and you could not help wondering if she slept in her clothes. She was serious and silent. When the next pause came, she stepped back to look at her work.

"I don't know why I'm having so much bother," she said. "But I mean to get it right." She turned to Philip. "How are you getting on?"

"Not at all," he answered, with a rueful smile.

She looked at what he had done.

"You can't expect to do anything that way. You must take measurements. And you must square out your paper."

She showed him rapidly how to set about the business. Philip was impressed by her earnestness, but repelled by her want of charm. He was grateful for the hints she gave him and set to work again. Meanwhile other people had come in, mostly men, for the women always arrived first, and the studio for the time of year (it was early yet) was fairly full. Presently there came in a young man with thin, black hair, an enormous nose, and a face so long that it reminded you of a horse. He sat down next to Philip and nodded across him to Miss Price.

"You're very late," she said. "Are you only just up?"

"It was such a splendid day, I thought I'd lie in bed and think how beautiful it was out."

Philip smiled, but Miss Price took the remark seriously.

"That seems a funny thing to do, I should have thought it would be more to the point to get up and enjoy it."

"The way of the humourist is very hard," said the young man gravely.

He did not seem inclined to work. He looked at his canvas; he was working in colour, and had sketched in the day before the model who was posing. He turned to Philip.

"Have you just come out from England?"

"Yes."

"How did you find your way to Amitrano's?"

"It was the only school I knew of."

"I hope you haven't come with the idea that you will learn anything here which will be of the smallest use to you."

"It's the best school in Paris," said Miss Price. "It's the only one where they take art seriously."

"Should art be taken seriously?" the young man asked; and since Miss Price replied only with a scornful shrug, he added: "But the point is, all schools are bad. They are academical, obviously. Why this is less injurious than most is that the teaching is more incompetent than elsewhere. Because you learn nothing. . . ."

"But why d'you come here then?" interrupted Philip.

"I see the better course, but do not follow it. Miss Price, who is cultured, will remember the Latin of that."

"I wish you would leave me out of your conversation, Mr. Clutton," said Miss Price brusquely.

"The only way to learn to paint," he went on, imperturbable, "is to take a studio, hire a model, and just fight it out for yourself."

"That seems a simple thing to do," said Philip.

"It only needs money," replied Clutton.

He began to paint, and Philip looked at him from the corner of his eye. He was long and desperately thin; his huge bones seemed to protrude from his body; his elbows were so sharp that they appeared to jut out through the arms of his shabby coat. His trousers were frayed at the bottom, and on each of his boots was a clumsy patch. Miss Price got up and went over to Philip's easel.

"If Mr. Clutton will hold his tongue for a moment, I'll just help you a little," she said.

"Miss Price dislikes me because I have humour," said Clutton, looking meditatively at his canvas, "but she detests me because I have genius."

He spoke with solemnity, and his colossal, misshapen nose made what he said very quaint. Philip was obliged to laugh, but Miss Price grew darkly red with anger.

"You're the only person who has ever accused you of genius."

"Also I am the only person whose opinion is of the least value to me."

Miss Price began to criticise what Philip had done. She talked glibly of anatomy and construction, planes and lines, and of much else which Philip did not understand. She had been at the studio a long time and knew the main points which the masters insisted upon, but though she could show what was wrong with Philip's work she could not tell him how to put it right.

"It's awfully kind of you to take so much trouble with me," said Philip.

"Oh, it's nothing," she answered, flushing awkwardly. "People did the same for me when I first came, I'd do it for anyone."

"Miss Price wants to indicate that she is giving you the advantage of her knowledge from a sense of duty rather than on account of any charms of your person," said Clutton.

Miss Price gave him a furious look, and went back to her own drawing. The clock struck twelve, and the model with a cry of relief stepped down from the stand.

Miss Price gathered up her things.

"Some of us go to Gravier's for lunch," she said to Philip, with a look at Clutton. "I always go home myself."

"I'll take you to Gravier's if you like," said Clutton.

Philip thanked him and made ready to go. On his way out Mrs. Otter asked him how he had been getting on.

"Did Fanny Price help you?" she asked. "I put you there because I know she can do it if she likes. She's a disagreeable, ill-natured girl, and she can't draw herself at all, but she knows the ropes, and she can be useful to a newcomer if she cares to take the trouble."

On the way down the street Clutton said to him:

"You've made an impression on Fanny Price. You'd better look out."

Philip laughed. He had never seen anyone on whom he wished less to make an impression. They came to the cheap little restaurant at which several of the students ate, and Clutton sat down at a table at which three or four men were already seated. For a franc, they got an egg, a plate of meat, cheese, and a small bottle of wine. Coffee was extra. They sat on the pavement, and yellow trams passed up and down the boulevard with a ceaseless ringing of bells.

"By the way, what's your name?" said Clutton, as they took their seats.

"Carey."

"Allow me to introduce an old and trusted friend, Carey by name," said Clutton gravely. "Mr. Flanagan, Mr. Lawson."

They laughed and went on with their conversation. They

talked of a thousand things, and they all talked at once. No one paid the smallest attention to anyone else. They talked of the places they had been to in the summer, of studios, of the various schools; they mentioned names which were unfamiliar to Philip, Monet, Manet, Renoir, Pissarro, Degas. Philip listened with all his ears, and though he felt a little out of it, his heart leaped with exultation. The time flew. When Clutton got up he said:

"I expect you'll find me here this evening if you care to come. You'll find this about the best place for getting dyspepsia at the lowest cost in the Quarter."

On Tuesdays and Fridays masters spent the morning at Amitrano's, criticising the work done. In France the painter earns little unless he paints portraits and is patronised by rich Americans; and men of reputation are glad to increase their incomes by spending two or three hours once a week at one of the numerous studios where art is taught. Tuesday was the day upon which Michel Rollin came to Amitrano's. He was an elderly man, with a white beard and a florid complexion, who had painted a number of decorations for the State, but these were an object of derision to the students he instructed; he was a disciple of Ingres, impervious to the progress of art and angrily impatient with that *tas de farceurs* whose names were Manet, Degas, Monet, and Sisley; but he was an excellent teacher, helpful, polite, and encouraging. Foinet, on the other hand, who visited the studio on Fridays, was a difficult man to get on with. He was a small, shrivelled person, with bad teeth and a bilious air, an untidy gray beard, and savage eyes; his voice was high and his tone sarcastic. He had had pictures bought by the Luxembourg, and at twenty-five looked forward to a great career; but his talent was due to youth rather than to personality, and for twenty years he had done nothing but repeat the landscape which had brought him his early success. When he was reproached with monotony, he answered:

"Corot only painted one thing. Why shouldn't I?"

He was envious of everyone's success, and had a peculiar, personal loathing of the impressionists; for he looked upon his own failure as due to the mad fashion which had attracted the public, *sale bête,* to their works. The genial disdain of Michel Rollin, who called them imposters, was answered by him with vituperation, of which *crapule* and *canaille* were the least violent items; he amused himself with abuse of their private lives, and with sardonic humour, with blasphemous and obscene detail, attacked the legitimacy of their births and the purity of their conjugal relations; he used an Oriental imagery and an Oriental emphasis to accentuate his ribald scorn. Nor did he conceal his contempt for the students whose work he examined. By them he was hated and feared; the women by his brutal sarcasm he reduced often to tears, which again aroused his ridicule; and he remained at the studio, notwithstanding the protests of those who suffered too bitterly from his attacks, because there could be no doubt that he was one of the best masters in Paris. Sometimes the old model who kept the school ventured to remonstrate with him, but his expostulations quickly gave way before the violent insolence of the painter to abject apologies.

It was Foinet with whom Philip first came in contact. He was already in the studio when Philip arrived. He went round from easel to easel, with Mrs. Otter, the *massière,* by his side to interpret his remarks for the benefit of those who could not understand French. Fanny Price, sitting next to Philip, was working feverishly. Her face was sallow with nervousness, and every now and then she stopped to wipe her hands on her blouse; for they were hot with anxiety. Suddenly she turned to Philip with an anxious look, which she tried to hide by a sullen frown.

"D'you think it's good?" she asked, nodding at her drawing.

Philip got up and looked at it. He was astounded; he felt she must have no eye at all; the thing was hopelessly out of drawing.

"I wish I could draw half as well myself," he answered.

"You can't expect to, you've only just come. It's a bit too much to expect that you should draw as well as I do. I've been here two years."

Fanny Price puzzled Philip. Her conceit was stupendous. Philip had already discovered that everyone in the studio cordially disliked her; and it was no wonder, for she seemed to go out of her way to wound people.

"I complained to Mrs. Otter about Foinet," she said now. "The last two weeks he hasn't looked at my drawings. He spends about half an hour on Mrs. Otter because she's the *massière*. After all I pay as much as anybody else, and I suppose my money's as good as theirs. I don't see why I shouldn't get as much attention as anybody else."

She took up her charcoal again, but in a moment put it down with a groan.

"I can't do any more now. I'm so frightfully nervous."

She looked at Foinet, who was coming towards them with Mrs. Otter. Mrs. Otter, meek, mediocre, and self-satisfied, wore an air of importance. Foinet sat down at the easel of an untidy little Englishwoman called Ruth Chalice. She had the fine black eyes, languid but passionate, the thin face, ascetic but sensual, the skin like old ivory, which under the influence of Burne-Jones were cultivated at that time by young ladies in Chelsea. Foinet seemed in a pleasant mood; he did not say much to her, but with quick, determined strokes of her charcoal pointed out her errors. Miss Chalice beamed with pleasure when he rose. He came to Clutton, and by this time Philip was nervous too but Mrs. Otter had promised to make things easy for him. Foinet stood for a moment in front of Clutton's work, biting his thumb si-

lently, then absent-mindedly spat out upon the canvas the
little piece of skin which he had bitten off.

"That's a fine line," he said at last, indicating with his
thumb what pleased him. "You're beginning to learn to
draw."

Clutton did not answer, but looked at the master with
his usual air of sardonic indifference to the world's opinion.

"I'm beginning to think you have at least a trace of talent."

Mrs. Otter, who did not like Clutton, pursed her lips. She
did not see anything out of the way in his work. Foinet sat
down and went into technical details. Mrs. Otter grew
rather tired of standing. Clutton did not say anything, but
nodded now and then, and Foinet felt with satisfaction that
he grasped what he said and the reasons of it; most of them
listened to him, but it was clear they never understood. Then
Foinet got up and came to Philip.

"He only arrived two days ago," Mrs. Otter hurried to
explain. "He's a beginner. He's never studied before."

"*Ça se voit,*" the master said. "One sees that."

He passed on, and Mrs. Otter murmured to him:

"This is the young lady I told you about."

He looked at her as though she were some repulsive animal, and his voice grew more rasping.

"It appears that you do not think I pay enough attention
to you. You have been complaining to the *massière*. Well,
show me this work to which you wish me to give attention."

Fanny Price coloured. The blood under her unhealthy
skin seemed to be of a strange purple. Without answering
she pointed to the drawing on which she had been at work
since the beginning of the week. Foinet sat down.

"Well, what do you wish me to say to you? Do you wish
me to tell you it is good? It isn't. Do you wish me to tell
you it is well drawn? It isn't. Do you wish me to say it has
merit? It hasn't. Do you wish me to show you what is

wrong with it? It is all wrong. Do you wish me to tell you what to do with it? Tear it up. Are you satisfied now?"

Miss Price became very white. She was furious because he had said all this before Mrs. Otter. Though she had been in France so long and could understand French well enough, she could hardly speak two words.

"He's got no right to treat me like that. My money's as good as anyone else's. I pay him to teach me. That's not teaching me."

"What does she say? What does she say?" asked Foinet.

Mrs. Otter hesitated to translate, and Miss Price repeated in execrable French.

"Je vous paye pour m'apprendre."

His eyes flashed with rage, he raised his voice and shook his fist.

"Mais, nom de Dieu, I can't teach you. I could more easily teach a camel." He turned to Mrs. Otter. "Ask her, does she do this for amusement, or does she expect to earn money by it?"

"I'm going to earn my living as an artist," Miss Price answered.

"Then it is my duty to tell you that you are wasting your time. It would not matter that you have no talent, talent does not run about the streets in these days, but you have not the beginning of an aptitude. How long have you been here? A child of five after two lessons would draw better than you do. I only say one thing to you, give up this hopeless attempt. You're more likely to earn your living as a *bonne à tout faire* than as a painter. Look."

He seized a piece of charcoal, and it broke as he applied it to the paper. He cursed, and with the stump drew great firm lines. He drew rapidly and spoke at the same time, spitting out the words with venom.

"Look, those arms are not the same length. That knee, it's grotesque. I tell you a child of five. You see, she's not standing on her legs. That foot!"

With each word the angry pencil made a mark, and in a moment the drawing upon which Fanny Price had spent so much time and eager trouble was unrecognisable, a confusion of lines and smudges. At last he flung down the charcoal and stood up.

"Take my advice, Mademoiselle, try dressmaking." He looked at his watch. "It's twelve. *A la semaine prochaine, messieurs.*"

Miss Price gathered up her things slowly. Philip waited behind after the others to say to her something consolatory. He could think of nothing but:

"I say, I'm awfully sorry. What a beast that man is!"

She turned on him savagely.

"Is that what you're waiting about for? When I want your sympathy I'll ask for it. Please get out of my way."

She walked past him, out of the studio, and Philip, with a shrug of the shoulders, limped along to Gravier's for luncheon.

"It served her right," said Lawson, when Philip told him what had happened. "Ill-tempered slut."

Philip did not find living in Paris as cheap as he had been led to believe and by February had spent most of the money with which he started. He was too proud to appeal to his guardian, nor did he wish Aunt Lousia to know that his circumstances were straitened, since he was certain she would make an effort to send him something from her own pocket, and he knew how little she could afford to. In three months he would attain his majority and come into possession of his small fortune. He tided over the interval by selling the few trinkets which he had inherited from his father.

At about this time Lawson suggested that they should take a small studio which was vacant in one of the streets that led out of the Boulevard Raspail. It was very cheap. It had a room attached, which they could use as a bed-room; and since Philip was at the school every morning Lawson could have the undisturbed use of the studio then; Lawson, after wandering from school to school, had come to the conclusion that he could work best alone, and proposed to get a model in three or four days a week. At first Philip hesitated on account of the expense, but they reckoned it out; and it seemed (they were so anxious to have a studio of their own that they calculated pragmatically) that the cost would not be much greater than that of living in a hotel. Though the rent and the cleaning by the *concierge* would come to a little more, they would save on the *petit déjeuner,* which they could make themselves. A year or two earlier Philip would have refused to share a room with anyone, since he was so sensitive about his deformed foot, but his morbid way of looking at it was growing less marked: in Paris it did not seem to matter so much, and, though he never by any chance forgot it himself, he ceased to feel that other people were constantly noticing it.

They moved in, bought a couple of beds, a washing-stand, a few chairs, and felt for the first time the thrill of possession. They were so excited that the first night they went to bed in what they could call a home they lay awake talking till three in the morning; and next day found lighting the fire and making their own coffee, which they had in pyjamas, such a jolly business that Philip did not get to Amitrano's till nearly eleven. He was in excellent spirits. He nodded to Fanny Price.

"How are you getting on?" he asked cheerily.

"What does that matter to you?" she asked in reply.

Philip could not help laughing.

"Don't jump down my throat. I was only trying to make myself polite."

"I don't want your politeness."

"D'you think it's worth while quarrelling with me too?" asked Philip mildly. "There are so few people you're on speaking terms with, as it is."

"That's my business, isn't it?"

"Quite."

He began to work, vaguely wondering why Fanny Price made herself so disagreeable. He had come to the conclusion that he thoroughly disliked her. Everyone did. People were only civil to her at all from fear of the malice of her tongue; for to their faces and behind their backs she said abominable things. But Philip was feeling so happy that he did not want even Miss Price to bear ill-feeling towards him. He used the artifice which had often before succeeded in banishing her ill-humour.

"I say, I wish you'd come and look at my drawing. I've got in an awful mess."

"Thank you very much, but I've got something better to do with my time."

Philip stared at her in surprise, for the one thing she could be counted upon to do with alacrity was to give advice. She went on quickly in a low voice, savage with fury.

"Now that Lawson's gone you think you'll put up with me. Thank you very much. Go and find somebody else to help you. I don't want anybody else's leavings."

Lawson had the pedagogic instinct; whenever he found anything out he was eager to impart it; and because he taught with delight he talked with profit. Philip, without thinking anything about it, had got into the habit of sitting by his side; it never occurred to him that Fanny Price was consumed with jealousy, and watched his acceptance of someone else's tuition with ever-increasing anger.

"You were very glad to put up with me when you knew nobody here," she said bitterly, "and as soon as you made friends with other people you threw me aside, like an old glove"—she repeated the stale metaphor with satisfaction—"like an old glove. All right, I don't care, but I'm not going to be made a fool of another time."

There was a suspicion of truth in what she said, and it made Philip angry enough to answer what first came into his head.

"Hang it all, I only asked your advice because I saw it pleased you."

She gave a gasp and threw him a sudden look of anguish. Then two tears rolled down her cheeks. She looked frowsy and grotesque. Philip, not knowing what on earth this new attitude implied, went back to his work. He was uneasy and conscience-stricken; but he would not go to her and say he was sorry if he had caused her pain, because he was afraid she would take the opportunity to snub him. For two or three weeks she did not speak to him, and, after Philip had got over the discomfort of being cut by her, he was somewhat relieved to be free from so difficult a friendship. He had been a little disconcerted by the air of proprietorship she assumed over him. She was an extraordinary woman. She came every day to the studio at eight o'clock, and was ready to start working when the model was in position; she worked steadily, talking to no one, struggling hour after hour with difficulties she could not overcome, and remained till the clock struck twelve. Her work was hopeless. There was not in it the smallest approach even to the mediocre achievement at which most of the young persons were able after some months to arrive. She wore every day the same ugly brown dress, with the mud of the last wet day still caked on the hem and with the raggedness, which Philip had noticed the first time he saw her, still unmended.

But one day she came up to him, and with a scarlet face asked whether she might speak to him afterwards.

"Of course, as much as you like," smiled Philip. "I'll wait behind at twelve."

He went to her when the day's work was over.

"Will you walk a little bit with me?" she said, looking away from him with embarrassment.

"Certainly."

They walked for two or three minutes in silence.

"D'you remember what you said to me the other day?" she asked then on a sudden.

"Oh, I say, don't let's quarrel," said Philip. "It really isn't worth while."

She gave a quick, painful inspiration.

"I don't want to quarrel with you. You're the only friend I had in Paris. I thought you rather liked me. I felt there was something between us. I was drawn towards you—you know what I mean, your club-foot."

Philip reddened and instinctively tried to walk without a limp. He did not like anyone to mention the deformity. He knew what Fanny Price meant. She was ugly and uncouth, and because he was deformed there was between them a certain sympathy. He was very angry with her, but he forced himself not to speak.

"You said you only asked my advice to please me. Don't you think my work's any good?"

"I've only seen your drawing at Amitrano's. It's awfully hard to judge from that."

"I was wondering if you'd come and look at my other work. I've never asked anyone else to look at it. I should like to show it to you."

"It's awfully kind of you. I'd like to see it very much."

"I live quite near here," she said apologetically. "It'll only take you ten minutes."

"Oh, that's all right," he said.

They were walking along the boulevard, and she turned down a side street, then led him into another, poorer still, with cheap shops on the ground floor, and at last stopped. They climbed flight after flight of stairs. She unlocked a door, and they went into a tiny attic with a sloping roof and a small window. This was closed and the room had a musty smell. Though it was very cold there was no fire and no sign that there had been one. The bed was unmade. A chair, a chest of drawers which served also as a washstand, and a cheap easel, were all the furniture. The place would have been squalid enough in any case, but the litter, the untidiness, made the impression revolting. On the chimney-piece, scattered over with paints and brushes, were a cup, a dirty plate, and a tea-pot.

"If you'll stand over there I'll put them on the chair so that you can see them better."

She showed him twenty small canvases, about eighteen by twelve. She placed them on the chair, one after the other, watching his face; he nodded as he looked at each one.

"You do like them, don't you?" she said anxiously, after a bit.

"I just want to look at them all first," he answered. "I'll talk afterwards."

He was collecting himself. He was panic-stricken. He did not know what to say. It was not only that they were ill-drawn, or that the colour was put on amateurishly by some-one who had no eye for it; but there was no attempt at get-ting the values, and the perspective was grotesque. It looked like the work of a child of five, but a child would have had some naïveté and might at least have made an attempt to put down what he saw; but here was the work of a vulgar mind chock full of recollections of vulgar pictures. Philip re-membered that she had talked enthusiastically about Monet and the Impressionists, but here were only the worst tradi-tions of the Royal Academy.

"There," she said at last, "that's the lot."

Philip was no more truthful than anybody else, but he had a great difficulty in telling a thundering, deliberate lie, and he blushed furiously when he answered:

"I think they're most awfully good."

A faint colour came into her unhealthy cheeks, and she smiled a little.

"You needn't say so if you don't think so, you know. I want the truth."

"But I do think so."

"Haven't you got any criticism to offer? There must be some you don't like as well as others."

Philip looked round helplessly. He saw a landscape, the

typical picturesque "bit" of the amateur, an old bridge, a creeper-clad cottage, and a leafy bank.

"Of course I don't pretend to know anything about it," he said. "But I wasn't quite sure about the values of that."

She flushed darkly and taking up the picture quickly turned its back to him.

"I don't know why you should have chosen that one to sneer at. It's the best thing I've ever done. I'm sure my values are all right. That's a thing you can't teach anyone, you either understand values or you don't."

"I think they're all most awfully good," repeated Philip.

She looked at them with an air of self-satisfaction.

"I don't think they're anything to be ashamed of."

Philip looked at his watch.

"I say, it's getting late. Won't you let me give you a little lunch?"

"I've got my lunch waiting for me here."

Philip saw no sign of it, but supposed perhaps the *concierge* would bring it up when he was gone. He was in a hurry to get away. The mustiness of the room made his head ache.

In March there was all the excitement of sending in to the Salon. Clutton, characteristically, had nothing ready, and he was very scornful of the two heads that Lawson sent; they were obviously the work of a student, straight-forward portraits of models, but they had a certain force; Clutton, aiming at perfection, had no patience wth efforts which betrayed hesitancy, and with a shrug of the shoulders told Lawson it was an impertinence to exhibit stuff which should never have been allowed out of his studio; he was not less contemptuous when the two heads were accepted. Flanagan tried his luck too, but his picture was refused. Mrs. Otter sent a blameless *Portrait de ma*

Mère, accomplished and second-rate; and was hung in a very good place.

Hayward, whom Philip had not seen since he left Heidelberg, arrived in Paris to spend a few days in time to come to the party which Lawson and Philip were giving in their studio to celebrate the hanging of Lawson's pictures. Philip had been eager to see Hayward again, but when at last they met, he experienced some disappointment. Hayward had altered a little in appearance: his fine hair was thinner, and with the rapid wilting of the very fair, he was becoming wizened and colourless; his blue eyes were paler than they had been, and there was a muzziness about his features. On the other hand, in mind he did not seem to have changed at all, and the culture which had impressed Philip at eighteen aroused somewhat the contempt of Philip at twenty-one. He had altered a good deal himself, and regarding with scorn all his old opinions of art, life, and letters, had no patience with anyone who still held them. He was scarcely conscious of the fact that he wanted to show off before Hayward, but when he took him round the galleries he poured out to him all the revolutionary opinions which he himself had so recently adopted. He took him to Manet's *Olympia* and said dramatically:

"I would give all the old masters except Velasquez, Rembrandt, and Vermeer for that one picture."

"Who was Vermeer?" asked Hayward.

"Oh, my dear fellow, don't you know Vermeer? You're not civilised. You mustn't live a moment longer without making his acquaintance. He's the one old master who painted like a modern."

He dragged Hayward out of the Luxembourg and hurried him off to the Louvre.

"But aren't there any more pictures here?" asked Hayward, with the tourist's passion for thoroughness.

"Nothing of the least consequence. You can come and look at them by yourself with your Baedeker."

When they arrived at the Louvre Philip led his friend down the Long Gallery.

"I should like to see *The Gioconda*," said Hayward.

"Oh, my dear fellow, it's only literature," answered Philip.

At last, in a small room, Philip stopped before *The Lacemaker* of Vermeer van Delft.

"There, that's the best picture in the Louvre. It's exactly like a Manet."

With an expressive, eloquent thumb Philip expatiated on the charming work. He used the jargon of the studios with overpowering effect.

"I don't know that I see anything so wonderful as all that in it," said Hayward.

"Of course it's a painter's picture," said Philip. "I can quite believe the layman would see nothing much in it."

"The what?" said Hayward.

"The layman."

Like most people who cultivate an interest in the arts, Hayward was extremely anxious to be right. He was dogmatic with those who did not venture to assert themselves, but with the self-assertive he was very modest. He was impressed by Philip's assurance, and accepted meekly Philip's implied suggestion that the painter's arrogant claim to be the sole possible judge of painting has anything but its impertinence to recommend it.

A day or two later Philip and Lawson gave their party. Miss Chalice offered to come and cook for them. She took no interest in her own sex and declined the suggestion that other girls should be asked for her sake. Clutton, Flanagan, Potter, and two others made up the party. Furniture was scarce, so the model stand was used as a table, and the guests were to sit on portmanteaux if they liked, and if they didn't on the floor. The feast consisted of a *pot-au-feu,* which Miss Chalice had made, of a leg of mutton roasted round the corner and brought round hot and savoury (Miss Chalice had cooked the potatoes, and the studio was redolent of

the carrots she had fried; fried carrots were her specialty);
and this was to be followed by *poires flambées,* pears with
burning brandy. The meal was to finish with an enormous
fromage de Brie, which stood near the window and added
fragrant odours to all the others which filled the studio.
Hayward in order to put the rest of them at their ease had
clothed himself in a tweed suit and a Trinity Hall tie. He
looked grotesquely British. The others were elaborately polite to him, and during the soup they talked of the weather
and the political situation. There was a pause while they
waited for the leg of mutton, and Miss Chalice lit a cigarette.

"Rapunzel, Rapunzel, let down your hair," she said
suddenly.

With an elegant gesture she untied a ribbon so that her
tresses fell over her shoulders. She shook her head.

"I always feel more comfortable with my hair down."

With her large brown eyes, thin, ascetic face, her pale skin,
and broad forehead, she might have stepped out of a picture
by Burne-Jones. She had long, beautiful hands, with fingers
deeply stained by nicotine. She wore sweeping draperies,
mauve and green. There was about her the romantic air of
High Street, Kensington. She was wantonly æsthetic; but
she was an excellent creature, kind and good natured; and
her affectations were but skin-deep. There was a knock at
the door, and they all gave a shout of exultation. Miss
Chalice rose and opened. She took the leg of mutton and
held it high above her, as though it were the head of John
the Baptist on a platter; and, the cigarette still in her mouth,
advanced with solemn, hieratic steps.

The mutton was eaten with gusto, and it did one good
to see what a hearty appetite the pale-faced lady had. Clutton and Potter sat on each side of her, and everyone knew
that neither had found her unduly coy. She grew tired of
most people in six weeks, but she knew exactly how to treat
afterwards the gentlemen who had laid their young hearts
at her feet. She bore them no ill-will, though having loved

them she had ceased to do so, and treated them with friendliness but without familiarity. Now and then she looked at Lawson with melancholy eyes. The *poires flambées* were a great success, partly because of the brandy, and partly because Miss Chalice insisted that they should be eaten with the cheese.

"I don't know whether it's perfectly delicious, or whether I'm just going to vomit," she said, after she had thoroughly tried the mixture.

Coffee and cognac followed with sufficient speed to prevent any untoward consequence, and they settled down to smoke in comfort. Ruth Chalice, who could do nothing that was not deliberately artistic, arranged herself in a graceful attitude. She looked into the dark abyss of time with brooding eyes, and now and then with a long meditative glance at Lawson she sighed deeply.

About this time Philip made a new friend. On Monday morning models assembled at the school in order that one might be chosen for the week, and one day a young man was taken who was plainly not a model by profession. Philip's attention was attracted by the manner in which he held himself: when he got on to the stand he stood firmly on both feet, square, with clenched hands, and with his head defiantly thrown forward; the attitude emphasised his fine figure; there was no fat on him, and his muscles stood out as though they were of iron. His head, close-cropped, was well-shaped, and he wore a short beard; he had large, dark eyes and heavy eyebrows. He held the pose hour after hour without appearance of fatigue. There was in his mien a mixture of shame and of determination. His air of passionate energy excited Philip's romantic imagination, and when, the sitting ended, he saw him in his clothes, it seemed to him that he wore them as though he were a king in rags. He was uncommunicative, but in a day or two Mrs. Otter told Philip that the model was a Spaniard and that he had never sat before.

"I suppose he was starving," said Philip.

"Have you noticed his clothes? They're quite neat and decent, aren't they?"

It chanced that Potter, one of the Americans who worked at Amitrano's, was going to Italy for a couple of months, and offered his studio to Philip. Philip was pleased. He was growing a little impatient of Lawson's peremptory advice and wanted to be by himself. At the end of the week he went up to the model and on the pretence that his drawing was not finished asked whether he could come and sit to him one day.

"I'm not a model," the Spaniard answered. "I have other things to do next week."

"Come and have luncheon with me now, and we'll talk about it," said Philip, and as the other hesitated, he added with a smile: "It won't hurt you to lunch with me."

With a shrug of the shoulders the model consented, and they went off to a *crémerie*. The Spaniard spoke broken French, fluent but difficult to follow, and Philip managed to get on well enough with him. He found out that he was a writer. He had come to Paris to write novels and kept himself meanwhile by all the expedients possible to a penniless man: he gave lessons, he did any translations he could get hold of, chiefly business documents, and at last had been driven to make money by his fine figure. Sitting was well paid, and what he had earned during the last week was enough to keep him for two more; he told Philip, amazed, that he could live easily on two francs a day; but it filled him with shame that he was obliged to show his body for money, and he looked upon sitting as a degradation which only hunger could excuse. Philip explained that he did not want him to sit for the figure, but only for the head; he wished to do a portrait of him which he might send to the next Salon.

"But why should you want to paint me?" asked the Spaniard.

Philip answered that the head interested him, he thought he could do a good portrait.

"I can't afford the time. I grudge every minute that I have to rob from my writing."

Philip, with his passion for the romantic, welcomed the opportunity to get in touch with a Spaniard; he used all his persuasiveness to overcome the man's reluctance.

"I'll tell you what I'll do," said the Spaniard at last. "I'll sit to you, but not for money, for my own pleasure."

Philip expostulated, but the other was firm, and at length they arranged that he should come on the following Monday at one o'clock. He gave Philip a card on which was printed his name: Miguel Ajuria.

One day he brought part of the manuscript, and in his bad French, translating excitedly as he went along so that Philip could scarcely understand, he read passages. It was lamentable. Philip, puzzled, looked at the picture he was painting; the mind behind that broad brow was trivial; and the flashing, passionate eyes saw nothing in life but the obvious. Philip was not satisfied with his portrait, and at the end of a sitting he nearly always scraped out what he had done. It was all very well to aim at the intention of the soul: who could tell what that was when people seemed a mass of contradictions? He liked Miguel, and it distressed him to realise that his magnificent struggle was futile; he had everything to make a good writer but talent. Philip looked at his own work. How could you tell whether there was anything in it or whether you were wasting your time? It was clear that the will to achieve could not help you and confidence in yourself meant nothing. Philip thought of Fanny Price; she had a vehement belief in her talent; her strength of will was extraordinary.

"If I thought I wasn't going to be really good, I'd rather

give up painting," said Philip. "I don't see any use in being a second-rate painter."

Then one morning when he was going out, the *concierge* called out to him that there was a letter. Nobody wrote to him but his Aunt Louisa and sometimes Hayward, and this was a handwriting he did not know. The letter was as follows:

> *Please come at once when you get this. I couldn't put up with it any more. Please come yourself. I can't bear the thought that anyone else should touch me. I want you to have everything.*
>
> ....   F. Price.
>
> *I have not had anything to eat for three days.*

Philip felt on a sudden sick with fear. He hurried to the house in which she lived. He was astonished that she was in Paris at all. He had not seen her for months and imagined she had long since returned to England. When he arrived he asked the *concierge* whether she was in.

"Yes, I've not seen her go out for two days."

Philip ran upstairs and knocked at the door. There was no reply. He called her name. The door was locked, and on bending down he found the key was in the lock.

"Oh, my God, I hope she hasn't done something awful," he cried aloud.

He ran down and told the porter that she was certainly in the room. He had had a letter from her and feared a terrible accident. He suggested breaking open the door. The porter, who had been sullen and disinclined to listen, became alarmed; he could not take the responsibility of breaking into the room; they must go for the *commissaire de police*. They walked together to the *bureau*, and then they fetched a locksmith. Philip found that Miss Price had not paid the last quarter's rent: on New Year's Day she had not given the *concierge* the present which old-established custom led him to regard as a right. The four of them went upstairs, and they knocked again at the door. There was no reply. The locksmith set to work, and at last they entered the room. Philip gave a cry and instinctively covered his eyes with his hands. The wretched woman was hanging with a rope round her neck, which she had tied to a hook in the ceiling fixed by some previous tenant to hold up the curtains of the bed. She had moved her own little bed out of the way and had stood on a chair, which had been kicked away. It was lying on its side on the floor. They cut her down. The body was quite cold.

Philip could not get the unhappy event out of his head. What troubled him most was the uselessness of Fanny's effort. No one could have worked harder than she, nor with more sincerity; she believed in herself with all her heart; but it was plain that self-confidence meant very little, all his friends had it, Miguel Ajuria among the rest; and Philip was shocked by the contrast between the Spaniard's heroic endeavour and the triviality of the thing he attempted. The unhappiness of Philip's life at school had called up in him the power of self-analysis; and this vice, as subtle as drug-taking, had taken possession of him so that he had now a peculiar keenness in the dissection of his feelings. He could not help seeing that art affected him differently from others. A fine picture gave Lawson an immediate thrill. His appreciation was instinctive. Even Flanagan felt certain things which Philip was obliged to think out. His own appreciation was intellectual. He could not help thinking that if he had in him the artistic temperament (he hated the phrase, but could discover no other) he would feel beauty in the emotional, unreasoning way in which they did. He began to wonder whether he had anything more than a superficial cleverness of the hand which enabled him to copy objects with accuracy. That was nothing. He had learned to despise technical dexterity. The important thing was to feel in terms of paint. He felt himself barren. He painted with the brain, and he could not help knowing that the only painting worth anything was done with the heart.

He had very little money, barely sixteen hundred pounds, and it would be necessary for him to practise the severest economy. He could not count on earning anything for ten years. The history of painting was full of artists who had earned nothing at all. He must resign himself to penury; and it was worth while if he produced work which was immortal; but he had a terrible fear that he would never be more than second-rate. Was it worth while for that to give up one's youth, and the gaiety of life, and the manifold chances of being? He knew the existence of foreign painters in Paris enough to see that the lives they led were narrowly provincial. He knew some who had dragged along for twenty years in the pursuit of a fame which always escaped them till they sunk into sordidness and alcoholism. Fanny's suicide had aroused memories, and Philip heard ghastly stories of the way in which one person or another had escaped from despair. He remembered the scornful advice which the master had given poor Fanny: it would have been well for her if she had taken it and given up an attempt which was hopeless.

It seemed to Philip, brooding over these matters, that in the true painters, writers, musicians, there was a power which drove them to such complete absorption in their work as to make it inevitable for them to subordinate life to art. Succumbing to an influence they never realised, they were merely dupes of the instinct that possessed them, and life slipped through their fingers unlived. But he had a feeling that life was to be lived rather than portrayed, and he wanted to search out the various experiences of it and wring from each moment all the emotion that it offered. He made up his mind at length to take a certain step and abide by the result, and, having made up his mind, he determined to take the step at once. Luckily enough the next morning was one of Foinet's days, and he resolved to ask him point-blank whether it was worth his while to go on with the study of art. He had never forgotten the master's brutal advice to Fanny Price. It had been sound. Philip could never get Fanny entirely out of his head. The studio seemed strange without her, and now and then the gesture of one of the women working there or the tone of a voice would give him a sudden start, reminding him of her: her presence was more noticeable now she was dead than it had ever been during her life; and he often dreamed of her at night, waking with a cry of terror. It was horrible to think of all the suffering she must have endured.

Philip knew that on the days Foinet came to the studio he lunched at a little restaurant in the Rue d'Odessa, and he hurried his own meal so that he could go and wait outside till the painter came out. Philip walked up and down the crowded street and at last saw Monsieur Foinet walking, with bent head, towards him; Philip was very nervous, but he forced himself to go up to him.

"Pardon, monsieur, I should like to speak to you for one moment."

Foinet gave him a rapid glance, recognised him, but did not smile a greeting.

"Speak," he said.

"I've been working here nearly two years now under you. I wanted to ask you to tell me frankly if you think it worth while for me to continue."

Philip's voice was trembling a little. Foinet walked on without looking up. Philip, watching his face, saw no trace of expression upon it.

"I don't understand."

"I'm very poor. If I have no talent I would sooner do something else."

"Don't you know if you have talent?"

"All my friends know they have talent, but I am aware some of them are mistaken."

Foinet's bitter mouth outlined the shadow of a smile, and he asked:

"Do you live near here?"

Philip told him where his studio was. Foinet turned round.

"Let us go there? You shall show me your work."

"Now?" cried Philip.

"Why not?"

Philip had nothing to say. He walked silently by the master's side. He felt horribly sick. It had never struck him that Foinet would wish to see his things there and then; he meant, so that he might have time to prepare himself, to ask him if he would mind coming at some future date or whether he might bring them to Foinet's studio. He was trembling with anxiety. In his heart he hoped that Foinet would look at his picture, and that rare smile would come into his face, and he would shake Philip's hand and say: "*Pas mal*. Go on, my lad. You have talent, real talent." Philip's heart swelled at the thought. It was such a relief, such a joy! Now he could go on with courage; and what did hardship matter, privation, and disappointment, if he arrived at last? He had worked very hard, it would be too cruel if all that industry were futile. And then with a start he remembered that he had heard Fanny Price say just that. They arrived at the house, and Philip was seized with fear. If he had dared he would have asked Foinet to go away. He did not want to know the truth. They went in and the *concierge* handed him a letter as they passed. He glanced at the envelope and recognised his uncle's handwriting. Foinet followed him up the stairs. Philip could think of nothing to say; Foinet was mute, and the silence got on his nerves. The professor sat down; and Philip without a word placed before him two portraits, two or three landscapes, and a number of sketches.

"That's all," he said presently, with a nervous laugh.

Monsieur Foinet rolled himself a cigarette and lit it.

"You have very little private means?" he asked at last.

"Very little," answered Philip, with a sudden feeling of cold at his heart. "Not enough to live on."

"There is nothing so degrading as the constant anxiety about one's means of livelihood. I have nothing but contempt for the people who despise money. They are hypocrites or fools. Money is like a sixth sense without which you cannot make a complete use of the other five. Without an adequate income half the possibilities of life are shut off. The only thing to be careful about is that you do not pay more than a shilling for the shilling you earn. You will hear people say that poverty is the best spur to the artist. They have never felt the iron of it in their flesh. They do not know how mean it makes you. It exposes you to endless humiliation, it cuts your wings, it eats into your soul like a cancer. It is not wealth one asks for, but just enough to preserve one's dignity, to work unhampered, to be generous, frank, and independent. I pity with all my heart the artist, whether he writes or paints, who is entirely dependent for subsistence upon his art."

Philip quietly put away the various things which he had shown.

"I'm afraid that sounds as if you didn't think I had much chance."

Monsieur Foinet slightly shrugged his shoulders.

"You have a certain manual dexterity. With hard work and perseverance there is no reason why you should not become a careful, not incompetent painter. You would find hundreds who painted worse than you, hundreds who painted as well. I see no talent in anything you have shown me. I see industry and intelligence. You will never be anything but mediocre."

Philip obliged himself to answer quite steadily.

"I'm very grateful to you for having taken so much trouble. I can't thank you enough."

Monsieur Foinet got up and made as if to go, but he

changed his mind and, stopping, put his hand on Philip's shoulder.

"But if you were to ask me my advice, I should say: take your courage in both hands and try your luck at something else. It sounds very hard, but let me tell you this: I would give all I have in the world if someone had given me that advice when I was your age and I had taken it."

Philip looked up at him with surprise. The master forced his lips into a smile, but his eyes remained grave and sad.

"It is cruel to discover one's mediocrity only when it is too late. It does not improve the temper."

He gave a little laugh as he said the last words and quickly walked out of the room.

Philip mechanically took up the letter from his uncle. The sight of his handwriting made him anxious, for it was his aunt who always wrote to him. She had been ill for the last three months, and he had offered to go over to England and see her; but she, fearing it would interfere with his work, had refused. She did not want him to put himself to inconvenience; she said she would wait till August and then she hoped he would come and stay at the vicarage for two or three weeks. If by any chance she grew worse she would let him know, since she did not wish to die without seeing him again. If his uncle wrote to him it must be because she was too ill to hold a pen. Philip opened the letter. It ran as follows:

My dear Philip,

I regret to inform you that your dear Aunt departed this life early this morning. She died very suddenly, but quite peacefully. The change for the worse was so rapid that we had no time to send for you. She was fully prepared for the end and entered into rest with the complete assurance of a blessed resurrection and with resignation to the divine will of our blessed Lord Jesus Christ. Your Aunt would have liked you to be present at the funeral so I trust you will come

OF HUMAN BONDAGE 137

as soon as you can. There is naturally a great deal of work
thrown upon my shoulders and I am very much upset. I
trust that you will be able to do everything for me.

Your affectionate uncle,
William Carey.

Next day Philip arrived at Blackstable. Since the death of
his mother he had never lost anyone closely connected with
him; his aunt's death shocked him and filled him also with
a curious fear; he felt for the first time his own mortality.
He could not realise what life would be for his uncle without the constant companionship of the woman who had
loved and tended him for forty years. He expected to find
him broken down with hopeless grief. He dreaded the first
meeting; he knew that he could say nothing which would
be of use. He rehearsed to himself a number of apposite
speeches.

He entered the vicarage by the side-door and went into
the dining-room. Uncle William was reading the paper.

"Your train was late," he said, looking up.

Philip was prepared to give way to his emotion, but the
matter-of-fact reception startled him. His uncle, subdued
but calm, handed him the paper.

"There's a very nice little paragraph about her in *The
Blackstable Times,*" he said.

Philip read it mechanically.

"Would you like to come up and see her?"

Philip nodded and together they walked upstairs. Aunt
Louisa was lying in the middle of the large bed, with flowers
all round her.

"Would you like to say a short prayer?" said the Vicar.

He sank on his knees, and because it was expected of
him Philip followed his example. He looked at the little
shrivelled face. He was only conscious of one emotion:
what a wasted life! In a minute Mr. Carey gave a cough, and
stood up. He pointed to a wreath at the foot of the bed.

"That's from the Squire," he said. He spoke in a low voice as though he were in church, but one felt that, as a clergyman, he found himself quite at home. "I expect tea is ready."

They went down again to the dining-room. The drawn blinds gave a lugubrious aspect. The Vicar sat at the end of the table at which his wife had always sat and poured out the tea with ceremony. Philip could not help feeling that neither of them should have been able to eat anything, but when he saw that his uncle's appetite was unimpaired he fell to with his usual heartiness. They did not speak for a while. Philip set himself to eat an excellent cake with the air of grief which he felt was decent.

"Things have changed a great deal since I was a curate," said the Vicar presently. "In my young days the mourners used always to be given a pair of black gloves and a piece of black silk for their hats. Poor Louisa used to make the silk into dresses. She always said that twelve funerals gave her a new dress."

Then he told Philip who had sent wreaths; there were twenty-four of them already; when Mrs. Rawlingson, wife of the Vicar at Ferne, had died she had had thirty-two; but probably a good many more would come the next day; the funeral would start at eleven o'clock from the vicarage, and they should beat Mrs. Rawlingson easily. Louisa never liked Mrs. Rawlingson.

"I shall take the funeral myself. I promised Louisa I would never let anyone else bury her."

Philip looked at his uncle with disapproval when he took a second piece of cake. Under the circumstances he could not help thinking it greedy.

"Mary Ann certainly makes capital cakes. I'm afraid no one else will make such good ones."

"She's not going?" cried Philip, with astonishment.

Mary Ann had been at the vicarage ever since he could remember. She never forgot his birthday, but made a point always of sending him a trifle, absurd but touching. He had a real affection for her.

"Yes," answered Mr. Carey. "I didn't think it would do to have a single woman in the house."

"But, good heavens, she must be over forty."

"Yes, I think she is. But she's been rather troublesome lately, she's been inclined to take too much on herself, and I thought this was a very good opportunity to give her notice."

"It's certainly one which isn't likely to recur," said Philip.

He took out a cigarette, but his uncle prevented him from lighting it.

"Not till after the funeral, Philip," he said gently.

"All right," said Philip.

"It wouldn't be quite respectful to smoke in the house so long as your poor Aunt Louisa is upstairs."

Josiah Graves, churchwarden and manager of the bank, came back to dinner at the vicarage after the funeral. The blinds had been drawn up, and Philip, against his will, felt a curious sensation of relief. The body in the house had made him uncomfortable: in life the poor woman had been all that was kind and gentle; and yet, when she lay upstairs in her bed-room, cold and stark, it seemed as though she cast upon the survivors a baleful influence. The thought horrified Philip.

He found himself alone for a minute or two in the dining-room with the churchwarden.

"I hope you'll be able to stay with your uncle a while," he said. "I don't think he ought to be left alone just yet."

"I haven't made any plans," answered Philip. "If he wants me I shall be very pleased to stay."

A few days later his uncle expressed the hope that he would spend the next few weeks at Blackstable.

"Yes, that will suit me very well," said Philip.

"I suppose it'll do if you go back to Paris in September."

Philip did not reply. He had thought much of what Foinet said to him, but he was still so undecided that he did not wish to speak of the future. There would be something fine in giving up art because he was convinced that he could not excel; but unfortunately it would seem so only to himself: to others it would be an admission of defeat, and he did not want to confess that he was beaten. He was an obstinate fellow, and the suspicion that his talent did not lie in one direction made him inclined to force circumstances and aim notwithstanding precisely in that direction. He could not bear that his friends should laugh at him. This might have prevented him from ever taking the definite step of abandoning the study of painting, but the different environment made him on a sudden see things differently. Like many another he discovered that crossing the Channel makes things which had seemed important singularly futile. The life which had been so charming that he could not bear to leave it now seemed inept; he was seized with a distaste for the cafés, the restaurants with their ill-cooked food, the shabby way in which they all lived. He did not care any more what his friends thought about him: Mrs. Otter with her respectability, Ruth Chalice with her affectations, Lawson and Clutton with their quarrels; he felt a revulsion from them all. He wrote to Lawson and asked him to send over all his belongings. A week later they arrived. When he unpacked his canvases he found himself able to examine his work without emotion. He noticed the fact with interest. His uncle was anxious to see his pictures. Though he had so greatly disapproved of Philip's desire to go to Paris, he accepted the situation now with equanimity. He was interested in the life of students and constantly put Philip questions about it. He was in fact a little proud of him because he was a painter, and when people were present made attempts to draw him out. He looked eagerly at the studies of models which Philip showed him. Philip set before him his portrait of Miguel Ajuria.

"Why did you paint him?" asked Mr. Carey.

"Oh, I wanted a model, and his head interested me."

"As you haven't got anything to do here I wonder you don't paint me."

"It would bore you to sit."

"I think I should like it."

"We must see about it."

Philip was amused at his uncle's vanity. It was clear that he was dying to have his portrait painted. To get something for nothing was a chance not to be missed. For two or three days he threw out little hints. He reproached Philip for laziness, asked him when he was going to start work, and finally began telling everyone he met that Philip was going to paint him. At last there came a rainy day, and after breakfast Mr. Carey said to Philip:

"Now, what d'you say to starting on my portrait this morning?" Philip put down the book he was reading and leaned back in his chair.

"I've given up painting," he said.

"Why?" asked his uncle in astonishment.

"I don't think there's much object in being a second-rate painter, and I came to the conclusion that I should never be anything else."

"You surprise me. Before you went to Paris you were quite certain that you were a genius."

"I was mistaken," said Philip.

"I should have thought now you'd taken up a profession you'd have the pride to stick to it. It seems to me that what you lack is perseverance."

Philip was a little annoyed that his uncle did not even see how truly heroic his determination was.

" 'A rolling stone gathers no moss,' " proceeded the clergyman. Philip hated that proverb above all, and it seemed to him perfectly meaningless. His uncle had repeated it often during the arguments which had preceded his departure from business. Apparently it recalled that occasion to his guardian.

"You're no longer a boy, you know; you must begin to think of settling down. First you insist on becoming a chartered accountant, and then you get tired of that and you want to become a painter. And now if you please you change your mind again. It points to . . ."

He hesitated for a moment to consider what defects of character exactly it indicated, and Philip finished the sentence.

"Irresolution, incompetence, want of foresight, and lack of determination."

The Vicar looked up at his nephew quickly to see whether he was laughing at him. Philip's face was serious, but there was a twinkle in his eyes which irritated him. Philip should really be getting more serious. He felt it right to give him a rap over the knuckles.

"Your money matters have nothing to do with me now. You're your own master; but I think you should remember that your money won't last for ever, and the unlucky deformity you have doesn't exactly make it easier for you to earn your living."

Philip knew by now that whenever anyone was angry with him his first thought was to say something about his club-foot. His estimate of the human race was determined by the fact that scarcely anyone failed to resist the temptation. But he had trained himself not to show any sign that the reminder wounded him. He had even acquired control over the blushing which in his boyhood had been one of his torments.

"As you justly remark," he answered, "my money matters have nothing to do with you and I am my own master."

"At all events you will do me the justice to acknowledge that I was justified in my opposition when you made up your mind to become an art-student."

"I don't know so much about that. I daresay one profits

more by the mistakes one makes off one's own bat than by doing the right thing on somebody's else advice. I've had my fling, and I don't mind settling down now."

"What at?"

Philip was not prepared for the question, since in fact he had not made up his mind. He had thought of a dozen callings.

"The most suitable thing you could do is to enter your father's profession and become a doctor."

"Oddly enough that is precisely what I intend."

He had thought of doctoring among other things, chiefly because it was an occupation which seemed to give a good deal of personal freedom, and his experience of life in an office had made him determined never to have anything more to do with one; his answer to the Vicar slipped out almost unawares, because it was in the nature of a repartee. It amused him to make up his mind in that accidental way, and he resolved then and there to enter his father's old hospital in the autumn.

"Then your two years in Paris may be regarded as so much wasted time?"

"I don't know about that. I had a very jolly two years, and I learned one or two useful things."

"What?"

Philip reflected for an instant, and his answer was not devoid of a gentle desire to annoy.

"I learned to look at hands, which I'd never looked at before. And instead of just looking at houses and trees I learned to look at houses and trees against the sky. And I learned also that shadows are not black but coloured."

"I suppose you think you're very clever. I think your flippancy is quite inane."

Taking the paper with him Mr. Carey retired to his study. Philip changed his chair for that in which his uncle had been sitting (it was the only comfortable one in the room), and looked out of the window at the pouring rain.

Even in that sad weather there was something restful about the green fields that stretched to the horizon. There was an intimate charm in the landscape which he did not remember ever to have noticed before. Two years in France had opened his eyes to the beauty of his own countryside.

He thought with a smile of his uncle's remark. It was lucky that the turn of his mind tended to flippancy. He had begun to realise what a great loss he had sustained in the death of his father and mother. That was one of the differences in his life which prevented him from seeing things in the same way as other people. The love of parents for their children is the only emotion which is quite disinterested. Among strangers he had grown up as best he could, but he had seldom been used with patience or forbearance. He prided himself on his self-control. It had been whipped into him by the mockery of his fellows. Then they called him cynical and callous. He had acquired calmness of demeanour and under most circumstances an unruffled exterior, so that now he could not show his feelings. People told him he was unemotional; but he knew that he was at the mercy of his emotions: an accidental kindness touched him so much that sometimes he did not venture to speak in order not to betray the unsteadiness of his voice. He remembered the bitterness of his life at school, the humiliation which he had endured, the banter which had made him morbidly afraid of making himself ridiculous; and he remembered the loneliness he had felt since, faced with the world, the disillusion and the disappointment caused by the difference between what it promised to his active imagination and what it gave. But notwithstanding he was able to look at himself from the outside and smile with amusement.

"By Jove, if I weren't flippant, I should hang myself," he thought cheerfully.

And so, on the last day of September, Philip, with sixteen hundred pounds and his club-foot, set out for the second time to London to make his third start in life.

The examination Philip had passed before he was articled to a chartered accountant was sufficient qualification for him to enter a medical school. He chose St. Luke's because his father had been a student there, and before the end of the summer session had gone up to London for a day in order to see the secretary. He got a list of rooms from him, and took lodgings in a dingy house which had the advantage of being within two minutes' walk of the hospital.

Philip's ideas of the life of medical students, like those of the public at large, were founded on the pictures which Charles Dickens drew in the middle of the nineteenth century. He soon discovered that Bob Sawyer, if he ever existed, was no longer at all like the medical student of the present.

It is a mixed lot which enters upon the medical profession, and naturally there are some who are lazy and reckless. They think it is an easy life, idle away a couple of years; and then, because their funds come to an end or because angry parents refuse any longer to support them, drift away from the hospital. Others find the examinations too hard for them; one failure after another robs them of their nerve; and, panic-stricken, they forget as soon as they come into the forbidding buildings of the Conjoint Board the knowledge which before they had so pat. They remain year after year, objects of good-humoured scorn to younger men: some of them crawl through the examination of the Apothecaries Hall; others become non-qualified assistants, a precarious position in which they are at the mercy of their employer; their lot is poverty, drunkenness, and Heaven only knows their end. But for the most part medical students are industrious young men of the middle-class with a sufficient allowance to live in the respectable fashion they have been used to; many are the sons of doctors who have already something of the professional manner; their career is mapped out: as soon as they are qualified they propose to apply for a hospital appointment, after holding which (and perhaps a trip to the Far East as a ship's doctor), they will join their father and spend the rest of their days in a country practice. One or two are marked out as exceptionally brilliant: they will take the various prizes and scholarships which are open each year to the deserving, get one appointment after another at the hospital, go on the staff, take a consulting-room in Harley Street, and, specialising in one subject or another, become prosperous, eminent, and titled.

Philip made himself at home in his tiny rooms. He arranged his books and hung on the walls such pictures and sketches as he possessed. Above him, on the drawing-room floor, lived a fifth-year man called Griffiths; but Philip saw little of him, partly because he was occupied chiefly in the wards and partly because he had been to Oxford. Such of the students as had been to a university kept a good deal together: they used a variety of means natural to the young in order to impress upon the less fortunate a proper sense of their inferiority; the rest of the students found their Olympian serenity rather hard to bear. Griffiths was a tall fellow, with a quantity of curly red hair and blue eyes, a white skin and a very red mouth; he was one of those fortunate people whom everybody liked, for he had high spirits and a constant gaiety. He strummed a little on the piano and sang comic songs with gusto; and evening after evening, while Philip was reading in his solitary room, he heard the shouts and the uproarious laughter of Griffiths' friends above him. He thought of those delightful evenings in Paris when they would sit in the studio, Lawson and he, Flanagan and Clutton, and talk of art and morals, the love-affairs of the present, and the fame of the future. He felt sick at heart. He found that it was easy to make a heroic gesture, but hard to abide by its results. The worst of

it was that the work seemed to him very tedious. He had
got out of the habit of being asked questions by demonstra-
tors. His attention wandered at lectures. Anatomy was a
dreary science, a mere matter of learning by heart an enormous number of facts; dissection bored him; he did not see
the use of dissecting out laboriously nerves and arteries when
with much less trouble you could see in the diagrams of a
book or in the specimens of the pathological museum exactly
where they were.

He made friends by chance, but not intimate friends, for
he seemed to have nothing in particular to say to his companions. When he tried to interest himself in their concerns,
he felt that they found him patronising. He was not of those
who can talk of what moves them without caring whether
it bores or not the people they talk to. One man, hearing
that he had studied art in Paris, and fancying himself on
his taste, tried to discuss art with him; but Philip was impatient of views which did not agree with his own; and,
finding quickly that the other's ideas were conventional,
grew monosyllabic. Philip desired popularity but could
bring himself to make no advances to others. A fear of
rebuff prevented him from affability, and he concealed his
shyness, which was still intense, under a frigid taciturnity.
He was going through the same experience as he had done
at school, but here the freedom of the medical students' life
made it possible for him to live a good deal by himself.

It was through no effort of his that he became friendly
with Dunsford. Dunsford attached himself to Philip merely
because he was the first person he had known at St. Luke's.
He had no friends in London, and on Saturday nights he
and Philip got into the habit of going together to the pit
of a music-hall or the gallery of a theatre. He was stupid,
but he was good-humoured and never took offence; he
always said the obvious thing, but when Philip laughed
at him merely smiled. He had a very sweet smile. Though
Philip made him his butt, he liked him; he was amused by

his candour and delighted with his agreeable nature: Dunsford had the charm which he himself was acutely conscious of not possessing.

They often went to have tea at a shop in Parliament Street, because Dunsford admired one of the young women who waited. Philip did not find anything attractive in her. She was tall and thin, with narrow hips and the chest of a boy.

"No one would look at her in Paris," said Philip scornfully.

"She's got a ripping face," said Dunsford.

"What *does* the face matter?"

She had the small regular features, the blue eyes, and the broad low brow, which the Victorian painters, Lord Leighton, Alma Tadema, and a hundred others, induced the world they lived in to accept as a type of Greek beauty. She seemed to have a great deal of hair: it was arranged with peculiar elaboration and done over the forehead in what she called an Alexandra fringe. She was very anæmic. Her thin lips were pale, and her skin was delicate, of a faint green colour, without a touch of red even in the cheeks. She had very good teeth. She took great pains to prevent her work from spoiling her hands, and they were small, thin, and white. She went about her duties with a bored look.

Dunsford, very shy with women, had never succeeded in getting into conversation with her; and he urged Philip to help him.

"All I want is a lead," he said, "and then I can manage for myself."

Philip, to please him, made one or two remarks, but she answered with monosyllables. She had taken their measure. They were boys, and she surmised they were students. She had no use for them. Dunsford noticed that a man with sandy hair and a bristly moustache, who looked like a German, was favoured with her attention whenever he came into the shop; and then it was only by calling her two or three times that they could induce her to take their order. She used the clients whom she did not know with frigid insolence, and when she was talking to a friend was perfectly indifferent to the calls of the hurried. She had the art of treating women who desired refreshment with just that degree of impertinence which irritated them without affording them an opportunity of complaining to the management. One day Dunsford told him her name was Mildred. He had heard one of the other girls in the shop address her.

"What an odius name," said Philip.

"Why?" asked Dunsford. "I like it."

"It's so pretentious."

It chanced that on this day the German was not there, and, when she brought the tea, Philip, smiling, remarked:

"Your friend's not here today."

"I don't know what you mean," she said coldly.

"I was referring to the nobleman with the sandy moustache. Has he left you for another?"

"Some people would do better to mind their own business," she retorted.

She left them, and, since for a minute or two there was no one to attend to, sat down and looked at the evening paper which a customer had left behind him.

"You are a fool to put her back up," said Dunsford.

"I'm really quite indifferent to the attitude of her vertebræ," replied Philip.

But he was piqued. It irritated him that when he tried to be agreeable with a woman she should take offence. When he asked for the bill, he hazarded a remark which he meant to lead further.

"Are we no longer on speaking terms?" he smiled.

"I'm here to take orders and to wait on customers. I've got nothing to say to them, and I don't want them to say anything to me."

She put down the slip of paper on which she had marked

the sum they had to pay, and walked back to the table at which she had been sitting. Philip flushed with anger.

"That's one in the eye for you, Carey," said Dunsford, when they got outside.

"Ill-mannered slut," said Philip. "I shan't go there again."

His influence with Dunsford was strong enough to get him to take their tea elsewhere, and Dunsford soon found another young woman to flirt with. But the snub which the waitress had inflicted on him rankled. If she had treated him with civility he would have been perfectly indifferent to her; but it was obvious that she disliked him rather than otherwise, and his pride was wounded. He could not suppress a desire to be even with her. He was impatient with himself because he had so petty a feeling, but three or four days' firmness, during which he would not go to the shop, did not help him to surmount it; and he came to the conclusion that it would be least trouble to see her. Having done so he would certainly cease to think of her. Pretexting an appointment one afternoon, for he was not a little ashamed of his weakness, he left Dunsford and went straight to the shop which he had vowed never again to enter. He saw the waitress the moment he came in and sat down at one of her tables. He expected her to make some reference to the fact that he had not been there for a week, but when she came up for his order she said nothing. He had heard her say to other customers:

"You're quite a stranger."

She gave no sign that she had ever seen him before. In order to see whether she had really forgotten him, when she brought his tea, he asked:

"Have you seen my friend tonight?"

"No, he's not been in here for some days."

He wanted to use this as the beginning of a conversation, but he was strangely nervous and could think of nothing to say. She gave him no opportunity, but at once went away. He had no chance of saying anything till he asked for his bill.

"Filthy weather, isn't it?" he said.

It was mortifying that he had been forced to prepare such a phrase as that. He could not make out why she filled him with such embarrassment.

"It don't make much difference to me what the weather is, having to be in here all day."

There was an insolence in her tone that peculiarly irritated him. A sarcasm rose to his lips, but he forced himself to be silent.

"I wish to God she'd say something really cheeky," he raged to himself, "so that I could report her and get her sacked. It would serve her damned well right."

He could not get her out of his mind. He laughed angrily at his own foolishness: it was absurd to care what an anæmic little waitress said to him; but he was strangely humiliated. Though no one knew of the humiliation but Dunsford, and he had certainly forgotten, Philip felt that he could have no peace till he had wiped it out. He thought over what he had better do. He made up his mind that he would go to the shop every day; it was obvious that he had made a disagreeable impression on her, but he thought he had the wits to eradicate it; he would take care not to say anything at which the most susceptible person could be offended. All this he did, but it had no effect. When he went in and said good-evening she answered with the same words, but when once he omitted to say it in order to see whether she would say it first, she said nothing at all. He murmured in his heart an expression which though frequently applicable to members of the female sex is not often used of them in polite society; but with an unmoved face he ordered his tea. He made up his mind not to speak a word, and left the shop without his usual good-night. He promised himself that he would not go any more, but the next day at tea-time he grew restless. He tried to think of other things, but he had no command over his thoughts. At last he said desperately:

"After all there's no reason why I shouldn't go if I want to."

The struggle with himself had taken a long time, and it was getting on for seven when he entered the shop.

"I thought you weren't coming," the girl said to him, when he sat down.

His heart leaped in his bosom and he felt himself reddening. "I was detained. I couldn't come before."

"Cutting up people, I suppose?"

"Not so bad as that."

"You are a stoodent, aren't you?"

"Yes."

But that seemed to satisfy her curiosity. She went away and, since at that late hour there was nobody else at her tables, she immersed herself in a novelette. This was before the time of the sixpenny reprints. There was a regular supply of inexpensive fiction written to order by poor hacks for the consumption of the illiterate. Philip was elated; she had addressed him of her own accord; he saw the time approaching when his turn would come and he would tell her exactly what he thought of her. It would be a great comfort to express the immensity of his contempt. He looked at her. It was true that her profile was beautiful; it was extraordinary how English girls of that class had so often a perfection of outline which took your breath away, but it was as cold as marble; and the faint green of her delicate skin gave an impression of unhealthiness. All the waitresses were dressed alike, in plain black dresses, with a white apron, cuffs, and a small cap. On a half sheet of paper that he had in his pocket Philip made a sketch of her as she sat leaning over her book (she outlined the words with her lips as she read), and left it on the table when he went away. It was an inspiration, for next day, when he came in, she smiled at him.

"I didn't know you could draw," she said.

"I was an art student in Paris for two years."

"I showed that drawing you left be'ind you last night to the manageress and she *was* struck with it. Was it meant to be me?"

"It was," said Philip.

When she went for his tea, one of the other girls came up to him.

"I saw that picture you done of Miss Rogers. It was the very image of her," she said.

That was the first time he had heard her name, and when he wanted his bill he called her by it.

"I see you know my name," she said, when she came.

"Your friend mentioned it when she said something to me about that drawing."

"She wants you to do one of her. Don't you do it. If you once begin you'll have to go on, and they'll all be wanting you to do them." Then without a pause, with peculiar inconsequence, she said: "Where's that young fellow that used to come with you? Has he gone away?"

"Fancy your remembering him," said Philip.

"He was a nice-looking young fellow."

Philip felt quite a peculiar sensation in his heart. He did not know what it was. Dunsford had jolly curling hair, a fresh complexion, and a beautiful smile. Philip thought of these advantages with envy.

"Oh, he's in love," said he, with a little laugh.

He was restless next day. He thought of going to lunch at the tea-shop, but he was certain there would be many people there then, and Mildred would not be able to talk to him. He had managed before this to get out of having tea with Dunsford, and, punctually at half past four (he had looked at his watch a dozen times), he went into the shop.

Mildred had her back turned to him. She was sitting down, talking to the German whom Philip had seen there every day till a fortnight ago and since then had not seen at all. She was laughing at what he said. Philip thought she had a common laugh, and it made him shudder. He called her, but she took no notice; he called her again; then, growing angry, for he was impatient, he rapped the table loudly with his stick. She approached sulkily.

"How d'you do?" he said.

"You seem to be in a great hurry."

She looked down at him with the insolent manner which he knew so well.

"I say, what's the matter with you?" he asked.

"If you'll kindly give your order I'll get what you want. I can't stand talking all night."

"Tea and toasted bun, please," Philip answered briefly.

He was furious with her. He had *The Star* with him and read it elaborately when she brought the tea.

"If you'll give me my bill now I needn't trouble you again," he said icily.

She wrote out the slip, placed it on the table, and went back to the German. Soon she was talking to him with animation. He was a man of middle height, with the round head of his nation and a sallow face; his moustache was large and bristling; he had on a tail-coat and gray trousers, and he wore a massive gold watch-chain. Philip thought the other girls looked from him to the pair at the table and exchanged significant glances. He felt certain they were laughing at him, and his blood boiled. He detested Mildred now with all his heart. He knew that the best thing he could do was to cease coming to the tea-shop, but he could not bear to think that he had been worsted in the affair, and he devised a plan to show her that he despised her. Next day he sat down at another table and ordered his tea from another waitress. Mildred's friend was there again and she was talking to him. She paid no attention to Philip, and so when he went out he chose a moment when she had to cross his path: as he passed he looked at her as though he had never seen her before. He repeated this for three or four days. He expected that presently she would take the opportunity to say something to him; he thought she would ask why he never came to one of her tables now, and he had prepared an answer charged with all the loathing he felt for her. He knew it was absurd to trouble, but he could not help himself. She had beaten him again. The German suddenly disappeared, but Philip still sat at other tables. She paid no attention to him. Suddenly he realised that what he did was a matter of complete indifference to her; he could go on in that way till doomsday, and it would have no effect.

"I've not finished yet," he said to himself.

The day after he sat down in his old seat, and when she came up said good-evening as though he had not ignored her for a week. His face was placid, but he could not prevent the mad beating of his heart. At that time the musical comedy had lately leaped into public favour, and he was sure that Mildred would be delighted to go to one.

"I say," he said suddenly, "I wonder if you'd dine with me one night and come to *The Belle of New York*. I'll get a couple of stalls."

He added the last sentence in order to tempt her. He knew that when the girls went to the play it was either in the pit, or, if some man took them, seldom to more expensive seats than the upper circle. Mildred's pale face showed no change of expression.

"I don't mind," she said.

"When will you come?"

"I get off early on Thursdays."

They made arrangements. Mildred lived with an aunt at Herne Hill. The play began at eight so they must dine at seven. She proposed that he should meet her in the second-class waiting-room at Victoria Station. She showed no pleasure, but accepted the invitation as though she conferred a favour. Philip was vaguely irritated.

Philip arrived at Victoria Station nearly half an hour before the time which Mildred had appointed, and sat down in the second-class waiting-room. He waited and she did not come. He began to grow anxious, and walked into the station watching the incoming suburban trains; the hour which she had fixed passed, and still there was no sign of her. Philip was impatient. He went into the other waiting-rooms and looked at the people sitting in them. Suddenly his heart gave a great thud.

"There you are. I thought you were never coming."

"I like that after keeping me waiting all this time. I had half a mind to go back home again."

"But you said you'd come to the second-class waiting-room."

"I didn't say any such thing. It isn't exactly likely I'd sit in the second-class room when I could sit in the first, is it?"

Though Philip was sure he had not made a mistake, he said nothing, and they got into a cab.

"Where are we dining?" she asked.

"I thought of the Adelphi Restaurant. Will that suit you?"

"I don't mind where we dine."

She spoke ungraciously. She was put out by being kept waiting and answered Philip's attempt at conversation with monosyllables. She wore a long cloak of some rough, dark material and a crochet shawl over her head. They reached the restaurant and sat down at a table. She looked round with satisfaction. The red shades to the candles on the tables, the gold of the decorations, the looking-glasses, lent the room a sumptuous air.

"I've never been here before."

She gave Philip a smile. She had taken off her cloak; and he saw that she wore a pale blue dress, cut square at the neck; and her hair was more elaborately arranged than ever. He had ordered champagne and when it came her eyes sparkled.

"You are going it," she said.

"Because I've ordered fiz?" he asked carelessly, as though he never drank anything else.

"I *was* surprised when you asked me to do a theatre with you."

Conversation did not go very easily, for she did not seem to have much to say; and Philip was nervously conscious that he was not amusing her. She listened carelessly to his remarks, with her eyes on other diners, and made no pretence that she was interested in him. He made one or two little jokes, but she took them quite seriously. The only sign of vivacity he got was when he spoke of the other girls in the shop; she could not bear the manageress and told him all her misdeeds at length.

They finished dinner and went to the play. Philip was a very cultured young man, and he looked upon musical comedy with scorn. He thought the jokes vulgar and the melodies obvious; it seemed to him that they did these things much better in France; but Mildred enjoyed herself thoroughly; she laughed till her sides ached, looking at Philip now and then when something tickled her to exchange a glance of pleasure; and she applauded rapturously.

"This is the seventh time I've been," she said, after the first act, "and I don't mind if I come seven times more."

She was much interested in the women who surrounded them in the stalls. She found no one to admire, and whenever she spoke of anyone it was to say something disagreeable. It made Philip uneasy. He supposed that next day she would tell the girls in the shop that he had taken her out and that he had bored her to death. He disliked her, and yet, he knew not why, he wanted to be with her. On the way home he asked:

"I hope you've enjoyed yourself?"

"Rather."

"Will you come out with me again one evening?"

"I don't mind."

He could never get beyond such expressions as that. Her indifference maddened him.

When he lay in bed it seemed impossible that he should be in love with Mildred Rogers. Her name was grotesque. He did not think her pretty; he hated the thinness of her, only that evening he had noticed how the bones of her chest stood out in evening-dress; he went over her features one by one; he did not like her mouth, and the unhealthiness of her colour vaguely repelled him. She was common. Her phrases, so bald and few, constantly repeated, showed the emptiness of her mind; he recalled her vulgar little laugh at the jokes of the musical comedy; and he remembered the little finger carefully extended when she held her glass to her mouth; her manners like her conversation, were odiously genteel. He remembered her insolence; sometimes he had felt inclined to box her ears; and suddenly, he knew not why, perhaps it was the thought of hitting her or the recollection of her tiny, beautiful ears, he was seized by an uprush of emotion. He yearned for her. He thought of taking her in his arms, the thin, fragile body, and kissing her pale mouth: he wanted to pass his fingers down the slightly greenish cheeks. He wanted her.

He had thought of love as a rapture which seized one so that all the world seemed spring-like, he had looked forward to an ecstatic happiness; but this was not happiness; it was a hunger of the soul, it was a painful yearning, it was a bitter anguish, he had never known before. He tried to think when it had first come to him. He did not know. He only remembered that each time he had gone into the shop, after the first two or three times, it had been with a little feeling in the heart that was pain; and he remembered that when she spoke to him he felt curiously breathless. When she left him it was wretchedness, and when she came to him again it was despair.

He stretched himself in his bed as a dog stretches himself. He wondered how he was going to endure that ceaseless aching of his soul.

Philip bought tickets for Saturday night. It was not one of the days on which she got off early and therefore she would have no time to go home and change; but she meant to bring a frock up with her in the morning and hurry into her clothes at the shop. If the manageress was in a good temper she would let her go at seven. Philip had agreed to wait outside from a quarter past seven onwards. He looked forward to the occasion with painful eagerness, for in the cab on the way from the theatre to the station he thought she would let him kiss her. The vehicle gave every facility for a man to put his arm round a girl's waist, (an advantage which the hansom had over the taxi of the present day,) and the delight of that was worth the cost of the evening's entertainment.

But on Saturday afternoon when he went in to have tea, in order to confirm the arrangements, he met the man with the fair moustache coming out of the shop. He knew by now that he was called Miller. He was a naturalized German, who had anglicised his name, and he had lived many years in England. Philip had heard him speak, and, though his English was fluent and natural, it had not quite the intonation of the native. Philip knew that he was flirting with Mildred, and he was horribly jealous of him; but he took comfort in the coldness of her temperament, which otherwise distressed him; and, thinking her incapable of passion, he looked upon his rival as no better off than himself. But his heart sank now, for his first thought was that Miller's sudden appearance might interfere with the jaunt which he had so looked forward to. He entered, sick with apprehension. The waitress came up to him, took his order for tea, and presently brought it.

"I'm awfully sorry," she said, with an expression on her face of real distress. "I shan't be able to come tonight after all."

"Why?" said Philip.

"Don't look so stern about it," she laughed. "It's not my fault. My aunt was taken ill last night, and it's the girl's night out so I must go and sit with her. She can't be left alone, can she?"

"It doesn't matter. I'll see you home instead."

"But you've got the tickets. It would be a pity to waste them."

He took them out of his pocket and deliberately tore them up.

"What are you doing that for?"

"You don't suppose I want to go and see a rotten musical comedy by myself, do you? I only took seats there for your sake."

"You can't see me home if that's what you mean."

"You've made other arrangements."

"I don't know what you mean by that. You're just as selfish as all the rest of them. You only think of yourself. It's not my fault if my aunt's queer."

She quickly wrote out his bill and left him. Philip knew very little about women, or he would have been aware that one should accept their most transparent lies. He made up his mind that he would watch the shop and see for certain whether Mildred went out with the German. He had an unhappy passion for certainty. At seven he stationed himself on the opposite pavement. He looked about for Miller, but did not see him. In ten minutes she came out, she had on the cloak and shawl which she had worn when he took her to the Shaftesbury Theatre. It was obvious that she was not going home. She saw him before he had time to move away, started a little, and then came straight up to him.

"What are you doing here?" she said.

"Taking the air," he answered.

"You're spying on me, you dirty little cad. I thought you was a gentleman."

"Did you think a gentleman would be likely to take any interest in you?" he murmured.

There was a devil within him which forced him to make matters worse. He wanted to hurt her as much as she was hurting him.

"I suppose I can change my mind if I like. I'm not obliged to come out with you. I tell you I'm going home, and I won't be followed or spied upon."

"Have you seen Miller today?"

"That's no business of yours. In point of fact I haven't, so you're wrong again."

"I saw him this afternoon. He'd just come out of the shop when I went in."

"Well, what if he did? I can go out with him if I want to, can't I? I don't know what you've got to say to it."

"He's keeping you waiting, isn't he?"

"Well, I'd rather wait for him than have you wait for me. Put that in your pipe and smoke it. And now p'raps you'll go off home and mind your own business in future."

His mood changed suddenly from anger to despair, and his voice trembled when he spoke.

"I say, don't be beastly with me, Mildred. You know I'm awfully fond of you. I think I love you with all my heart. Won't you change your mind? I was looking forward to this evening so awfully. You see, he hasn't come, and he can't care twopence about you really. Won't you dine with me? I'll get some more tickets, and we'll go anywhere you like."

"I tell you I won't. It's no good you talking. I've made up my mind, and when I make up my mind I keep to it."

He looked at her for a moment. His heart was torn with anguish. People were hurrying past them on the pavement, and cabs and omnibuses rolled by noisily. He saw that Mildred's eyes were wandering. She was afraid of missing Miller in the crowd.

"I can't go on like this," groaned Philip. "It's too degrading. If I go now I go for good. Unless you'll come with me tonight you'll never see me again."

"You seem to think that'll be an awful thing for me. All I say is, good riddance to bad rubbish."

"Then good-bye."

He nodded and limped away slowly, for he hoped with all his heart that she would call him back. At the next lamp-post he stopped and looked over his shoulder. He thought she might beckon to him—he was willing to forget everything, he was ready for any humiliation—but she had turned away, and apparently had ceased to trouble about him. He realised that she was glad to be quit of him.

He slept very badly. The next day was Sunday, and he worked at his biology. He sat with the book in front of him, forming the words with his lips in order to fix his attention, but he could remember nothing. He found his thoughts going back to Mildred every minute, and he repeated to himself the exact words of the quarrel they had had. He had to force himself back to his book. He went out for a walk. The streets on the South side of the river were dingy enough on week-days, but there was an energy, a coming and going, which gave them a sordid vivacity; but on Sundays, with no shops open, no carts in the roadway, silent and depressed, they were indescribably dreary. Philip thought that day would never end. But he was so tired that he slept heavily, and when Monday came he entered upon life with determination. Christmas was approaching, and a good many of the students had gone into the country for the short holiday between the two parts of the winter session; but Philip had refused his uncle's invitation to go down to Blackstable. He had given the approaching ex-

amination as his excuse, but in point of fact he had been
unwilling to leave London and Mildred. He had neglected
his work so much that now he had only a fortnight to learn
what the curriculum allowed three months for. He set to
work seriously. He found it easier each day not to think of
Mildred. He congratulated himself on his force of character. The pain he suffered was no longer anguish, but a
sort of soreness, like what one might be expected to feel if
one had been thrown off a horse and, though no bones were
broken, were bruised all over and shaken. Philip found that
he was able to observe with curiosity the condition he had
been in during the last few weeks. He analysed his feelings
with interest. He was a little amused at himself. One thing
that struck him was how little under those circumstances it
mattered what one thought; the system of personal philosophy, which had given him great satisfaction to devise, had
not served him. He was puzzled by this.

But sometimes in the street he would see a girl who
looked so like Mildred that his heart seemed to stop beating.
Then he could not help himself, he hurried on to catch her
up, eager and anxious, only to find that it was a total
stranger. Men came back from the country, and he went
with Dunsford to have tea at an A. B. C. shop. The well-
known uniform made him so miserable that he could not
speak. The thought came to him that perhaps she had been
transferred to another establishment of the firm for which
she worked, and he might suddenly find himself face to
face with her. The idea filled him with panic, so that he
feared Dunsford would see that something was the matter
with him: he could not think of anything to say; he pretended to listen to what Dunsford was talking about; the
conversation maddened him; and it was all he could do to
prevent himself from crying out to Dunsford for Heaven's
sake to hold his tongue.

Then came the day of his examination. Philip, when his
turn arrived, went forward to the examiner's table with the

utmost confidence. He answered three or four questions. Then they showed him various specimens; he had been to very few lectures and, as soon as he was asked about things which he could not learn from books, he was floored. He did what he could to hide his ignorance, the examiner did not insist, and soon his ten minutes were over. He felt certain he had passed; but next day, when he went up to the examination buildings to see the result posted on the door, he was astounded not to find his number among those who had satisfied the examiners. In amazement he read the list three times. Dunsford was with him.

"I say, I'm awfully sorry you're ploughed," he said.

He had just inquired Philip's number. Philip turned and saw by his radiant face that Dunsford had passed.

"Oh, it doesn't matter a bit," said Philip. "I'm jolly glad you're all right. I shall go up again in July."

He was very anxious to pretend he did not mind, but later on, he was seized with a feeling of utter loneliness. He seemed to himself absurd and futile. He had an urgent need of consolation, and the temptation to see Mildred was irresistible. He thought bitterly that there was small chance of consolation from her; but he wanted to see her even if he did not speak to her; after all, she was a waitress and would be obliged to serve him. She was the only person in the world he cared for. There was no use in hiding that fact from himself. Of course it would be humiliating to go back to the shop as though nothing had happened, but he had not much self-respect left. Though he would not confess it to himself, he had hoped each day that she would write to him; she knew that a letter addressed to the hospital would find him; but she had not written: it was evident that she cared nothing if she saw him again or not. And he kept on repeating to himself:

"I must see her. I must see her."

The desire was so great that he could not give the time necessary to walk, but jumped in a cab. He was too thrifty to use one when it could possibly be avoided. He stood outside the shop for a minute or two. The thought came to him that perhaps she had left, and in terror he walked in quickly. He saw her at once. He sat down and she came up to him.

"A cup of tea and a muffin, please," he ordered.

He could hardly speak. He was afraid for a moment that he was going to cry.

"I almost thought you was dead," she said.

She was smiling. Smiling! She seemed to have forgotten completely that last scene which Philip had repeated to himself a hundred times.

"I thought if you'd wanted to see me you'd write," he answered.

"I've got too much to do to think about writing letters."

It seemed impossible for her to say a gracious thing. Philip cursed the fate which chained him to such a woman. She went away to fetch his tea.

"Would you like me to sit down for a minute or two?" she said, when she brought it.

"Yes."

"Where have you been all this time?"

"I've been in London."

"I thought you'd gone away for the holidays. Why haven't you been in then?"

Philip looked at her with haggard, passionate eyes.

"Don't you remember that I said I'd never see you again?"

"What are you doing now then?"

She seemed anxious to make him drink up the cup of his humiliation; but he knew her well enough to know that she spoke at random; she hurt him frightfully, and never even tried to. He did not answer.

"It was a nasty trick you played on me, spying on me like that. I always thought you was a gentleman in every sense of the word."

"Don't be beastly to me, Mildred. I can't bear it."

"You are a funny feller. I can't make you out."

"It's very simple. I'm such a blasted fool as to love you with all my heart and soul, and I know that you don't care twopence for me."

"If you had been a gentleman I think you'd have come next day and begged my pardon."

She had no mercy. He looked at her neck and thought how he would like to jab it with the knife he had for his muffin. He knew enough anatomy to make pretty certain of getting the carotid artery. And at the same time he wanted to cover her pale, thin face with kisses.

"If I could only make you understand how frightfully I'm in love with you."

"You haven't begged my pardon yet."

He grew very white. She felt that she had done nothing wrong on that occasion. She wanted him now to humble himself. He was very proud. For one instant he felt inclined to tell her to go to hell, but he dared not. His passion made him abject. He was willing to submit to anything rather than not see her.

"I'm very sorry, Mildred. I beg your pardon."

He had to force the words out. It was a horrible effort.

"Now you've said that I don't mind telling you that I wish I had come out with you that evening. I thought Miller was a gentleman, but I've discovered my mistake now. I soon sent him about his business."

Philip gave a little gasp.

"Mildred, won't you come out with me tonight? Let's go and dine somewhere."

"Oh, I can't. My aunt'll be expecting me home."

"I'll send her a wire. You can say you've been detained in the shop; she won't know any better. Oh, do come, for God's sake. I haven't seen you for so long, and I want to talk to you."

She looked down at her clothes.

"Never mind about that. We'll go somewhere where it

doesn't matter how you're dressed. And we'll go to a music-hall afterwards. Please say yes. It would give me so much pleasure."

She hesitated a moment; he looked at her with pitifully appealing eyes.

"Well, I don't mind if I do. I haven't been out anywhere since I don't know how long."

It was with the greatest difficulty he could prevent himself from seizing her hand there and then to cover it with kisses.

Philip did not pass the examination in anatomy at the end of March. He and Dunsford had worked at the subject together on Philip's skeleton, asking each other questions till both knew by heart every attachment and the meaning of every nodule and groove on the human bones; but in the examination room Philip was seized with panic, and failed to give right answers to questions from a sudden fear that they might be wrong. He knew he was ploughed and did not even trouble to go up to the building next day to see whether his number was up. The second failure put him definitely among the incompetent and idle men of his year.

He did not care much. He had other things to think of. He told himself that Mildred must have senses like anybody else, it was only a question of awakening them; he had theories about woman, the rip at heart, and thought that there must come a time with everyone when she would yield to persistence. It was a question of watching for the opportunity, keeping his temper, wearing her down with small attentions, taking advantage of the physical exhaustion which opened the heart to tenderness, making himself a refuge from the petty vexations of her work. He talked to her of the relations between his friends in Paris and the fair ladies they admired. The life he described had a charm, an easy gaiety, in which was no grossness. Weav-

ing into his own recollections the adventures of Mimi and
Rodolphe, of Musette and the rest of them, he poured into
Mildred's ears a story of poverty made picturesque by song
and laughter, of lawless love made romantic by beauty and
youth. He never attacked her prejudices directly, but sought
to combat them by the suggestion that they were suburban.
He never let himself be disturbed by her inattention, nor
irritated by her indifference. He thought he had bored her.
By an effort he made himself affable and entertaining; he
never let himself be angry, he never asked for anything, he
never complained, he never scolded. When she made en-
gagements and broke them, he met her next day with a
smiling face; when she excused herself, he said it did not
matter. He never let her see that she pained him. He understood that his passionate grief had wearied her, and he took
care to hide every sentiment which could be in the least
degree troublesome. He was heroic.

Though she never mentioned the change, for she did not
take any conscious notice of it, it affected her nevertheless:
she became more confidential with him; she took her little
grievances to him, and she always had some grievance
against the manageress of the shop, one of her fellow-wait-
resses, or her aunt; she was talkative enough now, and
though she never said anything that was not trivial Philip
was never tired of listening to her.

"I like you when you don't want to make love to me,"
she told him once.

"That's flattering for me," he laughed.

She did not realise how her words made his heart sink
nor what an effort it needed for him to answer so lightly.

"Oh, I don't mind your kissing me now and then. It
doesn't hurt me and it gives you pleasure."

Occasionally she went so far as to ask him to take her
out to dinner, and the offer, coming from her, filled him
with rapture. "I wouldn't do it to anyone else," she said,
by way of apology. "But I know I can with you."

"You couldn't give me greater pleasure," he smiled.

She asked him to give her something to eat one evening towards the end of April.

"All right," he said. "Where would you like to go afterwards?"

"Oh, don't let's go anywhere. Let's just sit and talk. You don't mind, do you?"

"Rather not."

He thought she must be beginning to care for him. Three months before the thought of an evening spent in conversation would have bored her to death. It was a fine day, and the spring added to Philip's high spirits. He was content with very little now.

"I say, won't it be ripping when the summer comes along," he said, as they drove along on the top of a 'bus to Soho—she had herself suggested that they should not be so extravagant as to go by cab. "We shall be able to spend every Sunday on the River. We'll take our luncheon in a basket."

She smiled slightly, and he was encouraged to take her hand. She did not withdraw it.

"I really think you're beginning to like me a bit," he smiled.

"You *are* silly, you know I like you, or else I shouldn't be here, should I?"

They were old customers at the little restaurant in Soho by now, and the *patronne* gave them a smile as they came in. The waiter was obsequious.

"Let me order the dinner tonight," said Mildred.

Philip, thinking her more enchanting than ever, gave her the menu, and she chose her favourite dishes. The range was small, and they had eaten many times all that the restaurant could provide. Philip was gay. He looked into her eyes, and he dwelt on every perfection of her pale cheek. When they had finished Mildred by way of exception took a cigarette. She smoked very seldom.

"I don't like to see a lady smoking," she said.

She hesitated a moment and then spoke.

"Were you surprised, my asking you to take me out and give me a bit of dinner tonight?"

"I was delighted."

"I've got something to say to you, Philip."

He looked at her quickly, his heart sank, but he had trained himself well.

"Well, fire away," he said, smiling.

"You're not going to be silly about it, are you? The fact is I'm going to get married."

"Are you?" said Philip.

He could think of nothing else to say. He had considered the possibility often and had imagined to himself what he would do and say. He had suffered agonies when he thought of the despair he would suffer, he had thought of suicide, of the mad passion of anger that would seize him; but perhaps he had too completely anticipated the emotion he would experience, so that now he felt merely exhausted. He felt as one does in a serious illness when the vitality is so low that one is indifferent to the issue and wants only to be left alone.

"You see, I'm getting on," she said. "I'm twenty-four and it's time I settled down."

He was silent. He looked at the *patronne* sitting behind the counter, and his eye dwelt on a red feather one of the diners wore in her hat. Mildred was nettled.

"You might congratulate me," she said.

"I might, mightn't I? I can hardly believe it's true. I've dreamt it so often. It rather tickles me that I should have been so jolly glad that you asked me to take you out to dinner. Whom are you going to marry?"

"Miller," she answered, with a slight blush.

"Miller?" cried Philip, astounded. "But you've not seen him for months."

"He came in to lunch one day last week and asked me

then. He's earning very good money. He makes seven pounds a week now and he's got prospects."

Philip was silent again. He remembered that she had always liked Miller; he amused her; there was in his foreign birth an exotic charm which she felt unconsciously.

"I suppose it was inevitable," he said at last. "You were bound to accept the highest bidder. When are you going to marry?"

"On Saturday next. I have given notice."

Philip felt a sudden pang.

"As soon as that?"

"We're going to be married at a registry office. Emil prefers it."

Philip felt dreadfully tired. He wanted to get away from her. He thought he would go straight to bed. He called for the bill.

"I'll put you in a cab and send you down to Victoria. I daresay you won't have to wait long for a train."

"Won't you come with me?"

"I think I'd rather not if you don't mind."

"It's just as you please," she answered haughtily. "I suppose I shall see you at tea-time tomorrow?"

"No, I think we'd better make a full stop now. I don't see why I should go on making myself unhappy. I've paid the cab."

He nodded to her and forced a smile on his lips, then jumped on a 'bus and made his way home. He smoked a pipe before he went to bed, but he could hardly keep his eyes open. He suffered no pain. He fell into a heavy sleep almost as soon as his head touched the pillow.

*P*hilip had looked forward with apprehension to the day on which Mildred was to be married; he was expecting an intolerable anguish; and it was with relief that he got a letter from Hayward on Saturday morning to say

that he was coming up early on that very day and would
fetch Philip to help him to find rooms. Philip, anxious to
be distracted, looked up a time-table and discovered the only
train Hayward was likely to come by; he went to meet him,
and the reunion of the friends was enthusiastic. They left
the luggage at the station, and set off gaily. Hayward
characteristically proposed that first of all they should go
for an hour to the National Gallery; he had not seen pictures for some time, and he stated that it needed a glimpse
to set him in tune with life. Philip for months had had no
one with whom he could talk of art and books. Since the
Paris days Hayward had immersed himself in the modern
French versifiers, and, such a plethora of poets is there in
France, he had several new geniuses to tell Philip about.
They walked through the gallery pointing out to one another their favourite pictures; one subject led to another;
they talked excitedly. The sun was shining and the air
was warm.

"Let's go and sit in the Park," said Hayward. "We'll look
for rooms after luncheon."

The spring was pleasant there. It was a day upon which
one felt it good merely to live. The young green of the
trees was exquisite against the sky; and the sky, pale and
blue, was dappled with little white clouds. At the end of the
ornamental water was the gray mass of the Horse Guards.
The ordered elegance of the scene had the charm of an
eighteenth-century picture. It reminded you not of Watteau,
whose landscapes are so idyllic that they recall only the
woodland glens seen in dreams, but of the more prosaic
Jean-Baptiste Pater. Philip's heart was filled with lightness.
He realised, what he had only read before, that art (for
there was art in the manner in which he looked upon nature) might liberate the soul from pain.

They went to an Italian restaurant for luncheon and ordered themselves a *fiaschetto* of Chianti. Lingering over the
meal they talked on. They reminded one another of the

people they had known at Heidelberg, they spoke of Philip's friends in Paris, they talked of books, pictures, morals, life; and suddenly Philip heard a clock strike three. He remembered that by this time Mildred was married. He felt a sort of stitch in his heart, and for a minute or two he could not hear what Hayward was saying. But he filled his glass with Chianti. He was unaccustomed to alcohol and it had gone to his head. For the time at all events he was free from care. His quick brain had lain idle for so many months that he was intoxicated now with conversation. He was thankful to have someone to talk to who would interest himself in the things that interested him.

Hayward's visit did Philip a great deal of good. Each day his thoughts dwelt less on Mildred. He looked back upon the past with disgust. He could not understand how he had submitted to the dishonour of such a love; and when he thought of Mildred it was with angry hatred, because she had submitted him to so much humiliation. His imagination presented her to him now with her defects of person and manner exaggerated, so that he shuddered at the thought of having been connected with her.

"It just shows how damned weak I am," he said to himself. The adventure was like a blunder that one had committed at a party so horrible that one felt nothing could be done to excuse it: the only remedy was to forget. His horror at the degradation he had suffered helped him. He was like a snake casting its skin and he looked upon the old covering with nausea. He exulted in the possession of himself once more; he realised how much of the delight of the world he had lost when he was absorbed in that madness which they called love; he had had enough of it; he did not want to be in love any more if love was that. Philip told Hayward something of what he had gone through.

"Wasn't it Sophocles," he asked, "who prayed for the time when he would be delivered from the wild beast of passion that devoured his heart-strings?"

Philip seemed really to be born again. He breathed the circumambient air as though he had never breathed it before, and he took a child's pleasure in all the facts of the world. He called his period of insanity six months' hard labour.

Hayward had only been settled in London a few days when Philip received from Blackstable, where it had been sent, a card for a private view at some picture gallery. He took Hayward, and, on looking at the catalogue, saw that Lawson had a picture in it.

"I suppose he sent the card," said Philip. "Let's go and find him, he's sure to be in front of his picture."

This, a profile of Ruth Chalice, was tucked away in a corner, and Lawson was not far from it. He looked a little lost, in his large soft hat and loose, pale clothes, amongst the fashionable throng that had gathered for the private view. He greeted Philip with enthusiasm, and with his usual volubility told him that he had come to live in London, Ruth Chalice was a hussy, he had taken a studio, Paris was played out, he had a commission for a portrait, and they'd better dine together and have a good old talk. Philip reminded him of his acquaintance with Hayward, and was entertained to see that Lawson was slightly awed by Hayward's elegant clothes and grand manner. They sat upon him better than they had done in the shabby little studio which Lawson and Philip had shared.

Philip worked well and easily; he had a good deal to do, since he was taking in July the three parts of the First Conjoint examination, two of which he had failed in before; but he found life pleasant. He made a new friend. Lawson, on the look out for models, had discovered a girl who was understudying at one of the theatres, and in order to induce her to sit to him arranged a little luncheon-party one Sunday. She brought a chaperon with her; and to her Philip, asked to make a fourth, was instructed to confine his attentions. He found this easy, since she turned out to be an agreeable chatterbox with an amusing tongue. She asked Philip to go and see her; she had rooms in Vincent Square, and was always in to tea at five o'clock; he went, was delighted with his welcome, and went again. Mrs. Nesbit was not more than twenty-five, very small, with a pleasant, ugly face; she had very bright eyes, high cheek bones, and a large mouth: the excessive contrasts of her colouring reminded one of a portrait by one of the modern French painters; her skin was very white, her cheeks were very red, her thick eyebrows, her hair, were very black. The effect was odd, a little unnatural, but far from unpleasing. She was separated from her husband and earned her living and her child's by writing penny novelettes. There were one or two publishers who made a specialty of that sort of thing, and she had as much work as she could do. It was ill-paid, she received fifteen pounds for a story of thirty thousand words; but she was satisfied.

"After all, it only costs the reader twopence," she said, "and they like the same thing over and over again. I just change the names and that's all. When I'm bored I think of the washing and the rent and clothes for baby, and I go on again."

Besides, she walked on at various theatres where they wanted supers and earned by this when in work from sixteen shillings to a guinea a week. At the end of her day she was so tired that she slept like a top. She made the best of her difficult lot. Her keen sense of humour enabled her to get amusement out of every vexatious circumstance. Sometimes things went wrong, and she found herself with no money at all; then her trifling possessions found their way to a pawnshop in the Vauxhall Bridge Road, and she ate bread and butter till things grew brighter. She never lost her cheerfulness.

Philip was interested in her shiftless life, and she made him laugh with the fantastic narration of her struggles. He asked her why she did not try her hand at literary work of a better sort, but she knew that she had no talent, and the abominable stuff she turned out by the thousand words was not only tolerably paid, but was the best she could do. She had nothing to look forward to but a continuation of the life she led. She seemed to have no relations, and her friends were as poor as herself.

"I don't think of the future," she said. "As long as I have enough money for three weeks' rent and a pound or two over for food I never bother. Life wouldn't be worth living if I worried over the future as well as the present. When things are at their worst I find something always happens."

Soon Philip grew in the habit of going in to tea with her every day, and so that his visits might not embarrass her he took in a cake or a pound of butter or some tea. They started to call one another by their Christian names. Feminine sympathy was new to him, and he delighted in someone who gave a willing ear to all his troubles. The hours went quickly. He did not hide his admiration for her. She was a delightful companion. He could not help comparing her with Mildred; and he contrasted with the one's obstinate stupidity, which refused interest to everything she did not know, the other's quick appreciation and ready intelligence. His heart sank when he thought that he might have been tied for life to such a woman as Mildred. One evening he told Norah the whole story of his love. It was not one to give him much reason for self-esteem, and it was very pleasant to receive such charming sympathy.

"I think you're well out of it," she said, when he had finished.

She had a funny way at times of holding her head on one side like an Aberdeen puppy. She was sitting in an upright chair, sewing, for she had no time to do nothing, and Philip had made himself comfortable at her feet.

"I can't tell you how heartily thankful I am it's all over," he sighed.

"Poor thing, you must have had a rotten time," she murmured, and by way of showing her sympathy put her hand on his shoulder.

He took it and kissed it, but she withdrew it quickly.

"Why did you do that?" she asked, with a blush.

"Have you any objection?"

She looked at him for a moment with twinkling eyes, and she smiled.

"No," she said.

He got up on his knees and faced her. She looked into his eyes steadily, and her large mouth trembled with a smile.

"Well?" she said.

"You know, you are a ripper. I'm so grateful to you for being nice to me. I like you so much."

"Don't be idiotic," she said.

Philip took hold of her elbows and drew her towards him. She made no resistance, but bent forward a little, and he kissed her red lips.

"Why did you do that?" she asked again.

"Because it's comfortable."

She did not answer, but a tender look came into her eyes, and she passed her hand softly over his hair.

"You know, it's awfully silly of you to behave like this. We were such good friends. It would be so jolly to leave it at that."

"If you really want to appeal to my better nature," replied Philip, "you'll do well not to stroke my cheek while you're doing it."

She gave a little chuckle, but she did not stop.

"It's very wrong of me, isn't it?" she said.

Philip, surprised and a little amused, looked into her eyes, and as he looked he saw them soften and grow liquid, and there was an expression in them that enchanted him. His heart was suddenly stirred, and tears came to his eyes.

"Norah, you're not fond of me, are you?" he asked, incredulously.

"You clever boy, you ask such stupid questions."

"Oh, my dear, it never struck me that you could be."

He flung his arms round her and kissed her, while she, laughing, blushing, and crying, surrendered herself willingly to his embrace.

Presently he released her and sitting back on his heels looked at her curiously.

"Well, I'm blowed!" he said.

"Why?"

"I'm so surprised."

"And pleased?"

"Delighted," he cried with all his heart, "and so proud and so happy and so grateful."

He took her hands and covered them with kisses. This was the beginning for Philip of a happiness which seemed both solid and durable. They became lovers but remained friends. There was in Norah a maternal instinct which received satisfaction in her love for Philip; she wanted someone to pet, and scold, and make a fuss of; she had a domestic temperament and found pleasure in looking after his health and his linen. She pitied his deformity, over which he was so sensitive, and her pity expressed itself instinctively in tenderness. She was young, strong, and healthy, and it seemed quite natural to her to give her love. She had high spirits and a merry soul. She liked Philip because he laughed with her at all the amusing things in life that caught her fancy, and above all she liked him because he was he.

When she told him this he answered gaily:

"Nonsense. You like me because I'm a silent person and never want to get a word in."

Philip did not love her at all. He was extremely fond of her, glad to be with her, amused and interested by her conversation. She restored his belief in himself and put healing ointments, as it were, on all the bruises of his soul. He was immensely flattered that she cared for him. He admired her courage, her optimism, her impudent defiance of fate; she had a little philosophy of her own, ingenuous and practical.

"You know, I don't believe in churches and parsons and all that," she said, "but I believe in God, and I don't believe He minds much about what you do as long as you keep your end up and help a lame dog over a stile when you can. And I think people on the whole are very nice, and I'm sorry for those who aren't."

"And what about afterwards?" asked Philip.

"Oh, well, I don't know for certain, you know," she smiled, "but I hope for the best. And anyhow there'll be no rent to pay and no novelettes to write."

She had a feminine gift for delicate flattery. She thought that Philip did a brave thing when he left Paris because he was conscious he could not be a great artist; and he was enchanted when she expressed enthusiastic admiration for him. He had never been quite certain whether this action indicated courage or infirmity of purpose. It was delightful to realise that she considered it heroic. She ventured to tackle him on a subject which his friends instinctively avoided.

"It's very silly of you to be so sensitive about your club-foot," she said. She saw him flush darkly, but went on. "You know, people don't think about it nearly as much as you do. They notice it the first time they see you, and then they forget about it."

He would not answer.

"You're not angry with me, are you?"

"No."

She put her arm round his neck.

"You know, I only speak about it because I love you. I don't want it to make you unhappy."

"I think you can say anything you choose to me," he answered, smiling. "I wish I could do something to show you how grateful I am to you."

She took him in hand in other ways. She would not let him be bearish and laughed at him when he was out of temper. She made him more urbane.

"You can make me do anything you like," he said to her once.

"D'you mind?"

"No, I want to do what you like."

He had the sense to realise his happiness. It seemed to him that she gave him all that a wife could, and he preserved his freedom; she was the most charming friend he had ever had, with a sympathy that he had never found in a man. The sexual relationship was no more than the strongest link in their friendship. It completed it, but was not essential. And because Philip's appetites were satisfied, he became more equable and easier to live with. He felt in complete possession of himself. He thought sometimes of the winter, during which he had been obsessed by a hideous passion, and he was filled with loathing for Mildred and with horror of himself.

His examinations were approaching, and Norah was as interested in them as he. He was flattered and touched by her eagerness. She made him promise to come at once and tell her the results. He passed the three parts this time without mishap, and when he went to tell her she burst into tears.

"Oh, I'm so glad, I was so anxious."

"You silly little thing," he laughed, but he was choking.

No one could help being pleased with the way she took it.

One morning Philip on getting up felt his head swim, and going back to bed suddenly discovered he was ill. All his limbs ached and he shivered with cold. When the landlady brought in his breakfast he called to her through the open door that he was not well, and asked for a cup of tea and a piece of toast. A few minutes later there was a knock at his door, and Griffiths came in. They had lived in the same house for over a year, but had never done more than nod to one another in the passage.

"I say, I hear you're seedy," said Griffiths. "I thought I'd come in and see what was the matter with you."

Philip, blushing he knew not why, made light of the whole thing. He would be all right in an hour or two.

"Well, you'd better let me take your temperature," said Griffiths.

"It's quite unnecessary," answered Philip irritably.

"Come on."

Philip put the thermometer in his mouth. Griffiths sat on the side of the bed and chatted brightly for a moment, then he took it out and looked at it.

"Now, look here, old man, you must stay in bed, and I'll bring old Deacon in to have a look at you."

"Nonsense," said Philip. "There's nothing the matter. I wish you wouldn't bother about me."

"But it isn't any bother. You've got a temperature and you must stay in bed. You will, won't you?"

There was a peculiar charm in his manner, a mingling of gravity and kindliness, which was infinitely attractive.

"You've got a wonderful bed-side manner," Philip murmured, closing his eyes with a smile.

Griffiths shook out his pillow for him, deftly smoothed down the bed-clothes, and tucked him up. He went into Philip's sitting-room to look for a siphon, could not find one, and fetched it from his own room. He drew down the blind.

"Now, go to sleep and I'll bring the old man round as soon as he's done the wards."

It seemed hours before anyone came to Philip. His head felt as if it would split, anguish rent his limbs, and he was afraid he was going to cry. Then there was a knock at the door and Griffiths, healthy, strong, and cheerful, came in.

"Here's Doctor Deacon," he said.

The physician stepped forward, an elderly man with a bland manner, whom Philip knew only by sight. A few questions, a brief examination, and the diagnosis.

"What d'you make it?" he asked Griffiths, smiling.

"Influenza."

"Quite right."

Doctor Deacon looked round the dingy lodging-house room.

"Wouldn't you like to go to the hospital? They'll put you in a private ward, and you can be better looked after than you can here."

"I'd rather stay where I am," said Philip.

He did not want to be disturbed, and he was always shy of new surroundings. He did not fancy nurses fussing about him, and the dreary cleanliness of the hospital.

"I can look after him, sir," said Griffiths at once.

"Oh, very well."

He wrote a prescription, gave instructions, and left.

"Now you've got to do exactly as I tell you," said Griffiths. "I'm day-nurse and night-nurse all in one."

"It's very kind of you, but I shan't want anything," said Philip.

Griffiths put his hand on Philip's forehead, a large cool, dry hand, and the touch seemed to him good.

"I'm just going to take this round to the dispensary to have it made up, and then I'll come back."

In a little while he brought the medicine and gave Philip a dose. Then he went upstairs to fetch his books.

"You won't mind my working in your room this afternoon, will you?" he said, when he came down. "I'll leave the door open so that you can give me a shout if you want anything."

Later in the day Philip, awaking from an uneasy doze, heard voices in his sitting-room. A friend had come in to see Griffiths.

"I say, you'd better not come in tonight," he heard Griffiths saying.

And then a minute or two afterwards someone else entered the room and expressed his surprise at finding Griffiths there. Philip heard him explain.

"I'm looking after a second year's man who's got these rooms. The wretched blighter's down with influenza. No whist tonight, old man."

Presently Griffiths was left alone and Philip called him.

"I say, you're not putting off a party tonight, are you?" he asked.

"Not on your account. I must work at my surgery."

"Don't put it off. I shall be all right. You needn't bother about me."

"That's all right."

Philip grew **wor**se. As the night came on he became slightly delirious, but towards morning he awoke from a restless sleep. He saw Griffiths get out of an arm-chair, go down on his knees, and with his fingers put piece after piece of coal on the fire. He was in pyjamas and a dressing-gown.

"What are you doing here?" he asked.

"Did I wake you up? I tried to make up the fire without making a row."

"Why aren't you in bed? What's the time?"

"About five. I thought I'd better sit up with you tonight. I brought an arm-chair in as I thought if I put a mattress down I should sleep so soundly that I shouldn't hear you if you wanted anything."

"I wish you wouldn't be so good to me," groaned Philip. "Suppose you catch it?"

"Then you shall nurse me, old man," said Griffiths, with a laugh.

In the morning Griffiths drew up the blind. He looked pale and tired after his night's watch, but was full of spirits.

"Now, I'm going to wash you," he said to Philip cheerfully.

"I can wash myself," said Philip, ashamed.

"Nonsense. If you were in the small ward a nurse would wash you, and I can do it just as well as a nurse."

Philip, too weak and wretched to resist, allowed Griffiths to wash his hands and face, his feet, his chest and back. He did it with charming tenderness, carrying on meanwhile a stream of friendly chatter; then he changed the sheet just as they did at the hospital, shook out the pillow, and arranged the bed-clothes.

"I should like Sister Arthur to see me. It would make her sit up. Deacon's coming in to see you early."

"I can't imagine why you should be so good to me," said Philip.

"It's good practice for me. It's rather a lark having a patient."

Griffiths gave him his breakfast and went off to get dressed and have something to eat. A few minutes before ten he came back with a bunch of grapes and a few flowers.

"You are awfully kind," said Philip.

He was in bed for five days.

Norah and Griffiths nursed him between them. Though Griffiths was the same age as Philip he adopted towards him a humorous, motherly attitude. He was a thoughtful fellow, gentle and encouraging; but his greatest quality was a vitality which seemed to give health to everyone with whom he came in contact. Philip was unused to the petting which most people enjoy from mothers or sisters and he was deeply touched by the feminine tenderness of this strong young man. Philip grew better. Then Griffiths, sitting idly in Philip's room, amused him with gay stories of amorous adventure. He was a flirtatious creature, capable of carrying on three or four affairs at a time; and his account of the devices he was forced to in order to keep out of difficulties made excellent hearing. He had a gift for throwing a romantic glamour over everything that happened to him. He was crippled with debts, everything he had of any value was pawned, but he managed always to be cheerful, extravagant, and generous. He was the adventurer by nature. He loved people of doubtful occupations and shifty purposes; and his acquaintance among the riff-raff that frequents the bars of London was enormous. Loose women, treating him as a friend, told him the troubles, difficulties, and successes of their lives; and card-sharpers, respecting his impecuniosity, stood him dinners and lent him five-pound notes. He was ploughed in his examinations time after time; but he bore this cheerfully, and submitted with such a charming grace to the parental expostulations that his father, a doctor in practice at Leeds, had not the heart to be seriously angry with him.

"I'm an awful fool at books," he said cheerfuly, "but I *can't* work."

Life was much too jolly. But it was clear that when he had got through the exuberance of his youth, and was at last qualified, he would be a tremendous success in practice. He would cure people by the sheer charm of his manner.

Philip worshipped him as at school he had worshipped boys who were tall and straight and high of spirits. By the time he was well they were fast friends, and it was a peculiar satisfaction to Philip that Griffiths seemed to enjoy sitting in his little parlour, wasting Philip's time with his amusing chatter and smoking innumerable cigarettes. Philip took him sometimes to the tavern off Regent Street. Hayward found him stupid, but Lawson recognised his charm and was eager to paint him; he was a picturesque figure with his blue eyes, white skin, and curly hair. Often they discussed things he knew nothing about, and then he sat quietly, with a good-natured smile on his handsome face, feeling quite rightly that his presence was sufficient contribution to the entertainment of the company. When he discovered that Macalister was a stockbroker he was eager for tips; and Macalister, with his grave smile, told him what fortunes he could have made if he had bought certain stock at certain times. It made Philip's mouth water, for in one way and another he was spending more than he had expected, and it would have suited him very well to make a little money by the easy method Macalister suggested.

"Next time I hear of a really good thing I'll let you know," said the stockbroker. "They do come along sometimes. It's only a matter of biding one's time."

Philip could not help thinking how delightful it would be to make fifty pounds, so that he could give Norah the furs she so badly needed for the winter. He looked at the shops in Regent Street and picked out the articles he could buy for the money. She deserved everything. She made his life very happy.

One afternoon, when he went back to his rooms from the hospital to wash and tidy himself before going to tea as usual with Norah, as he let himself in with his latch-key, his landlady opened the door for him.

"There's a lady waiting to see you," she said.

"Me?" exclaimed Philip.

He was surprised. It would only be Norah, and he had no idea what had brought her.

"I shouldn't 'ave let her in, only she's been three times, and she seemed that upset at not finding you, so I told her she could wait."

He pushed past the explaining landlady and burst into the room. His heart turned sick. It was Mildred. She was sitting down, but got up hurriedly as he came in. She did not move towards him nor speak. He was so surprised that he did not know what he was saying.

"What the hell d'you want?" he asked.

She did not answer, but began to cry. She did not put her hands to her eyes, but kept them hanging by the side of her body. She looked like a housemaid applying for a situation. There was a dreadful humility in her bearing. Philip did not know what feelings came over him. He had a sudden impulse to turn round and escape from the room.

"I didn't think I'd ever see you again," he said at last.

"I wish I was dead," she moaned.

Philip left her standing where she was. He could only

think at the moment of steadying himself. His knees were shaking. He looked at her, and he groaned in despair.

"What's the matter?" he said.

"He's left me—Emil."

Philip's heart bounded. He knew then that he loved her as passionately as ever. He had never ceased to love her. She was standing before him humble and unresisting. He wished to take her in his arms and cover her tear-stained face with kisses. Oh, how long the separation had been! He did not know how he could have endured it.

"You'd better sit down. Let me give you a drink."

He drew the chair near the fire and she sat in it. He mixed her whiskey and soda, and, sobbing still, she drank it. She looked at him with great, mournful eyes. There were large black lines under them. She was thinner and whiter than when last he had seen her.

"I wish I'd married you when you asked me," she said.

Philip did not know why the remark seemed to swell his heart. He could not keep the distance from her which he had forced upon himself. He put his hand on her shoulder.

"I'm awfully sorry you're in trouble."

She leaned her head against his bosom and burst into hysterical crying. Her hat was in the way and she took it off. He had never dreamt that she was capable of crying like that. He kissed her again and again. It seemed to ease her a little.

"You were always good to me, Philip," she said. "That's why I knew I could come to you."

"Tell me what's happened."

"Oh, I can't, I can't," she cried out, breaking away from him.

He sank down on his knees beside her and put his cheek against hers.

"Don't you know that there's nothing you can't tell me? I can never blame you for anything."

She told him the story little by little, and sometimes she sobbed so much that he could hardly understand.

"Last Monday week he went up to Birmingham, and he promised to be back on Thursday, and he never came, and he didn't come on the Friday, so I wrote to ask what was the matter, and he never answered the letter. And I wrote and said that if I didn't hear from him by return I'd go up to Birmingham, and this morning I got a solicitor's letter to say I had no claim on him, and if I molested him he'd seek the protection of the law."

"But it's absurd," cried Philip. "A man can't treat his wife like that. Had you had a row?"

"Oh, yes, we'd had a quarrel on the Sunday, and he said he was sick of me, but he'd said it before, and he'd come back all right. I didn't think he meant it. He was frightened, because I told him a baby was coming. I kept it from him as long as I could. Then I had to tell him. He said it was my fault, and I ought to have known better. If you'd only heard the things he said to me! But I found out precious quick that he wasn't a gentleman. He left me without a penny. He hadn't paid the rent, and I hadn't got the money to pay it, and the woman who kept the house said such things to me —well, I might have been a thief the way she talked."

"I thought you were going to take a flat."

"That's what he said, but we just took furnished apartments in Highbury. He was that mean. He said I was extravagant, he didn't give me anything to be extravagant with."

She had an extraordinary way of mixing the trivial with the important. Philip was puzzled. The whole thing was incomprehensible.

"No man could be such a blackguard."

"You don't know him. I wouldn't go back to him now not if he was to come and ask me on his bended knees. I was a fool ever to think of him. And he wasn't earning the money he said he was. The lies he told me!"

Philip thought for a minute or two. He was so deeply moved by her distress that he could not think of himself.

"Would you like me to go to Birmingham? I could see him and try to make things up."

"Oh, there's no chance of that. He'll never come back now, I know him."

"But he must provide for you. He can't get out of that. I don't know anything about these things, you'd better go and see a solicitor."

"How can I? I haven't got the money."

"I'll pay all that. I'll write a note to my own solicitor, the sportsman who was my father's executor. Would you like me to come with you now? I expect he'll still be at his office."

"No, give me a letter to him. I'll go alone."

She was a little calmer now. He sat down and wrote a note. Then he remembered that she had no money. He had fortunately changed a cheque the day before and was able to give her five pounds.

"You are good to me, Philip," she said.

"I'm so happy to be able to do something for you."

"Are you fond of me still?"

"Just as fond as ever."

She put up her lips and he kissed her. There was a surrender in the action which he had never seen in her before. It was worth all the agony he had suffered.

She went away and he found that she had been there for two hours. He was extraordinarily happy.

"Poor thing, poor thing," he murmured to himself, his heart glowing with a greater love than he had ever felt before.

He never thought of Norah at all till about eight o'clock a telegram came. He knew before opening it that it was from her.

Is anything the matter? Norah.

He did not know what to do nor what to answer. He could fetch her after the play, in which she was walking on, was over and stroll home with her as he sometimes did; but his whole soul revolted against the idea of seeing her that evening. He thought of writing to her, but he could not bring himself to address her as usual, *dearest Norah*. He made up his mind to telegraph.

Sorry. Could not get away, Philip.

He visualised her. He was slightly repelled by the ugly little face, with its high cheek-bones and the crude colour. There was a coarseness in her skin which gave him goose-flesh. He knew that his telegram must be followed by some action on his part, but at all events it postponed it.

Next day he wired again.

Regret, unable to come. Will write.

Mildred had suggested coming at four in the afternoon, and he would not tell her that the hour was inconvenient. After all she came first. He waited for her impatiently. He watched for her at the window and opened the front-door himself.

"Well? Did you see Nixon?"

"Yes," she answered. "He said it wasn't any good. Nothing's to be done. I must just grin and bear it."

"But that's impossible," cried Philip.

She sat down wearily.

"Did he give any reasons?" he asked.

She gave him a crumpled letter.

"There's your letter, Philip. I never took it. I couldn't tell you yesterday, I really couldn't. Emil didn't marry me. He couldn't. He had a wife already and three children."

Philip felt a sudden pang of jealousy and anguish. It was almost more than he could bear.

"That's why I couldn't go back to my aunt. There's no one I can go to but you."

"What made you go away with him?" Philip asked, in a low voice which he struggled to make firm.

"I don't know. I didn't know he was a married man at first, and when he told me I gave him a piece of my mind. And then I didn't see him for months, and when he came to the shop again and asked me I don't know what came over me. I felt as if I couldn't help it. I had to go with him."

"Were you in love with him?"

"I don't know. I couldn't hardly help laughing at the things he said. And there was something about him—he said I'd never regret it, he promised to give me seven pounds a week—he said he was earning fifteen, and it was all a lie, he wasn't. And then I was sick of going to the shop every morning, and I wasn't getting on very well with my aunt; she wanted to treat me as a servant instead of a relation, said I ought to do my own room, and if I didn't do it nobody was going to do it for me. Oh, I wish I hadn't. But when he came to the shop and asked me I felt I couldn't help it."

Philip moved away from her. He sat down at the table and buried his face in his hands. He felt dreadfully humiliated.

"You're not angry with me, Philip?" she asked piteously.

"No," he answered, looking up but away from her, "only I'm awfully hurt."

"Why?"

"You see, I was so dreadfully in love with you. I did everything I could to make you care for me. I thought you were incapable of loving anyone. It's so horrible to know that you were willing to sacrifice everything for that bounder. I wonder what you saw in him."

"I'm awfully sorry, Philip. I regretted it bitterly afterwards, I promise you that."

He thought of Emil Miller, with his pasty, unhealthy look, his shifty blue eyes, and the vulgar smartness of his appearance; he always wore bright red knitted waistcoats. Philip sighed. She got up and went to him. She put her arm around his neck.

"I shall never forget that you offered to marry me, Philip."

He took her hand and looked up at her. She bent down and kissed him.

"Philip, if you want me still I'll do anything you like now. I know you're a gentleman in every sense of the word."

His heart stood still. Her words made him feel slightly sick.

"It's awfully good of you, but I couldn't."

"Don't you care for me any more?"

"Yes, I love you with all my heart."

"Then why shouldn't we have a good time while we've got the chance? You see, it can't matter now."

He released himself from her.

"You don't understand. I've been sick with love for you ever since I saw you, but now—that man. I've unfortunately got a vivid imagination. The thought of it simply disgusts me."

"You are funny," she said.

He took her hand again and smiled at her.

"You mustn't think I'm not grateful. I can never thank you enough, but you see, it's just stronger than I am."

"You are a good friend, Philip."

They went on talking, and soon they had returned to the familiar companionship of old days. It grew late. Philip suggested that they should dine together and go to a music-hall. She wanted some persuasion, for she had an idea of acting up to her situation, and felt instinctively that it did not accord with her distressed condition to go to a place of entertainment. At last Philip asked her to go simply to please him, and when she could look upon it as an act of self-sacrifice she accepted. She had a new thoughtfulness which delighted Philip. She asked him to take her to the little restaurant in Soho to which they had so often been; he was infinitely grateful to her, because her suggestion showed that happy memories were attached to it. She grew much more cheerful as dinner proceeded. The Burgundy from the public house at the corner warmed her heart, and she forgot that she ought to preserve a dolorous countenance. Philip thought it safe to speak to her of the future.

"I suppose you haven't got a brass farthing, have you?" he asked, when an opportunity presented itself.

"Only what you gave me yesterday, and I had to give the landlady three pounds of that."

"Well, I'd better give you a tenner to go on with. I'll go and see my solicitor and get him to write to Miller. We can make him pay up something, I'm sure. If we can get a hundred pounds out of him it'll carry you on till after the baby comes."

"I wouldn't take a penny from him. I'd rather starve."

"But it's monstrous that he should leave you in the lurch like this."

"I've got my pride to consider."

It was a little awkward for Philip. He needed rigid economy to make his own money last till he was qualified, and he must have something over to keep him during the year he intended to spend as house physician and house surgeon either at his own or at some other hospital. But Mildred had told him various stories of Emil's meanness, and he was afraid to remonstrate with her in case she accused him too of want of generosity.

"I wouldn't take a penny piece from him. I'd sooner beg my bread. I'd have seen about getting some work to do long before now, only it wouldn't be good for me in the state I'm in. You have to think of your health, don't you?"

"You needn't bother about the present," said Philip. "I can let you have all you want till you're fit to work again."

"I knew I could depend on you. I told Emil he needn't think I hadn't got somebody to go to. I told him you was a gentleman in every sense of the word."

By degrees Philip learned how the separation had come

about. It appeared that the fellow's wife had discovered the adventure he was engaged in during his periodical visits to London, and had gone to the head of the firm that employed him. She threatened to divorce him, and they announced that they would dismiss him if she did. He was passionately devoted to his children and could not bear the thought of being separated from them. When he had to choose between his wife and his mistress he chose his wife. He had been always anxious that there should be no child to make the entanglement more complicated; and when Mildred, unable longer to conceal its approach, informed him of the fact, he was seized with panic. He picked a quarrel and left her without more ado.

"When d'you expect to be confined?" asked Philip.

"At the beginning of March."

"Three months."

It was necessary to discuss plans. Mildred declared she would not remain in the rooms at Highbury, and Philip thought it more convenient too that she should be nearer to him. He promised to look for something next day. She suggested the Vauxhall Bridge Road as a likely neighbourhood.

"And it would be near for afterwards," she said.

"What do you mean?"

"Well, I should only be able to stay there about two months or a little more, and then I should have to go into a house. I know a very respectable place, where they have a most superior class of people, and they take you for four guineas a week and no extras. Of course the doctor's extra, but that's all. A friend of mine went there, and the lady who keeps it is a thorough lady. I mean to tell her that my husband's an officer in India and I've come to London for my baby, because it's better for my health."

It seemed extraordinary to Philip to hear her talking in this way. With her delicate little features and her pale face she looked cold and maidenly. When he thought of the passions that burnt within her, so unexpected, his heart was strangely troubled. His pulse beat quickly.

Philip expected to find a letter from Norah when he got back to his rooms, but there was nothing; nor did he receive one the following morning. The silence irritated and at the same time alarmed him. They had seen one another every day he had been in London since the previous June; and it must seem odd to her that he should let two days go by without visiting her or offering a reason for his absence; he wondered whether by an unlucky chance she had seen him with Mildred. He could not bear to think that she was hurt or unhappy, and he made up his mind to call on her that afternoon. He was almost inclined to reproach her because he had allowed himself to get on such intimate terms with her. The thought of continuing them filled him with disgust.

He found two rooms for Mildred on the second floor of a house in the Vauxhall Bridge Road. They were noisy, but he knew that she liked the rattle of traffic under her windows.

"I don't like a dead and alive street where you don't see a soul pass all day," she said. "Give me a bit of life."

Then he forced himself to go to Vincent Square. He was sick with apprehension when he rang the bell. He had an uneasy sense that he was treating Norah badly; he dreaded reproaches; he knew she had a quick temper, and he hated scenes: perhaps the best way would be to tell her frankly that Mildred had come back to him and his love for her was as violent as it had ever been; he was very sorry, but he had nothing to offer Norah any more. Then he thought of her anguish, for he knew she loved him; it had flattered him before, and he was immensely grateful; but now it was horrible. She had not deserved that he should inflict pain upon her. He asked himself how she would greet him now, and as he walked up the stairs all possible forms of her behaviour flashed across his mind. He knocked at the door. He felt that he was pale, and wondered how to conceal his nervousness.

She was writing away industriously, but she sprang to her feet as he entered.

"I recognised your step," she cried. "Where have you been hiding yourself, you naughty boy?"

She came towards him joyfully and put her arms round his neck. She was delighted to see him. He kissed her, and then, to give himself countenance, said he was dying for tea. She bustled the fire to make the kettle boil.

"I've been awfully busy," he said lamely.

She began to chatter in her bright way, telling him of a new commission she had to provide a novelette for a firm which had not hitherto employed her. She was to get fifteen guineas for it.

"It's money from the clouds. I'll tell you what we'll do, we'll stand ourselves a little jaunt. Let's go and spend a day at Oxford, shall we? I'd love to see the colleges."

He looked at her to see whether there was any shadow of reproach in her eyes; but they were as frank and merry as ever: she was overjoyed to see him. His heart sank. He could not tell her the brutal truth. She made some toast for him, and cut it into little pieces, and gave it him as though he were a child.

"Is the brute fed?" she asked.

He nodded, smiling; and she lit a cigarette for him. Then, as she loved to do, she came and sat on his knees. She was very light. She leaned back in his arms with a sigh of delicious happiness.

"Say something nice to me," she murmured.

"What shall I say?"

"You might by an effort of imagination say that you rather liked me."

"You know I do that."

He had not the heart to tell her then. He would give her peace at all events for that day, and perhaps he might write to her. That would be easier. He could not bear to think of her crying. She made him kiss her, and as he kissed her he thought of Mildred and Mildred's pale, thin lips. The recollection of Mildred remained with him all the time, like an incorporated form, but more substantial than a shadow; and the sight continually distracted his attention.

"You're very quiet today," Norah said.

Her loquacity was a standing joke between them, and he answered:

"You never let me get a word in, and I've got out of the habit of talking."

"But you're not listening, and that's bad manners."

He reddened a little, wondering whether she had some inkling of his secret; he turned away his eyes uneasily. The weight of her irked him this afternoon, and he did not want her to touch him.

"My foot's gone to sleep," he said.

"I'm so sorry," she cried, jumping up. "I shall have to bant if I can't break myself of this habit of sitting on gentlemen's knees."

He went through an elaborate form of stamping his foot and walking about. Then he stood in front of the fire so that she should not resume her position. While she talked he thought that she was worth ten of Mildred; she amused him much more and was jollier to talk to; she was cleverer, and she had a much nicer nature. She was a good, brave, honest little woman; and Mildred, he thought bitterly, deserved none of these epithets. If he had any sense he would stick to Norah, she would make him much happier than he would ever be with Mildred: after all she loved him, and Mildred was only grateful for his help. But when all was said the important thing was to love rather than to be loved; and he yearned for Mildred with his whole soul. He would

sooner have ten minutes with her than a whole afternoon
with Norah, he prized one kiss of her cold lips more than
all Norah could give him.

"I can't help myself," he thought. "I've just got her in
my bones."

He did not care if she was heartless, vicious and vulgar,
stupid and grasping, he loved her. He would rather have
misery with the one than happiness with the other.

When he got up to go Norah said casually:

"Well, I shall see you tomorrow, shan't I?"

"Yes," he answered.

He knew that he would not be able to come, since he was
going to help Mildred with her moving, but he had not the
courage to say so. He made up his mind that he would send
a wire. Mildred saw the rooms in the morning, was satisfied
with them, and after luncheon Philip went up with her to
Highbury. She had a trunk for her clothes and another for
the various odds and ends, cushions, lampshades, photograph frames, with which she had tried to give the apartments a home-like air; she had two or three large cardboard
boxes besides, but in all there was no more than could be
put on the roof of a four-wheeler. As they drove through
Victoria Street Philip sat well back in the cab in case Norah
should happen to be passing. He had not had an opportunity to telegraph and could not do so from the post-office
in the Vauxhall Bridge Road, since she would wonder what
he was doing in that neighbourhood; and if he was there he
could have no excuse for not going into the neighbouring
square where she lived. He made up his mind that he had
better go in and see her for half an hour; but the necessity
irritated him: he was angry with Norah, because she forced
him to vulgar and degrading shifts. But he was happy to be
with Mildred. It amused him to help her with the unpack-
ing; and he experienced a charming sense of possession in
installing her in these lodgings which he had found and was

paying for. He would not let her exert herself. It was a pleasure to do things for her, and she had no desire to do what somebody else seemed desirous to do for her. He unpacked her clothes and put them away. She was not proposing to go out again, so he got her slippers and took off her boots. It delighted him to perform menial offices.

"You do spoil me," she said, running her fingers affectionately through his hair, while he was on his knees unbuttoning her boots.

He took her hands and kissed them.

"It is nipping to have you here."

He arranged the cushions and the photograph frames. She had several jars of green earthenware.

"I'll get you some flowers for them," he said.

He looked round at his work proudly.

"As I'm not going out any more I think I'll get into a tea-gown," she said. "Undo me behind, will you?"

She turned round as unconcernedly as though he were a woman. His sex meant nothing to her. But his heart was filled with gratitude for the intimacy her request showed. He undid the hooks and eyes with clumsy fingers.

"That first day I came into the shop I never thought I'd be doing this for you now," he said, with a laugh which he forced.

"Somebody must do it," she answered.

She went into the bed-room and slipped into a pale blue tea-gown decorated with a great deal of cheap lace. Then Philip settled her on a sofa and made tea for her.

"I'm afraid I can't stay and have it with you," he said regretfully. "I've got a beastly appointment. But I shall be back in half an hour."

He wondered what he should say if she asked him what the appointment was, but she showed no curiosity. He had ordered dinner for the two of them when he took the rooms, and proposed to spend the evening with her quietly. He was in such a hurry to get back that he took a tram along the Vauxhall Bridge Road. He thought he had better break the fact to Norah at once that he could not stay more than a few minutes.

"I say, I've got only just time to say how d'you do," he said, as soon as he got into her rooms. "I'm frightfully busy."

Her face fell.

"Why, what's the matter?"

It exasperated him that she should force him to tell lies, and he knew that he reddened when he answered that there was a demonstration at the hospital which he was bound to go to. He fancied that she looked as though she did not believe him, and this irritated him all the more.

"Oh, well, it doesn't matter," she said. "I shall have you all tomorrow."

He looked at her blankly. It was Sunday, and he had been looking forward to spending the day with Mildred. He told himself that he must do that in common decency; he could not leave her by herself in a strange house.

"I'm awfully sorry, I'm engaged tomorrow."

He knew this was the beginning of a scene which he would have given anything to avoid. The colour on Norah's cheeks grew brighter.

"But I've asked the Gordons to lunch"—they were an actor and his wife who were touring the provinces and in London for Sunday—"I told you about it a week ago."

"I'm awfully sorry, I forgot." He hesitated. "I'm afraid I can't possibly come. Isn't there somebody else you can get?"

"What are you doing tomorrow then?"

"I wish you wouldn't cross-examine me."

"Don't you want to tell me?"

"I don't in the least mind telling you, but it's rather annoying to be forced to account for all one's movements."

Norah suddenly changed. With an effort of self-control

she got the better of her temper, and going up to him took his hands.

"Don't disappoint me tomorrow, Philip, I've been looking forward so much to spending the day with you. The Gordons want to see you, and we'll have such a jolly time."

"I'd love to if I could."

"I'm not very exacting, am I? I don't often ask you to do anything that's a bother. Won't you get out of your horrid engagement—just this once?"

"I'm awfully sorry, I don't see how I can," he replied sullenly.

"Tell me what it is," she said coaxingly.

He had had time to invent something.

"Griffiths' two sisters are up for the week-end and we're taking them out."

"Is that all?" she said joyfully. "Griffiths can so easily get another man."

He wished he had thought of something more urgent than that. It was a clumsy lie.

"No, I'm awfully sorry, I can't—I've promised and I mean to keep my promise."

"But you promised me too. Surely I come first."

"I wish you wouldn't persist," he said.

She flared up.

"You won't come because you don't want to. I don't know what you've been doing the last few days, you've been quite different."

He looked at his watch.

"I'm afraid I'll have to be going," he said.

"You won't come tomorrow?"

"No."

"In that case you needn't trouble to come again," she cried, losing her temper for good.

"That's just as you like," he answered.

"Don't let me detain you any longer," she added ironically.

He shrugged his shoulders and walked out. He was re-

lieved that it had gone no worse. There had been no tears.
As he walked along he congratulated himself on getting out
of the affair so easily. He went into Victoria Street and
bought a few flowers to take in to Mildred.

The little dinner was a great success. Philip had sent in a
small pot of caviare, which he knew she was very fond of,
and the landlady brought them up some cutlets with vege-
tables and a sweet. Philip had ordered Burgundy, which was
her favourite wine. With the curtains drawn, a bright fire,
and one of Mildred's shades on the lamp, the room was
cosy.

"It's really just like home," smiled Philip.

"I might be worse off, mightn't I?" she answered.

When they finished, Philip drew two arm-chairs in front
of the fire, and they sat down. He smoked his pipe comfortably. He felt happy and generous.

"What would you like to do tomorrow?" he asked.

"Oh, I'm going to Tulse Hill. You remember the manageress at the shop, well, she's married now, and she's asked
me to go and spend the day with her. Of course she thinks
I'm married too."

Philip's heart sank.

"But I refused an invitation so that I might spend Sunday with you."

He thought that if she loved him she would say that in
that case she would stay with him. He knew very well that
Norah would not have hesitated.

"Well, you were a silly to do that. I've promised to go for
three weeks and more."

"But how can you go alone?"

"Oh, I shall say that Emil's away on business. Her husband's in the glove trade, and he's a very superior fellow."

Philip was silent, and bitter feelings passed through his
heart. She gave him a sidelong glance.

"You don't grudge me a little pleasure, Philip? You see,

it's the last time I shall be able to go anywhere for I don't know how long, and I had promised."

He took her hand and smiled.

"No, darling, I want you to have the best time you can. I only want you to be happy."

There was a little book bound in blue paper lying open, face downwards, on the sofa, and Philip idly took it up. It was a two-penny novelette, and the author was Courtenay Paget. That was the name under which Norah wrote.

"I do like his books," said Mildred. "I read them all. They're so refined."

He remembered what Norah had said of herself.

"I have an immense popularity among kitchen-maids. They think me so genteel."

*P*hilip, in return for Griffiths' confidences, had told him the details of his own complicated amours, and on Sunday morning, after breakfast when they sat by the fire in their dressing-gowns and smoked, he recounted the scene of the previous day. Griffiths congratulated him because he had got out of his difficulties so easily.

"It's the simplest thing in the world to have an affair with a woman," he remarked sententiously, "but it's a devil of a nuisance to get out of it."

Philip felt a little inclined to pat himself on the back for his skill in managing the business. At all events he was immensely relieved. He thought of Mildred enjoying herself in Tulse Hill, and he found in himself a real satisfaction because she was happy. It was an act of self-sacrifice on his part that he did not grudge her pleasure even though paid for by his own disappointment, and it filled his heart with a comfortable glow.

But on Monday morning he found on his table a letter from Norah. She wrote:

Dearest,

I'm sorry I was cross on Saturday. Forgive me and come to tea in the afternoon as usual. I love you.

Your Norah.

His heart sank, and he did not know what to do. He took the note to Griffiths and showed it to him.

"You'd better leave it unanswered," said he.

"Oh, I can't," cried Philip. "I should be miserable if I thought of her waiting and waiting. You don't know what it is to be sick for the postman's knock. I do, and I can't expose anybody else to that torture."

"My dear fellow, one can't break that sort of affair off without somebody suffering. You must just set your teeth to that. One thing is, it doesn't last very long."

Philip felt that Norah had not deserved that he should make her suffer; and what did Griffiths know about the degrees of anguish she was capable of? He remembered his own pain when Mildred had told him she was going to be married. He did not want anyone to experience what he had experienced then.

"If you're so anxious not to give her pain, go back to her," said Griffiths.

"I can't do that."

He got up and walked up and down the room nervously. He was angry with Norah because she had not let the matter rest. She must have seen that he had no more love to give her. They said women were so quick at seeing those things.

"You might help me," he said to Griffiths.

"My dear fellow, don't make such a fuss about it. People do get over these things, you know. She probably isn't so wrapped up in you as you think, either. One's always rather apt to exaggerate the passion one's inspired other people with."

He paused and looked at Philip with amusement.

"Look here, there's only one thing you can do. Write to

her, and tell her the thing's over. Put it so that there can be no mistake about it. It'll hurt her, but it'll hurt her less if you do the thing brutally than if you try half-hearted ways."

Philip sat down and wrote the following letter:

My dear Norah,
I am sorry to make you unhappy, but I think we had better let things remain where we left them on Saturday. I don't think there's any use in letting these things drag on when they've ceased to be amusing. You told me to go and I went. I do not propose to come back. Good-bye.
Philip Carey.

He showed the letter to Griffiths and asked him what he thought of it. Griffiths read it and looked at Philip with twinkling eyes. He did not say what he felt.

"I think that'll do the trick," he said.

Philip went out and posted it. He passed an uncomfortable morning, for he imagined with great detail what Norah would feel when she received his letter. He tortured himself with the thought of her tears. But at the same time he was relieved. Imagined grief was more easy to bear than grief seen, and he was free now to love Mildred with all his soul. His heart leaped at the thought of going to see her that afternoon, when his day's work at the hospital was over.

When as usual he went back to his rooms to tidy himself, he had no sooner put the latch-key in his door than he heard a voice behind him.

"May I come in? I've been waiting for you for half an hour."

It was Norah. He felt himself blush to the roots of his hair. She spoke gaily. There was no trace of resentment in her voice and nothing to indicate that there was a rupture between them. He felt himself cornered. He was sick with fear, but he did his best to smile.

"Yes, do," he said.

He opened the door, and she preceded him into his sitting-room. He was nervous and, to give himself countenance, offered her a cigarette and lit one for himself. She looked at him brightly.

"Why did you write me such a horrid letter, you naughty boy? If I'd taken it seriously it would have made me perfectly wretched."

"It was meant seriously," he answered gravely.

"Don't be so silly. I lost my temper the other day, and I wrote and apologised. You weren't satisfied, so I've come here to apologise again. After all, you're your own master and I have no claims upon you. I don't want you to do anything you don't want to."

She got up from the chair in which she was sitting and went towards him impulsively, with outstretched hands.

"Let's make friends again, Philip. I'm so sorry if I offended you."

He could not prevent her from taking his hands, but he could not look at her.

"I'm afraid it's too late," he said.

She let herself down on the floor by his side and clasped his knees.

"Philip, don't be silly. I'm quick-tempered too and I can understand that I hurt you, but it's so stupid to sulk over it. What's the good of making us both unhappy? It's been so jolly, our friendship." She passed her fingers slowly over his hand. "I love you, Philip."

He got up, disengaging himself from her, and went to the other side of the room.

"I'm awfully sorry, I can't do anything. The whole thing's over."

"D'you mean to say you don't love me any more?"

"I'm afraid so."

"You were just looking for an opportunity to throw me over and you took that one?"

He did not answer. She looked at him steadily for a time which seemed intolerable. She was sitting on the floor where he had left her, leaning against the arm-chair. She began to cry quite silently, without trying to hide her face, and the large tears rolled down her cheeks one after the other. She did not sob. It was horribly painful to see her. Philip turned away.

"I'm awfully sorry to hurt you. It's not my fault if I don't love you."

She did not answer. She merely sat there, as though she were overwhelmed, and the tears flowed down her cheeks. It would have been easier to bear if she had reproached him. He had thought her temper would get the better of her, and he was prepared for that. At the back of his mind was a feeling that a real quarrel, in which each said to the other cruel things, would in some way be a justification of his behaviour. The time passed. At last he grew frightened by her silent crying; he went into his bed-room and got a glass of water; he leaned over her.

"Won't you drink a little? It'll relieve you."

She put her lips listlessly to the glass and drank two or three mouthfuls. Then in an exhausted whisper she asked him for a handkerchief. She dried her eyes.

"Of course I knew you never loved me as much as I loved you," she moaned.

"I'm afraid that's always the case," he said. "There's always one who loves and one who lets himself be loved."

He thought of Mildred, and a bitter pain traversed his heart. Norah did not answer for a long time.

"I'd been so miserably unhappy, and my life was so hateful," she said at last.

She did not speak to him, but to herself. He had never heard her before complain of the life she had led with her husband or of her poverty. He had always admired the bold front she displayed to the world.

"And then you came along and you were so good to me.

And I admired you because you were clever and it was so heavenly to have someone I could put my trust in. I loved you. I never thought it could come to an end. And without any fault of mine at all."

Her tears began to flow again, but now she was more mistress of herself, and she hid her face in Philip's handkerchief. She tried hard to control herself.

"Give me some more water," she said.

She wiped her eyes.

"I'm sorry to make such a fool of myself. I was so unprepared."

"I'm awfully sorry, Norah. I want you to know that I'm very grateful for all you've done for me."

He wondered what it was she saw in him.

"Oh, it's always the same," she sighed, "if you want men to behave well to you, you must be beastly to them; if you treat them decently they make you suffer for it."

She got up from the floor and said she must go. She gave Philip a long, steady look. Then she sighed.

"It's so inexplicable. What does it all mean?"

Philip took a sudden determination.

"I think I'd better tell you, I don't want you to think too badly of me, I want you to see that I can't help myself. Mildred's come back."

The colour came to her face.

"Why didn't you tell me at once? I deserved that surely."

"I was afraid to."

She looked at herself in the glass and set her hat straight.

"Will you call me a cab," she said. "I don't feel I *can* walk."

He went to the door and stopped a passing hansom; but when she followed him into the street he was startled to see how white she was. There was a heaviness in her movements as though she had suddenly grown older. She looked so ill that he had not the heart to let her go alone.

"I'll drive back with you if you don't mind."

She did not answer, and he got into the cab. They drove along in silence over the bridge, through shabby streets in which children, with shrill cries, played in the road. When they arrived at her door she did not immediately get out. It seemed as though she could not summon enough strength to her legs to move.

"I hope you'll forgive me, Norah," he said.

She turned her eyes towards him, and he saw that they were bright again with tears, but she forced a smile to her lips.

"Poor fellow, you're quite worried about me. You mustn't bother. I don't blame you. I shall get over it all right."

Lightly and quickly she stroked his face to show him that she bore no ill-feeling, the gesture was scarcely more than suggested; then she jumped out of the cab and let herself into her house.

Philip paid the hansom and walked to Mildred's lodgings. There was a curious heaviness in his heart. He was inclined to reproach himself. But why? He did not know what else he could have done. Passing a fruiterer's, he remembered that Mildred was fond of grapes. He was so grateful that he could show his love for her by recollecting every whim she had.

For the next three months Philip went every day to see Mildred. He took his books with him and after tea worked, while Mildred lay on the sofa reading novels. Sometimes he would look up and watch her for a minute. A happy smile crossed his lips. She would feel his eyes upon her.

"Don't waste your time looking at me, silly. Go on with your work," she said.

"Tyrant," he answered gaily.

At the bottom of her heart was the hope that the child would be still-born. She did no more than hint it, but Philip saw that the thought was there. He was shocked at first;

and then, reasoning with himself, he was obliged to confess that for all concerned such an event was to be desired.

"It's all very fine to say this and that," Mildred remarked querulously, "but it's jolly difficult for a girl to earn her living by herself; it doesn't make it any easier when she's got a baby."

"Fortunately you've got me to fall back on," smiled Philip, taking her hand.

"You've been good to me, Philip."

"Oh, what rot!"

"You can't say I didn't offer anything in return for what you've done."

"Good heavens, I don't want a return. If I've done anything for you, I've done it because I love you. You owe me nothing. I don't want you to do anything unless you love me."

He was a little horrified by her feeling that her body was a commodity which she could deliver indifferently as an acknowledgment for services rendered.

"But I do want to, Philip. You've been so good to me."

"Well, it won't hurt for waiting. When you're all right again we'll go for our little honeymoon."

"You are naughty," she said, smiling.

Presently the time came for her to move to the nursing-home where she was to be confined. Philip was then able to visit her only in the afternoons. Mildred changed her story and represented herself as the wife of a soldier who had gone to India to join his regiment, and Philip was introduced to the mistress of the establishment as her brother-in-law.

"I have to be rather careful what I say," she told him, "as there's another lady here whose husband's in the Indian Civil."

"I wouldn't let that disturb me if I were you," said Philip. "I'm convinced that her husband and yours went out on the same boat."

"What boat?" she asked innocently.

"The Flying Dutchman."

Mildred was safely delivered of a daughter, and when Philip was allowed to see her the child was lying by her side. Mildred was very weak, but relieved that everything was over. She showed him the baby, and herself looked at it curiously.

"It's a funny-looking little thing, isn't it? I can't believe it's mine."

It was red and wrinkled and odd. Philip smiled when he looked at it. He did not quite know what to say; and it embarrassed him because the nurse who owned the house was standing by his side; and he felt by the way she was looking at him that, disbelieving Mildred's complicated story, she thought he was the father.

"What are you going to call her?" asked Philip.

"I can't make up my mind if I shall call her Madeleine or Cecilia."

The nurse left them alone for a few minutes, and Philip bent down and kissed Mildred on the mouth.

"I'm so glad it's all over happily, darling."

She put her thin arms round his neck.

"You have been a brick to me, Phil dear."

"Now I feel that you're mine at last. I've waited so long for you, my dear."

They heard the nurse at the door, and Philip hurriedly got up. The nurse entered. There was a slight smile on her lips.

Three weeks later Philip saw Mildred and her baby off to Brighton. She had made a quick recovery and looked better than he had ever seen her. She was going to a board-ing-house where she had spent a couple of week-ends with Emil Miller, and had written to say that her husband was obliged to go to Germany on business and she was coming down with her baby. She got pleasure out of the stories she invented, and she showed a certain fertility of invention in the working out of the details. Mildred proposed to find in Brighton some woman who would be willing to take charge of the baby. Philip was startled at the callousness with which she insisted on getting rid of it so soon, but she argued with common sense that the poor child had much better be put somewhere before it grew used to her. Philip had expected the maternal instinct to make itself felt when she had had the baby two or three weeks and had counted on this to help him persuade her to keep it; but nothing of the sort occurred. Mildred was not unkind to her baby; she did all that was necessary; it amused her sometimes, and she talked about it a good deal; but at heart she was indifferent to it. She could not look upon it as part of herself. She fancied it resembled its father already. She was continually wondering how she would manage when it grew older; and she was exasperated with herself for being such a fool as to have it at all.

"If I'd only known then all I do now," she said.

She laughed at Philip, because he was anxious about its welfare.

"You couldn't make more fuss if you was the father," she said. "I'd like to see Emil getting into such a stew about it."

"You will write to me, darling, won't you? And I shall look forward to your coming back with oh! such impatience."

"Mind you get through your exam."

He had been working for it industriously, and now with only ten days before him he made a final effort. He was very anxious to pass, first to save himself time and expense, for money had been slipping through his fingers during the last four months with incredible speed; and then because this examination marked the end of the drudgery: after that the student had to do with medicine, midwifery, and surgery, the interest of which was more vivid than the anatomy and physiology with which he had been hitherto concerned. Philip looked forward with interest to the rest of the curriculum. Nor did he want to have to confess to Mildred that he had failed: though the examination was difficult and the majority of the candidates were ploughed at the first attempt, he knew that she would think less well of him if he did not succeed; she had a peculiarly humiliating way of showing what she thought.

He went into the examination with happy confidence. There was nothing in either of the papers that gave him trouble. He knew that he had done well, and though the second part of the examination was *viva voce* and he was more nervous, he managed to answer the questions adequately. He sent a triumphant telegram to Mildred when the result was announced.

He wrote to her next day, sent her a five-pound note, and at the end of his letter said that if she were very nice and cared to see him for the week-end he would be glad to run down; but she was by no means to alter any plans she had made. He awaited her answer with impatience. In it she said that if she had only known before she could have arranged it, but she had promised to go to a music-hall on the Saturday night; besides, it would make the people at the boarding-house talk if he stayed there. Why did he not come on Sunday morning and spend the day? They could lunch at the Metropole, and she would take him afterwards to see the very superior lady-like person who was going to take the baby.

Sunday. He blessed the day because it was fine. As the train approached Brighton the sun poured through the carriage window. Mildred was waiting for him on the platform.

"How jolly of you to come and meet me!" he cried, as he seized her hands.

"You expected me, didn't you?"

"I hoped you would. I say, how well you're looking."

"It's done me a rare lot of good, but I think I'm wise to

stay here as long as I can. And there are a very nice class of people at the boarding-house. I wanted cheering up after seeing nobody all these months. It was dull sometimes."

She looked very smart in her new hat, a large black straw with a great many inexpensive flowers on it; and round her neck floated a long boa of imitation swansdown. She was still very thin, and she stooped a little when she walked, (she had always done that,) but her eyes did not seem so large; and though she never had any colour, her skin had lost the earthy look it had. They walked down to the sea. Philip, remembering he had not walked with her for months, grew suddenly conscious of his limp and walked stiffly in the attempt to conceal it.

"Are you glad to see me?" he asked, love dancing madly in his heart.

"Of course I am. You needn't ask that."

"By the way, Griffiths sends you his love."

"What cheek!"

He had talked to her a great deal of Griffiths. He had told her how flirtatious he was and had amused her often with the narration of some adventure which Griffiths under the seal of secrecy had imparted to him. Mildred had listened, with some pretense of disgust sometimes, but generally with curiosity; and Philip, admiringly, had enlarged upon his friend's good looks and charm.

"I'm sure you'll like him just as much as I do. He's so jolly and amusing, and he's such an awfully good sort."

Philip told her how, when they were perfect strangers, Griffiths had nursed him through an illness; and in the telling Griffiths' self-sacrifice lost nothing.

"You can't help liking him," said Philip.

"I don't like good-looking men," said Mildred. "They're too conceited for me."

"He wants to know you. I've talked to him about you an awful lot."

"What have you said?" asked Mildred.

Philip had no one but Griffiths to talk to of his love for Mildred, and little by little had told him the whole story of his connection with her. He described her to him fifty times. He dwelt amorously on every detail of her appearance, and Griffiths knew exactly how her thin hands were shaped and how white her face was, and he laughed at Philip when he talked of the charm of her pale, thin lips.

"By Jove, I'm glad I don't take things so badly as that," he said. "Life wouldn't be worth living."

Philip smiled. Griffiths did not know the delight of being so madly in love that it was like meat and wine and the air one breathed and whatever else was essential to existence. Griffiths knew that Philip had looked after the girl while she was having her baby and was now going away with her.

"Well, I must say you've deserved to get something," he remarked. "It must have cost you a pretty penny. It's lucky you can afford it."

"I can't," said Philip. "But what do I care!"

After dinner they walked down to the station, and Philip took her arm. He told her what arrangements he had made for their journey to France. She was to come up to London at the end of the week, but she told him that she could not go away till the Saturday of the week after that. He had already engaged a room in a hotel in Paris. He was looking forward eagerly to taking the tickets.

"You won't mind going second-class, will you? We mustn't be extravagant, and it'll be all the better if we can do ourselves pretty well when we get there."

He had talked to her a hundred times of the Quarter. They would wander through its pleasant old streets, and they would sit idly in the charming gardens of the Luxembourg. If the weather was fine perhaps, when they had had enough of Paris, they might go to Fontainebleau. The trees would be just bursting into leaf. The green of the forest in spring was more beautiful than anything he knew; it was like a song, and it was like the happy pain of love. Mildred listened quietly. He turned to her and tried to look deep into her eyes.

"You do want to come, don't you?" he said.

"Of course I do," she smiled.

"You don't know how I'm looking forward to it. I don't know how I shall get through the next days. I'm so afraid something will happen to prevent it. It maddens me sometimes that I can't tell you how much I love you. And at last, at last . . ."

He broke off. They reached the station, but they had dawdled on the way, and Philip had barely time to say good-night. He kissed her quickly and ran towards the wicket as fast as he could. She stood where he left her. He was strangely grotesque when he ran.

The following Saturday Mildred returned, and that evening Philip kept her to himself. He took seats for the play, and they drank champagne at dinner. It was her first gaiety in London for so long that she enjoyed everything ingenuously. She cuddled up to Philip when they drove from the theatre to the room he had taken for her in Pimlico.

"I really believe you're quite glad to see me," he said.

She did not answer, but gently pressed his hand. Demonstrations of affection were so rare with her that Philip was enchanted.

"I've asked Griffiths to dine with us tomorrow," he told her.

"Oh, I'm glad you've done that. I wanted to meet him."

There was no place of entertainment to take her to on Sunday night, and Philip was afraid she would be bored if she were alone with him all day. Griffiths was amusing; he would help them to get through the evening; and Philip was so fond of them both that he wanted them to know and to like one another. He left Mildred with the words:

"Only six days more."

They had arranged to dine in the gallery at Romano's on Sunday, because the dinner was excellent and looked as though it cost a good deal more than it did. Philip and Mildred arrived first and had to wait some time for Griffiths.

"He's an unpunctual devil," said Philip. "He's probably making love to one of his numerous flames."

But presently he appeared. He was a handsome creature, tall and thin; his head was placed well on the body, it gave him a conquering air which was attractive; and his curly hair, his bold, friendly blue eyes, his red mouth, were charming. Philip saw Mildred look at him with appreciation, and he felt a curious satisfaction. Griffiths greeted them with a smile.

"I've heard a great deal about you," he said to Mildred, as he took her hand.

"Not so much as I've heard about you," she answered.

"Nor so bad," said Philip.

"Has he been blackening my character?"

Griffiths laughed, and Philip saw that Mildred noticed how white and regular his teeth were and how pleasant his smile.

"You ought to feel like old friends," said Philip. "I've talked so much about you to one another."

Griffiths was in the best possible humour, for, having at length passed his final examination, he was qualified, and he had just been appointed house-surgeon at a hospital in the North of London. He was taking up his duties at the beginning of May and meanwhile was going home for a holiday; this was his last week in town, and he was determined to get as much enjoyment into it as he could. He began to talk the gay nonsense which Philip admired because he could not copy it. There was nothing much in what he said, but his vivacity gave it point. There flowed from him a force of life which affected everyone who knew him; it was almost as sensible as bodily warmth. Mildred was more lively than Philip had ever known her, and he was delighted

to see that his little party was a success. She was amusing
herself enormously. She laughed louder and louder. She
quite forgot the genteel reserve which had become second
nature to her.

Presently Griffiths said:

"I say, it's dreadfully difficult for me to call you Mrs.
Miller. Philip never calls you anything but Mildred."

"I daresay she won't scratch your eyes out if you call her
that too," laughed Philip.

"Then she must call me Harry."

Philip sat silent while they chattered away and thought
how good it was to see people happy. Now and then Griffiths teased him a little, kindly, because he was always so
serious.

"I believe he's quite fond of you, Philip," smiled Mildred.

"He isn't a bad old thing," answered Griffiths, and taking
Philip's hand he shook it gaily.

It seemed an added charm in Griffiths that he liked
Philip. They were all sober people, and the wine they had
drunk went to their heads. Griffiths became more talkative
and so boisterous that Philip, amused, had to beg him to
be quiet. He had a gift for story-telling, and his adventures
lost nothing of their romance and their laughter in his narration. He played in all of them a gallant, humorous part.
Mildred, her eyes shining with excitement, urged him on.
He poured out anecdote after anecdote. When the lights
began to be turned out she was astonished.

"My word, the evening has gone quickly. I thought it
wasn't more than half past nine."

They got up to go and when she said good-bye, she
added:

"I'm coming to have tea at Philip's room tomorrow.
You might look in if you can."

"All right," he smiled.

On the way back to Pimlico Mildred talked of nothing

but Griffiths. She was taken with his good looks, his well-cut clothes, his voice, his gaiety.

"I *am* glad you like him," said Philip. "D'you remember you were rather sniffy about meeting him?"

"I think it's so nice of him to be so fond of you, Philip. He is a nice friend for you to have."

She put up her face to Philip for him to kiss her. It was a thing she did rarely.

"I have enjoyed myself this evening, Philip. Thank you so much."

"Don't be so absurd," he laughed, touched by her appreciation so that he felt the moisture come to his eyes.

She opened her door and just before she went in, turned again to Philip.

"Tell Harry I'm madly in love with him," she said.

"All right," he laughed. "Good-night."

Next day, when they were having tea, Griffiths came in. He sank lazily into an arm-chair. There was something strangely sensual in the slow movements of his large limbs. Philip remained silent, while the others chattered away, but he was enjoying himself. He admired them both so much that it seemed natural enough for them to admire one another. He did not care if Griffiths absorbed Mildred's attention, he would have her to himself during the evening: he had something the attitude of a loving husband, confident in his wife's affection, who looks on with amusement while she flirts harmlessly with a stranger. But at half past seven he looked at his watch and said:

"It's about time we went out to dinner, Mildred."

There was a moment's pause, and Griffiths seemed to be considering.

"Well, I'll be getting along," he said at last. "I didn't know it was so late."

"Are you doing anything tonight?" asked Mildred.

"No."

There was another silence. Philip felt slightly irritated.

"I'll just go and have a wash," he said, and to Mildred he added: "Would you like to wash your hands?"

She did not answer him.

"Why don't you come and dine with us?" she said to Griffiths.

He looked at Philip and saw him staring at him sombrely.

"I dined with you last night," he laughed. "I should be in the way."

"Oh, that doesn't matter," insisted Mildred. "Make him come, Philip. He won't be in the way, will he?"

"Let him come by all means if he'd like to."

"All right, then," said Griffiths promptly. "I'll just go upstairs and tidy myself."

The moment he left the room Philip turned to Mildred angrily.

"Why on earth did you ask him to dine with us?"

"I couldn't help myself. It would have looked so funny to say nothing when he said he wasn't doing anything."

"Oh, what rot! And why the hell did you ask him if he was doing anything?"

Mildred's pale lips tightened a little.

"I want a little amusement sometimes. I get tired always being alone with you."

They heard Griffiths coming heavily down the stairs, and Philip went into his bed-room to wash. They dined in the neighbourhood in an Italian restaurant. Philip was cross and silent, but he quickly realised that he was showing to disadvantage in comparison with Griffiths, and he forced himself to hide his annoyance. He drank a good deal of wine to destroy the pain that was gnawing at his heart, and he set himself to talk. Mildred, as though remorseful for what she had said, did all she could to make herself pleasant to him. She was kindly and affectionate. Presently Philip began to think he had been a fool to surrender to a feeling of jealousy. After dinner when they got into a hansom to drive to a music-hall Mildred, sitting between the two men, of her own accord gave him her hand. His anger vanished. Suddenly, he knew not how, he grew conscious that Griffiths was holding her other hand. The pain seized him again violently, it was a real physical pain, and he asked himself, panic-stricken, what he might have asked himself before, whether Mildred and Griffiths were in love with one another. He could not see anything of the performance on account of the mist of suspicion, anger, dismay, and wretchedness which seemed to be before his eyes; but he forced himself to conceal the fact that anything was the matter; he went on talking and laughing. Then a strange desire to torture himself seized him, and he got up, saying he wanted to go and drink something. Mildred and Griffiths had never been alone together for a moment. He wanted to leave them by themselves.

"I'll come too," said Griffiths. "I've got rather a thirst on."

"Oh, nonsense, you stay and talk to Mildred."

Philip did not know why he said that. He was throwing them together now to make the pain he suffered more intolerable. He did not go to the bar, but up into the balcony, from where he could watch them and not be seen. They had ceased to look at the stage and were smiling into one another's eyes. Griffiths was talking with his usual happy fluency and Mildred seemed to hang on his lips. Philip's head began to ache frightfully. He stood there motionless. He knew he would be in the way if he went back. They were enjoying themselves without him, and he was suffering, suffering. Time passed, and now he had an extraordinary shyness about rejoining them. He knew they had not thought of him at all, and he reflected bitterly that he had paid for the dinner and their seats in the music-hall. What a fool they were making of him! He was hot with shame. He could see how happy they were without him. His instinct was to leave them to themselves and go home, but he had not his hat and coat, and it would necessitate endless explanations. He went back. He felt a shadow of annoyance in Mildred's eyes when she saw him, and his heart sank.

"You've been a devil of a time," said Griffiths, with a smile of welcome.

"I met some men I knew. I've been talking to them, and I couldn't get away. I thought you'd be all right together."

"I've been enjoying myself thoroughly," said Griffiths. "I don't know about Mildred."

She gave a little laugh of happy complacency. There was a vulgar sound in the ring of it that horrified Philip. He suggested that they should go.

"Come on," said Griffiths, "we'll both drive you home."

Philip suspected that she had suggested that arrangement so that she might not be left alone with him. In the cab he did not take her hand nor did she offer it, and he knew all the time that she was holding Griffiths'. His chief thought was that it was all so horribly vulgar. As they drove along he asked himself what plans they had made to meet without his knowledge, he cursed himself for having left them alone, he had actually gone out of his way to enable them to arrange things.

"Let's keep the cab," said Philip, when they reached the house in which Mildred was lodging. "I'm too tired to walk home."

On the way back Griffiths talked gaily and seemed indifferent to the fact that Philip answered in monosyllables. Philip felt he must notice that something was the matter. Philip's silence at last grew too significant to struggle against, and Griffiths, suddenly nervous, ceased talking. Philip wanted to say something, but he was so shy he could hardly bring himself to, and yet the time was passing and the opportunity would be lost. It was best to get at the truth at once. He forced himself to speak.

"Are you in love with Mildred?" he asked suddenly.

"I?" Griffiths laughed. "Is that what you've been so funny about this evening? Of course not, my dear old man."

He tried to slip his hand through Philip's arm, but Philip
drew himself away. He knew Griffiths was lying. He could
not bring himself to force Griffiths to tell him that he had
not been holding the girl's hand. He suddenly felt very
weak and broken.

"It doesn't matter to you, Harry," he said. "You've got so
many women—don't take her away from me. It means my
whole life. I've been so awfully wretched."

His voice broke, and he could not prevent the sob that
was torn from him. He was horribly ashamed of himself.

"My dear old boy, you know I wouldn't do anything to
hurt you. I'm far too fond of you for that. I was only playing the fool. If I'd known you were going to take it like that
I'd have been more careful."

"Is that true?" asked Philip.

"I don't care a twopenny damn for her. I give you my
word of honour."

Philip gave a sigh of relief. The cab stopped at their door.

Next day Philip was in a good temper. He was very
anxious not to bore Mildred with too much of his
society, and so had arranged that he should not see her till
dinner-time. She was ready when he fetched her, and he
chaffed her for her unwonted punctuality. She was wearing
a new dress he had given her. He remarked on its smartness.

"It'll have to go back and be altered," she said. "The
skirt hangs all wrong."

"You'll have to make the dressmaker hurry up if you
want to take it to Paris with you."

"It'll be ready in time for that."

"Only three more whole days. We'll go over by the eleven
o'clock, shall we?"

"If you like."

He would have her for nearly a month entirely to himself. His eyes rested on her with hungry adoration. He was able to laugh a little at his own passion.

"I wonder what it is I see in you," he smiled.

"That's a nice thing to say," she answered.

Her body was so thin that one could almost see her skeleton. Her chest was as flat as a boy's. Her mouth, with its narrow pale lips, was ugly, and her skin was faintly green.

"I shall give you Blaud's Pills in quantities when we're away," said Philip, laughing. "I'm going to bring you back fat and rosy."

"I don't want to get fat," she said.

She did not speak of Griffiths, and presently while they were dining Philip half in malice, for he felt sure of himself and his power over her, said:

"It seems to me you were having a great flirtation with Harry last night?"

"I told you I was in love with him," she laughed.

"I'm glad to know that he's not in love with you."

"How d'you know?"

"I asked him."

She hesitated a moment, looking at Philip, and a curious gleam came into her eyes.

"Would you like to read a letter I had from him this morning?"

She handed him an envelope and Philip recognised Griffiths' bold, legible writing. There were eight pages. It was well written, frank and charming; it was the letter of a man who was used to making love to women. He told Mildred that he loved her passionately, he had fallen in love with her the first moment he saw her; he did not want to love her, for he knew how fond Philip was of her, but he could not help himself. Philip was such a dear, and he was very much ashamed of himself, but it was not his fault, he was just carried away. He paid her delightful compliments. Finally he thanked her for consenting to lunch with him next day and said he was dreadfully impatient to see her. Philip noticed that the letter was dated the night before; Griffiths must have written it after leaving Philip, and had taken the trouble to go out and post it when Philip thought he was in bed.

He read it with a sickening palpitation of his heart, but gave no outward sign of surprise. He handed it back to Mildred with a smile, calmly.

"Did you enjoy your lunch?"

"Rather," she said emphatically.

He felt that his hands were trembling, so he put them under the table.

"You mustn't take Griffiths too seriously. He's just a butterfly, you know."

She took the letter and looked at it again.

"I can't help it either," she said, in a voice which she tried to make nonchalant. "I don't know what's come over me."

"It's a little awkward for me, isn't it?" said Philip.

She gave him a quick look.

"You're taking it pretty calmly, I must say."

"What do you expect me to do? Do you want me to tear out my hair in handfuls?"

"I knew you'd be angry with me."

"The funny thing is, I'm not at all. I ought to have known this would happen. I was a fool to bring you together. I know perfectly well that he's got every advantage over me; he's much jollier, and he's very handsome, he's more amusing, he can talk to you about the things that interest you."

"I don't know what you mean by that. If I'm not clever I can't help it, but I'm not the fool you think I am, not by a long way, I can tell you. You're a bit too superior for me, my young friend."

"D'you want to quarrel with me?" he asked mildly.

"No, but I don't see why you should treat me as if I was I don't know what."

"I'm sorry, I didn't mean to offend you. I just wanted to talk things over quietly. We don't want to make a mess of them if we can help it. I saw you were attracted by him and it seemed to me very natural. The only thing that really hurts me is that he should have encouraged you. He knew how awfully keen I was on you. I think it's rather shabby of him to have written that letter to you five minutes after he told me he didn't care twopence about you."

"If you think you're going to make me like him any the less by saying nasty things about him, you're mistaken."

Philip was silent for a moment. He did not know what words he could use to make her see his point of view. He wanted to speak coolly and deliberately, but he was in such a turmoil of emotion that he could not clear his thoughts.

"It's not worth while sacrificing everything for an infatuation that you know can't last. After all, he doesn't care for anyone more than ten days, and you're rather cold; that sort of thing doesn't mean very much to you."

"That's what you think."

She made it more difficult for him by adopting a cantankerous tone.

"If you're in love with him you can't help it. I'll just bear it as best I can. We get on very well together, you and I, and I've not behaved badly to you, have I? I've always known that you're not in love with me, but you like me all right, and when we get over to Paris you'll forget about Griffiths. If you make up your mind to put him out of your thoughts you won't find it so hard as all that, and I've deserved that you should do something for me."

She did not answer, and they went on eating their dinner. When the silence grew oppressive Philip began to talk of indifferent things. He pretended not to notice that Mildred was inattentive. Her answers were perfunctory, and she volunteered no remarks of her own. At last she interrupted abruptly what he was saying:

"Philip, I'm afraid I shan't be able to go away on Saturday. The doctor says I oughtn't to."

He knew this was not true, but he answered:

"When will you be able to come away?"

She glanced at him, saw that his face was white and rigid, and looked nervously away. She was at that moment a little afraid of him.

"I may as well tell you and have done with it, I can't come away with you at all."

"I thought you were driving at that. It's too late to change your mind now. I've got the tickets and everything."

"You said you didn't wish me to go unless I wanted it too, and I don't."

"I've changed my mind. I'm not going to have any more tricks played with me. You must come."

"I like you very much, Philip, as a friend. But I can't bear to think of anything else. I don't like you that way. I couldn't, Philip."

"You were quite willing to a week ago."

"It was different then."

"You hadn't met Griffiths?"

"You said yourself I couldn't help it if I'm in love with him."

Her face was set into a sulky look, and she kept her eyes fixed on her plate. Philip was white with rage. He would have liked to hit her in the face with his clenched fist, and in fancy he saw how she would look with a black eye. There were two lads of eighteen dining at a table near them, and now and then they looked at Mildred; he wondered if they envied him dining with a pretty girl; perhaps they were wishing they stood in his shoes. It was Mildred who broke the silence.

"What's the good of our going away together? I'd be thinking of him all the time. It wouldn't be much fun for you."

"That's my business," he answered.

She thought over all his reply implicated, and she reddened.

"But that's just beastly."

"What of it?"

"I thought you were a gentleman in every sense of the word."

"You were mistaken."

His reply entertained him, and he laughed as he said it.

"For God's sake don't laugh," she cried. "I can't come away with you, Philip. I'm awfully sorry. I know I haven't behaved well to you, but one can't force themselves."

"Have you forgotten that when you were in trouble I did everything for you? I planked out the money to keep you till your baby was born, I paid for your doctor and everything, I paid for you to go to Brighton, and I'm paying for the keep of your baby, I'm paying for your clothes, I'm paying for every stitch you've got on now."

"If you was a gentleman you wouldn't throw what you've done for me in my face."

"Oh, for goodness' sake, shut up. What d'you suppose I care if I'm a gentleman or not? If I were a gentleman I shouldn't waste my time with a vulgar slut like you. I don't care a damn if you like me or not. I'm sick of being made a blasted fool of. You're jolly well coming to Paris with me on Saturday or you can take the consequences."

Her cheeks were red with anger, and when she answered her voice had the hard commonness which she concealed generally by a genteel enunciation.

"I never liked you, not from the beginning, but you forced yourself on me, I always hated it when you kissed me. I wouldn't let you touch me now not if I was starving."

Philip tried to swallow the food on his plate, but the muscles of his throat refused to act. He gulped down something to drink and lit a cigarette. He was trembling in every part. He did not speak. He waited for her to move, but she sat in silence, staring at the white tablecloth. If they had been alone he would have flung his arms round her and kissed her passionately; he fancied the throwing back of her long white throat as he pressed upon her mouth with his lips.

They passed an hour without speaking, and at last Philip thought the waiter began to stare at them curiously. He called for the bill.

"Shall we go?" he said then, in an even tone.

She did not reply, but gathered together her bag and her gloves. She put on her coat.

"When are you seeing Griffiths again?"

"Tomorrow," she answered indifferently.

"You'd better talk it over with him."

She opened her bag mechanically and saw a piece of paper in it. She took it out.

"Here's the bill for this dress," she said hesitatingly.

"What of it?"

"I promised I'd give her the money tomorrow."

"Did you?"

"Does that mean you won't pay for it after having told me I could get it?"

"It does."

"I'll ask Harry," she said, flushing quickly.

"He'll be glad to help you. He owes me seven pounds at the moment, and he pawned his microscope last week, because he was so broke."

"You needn't think you can frighten me by that. I'm quite capable of earning my own living."

"It's the best thing you can do. I don't propose to give you a farthing more."

She thought of her rent due on Saturday and the baby's keep, but did not say anything. They left the restaurant, and in the street Philip asked her:

"Shall I call a cab for you? I'm going to take a little stroll."

"I haven't got any money. I had to pay a bill this afternoon."

"It won't hurt you to walk. If you want to see me tomorrow I shall be in about tea-time."

He took off his hat and sauntered away. He looked round

in a moment and saw that she was standing helplessly where he had left her, looking at the traffic. He went back and with a laugh pressed a coin into her hand.

"Here's two bob for you to get home with."

Before she could speak he hurried away.

Next day, in the afternoon, Philip sat in his room and wondered whether Mildred would come. He had slept badly. He had spent the morning in the club of the Medical School, reading one newspaper after another. It was the vacation and few students he knew were in London, but he found one or two people to talk to, he played a game of chess, and so wore out the tedious hours. After luncheon he felt so tired, his head was aching so, that he went back to his lodgings and lay down; he tried to read a novel. He had not seen Griffiths. He was not in when Philip returned the night before; he heard him come back, but he did not as usual look into Philip's room to see if he was asleep; and in the morning Philip heard him go out early. It was clear that he wanted to avoid him. Suddenly there was a light tap at his door. Philip sprang to his feet and opened it. Mildred stood on the threshold. She did not move.

"Come in," said Philip.

He closed the door after her. She sat down. She hesitated to begin.

"Thank you for giving me that two shillings last night," she said.

"Oh, that's all right."

She gave him a faint smile. It reminded Philip of the timid, ingratiating look of a puppy that has been beaten for naughtiness and wants to reconcile himself with his master.

"I've been lunching with Harry," she said.

"Have you?"

"If you still want me to go away with you on Saturday, Philip, I'll come."

A quick thrill of triumph shot through his heart, but it was a sensation that only lasted an instant; it was followed by a suspicion.

"Because of the money?" he asked.

"Partly," she answered simply. "Harry can't do anything. He owes five weeks here, and he owes you seven pounds, and his tailor's pressing him for money. He'd pawn anything he could, but he's pawned everything already. I had a job to put the woman off about my new dress, and on Saturday there's the book at my lodgings, and I can't get work in five minutes. It always means waiting some little time till there's a vacancy."

She said all this in an even, querulous tone, as though she were recounting the injustices of fate, which had to be borne as part of the natural order of things. Philip did not answer. He knew what she told him well enough.

"You said partly," he observed at last.

"Well, Harry says you've been a brick to both of us. You've been a real good friend to him, he says, and you've done for me what p'raps no other man would have done. We must do the straight thing, he says. And he said what you said about him, that he's fickle by nature, he's not like you, and I should be a fool to throw you away for him. He won't last and you will, he says so himself."

"D'you *want* to come away with me?" asked Philip.

"I don't mind."

He looked at her, and the corners of his mouth turned down in an expression of misery. He had triumphed indeed, and he was going to have his way. He gave a little laugh of derision at his own humiliation. She looked at him quickly, but did not speak.

"I've looked forward with all my soul to going away with you, and I thought at last, after all that wretchedness, I was going to be happy . . ."

He did not finish what he was going to say. And then on a sudden, without warning, Mildred broke into a storm of tears. She was sitting in the chair in which Norah had sat and wept, and like her she hid her face on the back of it, towards the side where there was a little bump formed by the sagging in the middle, where the head had rested.

"I'm not lucky with women," thought Philip.

Her thin body was shaken with sobs. Philip had never seen a woman cry with such an utter abandonment. It was horribly painful, and his heart was torn. Without realising what he did, he went up to her and put his arms round her; she did not resist, but in her wretchedness surrendered herself to his comforting. He whispered to her little words of solace. He scarcely knew what he was saying, he bent over her and kissed her repeatedly.

"Are you awfully unhappy?" he said at last.

"I wish I was dead," she moaned. "I wish I'd died when the baby come."

Her hat was in her way, and Philip took it off for her. He placed her head more comfortably in the chair, and then he went and sat down at the table and looked at her.

"It is awful, love, isn't it?" he said. "Fancy anyone wanting to be in love."

Presently the violence of her sobbing diminished and she sat in the chair, exhausted, with her head thrown back and her arms hanging by her side. She had the grotesque look of one of those painters' dummies used to hang draperies on.

"I didn't know you loved him so much as all that," said Philip.

He understood Griffiths' love well enough, for he put himself in Griffiths' place and saw with his eyes, touched with his hands; he was able to think himself in Griffiths' body, and he kissed her with his lips, smiled at her with his smiling blue eyes. It was her emotion that surprised him. He had never thought her capable of passion, and this was passion: there was no mistaking it. Something seemed to give way in his heart; it really felt to him as though something were breaking, and he felt strangely weak.

"I don't want to make you unhappy. You needn't come away with me if you don't want to. I'll give you the money all the same."

She shook her head.

"No, I said I'd come, and I'll come."

"What's the good, if you're sick with love for him?"

"Yes, that's the word. I'm sick with love. I know it won't last, just as well as he does, but just now . . ."

She paused and shut her eyes as though she were going to faint. A strange idea came to Philip, and he spoke it as it came, without stopping to think it out.

"Why don't you go away with him?"

"How can I? You know we haven't got the money."

"I'll give you the money."

"You?"

She sat up and looked at him. Her eyes began to shine, and the colour came into her cheeks.

"Perhaps the best thing would be to get it over, and then you'd come back to me."

Now that he had made the suggestion he was sick with anguish, and yet the torture of it gave him a strange, subtle sensation. She stared at him with open eyes.

"Oh, how could we, on your money? Harry wouldn't think of it."

"Oh yes, he would, if you persuaded him."

Her objections made him insist, and yet he wanted her with all his heart to refuse vehemently.

"I'll give you a fiver, and you can go away from Saturday to Monday. You could easily do that. On Monday he's going home till he takes up his appointment at the North London."

"Oh, Philip, do you mean that?" she cried, clasping her hands. "If you could only let us go—I would love you so much afterwards, I'd do anything for you. I'm sure I shall get over it if you'll only do that. Would you really give us the money?"

"Yes," he said.

She was entirely changed now. She began to laugh. He could see that she was insanely happy. She got up and knelt down by Philip's side, taking his hands.

"You are a brick, Philip. You're the best fellow I've ever known. Won't you be angry with me afterwards?"

He shook his head, smiling, but with what agony in his heart!

"May I go and tell Harry now? And can I say to him that you don't mind? He won't consent unless you promise it doesn't matter. Oh, you don't know how I love him! And afterwards I'll do anything you like. I'll come over to Paris with you or anywhere on Monday."

She got up and put on her hat.

"Where are you going?"

"I'm going to ask him if he'll take me."

"Already?"

"D'you want me to stay? I'll stay if you like."

She sat down, but he gave a little laugh.

"No, it doesn't matter, you'd better go at once. There's only one thing: I can't bear to see Griffiths just now, it would hurt me too awfully. Say I have no ill-feeling towards him or anything like that, but ask him to keep out of my way."

"All right." She sprang up and put on her gloves. "I'll let you know what he says."

After lunching in the basement of the Medical School Philip went back to his rooms. It was Saturday afternoon, and the landlady was cleaning the stairs.

"Is Mr. Griffiths in?" he asked.

"No, sir. He went away this morning, soon after you went out."

"Isn't he coming back?"

"I don't think so, sir. He's taken his luggage."

Philip wondered what this could mean. He took a book and began to read. It was Burton's *Journey to Meccah,* which he had just got out of the Westminster Public Library; and he read the first page, but could make no sense of it, for his mind was elsewhere; he was listening all the time for a ring at the bell. He dared not hope that Griffiths had gone away already, without Mildred, to his home in Cumberland. Mildred would be coming presently for the money. He set his teeth and read on; he tried desperately to concentrate his attention; the sentences etched themselves in his brain by the force of his effort, but they were distorted by the agony he was enduring. He wished with all his heart that he had not made the horrible proposition to give them money; but now that he had made it he lacked the strength to go back on it, not on Mildred's account, but on his own. There was a morbid obstinacy in him which forced him to do the thing he had determined. He discovered that the three pages he had read had made no impression on him at all; and he went back and started from the beginning: he found himself reading one sentence over and over again; and now it weaved itself in with his thoughts, horribly, like some formula in a nightmare. One thing he could do was to go out and keep away till midnight; they could not go then; and he saw them calling at the house every hour to ask if he was in. He enjoyed the thought of their disappointment. He repeated that sentence to himself mechanically. But he could not do that. Let them come and take the money, and he would know then to what depths of infamy it was possible for men to descend. He could not read any more now. He simply could not see the words. He leaned back in his chair, closing his eyes, and, numb with misery, waited for Mildred.

The landlady came in.

"Will you see Mrs. Miller, sir?"

"Show her in."

Philip pulled himself together to receive her without any sign of what he was feeling. He had an impulse to throw himself on his knees and seize her hands and beg her not to go; but he knew there was no way of moving her; she would tell Griffiths what he had said and how he acted. He was ashamed.

"Well, how about the little jaunt?" he said gaily.

"We're going. Harry's outside. I told him you didn't want to see him, so he's kept out of your way. But he wants to know if he can come in just for a minute to say good-bye to you."

"No, I won't see him," said Philip.

He could see she did not care if he saw Griffiths or not. Now that she was there he wanted her to go quickly.

"Look here, here's the fiver. I'd like you to go now."

She took it and thanked him. She turned to leave the room.

"When are you coming back?" he asked.

"Oh, on Monday. Harry must go home then."

He knew what he was going to say was humiliating, but he was broken down with jealousy and desire.

"Then I shall see you, shan't I?"

He could not help the note of appeal in his voice.

"Of course. I'll let you know the moment I'm back."

He shook hands with her. Through the curtains he watched her jump into a four-wheeler that stood at the door. It rolled away. Then he threw himself on his bed and hid his face in his hands. He felt tears coming to his eyes, and he was angry with himself; he clenched his hands and screwed up his body to prevent them; but he could not; and great painful sobs were forced from him.

At last Monday came. Philip felt a bitter hatred for Griffiths, but for Mildred, notwithstanding all that had passed, only a heart-rending desire. What did he care if it was shocking or disgusting? He was ready for any compromise, prepared for more degrading humiliations still, if he could only gratify his desire.

Towards the evening his steps took him against his will to the house in which she lived, and he looked up at her window. It was dark. He did not venture to ask if she was back. He was confident in her promise. But there was no letter from her in the morning, and, when about mid-day he called, the maid told him she had not arrived. He could not understand it. He knew that Griffiths would have been obliged to go home the day before, for he was to be best man at a wedding, and Mildred had no money. He turned over in his mind every possible thing that might have happened. He went again in the afternoon and left a note, asking her to dine with him that evening as calmly as though the events of the last fortnight had not happened. He mentioned the place and time at which they were to meet, and hoping against hope kept the appointment: though he waited for an hour she did not come. On Wednesday morning he was ashamed to ask at the house and sent a messenger-boy with a letter and instructions to bring back a reply; but in an hour the boy came back with Philip's letter unopened and the answer that the lady had not returned from the country. Philip was beside himself. The last deception was more than he could bear. He repeated to himself over and over again that he loathed Mildred, and, ascribing to Griffiths this new disappointment, he hated him so much that he knew what was the delight of murder: he walked about considering what a joy it would be to come upon him on a dark night and stick a knife into his throat, just about the carotid artery, and leave him to die in the street like a dog. Philip was out of his senses with grief and rage. He did not like whiskey, but he drank to stupefy himself. He went to bed drunk on the Tuesday and on the Wednesday night.

On Thursday morning he got up very late and dragged himself, blear-eyed and sallow, into his sitting-room to see if there were any letters. A curious feeling shot through his heart when he recognised the handwriting of Griffiths.

Dear old man:

*I hardly know how to write to you and yet I feel I must
write. I hope you're not awfully angry with me. I know I
oughtn't to have gone away with Milly, but I simply couldn't
help myself. She simply carried me off my feet and I would
have done anything to get her. When she told me you had
offered us the money to go I simply couldn't resist. And
now it's all over I'm awfully ashamed of myself and I wish
I hadn't been such a fool. I wish you'd write and say you're
not angry with me, and I want you to let me come and see
you. I was awfully hurt at your telling Milly you didn't want
to see me. Do write me a line, there's a good chap, and tell
me you forgive me. It'll ease my conscience. I thought you
wouldn't mind or you wouldn't have offered the money.
But I know I oughtn't to have taken it. I came home on
Monday and Milly wanted to stay a couple of days at Oxford by herself. She's going back to London on Wednesday,
so by the time you receive this letter you will have seen her
and I hope everything will go off all right. Do write and say
you forgive me. Please write at once.*

Yours ever,

Harry.

Philip tore up the letter furiously. He did not mean to
answer it. He despised Griffiths for his apologies, he had
no patience with his prickings of conscience: one could do
a dastardly thing if one chose, but it was contemptible to
regret it afterwards. He thought the letter cowardly and
hypocritical. He was disgusted at its sentimentality.

"It would be very easy if you could do a beastly thing," he
muttered to himself, "and then say you were sorry, and that
put it all right again."

He hoped with all his heart he would have the chance one
day to do Griffiths a bad turn.

But at all events he knew that Mildred was in town. He
dressed hurriedly, not waiting to shave, drank a cup of tea,

and took a cab to her rooms. The cab seemed to crawl. He was painfully anxious to see her, and unconsciously he uttered a prayer to the God he did not believe in to make her receive him kindly. He only wanted to forget. With beating heart he rang the bell. He forgot all his suffering in the passionate desire to enfold her once more in his arms.

"Is Mrs. Miller in?" he asked joyously.

"She's gone," the maid answered.

He looked at her blankly.

"She came about an hour ago and took away her things."

For a moment he did not know what to say.

"Did you give her my letter? Did she say where she was going?"

Then he understood that Mildred had deceived him again. She was not coming back to him. He made an effort to save his face.

"Oh, well, I daresay I shall hear from her. She may have sent a letter to another address."

He turned away and went back hopeless to his rooms. He might have known that she would do this; she had never cared for him, she had made a fool of him from the beginning; she had no pity, she had no kindness, she had no charity. The only thing was to accept the inevitable. The pain he was suffering was horrible, he would sooner be dead than endure it; and the thought came to him that it would be better to finish with the whole thing: he might throw himself in the river or put his neck on a railway line; but he had no sooner set the thought into words than he rebelled against it. His reason told him that he would get over his unhappiness in time; if he tried with all his might he could forget her; and it would be grotesque to kill himself on account of a vulgar slut. He had only one life, and it was madness to fling it away. He *felt* that he would never overcome his passion, but he *knew* that after all it was only a matter of time.

He would not stay in London. There everything reminded

him of his unhappiness. He telegraphed to his uncle that he was coming to Blackstable, and, hurrying to pack, took the first train he could. He wanted to get away from the sordid rooms in which he had endured so much suffering. He wanted to breathe clean air. He was disgusted with himself. He felt that he was a little mad.

Philip went up to London a couple of days before the session began in order to find himself rooms. He hunted about the streets that led out of the Westminster Bridge Road, but their dinginess was distasteful to him; and at last he found one in Kennington which had a quiet and old-world air. It reminded one a little of the London which Thackeray knew on that side of the river, and in the Kennington Road, through which the great barouche of the Newcomes must have passed as it drove the family to the West of London, the plane-trees were bursting into leaf. The houses in the street which Philip fixed upon were two-storied, and in most of the windows was a notice to state that lodgings were to let. He knocked at one which announced that the lodgings were unfurnished, and was shown by an austere, silent woman four very small rooms, in one of which there was a kitchen range and a sink. The rent was nine shillings a week. Philip did not want so many rooms, but the rent was low and he wished to settle down at once. He asked the landlady if she could keep the place clean for him and cook his breakfast, but she replied that she had enough work to do without that; and he was pleased rather than otherwise because she intimated that she wished to have nothing more to do with him than to receive his rent. She told him that, if he inquired at the grocer's round the corner, which was also a post-office, he might hear of a woman who would 'do' for him.

Philip had a little furniture which he had gathered as he went along, an arm-chair that he had bought in Paris, a table, a few drawings. His uncle had offered a fold-up bed for which, now that he no longer let his house in August, he had no further use; and by spending another ten pounds Philip bought himself whatever else was essential. He spent ten shillings on putting a corn-coloured paper in the room he was making his parlour; and he hung on the walls a sketch which Lawson had given him of the Quai des Grands Augustins, and the photograph of the *Odalisque* by Ingres and Manet's *Olympia* which in Paris had been the objects of his contemplation while he shaved. To remind himself that he too had once been engaged in the practice of art, he put up a charcoal drawing of the young Spaniard Miguel Ajuria: it was the best thing he had ever done, a nude standing with clenched hands, his feet gripping the floor with a peculiar force, and on his face that air of determination which had been so impressive; and though Philip after the long interval saw very well the defects of his work its associations made him look upon it with tolerance. He wondered what had happened to Miguel. There is nothing so terrible as the pursuit of art by those who have no talent. Perhaps, worn out by exposure, starvation, disease, he had found an end in some hospital, or in an access of despair had sought death in the turbid Seine; but perhaps with his Southern instability he had given up the struggle of his own accord, and now, a clerk in some office in Madrid, turned his fervent rhetoric to politics and bull-fighting.

Philip asked Lawson and Hayward to come and see his new rooms, and they came, one with a bottle of whiskey, the other with a *pâté de foie gras;* and he was delighted when they praised his taste. He would have invited the Scotch stockbroker, too, but he had only three chairs, and thus could entertain only a definite number of guests.

Philip attended now lectures on medicine and on surgery. On certain mornings in the week he practised bandaging on out-patients glad to earn a little money, and he was taught auscultation and how to use the stethoscope. He learned dispensing. He was taking the examination in *Materia*

Medica in July, and it amused him to play with various drugs, concocting mixtures, rolling pills, and making ointments. He seized avidly upon anything from which he could extract a suggestion of human interest.

He saw Griffiths once in the distance, but, not to have the pain of cutting him dead, avoided him. Philip had felt a certain self-consciousness with Griffiths' friends, some of whom were now friends of his, when he realised they knew of his quarrel with Griffiths and surmised they were aware of the reason. One of them, a very tall fellow, with a small head and a languid air, a youth called Ramsden, who was one of Griffiths' most faithful admirers, copied his ties, his boots, his manner of talking and his gestures, told Philip that Griffiths was very much hurt because Philip had not answered his letter. He wanted to be reconciled with him.

"Has he asked you to give me the message?" asked Philip.

"Oh, no. I'm saying this entirely on my own," said Ramsden. "He's awfully sorry for what he did, and he says you always behaved like a perfect brick to him. I know he'd be glad to make it up. He doesn't come to the hospital because he's afraid of meeting you, and he thinks you'd cut him."

"I should."

"It makes him feel rather wretched, you know."

"I can bear the trifling inconvenience that he feels with a good deal of fortitude," said Philip.

"He'll do anything he can to make it up."

"How childish and hysterical! Why should he care? I'm a very insignificant person, and he can do very well without my company. I'm not interested in him any more."

Ramsden thought Philip hard and cold. He paused for a moment or two, looking about him in a perplexed way.

"Harry wishes to God he'd never had anything to do with the woman."

"Does he?" asked Philip.

He spoke with an indifference which he was satisfied

with. No one could have guessed how violently his heart was beating. He waited impatiently for Ramsden to go on.

"I suppose you've quite got over it now, haven't you?"

"I?" said Philip. "Quite."

Little by little he discovered the history of Mildred's relations with Griffiths. He listened with a smile on his lips, feigning an equanimity which quite deceived the dull-witted boy who talked to him. The week-end she spent with Griffiths at Oxford inflamed rather than extinguished her sudden passion; and when Griffiths went home, with a feeling that was unexpected in her she determined to stay in Oxford by herself for a couple of days, because she had been so happy in it. She felt that nothing could induce her to go back to Philip. He revolted her. Griffiths was taken aback at the fire he had aroused, for he had found his two days with her in the country somewhat tedious; and he had no desire to turn an amusing episode into a tiresome affair. She made him promise to write to her, and, being an honest, decent fellow, with natural politeness and a desire to make himself pleasant to everybody, when he got home he wrote her a long and charming letter. She answered it with reams of passion, clumsy, for she had no gift of expression, ill-written, and vulgar; the letter bored him, and when it was followed next day by another, and the day after by a third, he began to think her love no longer flattering but alarming. He did not answer; and she bombarded him with telegrams, asking him if he were ill and had received her letters; she said his silence made her dreadfully anxious. He was forced to write, but he sought to make his reply as casual as was possible without being offensive: he begged her not to wire, since it was difficult to explain telegrams to his mother, an old-fashioned person for whom a telegram was still an event to excite tremor. She answered by return of post that she must see him and announced her intention to pawn things (she had the dressing-case which Philip had given her as a wedding-present and could raise eight pounds on that) in order to come up and stay at the market town four miles from which was the village in which his father practised. This frightened Griffiths; and he, this time, made use of the telegraph wires to tell her that she must do nothing of the kind. He promised to let her know the moment he came up to London, and, when he did, found that she had already been asking for him at the hospital at which he had an appointment. He did not like this, and, on seeing her, told Mildred that she was not to come there on any pretext; and now, after an absence of three weeks, he found that she bored him quite decidedly; he wondered why he had ever troubled about her, and made up his mind to break with her as soon as he could. He was a person who dreaded quarrels, nor did he want to give pain; but at the same time he had other things to do, and he was quite determined not to let Mildred bother him. When he met her he was pleasant, cheerful, amusing, affectionate; he invented convincing excuses for the interval since last he had seen her; but he did everything he could to avoid her. When she forced him to make appointments he sent telegrams to her at the last moment to put himself off; and his landlady (the first three months of his appointment he was spending in rooms) had orders to say he was out when Mildred called. She would waylay him in the street and, knowing she had been waiting about for him to come out of the hospital for a couple of hours, he would give her a few charming, friendly words and bolt off with the excuse that he had a business engagement. He grew very skilful in slipping out of the hospital unseen. Once, when he went back to his lodgings at midnight, he saw a woman standing at the area railings and suspecting who it was went to beg a shake-down in Ramsden's rooms; next day the landlady told him that Mildred had sat crying on the doorsteps for hours, and she had been obliged to tell her at last that if she did not go away she would send for a policeman.

"I tell you, my boy," said Ramsden, "you're jolly well out

of it. Harry says that if he'd suspected for half a second she was going to make such a blooming nuisance of herself he'd have seen himself damned before he had anything to do with her."

Philip thought of her sitting on that doorstep through the long hours of the night. He saw her face as she looked up dully at the landlady who sent her away.

"I wonder what she's doing now."

"Oh, she's got a job somewhere, thank God. That keeps her busy all day."

The last thing he heard, just before the end of the summer session, was that Griffiths' urbanity had given way at length under the exasperation of the constant persecution. He had told Mildred that he was sick of being pestered, and she had better take herself off and not bother him again.

"It was the only thing he could do," said Ramsden. "It was getting a bit too thick."

"Is it all over then?" asked Philip.

"Oh, he hasn't seen her for ten days. You know, Harry's wonderful at dropping people. This is about the toughest nut he's ever had to crack, but he's cracked it all right."

Then Philip heard nothing more of her at all. She vanished into the vast anonymous mass of the population of London.

In the spring Philip, having finished his dressing in the out-patients' department, became an in-patients' clerk. This appointment lasted six months. The clerk spent every morning in the wards, first in the men's, then in the women's, with the house-physician; he wrote up cases, made tests, and passed the time of day with the nurses. On two afternoons a week the physician in charge went round with a little knot of students, examined the cases, and dispensed information. The work had not the excitement, the constant change, the intimate contact with reality, of the work in the out-patients' department; but Philip picked up a good deal of knowledge.

He got on very well with the patients, and he was a little flattered at the pleasure they showed in his attendance on them. He was not conscious of any deep sympathy in their sufferings, but he liked them; and because he put on no airs he was more popular with them than others of the clerks. He was pleasant, encouraging, and friendly. Like everyone connected with hospitals he found that male patients were more easy to get on with than female. The women were often querulous and ill-tempered. They complained bitterly of the hard-worked nurses, who did not show them the attention they thought their right; and they were troublesome, ungrateful, and rude.

Presently Philip was fortunate enough to make a friend. One morning the house-physician gave him a new case, a man; and, seating himself at the bedside, Philip proceeded to write down particulars on the 'letter.' He noticed on looking at this that the patient was described as a journalist: his name was Thorpe Athelny, an unusual one for a hospital patient, and his age was forty-eight. He was suffering from a sharp attack of jaundice, and had been taken into the ward on account of obscure symptoms which it seemed necessary to watch. He answered the various questions which it was Philip's duty to ask him in a pleasant, educated voice. Since he was lying in bed it was difficult to tell if he was short or tall, but his small head and small hands suggested that he was a man of less than average height. Philip had the habit of looking at people's hands, and Athelny's astonished him: they were very small, with long, tapering fingers and beautiful, rosy finger-nails; they were very smooth and except for the jaundice would have been of a surprising whiteness. The patient kept them outside the bed-clothes, one of them slightly spread out, the second and third fingers together, and, while he spoke to Philip, seemed to contemplate them with satisfaction. With a twinkle in his eyes Philip glanced at the man's face. Notwithstanding the yellowness it was distinguished; he had blue eyes, a nose of an imposing boldness, hooked, aggressive but not clumsy, and a small beard, pointed and gray: he was rather bald, but his hair had evidently been quite fine, curling prettily, and he still wore it long.

"I see you're a journalist," said Philip. "What papers d'you write for?"

"I write for all the papers. You cannot open a paper without seeing some of my writing."

There was one by the side of the bed and reaching for it he pointed out an advertisement. In large letters was the name of a firm well-known to Philip, Lynn and Sedley, Regent Street, London; and below, in type smaller but still of some magnitude, was the dogmatic statement: Procrastination is the Thief of Time. Then a question, startling because of its reasonableness: Why not order today? There was a repetition, in large letters, like the hammering of conscience on a murderer's heart: Why not? Then, boldly: Thousands of pairs of gloves from the leading markets of the world at astounding prices. Thousands of pairs of stockings from the most reliable manufacturers of the universe at sensational reductions. Finally the question recurred, but flung now like a challenging gauntlet in the lists: Why not order today?

"I'm the press representative of Lynn and Sedley." He gave a little wave of his beautiful hand. "To what base uses . . ."

Philip went on asking the regulation questions, some a mere matter of routine, others artfully devised to lead the patient to discover things which he might be expected to desire to conceal.

"Have you ever lived abroad?" asked Philip.

"I was in Spain for eleven years."

"What were you doing there?"

"I was secretary of the English water company at Toledo."

The journalist's answer made him look at him with more interest; but he felt it would be improper to show this: it was necessary to preserve the distance between the hospital patient and the staff. When he had finished his examination he went on to other beds.

Thorpe Athelny's illness was not grave, and, though remaining very yellow, he soon felt much better: he stayed in bed only because the physician thought he should be kept under observation till certain reactions became normal.

During the next few days, in moments snatched whenever there was opportunity, Philip's acquaintance with the journalist increased. Thorpe Athelny was a good talker. He did not say brilliant things, but he talked inspiringly, with an eager vividness which fired the imagination; Philip, living so much in a world of make-believe, found his fancy teeming with new pictures. Athelny had very good manners. He knew much more than Philip, both of the world and of books; he was a much older man; and the readiness of his conversation gave him a certain superiority; but he was in the hospital a recipient of charity, subject to strict rules; and he held himself between the two positions with ease and humour. Once Philip asked him why he had come to the hospital.

"Oh, my principle is to profit by all the benefits that society provides. I take advantage of the age I live in. When I'm ill I get myself patched up in a hospital and I have no false shame, and I send my children to be educated at the board-school."

"Do you really?" said Philip.

"And a capital education they get too, much better than I got at Winchester. How else do you think I could educate them at all? I've got nine. You must come and see them all when I get home again. Will you?"

"I'd like to very much," said Philip.

Ten days later Thorpe Athelny was well enough to leave the hospital. He gave Philip his address, and Philip promised to dine with him at one o'clock on the following Sunday.

Athelny had told him that he lived in a house built by Inigo Jones; he had raved, as he raved over everything, over the balustrade of old oak; and when he came down to open the door for Philip he made him at once admire the elegant carving of the lintel. It was a shabby house, badly needing a coat of paint, but with the dignity of its period, in a little street between Chancery Lane and Holborn, which had once been fashionable but was now little better than a slum: there was a plan to pull it down in order to put up handsome offices; meanwhile the rents were small, and Athelny was able to get the two upper floors at a price which suited his income. Philip had not seen him up before and was surprised at his small size; he was not more than five feet and five inches high. He was dressed fantastically in blue linen trousers of the sort worn by working men in France, and a very old brown velvet coat; he wore a bright red sash round his waist, a low collar, and for tie a flowing bow of the kind used by the comic Frenchman in the pages of *Punch*. He greeted Philip with enthusiasm. He began talking at once of the house and passèd his hand lovingly over the balusters.

"Look at it, feel it, it's like silk. What a miracle of grace! And in five years the house-breaker will sell it for firewood."

He insisted on taking Philip into a room on the first floor, where a man in shirt sleeves, a blousy woman, and three children were having their Sunday dinner.

"I've just brought this gentleman in to show him your ceiling. Did you ever see anything so wonderful? How are you, Mrs. Hodgson? This is Mr. Carey, who looked after me when I was in the hospital."

"Come in, sir," said the man. "Any friend of Mr. Athelny's is welcome. Mr. Athelny shows the ceiling to all his friends. And it don't matter what we're doing, if we're in bed or if I'm 'aving a wash, in 'e comes."

Philip could see that they looked upon Athelny as a little queer; but they liked him none the less and they listened open-mouthed while he discoursed with his impetuous fluency on the beauty of the seventeenth-century ceiling.

"What a crime to pull this down, eh, Hodgson? You're an influential citizen, why don't you write to the papers and protest?"

The man in shirt sleeves gave a laugh and said to Philip:

"Mr. Athelny will 'ave his little joke. They do say these 'ouses are that unsanitary, it's not safe to live in them."

"Sanitation be damned, give me art," cried Athelny. "I've got nine children and they thrive on bad drains. No, no, I'm not going to take any risk. None of your new-fangled notions for me! When I move from here I'm going to make sure the drains are bad before I take anything."

There was a knock at the door, and a little fair-haired girl opened it.

"Daddy, mummy says, do stop talking and come and eat your dinner."

"This is my third daughter," said Athelny, pointing to her with a dramatic forefinger. "She is called Maria del Pilar, but she answers more willingly to the name of Jane. Jane, your nose wants blowing."

"I haven't got a hanky, daddy."

"Tut, tut, child," he answered, as he produced a vast, brilliant bandanna, "what do you suppose the Almighty gave you fingers for?"

They went upstairs, and Philip was taken into a room with walls panelled in dark oak. In the middle was a narrow table of teak on trestle legs, with two supporting bars of iron, of the kind called in Spain *mesa de hieraje*. They were to dine there, for two places were laid, and there were two large arm-chairs, with broad flat arms of oak and leathern backs, and leathern seats. They were severe, elegant, and uncomfortable. The only other piece of furniture was a *bargueño,* elaborately ornamented with gilt iron-work, on a stand of ecclesiastical design roughly but very finely carved. There stood on this two or three lustre plates, much broken but rich in colour; and on the walls were old masters of the Spanish school in beautiful though dilapidated frames: though gruesome in subject, ruined by age and bad treatment, and second rate in their conception, they had a glow of passion. There was nothing in the room of any value, but the effect was lovely. It was magnificent and yet austere. Philip felt that it offered the very spirit of old Spain Athelny was in the middle of showing him the inside of the *bargueño*, with its beautiful ornamentation and secret drawers, when a tall girl, with two plaits of bright brown hair hanging down her back, came in.

"Mother says dinner's ready and waiting and I'm to bring it in as soon as you sit down."

"Come and shake hands with Mr. Carey, Sally." He turned to Philip. "Isn't she enormous? She's my eldest. How old are you, Sally?"

"Fifteen, father, come next June."

"I christened her Maria del Sol, because she was my first child and I dedicated her to the glorious sun of Castile; but her mother calls her Sally and her brother Pudding-Face."

The girl smiled shyly, she had even, white teeth, and blushed. She was well set-up, tall for her age, with pleasant gray eyes and a broad forehead. She had red cheeks.

"Go and tell your mother to come in and shake hands with Mr. Carey before he sits down."

"Mother says she'll come in after dinner. She hasn't washed herself yet."

"Then we'll go in and see her ourselves. He mustn't eat the Yorkshire pudding till he's shaken the hand that made it."

Philip followed his host into the kitchen. It was small and much overcrowded. There had been a lot of noise, but it stopped as soon as the stranger entered. There was a large table in the middle and round it, eager for dinner, were seated Athelny's children. A woman was standing at the oven, taking out baked potatoes one by one.

"Here's Mr. Carey, Betty," said Athelny.

"Fancy bringing him in here. What will he think?"

She wore a dirty apron, and the sleeves of her cotton dress were turned up above her elbows; she had curling pins in her hair. Mrs. Athelny was a large woman, a good three inches taller than her husband, fair, with blue eyes and a kindly expression; she had been a handsome creature, but advancing years and the bearing of many children had made her fat and blousy; her blue eyes had become pale, her skin was coarse and red, the colour had gone out of her hair. She straightened herself, wiped her hand on her apron, and held it out.

"You're welcome, sir," she said, in a slow voice, with an accent that seemed oddly familiar to Philip. "Athelny said you was very kind to him in the 'orspital."

"Now you must be introduced to the live stock," said Athelny. "That is Thorpe," he pointed to a chubby boy with curly hair, "he is my eldest son, heir to the title, estates, and responsibilities of the family. There is Athelstan, Harold, Edward." He pointed with his forefinger to three smaller boys, all rosy, healthy, and smiling, though when they felt Philip's smiling eyes upon them they looked shyly down at their plates. "Now the girls in order: Maria del Sol . . ."

"Pudding-Face," said one of the small boys.

"Your sense of humour is rudimentary, my son. Maria de los Mercedes, Maria del Pilar, Maria de la Concepcion, Maria del Rosario."

"I call them Sally, Molly, Connie, Rosie, and Jane," said Mrs. Athelny. "Now, Athelny, you go into your own room and I'll send you your dinner. I'll let the children come in afterwards for a bit when I've washed them."

"My dear, if I'd had the naming of you I should have called you Maria of the Soapsuds. You're always torturing these wretched brats with soap."

"You go first, Mr. Carey, or I shall never get him to sit down and eat his dinner."

Athelny and Philip installed themselves in the great monkish chairs, and Sally brought them in two plates of beef, Yorkshire pudding, baked potatoes, and cabbage. Athelny took sixpence out of his pocket and sent her for a jug of beer.

"I hope you didn't have the table laid here on my account," said Philip. "I should have been quite happy to eat with the children."

"Oh no, I always have my meals by myself I like these antique customs. I don't think that women ought to sit down at table with men. It ruins conversation and I'm sure it's very bad for them. It puts ideas in their heads, and women are never at ease with themselves when they have ideas."

Both host and guest ate with a hearty appetite.

"Did you ever taste such Yorkshire pudding? No one can make it like my wife. That's the advantage of not marrying a lady. You noticed she wasn't a lady, didn't you?"

It was an awkward question, and Philip did not know how to answer it.

"I never thought about it," he said lamely.

Athelny laughed. He had a peculiarly joyous laugh.

"No, she's not a lady, nor anything like it. Her father was a farmer, and she's never bothered about aitches in her life. We've had twelve children and nine of them are alive. I tell her it's about time she stopped, but she's an obstinate woman, she's got into the habit of it now, and I don't believe she'll be satisfied till she's had twenty."

At that moment Sally came in with the beer, and, having poured out a glass for Philip, went to the other side of the table to pour some out for her father. He put his hand round her waist.

"Did you ever see such a handsome, strapping girl? Only fifteen and she might be twenty. Look at her cheeks. She's never had a day's illness in her life. It'll be a lucky man who marries her, won't it, Sally?"

Sally listened to all this with a slight, slow smile, not much embarrassed, for she was accustomed to her father's outbursts, but with an easy modesty which was very attractive.

"Don't let your dinner get cold, father," she said, drawing herself away from his arm. "You'll call when you're ready for your pudding, won't you?"

They were left alone, and Athelny lifted the pewter tankard to his lips. He drank long and deep.

"My word, is there anything better than English beer?" he said. "Let us thank God for simple pleasures, roast beef and rice pudding, a good appetite and beer. I was married to a lady once. My God! Don't marry a lady, my boy."

Philip laughed. He was exhilarated by the scene, the funny little man in his odd clothes, the panelled room and the Spanish furniture, the English fare: the whole thing had an exquisite incongruity.

"You laugh, my boy, you can't imagine marrying beneath you. You want a wife who's an intellectual equal. Your head is crammed full of ideas of comradeship. Stuff and nonsense, my boy! A man doesn't want to talk politics to his wife, and what do you think I care for Betty's views upon the Differential Calculus? A man wants a wife who can cook his dinner and look after his children. I've tried both and I know. Let's have the pudding in."

He clapped his hands and presently Sally came. When she took away the plates, Philip wanted to get up and help her, but Athelny stopped him.

"Let her alone, my boy. She doesn't want you to fuss about, do you, Sally? And she won't think it rude of you to sit still while she waits upon you. She don't care a damn for chivalry, do you, Sally?"

"No, father," answered Sally demurely.

"Do you know what I'm talking about, Sally?"

"No, father. But you know mother doesn't like you to swear."

Athelny laughed boisterously. Sally brought them plates of rice pudding, rich, creamy, and luscious. Athelny attacked his with gusto.

"One of the rules of this house is that Sunday dinner should never alter. It is a ritual. Roast beef and rice pudding for fifty Sundays in the year. On Easter Sunday lamb and green peas, and at Michaelmas roast goose and apple sauce. Thus we preserve the traditions of our people. When Sally marries she will forget many of the wise things I have taught her, but she will never forget that if you want to be good and happy you must eat on Sundays roast beef and rice pudding."

"You'll call when you're ready for cheese," said Sally impassively.

"D'you know the legend of the halcyon?" said Athelny: Philip was growing used to his rapid leaping from one subject to another. "When the kingfisher, flying over the sea, is exhausted, his mate places herself beneath him and bears him along upon her stronger wings. That is what a man wants in a wife, the halcyon. I lived with my first wife for three years. She was a lady, she had fifteen hundred a year, and we used to give nice little dinner parties in our little red brick house in Kensington. She was a charming woman; they all said so, the barristers and their wives who dined with us, and the literary stockbrokers, and the budding politicians; oh, she was a charming woman. She made me go to church in a silk hat and a frock coat, she took me to classical concerts, and she was very fond of lectures on Sunday afternoon; and she sat down to breakfast every morning at eight-thirty, and if I was late breakfast was cold; and she read the right books, admired the right pictures, and adored the right music. My God, how that woman bored me! She is charming still, and she lives in the little red brick house in Kensington, with Morris papers and Whistler's etchings on the walls, and gives the same nice little dinner

parties, with veal creams and ices from Gunter's, as she did
twenty years ago."

Philip did not ask by what means the ill-matched couple
had separated, but Athelny told him.

"Betty's not my wife, you know; my wife wouldn't divorce me. The children are bastards, every jack one of them,
and are they any the worse for that? Betty was one of the
maids in the little red brick house in Kensington. Four or
five years ago I was on my uppers, and I had seven children,
and I went to my wife and asked her to help me. She said
she'd make me an allowance if I'd give Betty up and go
abroad. Can you see me giving Betty up? We starved for a
while instead. My wife said I loved the gutter. I've degener-
ated; I've come down in the world; I earn three pounds a
week as press agent to a linen-draper, and every day I thank
God that I'm not in the little red brick house in Kensington."

Sally brought in Cheddar cheese, and Athelny went on
with his fluent conversation.

"It's the greatest mistake in the world to think that one
needs money to bring up a family. You need money to make
them gentlemen and ladies, but I don't want my children to
be ladies and gentlemen. Sally's going to earn her living in
another year. She's to be apprenticed to a dressmaker, aren't
you, Sally? And the boys are going to serve their country.
I want them all to go into the Navy; it's a jolly life and a
healthy life, good food, good pay, and a pension to end their
days on."

Philip lit his pipe. Athelny smoked cigarettes of Havana
tobacco, which he rolled himself. Sally cleared away. Philip
was reserved, and it embarrassed him to be the recipient of
so many confidences. Athelny, with his powerful voice in
the diminutive body, with his bombast, with his foreign
look, with his emphasis, was an astonishing creature. Athelny was very proud of the county family to which he be-

longed; he showed Philip photographs of an Elizabethan mansion, and told him:

"The Athelnys have lived there for seven centuries, my boy. Ah, if you saw the chimney-pieces and the ceilings!"

There was a cupboard in the wainscoting and from this he took a family tree. He showed it to Philip with child-like satisfaction. It was indeed imposing.

"You see how the family names recur, Thorpe, Athelstan, Harold, Edward; I've used the family names for my sons. And the girls, you see, I've given Spanish names to."

An uneasy feeling came to Philip that possibly the whole story was an elaborate imposture, not told with any base motive, but merely from a wish to impress, startle, and amaze. Athelny had told him that he was at Winchester; but Philip, sensitive to differences of manner, did not feel that his host had the characteristics of a man educated at a great public school. While he pointed out the great alliances which his ancestors had formed, Philip amused himself by wondering whether Athelny was not the son of some trades-man in Winchester, auctioneer or coal-merchant, and whether a similarity of surname was not his only connection with the ancient family whose tree he was displaying.

There was a knock at the door and a troop of children came in. They were clean and tidy now; their faces shone with soap, and their hair was plastered down; they were going to Sunday school under Sally's charge. Athelny joked with them in his dramatic, exuberant fashion, and you could see that he was devoted to them all. His pride in their good health and their good looks was touching. Philip felt that they were a little shy in his presence, and when their father sent them off they fled from the room in evident re-lief. In a few minutes Mrs. Athelny appeared. She had taken her hair out of the curling pins and now wore an elaborate fringe. She had on a plain black dress, a hat with cheap flowers, and was forcing her hands, red and coarse from much work, into black kid gloves.

"I'm going to church, Athelny," she said. "There's nothing you'll be wanting, is there?"

"Only your prayers, my Betty."

"They won't do you much good, you're too far gone for that," she smiled. Then, turning to Philip, she drawled: "I can't get him to go to church. He's no better than an atheist."

"Doesn't she look like Rubens' second wife?" cried Athelny. "Wouldn't she look splendid in a seventeenth-century costume? That's the sort of wife to marry, my boy. Look at her."

"I believe you'd talk the hind leg off a donkey, Athelny," she answered calmly.

She succeeded in buttoning her gloves, but before she went she turned to Philip with a kindly, slightly embarrassed smile.

"You'll stay to tea, won't you? Athelny likes someone to talk to, and it's not often he gets anybody who's clever enough."

"Of course he'll stay to tea," said Athelny. Then when his wife had gone: "I make a point of the children going to Sunday school, and I like Betty to go to church. I think women ought to be religious. I don't believe myself, but I like women and children to."

Philip did not leave the Athelnys' till ten o'clock. The children came in to say good-night at eight and quite naturally put up their faces for Philip to kiss. His heart went out to them. Sally only held out her hand.

"Sally never kisses gentlemen till she's seen them twice," said her father.

"You must ask me again then," said Philip.

"You mustn't take any notice of what father says," remarked Sally, with a smile.

"She's a most self-possessed young woman," added her parent.

They had supper of bread and cheese and beer, while Mrs. Athelny was putting the children to bed; and when Philip went into the kitchen to bid her good-night (she had been sitting there, resting herself and reading *The Weekly Despatch*) she invited him cordially to come again.

"There's always a good dinner on Sundays so long as Athelny's in work," she said, "and it's a charity to come and talk to him."

On the following Saturday Philip received a postcard from Athelny saying that they were expecting him to dinner next day; but fearing their means were not such that Mr. Athelny would desire him to accept, Philip wrote back that he would only come to tea. He bought a large plum cake so that his entertainment should cost nothing. He found the whole family glad to see him, and the cake completed his conquest of the children. He insisted that they should all have tea together in the kitchen, and the meal was noisy and hilarious.

Soon Philip got into the habit of going to Athelny's every Sunday. He became a great favourite with the children, because he was simple and unaffected and because it was so plain that he was fond of them. As soon as they heard his ring at the door one of them popped a head out of window to make sure it was he, and then they all rushed downstairs tumultuously to let him in. They flung themselves into his arms. At tea they fought for the privilege of sitting next to him. Soon they began to call him Uncle Philip.

Athelny was very communicative, and little by little Philip learned the various stages of his life. He had followed many occupations, and it occurred to Philip that he managed to make a mess of everything he attempted. He had been on a tea plantation in Ceylon and a traveller in America for Italian wines; his secretaryship of the water company in Toledo had lasted longer than any of his employments; he

had been a journalist and for some time had worked as
police-court reporter for an evening paper; he had been
sub-editor of a paper in the Midlands and editor of another
on the Riviera. From all his occupations he had gathered
amusing anecdotes, which he told with a keen pleasure in
his own powers of entertainment. He had read a great deal,
chiefly delighting in books which were unusual; and he
poured forth his stores of abstruse knowledge with childlike
enjoyment of the amazement of his hearers. Three or four
years before abject poverty had driven him to take the job
of press-representative to a large firm of drapers; and though
he felt the work unworthy his abilities, which he rated high-
ly, the firmness of his wife and the needs of his family had
made him stick to it.

When he left the Athelnys' Philip walked down Chancery
Lane and along the Strand to get a 'bus at the top of Parliament Street. One Sunday, when he had known them
about six weeks, he did this as usual, but he found the Kennington 'bus full. It was June, but it had rained during the
day and the night was raw and cold. He walked up to Piccadilly Circus in order to get a seat; the 'bus waited at the
fountain, and when it arrived there seldom had more than
two or three people in it. This service ran every quarter of
an hour, and he had some time to wait. He looked idly at
the crowd. The public-houses were closing, and there were
many people about. His mind was busy with the ideas
Athelny had the charming gift of suggesting.

Suddenly his heart stood still. He saw Mildred. He had
not thought of her for weeks. She was crossing over from
the corner of Shaftesbury Avenue and stopped at the shelter
till a string of cabs passed by. She was watching her opportunity and had no eyes for anything else. She wore a large
black straw hat with a mass of feathers on it and a black silk
dress; at that time it was fashionable for women to wear
trains; the road was clear, and Mildred crossed, her skirt
trailing on the ground, and walked down Piccadilly. Philip,

his heart beating excitedly, followed her. He did not wish to speak to her, but he wondered where she was going at that hour; he wanted to get a look at her face. She walked slowly along and turned down Air Street and so got through into Regent Street. She walked up again towards the Circus. Philip was puzzled. He could not make out what she was doing. Perhaps she was waiting for somebody, and he felt a great curiosity to know who it was. She overtook a short man in a bowler hat, who was strolling very slowly in the same direction as herself; she gave him a sidelong glance as she passed. She walked a few steps more till she came to Swan and Edgar's, then stopped and waited, facing the road. When the man came up she smiled. The man stared at her for a moment, turned away his head, and sauntered on. Then Philip understood.

He was overwhelmed with horror. For a moment he felt such a weakness in his legs that he could hardly stand; then he walked after her quickly; he touched her on the arm.

"Mildred."

She turned round with a violent start. He thought that she reddened, but in the obscurity he could not see very well. For a while they stood and looked at one another without speaking. At last she said:

"Fancy seeing you!"

He did not know what to answer; he was horribly shaken; and the phrases that chased one another through his brain seemed incredibly melodramatic.

"It's awful," he gasped, almost to himself.

She did not say anything more, she turned away from him, and looked down at the pavement. He felt that his face was distorted with misery.

"Isn't there anywhere we can go and talk?"

"I don't want to talk," she said sullenly. "Leave me alone, can't you?"

The thought struck him that perhaps she was in urgent

need of money and could not afford to go away at that hour.

"I've got a couple of sovereigns on me if you're hard up," he blurted out.

"I don't know what you mean. I was just walking along here on my way back to my lodgings. I expected to meet one of the girls from where I work."

"For God's sake don't lie now," he said.

Then he saw that she was crying, and he repeated his question.

"Can't we go and talk somewhere? Can't I come back to your rooms?"

"No, you can't do that," she sobbed. "I'm not allowed to take gentlemen in there. If you like I'll meet you tomorrow."

He felt certain that she would not keep an appointment. He was not going to let her go.

"No. You must take me somewhere now."

"Well, there is a room I know, but they'll charge six shillings for it."

"I don't mind that. Where is it?"

She gave him the address, and he called a cab. They drove to a shabby street beyond the British Museum in the neighbourhood of the Gray's Inn Road, and she stopped the cab at the corner.

"They don't like you to drive up to the door," she said.

They were the first words either of them had spoken since getting into the cab. They walked a few yards and Mildred knocked three times, sharply, at a door. Philip noticed in the fanlight a cardboard on which was an announcement that apartments were to let. The door was opened quietly, and an elderly, tall woman let them in. She gave Philip a stare and then spoke to Mildred in an undertone. Mildred led Philip along a passage to a room at the back. It was quite dark; she asked him for a match, and lit the gas; there was no globe, and the gas flared shrilly. Philip saw that he was in a dingy little bedroom with a suite of furniture painted to look like pine much too large for it; the

lace curtains were very dirty; the grate was hidden by a large
paper fan. Mildred sank on the chair which stood by the side
of the chimney-piece. Philip sat on the edge of the bed. He
felt ashamed. He saw now that Mildred's cheeks were
thick with rouge, her eyebrows were blackened; but she
looked thin and ill, and the red on her cheeks exaggerated
the greenish pallor of her skin. She stared at the paper fan
in a listless fashion. Philip could not think what to say,
and he had a choking in his throat as if he were going to
cry. He covered his eyes with his hands.

"My God, it is awful," he groaned.

"I don't know what you've got to fuss about. I should
have thought you'd have been rather pleased."

Philip did not answer, and in a moment she broke into
a sob.

"You don't think I do it because I like it, do you?"

"Oh, my dear," he cried. "I'm so sorry, I'm so awfully
sorry."

"That'll do me a fat lot of good."

Again Philip found nothing to say. He was desperately
afraid of saying anything which she might take for a reproach or a sneer.

"Where's the baby?" he asked at last.

"I've got her with me in London. I hadn't got the money
to keep her on at Brighton, so I had to take her. I've got a
room up Highbury way. I told them I was on the stage. It's
a long way to have to come down to the West End every
day, but it's a rare job to find anyone who'll let to ladies at
all."

"Wouldn't they take you back at the shop?"

"I couldn't get any work to do anywhere. I walked my
legs off looking for work. I did get a job once, but I was
off for a week because I was queer, and when I went back
they said they didn't want me any more. You can't blame
them either, can you? Them places, they can't afford to have
girls that aren't strong."

"You don't look very well now," said Philip.

"I wasn't fit to come out tonight, but I couldn't help myself, I wanted the money. I wrote to Emil and told him I was broke, but he never even answered the letter."

"You might have written to me."

"I didn't like to, not after what happened, and I didn't want you to know I was in difficulties. I shouldn't have been surprised if you'd just told me I'd only got what I deserved."

"You don't know me very well, do you, even now?"

For a moment he remembered all the anguish he had suffered on her account, and he was sick with the recollection of his pain. But it was no more than recollection. When he looked at her he knew that he no longer loved her. He was very sorry for her, but he was glad to be free. Watching her gravely, he asked himself why he had been so besotted with passion for her.

"You're a gentleman in every sense of the word," she said. "You're the only one I've ever met." She paused for a minute and then flushed. "I hate asking you, Philip, but can you spare me anything?"

"It's lucky I've got some money on me. I'm afraid I've only got two pounds."

He gave her the sovereigns.

"I'll pay you back, Philip."

"Oh, that's all right," he smiled. "You needn't worry."

He had said nothing that he wanted to say. They had talked as if the whole thing were natural; and it looked as though she would go now, back to the horror of her life, and he would be able to do nothing to prevent it. She had got up to take the money, and they were both standing.

"Am I keeping you?" she asked. "I suppose you want to be getting home."

"No, I'm in no hurry," he answered.

"I'm glad to have a chance of sitting down."

Those words, with all they implied, tore his heart, and

it was dreadfully painful to see the weary way in which she sank back into the chair. The silence lasted so long that Philip in his embarrassment lit a cigarette.

"It's very good of you not to have said anything disagreeable to me, Philip. I thought you might say I didn't know what all."

He saw that she was crying again. He remembered how she had come to him when Emil Miller had deserted her and how she had wept. The recollection of her suffering and of his own humiliation seemed to render more overwhelming the compassion he felt now.

"If I could only get out of it!" she moaned. "I hate it so. I'm unfit for the life. I'm not the sort of girl for that. I'd do anything to get away from it, I'd be a servant if I could. Oh, I wish I was dead."

And in pity for herself she broke down now completely. She sobbed hysterically, and her thin body was shaken.

"Oh, you don't know what it is. Nobody knows till they've done it."

Philip could not bear to see her cry. He was tortured by the horror of her position.

"Poor child," he whispered. "Poor child."

He was deeply moved. Suddenly he had an inspiration. It filled him with a perfect ecstasy of happiness.

"Look here, if you want to get away from it, I've got an idea. I'm frightfully hard up just now, I've got to be as economical as I can; but I've got a sort of little flat now in Kennington and I've got a spare room. If you like you and the baby can come and live there. I pay a woman three and sixpence a week to keep the place clean and to do a little cooking for me. You could do that and your food wouldn't come to much more than the money I should save on her. It doesn't cost any more to feed two than one, and I don't suppose the baby eats much."

She stopped crying and looked at him.

"D'you mean to say that you could take me back after all that's happened?"

Philip flushed a little in embarrassment at what he had to say.

"I don't want you to mistake me. I'm just giving you a room which doesn't cost me anything and your food. I don't expect anything more from you than that you should do exactly the same as the woman I have in does. Except for that I don't want anything from you at all. I daresay you can cook well enough for that."

She sprang to her feet and was about to come towards him.

"You are good to me, Philip."

"No, please stop where you are," he said hurriedly, putting out his hand as though to push her away.

He did not know why it was, but he could not bear the thought that she should touch him.

"I don't want to be anything more than a friend to you."

"You are good to me," she repeated. "You are good to me."

"Does that mean you'll come?"

"Oh, yes, I'd do anything to get away from this. You'll never regret what you've done, Philip, never. When can I come, Philip?"

"You'd better come tomorrow."

Suddenly she burst into tears again.

"What on earth are you crying for now?" he smiled.

"I'm so grateful to you. I don't know how I can ever make it up to you."

"Oh, that's all right. You'd better go home now."

He wrote out the address and told her that if she came at half past five he would be ready for her. It was so late that he had to walk home, but it did not seem a long way, for he was intoxicated with delight; he seemed to walk on air.

Next day he got up early to make the room ready for Mildred. He told the woman who had looked after him that he would not want her any more. Mildred came about six, and Philip, who was watching from the window, went down to let her in and help her to bring up the luggage: it consisted now of no more than three large parcels wrapped in brown paper, for she had been obliged to sell everything that was not absolutely needful. She wore the same black silk dress she had worn the night before, and, though she had now no rouge on her cheeks, there was still about her eyes the black which remained after a perfunctory wash in the morning: it made her look very ill. She was a pathetic figure as she stepped out of the cab with the baby in her arms. She seemed a little shy, and they found nothing but commonplace things to say to one another.

"So you've got here all right."

"I've never lived in this part of London before."

The baby was sleeping placidly.

"You don't recognise her, I expect," said Mildred.

"I've not seen her since we took her down to Brighton."

"Where shall I put her? She's so heavy I can't carry her very long."

"I'm afraid I haven't got a cradle," said Philip, with a nervous laugh.

"Oh, she'll sleep with me. She always does."

Mildred put the baby in an arm-chair and looked round the room. She recognised most of the things which she had known in his old diggings. Only one thing was new, a head and shoulders of Philip which Lawson had painted at the end of the preceding summer; it hung over the chimney-piece; Mildred looked at it critically.

"In some ways I like it and in some ways I don't. I think you're better looking than that."

"Things are looking up," laughed Philip. "You've never told me I was good-looking before."

"I'm not one to worry myself about a man's looks. I don't like good-looking men. They're too conceited for me."

Her eyes travelled round the room in an instinctive search for a looking-glass, but there was none; she put up her hand and patted her large fringe.

"What'll the other people in the house say to my being here?" she asked suddenly.

"Oh, there's only a man and his wife living here. He's out all day, and I never see her except on Saturday to pay my rent. They keep entirely to themselves. I've not spoken two words to either of them since I came."

Mildred went into the bedroom to undo her things and put them away. Philip tried to read, but his spirits were too high: he leaned back in his chair, smoking a cigarette, and with smiling eyes looked at the sleeping child. He felt very happy. He was quite sure that he was not at all in love with Mildred. He was surprised that the old feeling had left him so completely; he discerned in himself a faint physical repulsion from her; and he thought that if he touched her it would give him goose-flesh. He could not understand himself. Presently, knocking at the door, she came in again.

"I say, you needn't knock," he said. "Have you made the tour of the mansion?"

"It's the smallest kitchen I've ever seen."

"You'll find it large enough to cook our sumptuous repasts," he retorted lightly.

"I see there's nothing in. I'd better go out and get something."

"Yes, but I venture to remind you that we must be devilish economical."

"What shall I get for supper?"

"You'd better get what you think you can cook," laughed Philip.

He gave her some money and she went out. She came in half an hour later and put her purchases on the table. She was out of breath from climbing the stairs.

"I say, you are anæmic," said Philip. "I'll have to dose you with Blaud's Pills."

"It took me some time to find the shops. I bought some liver. That's tasty, isn't it? And you can't eat much of it, so it's more economical than butcher's meat."

There was a gas stove in the kitchen, and when she had put the liver on, Mildred came into the sitting-room to lay the cloth.

"Why are you only laying one place?" asked Philip. "Aren't you going to eat anything?"

Mildred flushed.

"I thought you mightn't like me to have my meals with you."

"Why on earth not?"

"Well, I'm only a servant, aren't I?"

"Don't be an ass. How can you be so silly?"

He smiled, but her humility gave him a curious twist in his heart. Poor thing! He remembered what she had been when first he knew her. He hesitated for an instant.

"Don't think I'm conferring any benefit on you," he said. "It's simply a business arrangement, I'm giving you board and lodging in return for your work. You don't owe me anything. And there's nothing humiliating to you in it."

She did not answer, but tears rolled heavily down her cheeks. Philip knew from his experience at the hospital that women of her class looked upon service as degrading: he could not help feeling a little impatient with her; but he blamed himself, for it was clear that she was tired and ill. He got up and helped her to lay another place at the table. The baby was awake now, and Mildred had prepared some Mellin's Food for it. The liver and bacon were ready and they sat down. For economy's sake Philip had given up drinking anything but water, but he had in the house a half a bottle of whiskey, and he thought a little would do Mildred good. He did his best to make the supper pass cheerfully, but Mildred was subdued and exhausted. When they had finished she got up to put the baby to bed.

"I think you'll do well to turn in early yourself," said Philip. "You look absolutely done up."

"I think I will after I've washed up."

Philip lit his pipe and began to read. It was pleasant to hear somebody moving about in the next room. Sometimes his loneliness had oppressed him. Mildred came in to clear the table, and he heard the clatter of plates as she washed up. Philip smiled as he thought how characteristic it was of her that she should do all that in a black silk dress. But he had work to do, and he brought his book up to the table. He was reading Osler's *Medicine,* which had recently taken the place in the students' favour of Taylor's work, for many years the text-book most in use. Presently Mildred came in, rolling down her sleeves. Philip gave her a casual glance, but did not move; the occasion was curious, and he felt a little nervous. He feared that Mildred might imagine he was going to make a nuisance of himself, and he did not quite know how without brutality to reassure her.

"By the way, I've got a lecture at nine, so I should want breakfast at a quarter past eight. Can you manage that?"

"Oh, yes. Why, when I was in Parliament Street I used to catch the eight-twelve from Herne Hill every morning."

"I hope you'll find your room comfortable. You'll be a different woman tomorrow after a long night in bed."

"I suppose you work till late?"

"I generally work till about eleven or half-past."

"I'll say good-night then."

"Good-night."

The table was between them. He did not offer to shake hands with her. She shut the door quietly. He heard her moving about in the bedroom, and in a little while he heard the creaking of the bed as she got in.

The following day was Tuesday. Philip as usual hurried through his breakfast and dashed off to get to his lecture at nine. He had only time to exchange a few words with Mildred. When he came back in the evening he found her seated at the window, darning his socks.

"I say, you are industrious," he smiled. "What have you been doing with yourself all day?"

"Oh, I gave the place a good cleaning and then I took baby out for a little."

She was wearing an old black dress, the same as she had worn as uniform when she served in the tea-shop; it was shabby, but she looked better in it than in the silk of the day before. The baby was sitting on the floor. She looked up at Philip with large, mysterious eyes and broke into a laugh when he sat down beside her and began playing with her bare toes. The afternoon sun came into the room and shed a mellow light.

"It's rather jolly to come back and find someone about the place. A woman and a baby make very good decoration in a room."

He had gone to the hospital dispensary and got a bottle of Blaud's Pills. He gave them to Mildred and told her she must take them after each meal. It was a remedy she was used to, for she had taken it off and on ever since she was sixteen.

"I'm sure Lawson would love that green skin of yours," said Philip. "He'd say it was so paintable, but I'm terribly matter of fact nowadays, and I shan't be happy till you're as pink and white as a milkmaid."

"I feel better already."

After a frugal supper Philip filled his pouch with tobacco and put on his hat. It was on Tuesdays that he generally went to the tavern in Beak Street, and he was glad that this day came so soon after Mildred's arrival, for he wanted to make his relations with her perfectly clear.

"Are you going out?" she said.

"Yes, on Tuesdays I give myself a night off. I shall see you tomorrow. Good-night."

Philip always went to the tavern with a sense of pleasure. Macalister, the philosophic stockbroker, was generally there and glad to argue upon any subject under the sun; Hayward came regularly when he was in London; and though he and Macalister disliked one another they continued out of habit to meet on that one evening in the week. Macalister thought Hayward a poor creature, and sneered at his delicacies of sentiment; he asked satirically about Hayward's literary work and received with scornful smiles his vague suggestions of future masterpieces; their arguments were often heated; but the punch was good, and they were both fond of it; towards the end of the evening they generally composed their differences and thought each other capital fellows. This evening Philip found them both there, and Lawson also; Lawson came more seldom now that he was beginning to know people in London and went out to dinner a good deal. They were all on excellent terms with themselves, for Macalister had given them a good thing on the Stock Exchange, and Hayward and Lawson had made fifty pounds apiece. It was a great thing for Lawson, who was extravagant and earned little money: he had arrived at that stage of the portrait-painter's career when he was noticed a good deal by the critics and found a number of aristocratic ladies who were willing to allow him to paint them for nothing (it advertised them both, and gave the great ladies quite an air of patronesses of the arts); but he very seldom got hold of the solid philistine who was ready to pay good money for a portrait of his wife. Lawson was brimming over with satisfaction.

"It's the most ripping way of making money that I've ever struck," he cried. "I didn't have to put my hand in my pocket for sixpence."

"You lost something by not being here last Tuesday, young man," said Macalister to Philip.

"My God, why didn't you write to me?" said Philip. "If you only knew how useful a hundred pounds would be to me."

"Oh, there wasn't time for that. One has to be on the spot. I heard of a good thing last Tuesday, and I asked these fellows if they'd like to have a flutter, I bought them a thousand shares on Wednesday morning, and there was a rise in the afternoon so I sold them at once. I made fifty pounds for each of them and a couple of hundred for myself."

Philip was sick with envy. He had recently sold the last mortgage in which his small fortune had been invested and now had only six hundred pounds left. He was panic-stricken sometimes when he thought of the future. He had still to keep himself for two years before he could be qualified, and then he meant to try for hospital appointments, so that he could not expect to earn anything for three years at least. With the most rigid economy he would not have more than a hundred pounds left then. It was very little to have as a stand-by in case he was ill and could not earn money or found himself at any time without work. A lucky gamble would make all the difference to him.

"Oh, well, it doesn't matter," said Macalister. "Something is sure to turn up soon. There'll be a boom in South Africans again one of these days, and then I'll see what I can do for you."

Macalister was in the Kaffir market and often told them stories of the sudden fortunes that had been made in the great boom of a year or two back.

"Well, don't forget next time."

They sat on talking till nearly midnight, and Philip, who lived furthest off, was the first to go. If he did not catch the last tram he had to walk, and that made him very late. As it was he did not reach home till nearly half past twelve. When he got upstairs he was surprised to find Mildred still sitting in his arm-chair.

"Why on earth aren't you in bed?" he cried.

"I wasn't sleepy."

"You ought to go to bed all the same. It would rest you."

She did not move. He noticed that since supper she had changed into her black silk dress.

"I thought I'd rather wait up for you in case you wanted anything."

She looked at him, and the shadow of a smile played upon her thin pale lips. Philip was not sure whether he understood or not. He was slightly embarrassed, but assumed a cheerful, matter-of-fact air.

"Well, good-night."

"D'you want to go to bed already?"

"It's nearly one. I'm not used to late hours these days," said Philip.

She took his hand and holding it looked into his eyes with a little smile.

"Phil, the other night in that room, when you asked me to come and stay here, I didn't mean what you thought I meant, when you said you didn't want me to be anything to you except just to cook and that sort of thing."

"Didn't you?" answered Philip, withdrawing his hand. "I did."

"Don't be such an old silly," she laughed.

He shook his head.

"I meant it quite seriously. I shouldn't have asked you to stay here on any other condition."

"Why not?"

"I feel I couldn't. I can't explain it, but it would spoil it all."

She shrugged her shoulders.

"Oh, very well, it's just as you choose. I'm not one to go down on my hands and knees for that, and chance it."

She went out, slamming the door behind her.

Life went smoothly enough with them. Philip spent all day at the hospital and worked at home in the evening except when he went to the Athelnys' or to the tavern in Beak Street. Once the physician for whom he clerked asked him to a solemn dinner, and two or three times he went to parties given by fellow-students. Mildred accepted the monotony of her life. If she minded that Philip left her sometimes by herself in the evening she never mentioned it. Occasionally he took her to a music-hall. He carried out his intention that the only tie between them should be the domestic service she did in return for board and lodging. She had made up her mind that it was no use trying to get work that summer, and with Philip's approval determined to stay where she was till the autumn. She thought it would be easy to get something to do then.

"As far as I'm concerned you can stay on here when you've got a job if it's convenient. The room's there, and the woman who did for me before can come in to look after the baby."

Towards the end of his second term as in-patients' clerk a piece of good fortune befell Philip. It was the middle of July. He went one Tuesday evening to the tavern in Beak Street and found nobody there but Macalister. They sat together, chatting about their absent friends, and after a while Macalister said to him:

"Oh, by the way, I heard of a rather good thing today, New Kleinfonteins; it's a gold mine in Rhodesia. If you'd like to have a flutter you might make a bit."

Philip had been waiting anxiously for such an opportunity, but now that it came he hesitated. He was desperately afraid of losing money. He had little of the gambler's spirit.

"I'd love to, but I don't know if I dare risk it. How much could I lose if things went wrong?"

"I shouldn't have spoken of it, only you seemed so keen about it," Macalister answered coldly.

Philip felt that Macalister looked upon him as rather a donkey.

"I'm awfully keen on making a bit," he laughed.

"You can't make money unless you're prepared to risk money."

Macalister began to talk of other things and Philip, while he was answering him, kept thinking that if the venture turned out well the stockbroker would be very facetious at his expense next time they met. Macalister had a sarcastic tongue.

"I think I will have a flutter if you don't mind," said Philip anxiously.

"All right. I'll buy you two hundred and fifty shares and if I see a half-crown rise I'll sell them at once."

Philip quickly reckoned out how much that would amount to, and his mouth watered; thirty pounds would be a godsend just then, and he thought the fates owed him something. He told Mildred what he had done when he saw her at breakfast next morning. She thought him very silly.

"I never knew anyone who made money on the Stock Exchange," she said. "That's what Emil always said, you can't expect to make money on the Stock Exchange, he said."

Philip bought an evening paper on his way home and turned at once to the money columns. He knew nothing about these things and had difficulty in finding the stock which Macalister had spoken of. He saw they had advanced a quarter. His heart leaped, and then he felt sick with apprehension in case Macalister had forgotten or for some reason had not bought. Macalister had promised to telegraph. Philip could not wait to take a tram home. He jumped into a cab. It was an unwonted extravagance.

"Is there a telegram for me?" he said, as he burst in.

"No," said Mildred.

His face fell, and in bitter disappointment he sank heavily into a chair.

"Then he didn't buy them for me after all. Curse him,"

he added violently. "What cruel luck! And I've been thinking all day of what I'd do with the money."

"Why, what were you going to do?" she asked.

"What's the good of thinking about that now? Oh, I wanted the money so badly."

She gave a laugh and handed him a telegram.

"I was only having a joke with you. I opened it."

He tore it out of her hands. Macalister had bought him two hundred and fifty shares and sold them at the half-crown profit he had suggested. The commission note was to follow next day. For one moment Philip was furious with Mildred for her cruel jest, but then he could only think of his joy.

"It makes such a difference to me," he cried. "I'll stand you a new dress if you like."

"I want it badly enough," she answered.

Money was occupying Philip's thoughts a good deal. He discovered the little truth there was in the airy saying which himself had repeated, that two could live as cheaply as one, and his expenses were beginning to worry him. Mildred was not a good manager, and it cost them as much to live as if they had eaten in restaurants; the child needed clothes, and Mildred boots, an umbrella, and other small things which it was impossible for her to do without. She had announced her intention of getting a job, but she took no definite steps, and presently a bad cold laid her up for a fortnight. When she was well she answered one or two advertisements, but nothing came of it: either she arrived too late and the vacant place was filled, or the work was more than she felt strong enough to do. Once she got an offer, but the wages were only fourteen shillings a week, and she thought she was worth more than that.

"It's no good letting oneself be put upon," she remarked. "People don't respect you if you let yourself go too cheap."

"I don't think fourteen shillings is so bad," answered Philip, drily.

He could not help thinking how useful it would be towards the expenses of the household, and Mildred was already beginning to hint that she did not get a place because she had not got a decent dress to interview employers in. He gave her the dress, and she made one or two more attempts, but Philip came to the conclusion that they were not serious. She did not want to work. The only way he knew to make money was on the Stock Exchange, and he was very anxious to repeat the lucky experiment of the summer; but war had broken out with the Transvaal and nothing was doing in South Africans. Macalister told him that Redvers Buller would march into Pretoria in a month and then everything would boom. The only thing was to wait patiently. What they wanted was a British reverse to knock things down a bit, and then it might be worth while buying. Philip began reading assiduously the "city chat" of his favourite newspaper. He was worried and irritable. Once or twice he spoke sharply to Mildred, and since she was neither tactful nor patient she answered with temper, and they quarrelled. Philip always expressed his regret for what he had said, but Mildred had not a forgiving nature, and she would sulk for a couple of days. She got on his nerves in all sorts of ways; by the manner in which she ate, and by the untidiness which made her leave articles of clothing about their sitting-room.

Philip was exasperated by Mildred's stupidity; but he was so indifferent to her now that it was only at times she made him angry. He grew used to having her about. Christmas came, and with it a couple of days holiday for Philip. He brought some holly in and decorated the flat, and on Christmas Day he gave small presents to Mildred and the baby. There were only two of them so they could not have a turkey, but Mildred roasted a chicken and boiled a Christmas pudding which she had bought at a local grocer's. They stood themselves a bottle of wine. When they had dined Philip sat in his arm-chair by the fire, smoking his pipe;

and the unaccustomed wine had made him forget for a
while the anxiety about money which was so constantly
with him. He felt happy and comfortable. Presently Mildred came in to tell him that the baby wanted him to kiss
her good-night, and with a smile he went into Mildred's
bed-room. Then, telling the child to go to sleep, he turned
down the gas and, leaving the door open in case she cried,
went back into the sitting-room.

"Where are you going to sit?" he asked Mildred.

"You sit in your chair. I'm going to sit on the floor."

When he sat down she settled herself in front of the fire
and leaned against his knees. He could not help remembering that this was how they had sat together in her rooms in
the Vauxhall Bridge Road, but the positions had been re-
versed; it was he who had sat on the floor and leaned his
head against her knee. How passionately he had loved her
then! Now he felt for her a tenderness he had not known
for a long time. He seemed still to feel twined round his
neck the baby's soft little arms.

"Are you comfy?" he asked.

She looked up at him, gave a slight smile, and nodded.
They gazed into the fire dreamily, without speaking to one
another. At last she turned round and stared at him curiously.

"D'you know that you haven't kissed me once since I
came here?" she said suddenly.

"D'you want me to?" he smiled.

"I suppose you don't care for me in that way any more?"

"I'm very fond of you."

"You're much fonder of baby."

He did not answer, and she laid her cheek against his
hand.

"You're not angry with me any more?" she asked presently, with her eyes cast down.

"Why on earth should I be?"

"I've never cared for you as I do now. It's only since I passed through the fire that I've learnt to love you."

It chilled Philip to hear her make use of the sort of phrase she read in the penny novelettes which she devoured. Then he wondered whether what she said had any meaning for her: perhaps she knew no other way to express her genuine feelings than the stilted language of *The Family Herald*.

"It seems so funny our living together like this."

He did not reply for quite a long time, and silence fell upon them again; but at last he spoke and seemed conscious of no interval.

"You mustn't be angry with me. One can't help these things. I remember that I thought you wicked and cruel because you did this, that, and the other; but it was very silly of me. You didn't love me, and it was absurd to blame you for that. I thought I could make you love me, but I know now that was impossible. I don't know what it is that makes someone love you, but whatever it is, it's the only thing that matters, and if it isn't there you won't create it by kindness, or generosity, or anything of that sort."

"I should have thought if you'd loved me really you'd have loved me still."

"I should have thought so too. I remember how I used to think that it would last for ever, I felt I would rather die than be without you, and I used to long for the time when you would be faded and wrinkled so that nobody cared for you any more and I should have you all to myself."

She did not answer, and presently she got up and said she was going to bed. She gave a timid little smile.

"It's Christmas Day, Philip, won't you kiss me goodnight?"

He gave a laugh, blushed slightly, and kissed her. She went to her bed-room and he began to read.

The climax came two or three weeks later. Mildred was driven by Philip's behaviour to a pitch of strange exasperation. There were many different emotions in her soul, and she passed from mood to mood with facility. She spent a great deal of time alone and brooded over her position. She did not put all her feelings into words, she did not even know what they were, but certain things stood out in her mind, and she thought of them over and over again. She had never understood Philip, nor had very much liked him; but she was pleased to have him about her because she thought he was a gentleman. She was impressed because his father had been a doctor and his uncle was a clergyman. She despised him a little because she had made such a fool of him, and at the same time was never quite comfortable in his presence; she could not let herself go, and she felt that he was criticising her manners.

When she first came to live in the little rooms in Kennington she was tired out and ashamed. She was glad to be left alone. It was a comfort to think that there was no rent to pay; she need not go out in all weathers, and she could lie quietly in bed if she did not feel well. She had hated the life she led. It was horrible to have to be affable and sub-servient; and even now when it crossed her mind she cried with pity for herself as she thought of the roughness of men and their brutal language. But it crossed her mind very seldom. She was grateful to Philip for coming to her rescue, and when she remembered how honestly he had loved her and how badly she had treated him, she felt a pang of remorse. It was easy to make it up to him. It meant very little to her. She was surprised when he refused her suggestion, but she shrugged her shoulders: let him put on airs if he liked, she did not care, he would be anxious enough in a little while, and then it would be her turn to refuse; if he thought it was any deprivation to her he was very much mistaken. She had no doubt of her power over him. He was peculiar, but she knew him through and through. He had so often

281

quarrelled with her and sworn he would never see her again,
and then in a little while he had come on his knees begging
to be forgiven. It gave her a thrill to think how he had
cringed before her. He would have been glad to lie down on
the ground for her to walk on him. She had seen him cry.
She knew exactly how to treat him, pay no attention to
him, just pretend you didn't notice his tempers, leave him
severely alone, and in a little while he was sure to grovel.
She laughed a little to herself, good-humouredly, when she
thought how he had come and eaten dirt before her. She
had had her fling now. She knew what men were and did
not want to have anything more to do with them. She was
quite ready to settle down with Philip. When all was said,
he was a gentleman in every sense of the word, and that was
something not to be sneezed at, wasn't it? Anyhow she was
in no hurry, and she was not going to take the first step.
She was glad to see how fond he was growing of the baby,
though it tickled her a good deal; it was comic that he
should set so much store on another man's child. He *was*
peculiar and no mistake.

But one or two things surprised her. She had been used
to his subservience: he was only too glad to do anything
for her in the old days, she was accustomed to see him cast
down by a cross word and in ecstasy at a kind one; he was
different now, and she said to herself that he had not im-
proved in the last year. It never struck her for a moment
that there could be any change in his feelings, and she
thought it was only acting when he paid no heed to her bad
temper. He wanted to read sometimes and told her to stop
talking: she did not know whether to flare up or to sulk,
and was so puzzled that she did neither. Then came the conversation in which he told her that he intended their relations to be platonic, and, remembering an incident of their
common past, it occurred to her that he dreaded the possibility of her being pregnant. She took pains to reassure him.
It made no difference. She was the sort of woman who was

unable to realise that a man might not have her own obsession with sex; her relations with men had been purely on those lines; and she could not understand that they ever had other interests. The thought struck her that Philip was in love with somebody else, and she watched him, suspecting nurses at the hospital or people he met out; but artful questions led her to the conclusion that there was no one dangerous in the Athelny household; and it forced itself upon her also that Philip, like most medical students, was unconscious of the sex of the nurses with whom his work threw him in contact. They were associated in his mind with a faint odour of iodoform. Philip received no letters, and there was no girl's photograph among his belongings. If he was in love with someone, he was very clever at hiding it; and he answered all Mildred's questions with frankness and apparently without suspicion that there was any motive in them.

"I don't believe he's in love with anybody else," she said to herself at last.

It was a relief, for in that case he was certainly still in love with her; but it made his behaviour very puzzling. If he was going to treat her like that why did he ask her to come and live at the flat? It was unnatural. Mildred was not a woman who conceived the possibility of compassion, generosity, or kindness. Her only conclusion was that Philip was queer. She took it into her head that the reasons for his conduct were chivalrous; and, her imagination filled with the extravagances of cheap fiction, she pictured to herself all sorts of romantic explanations for his delicacy. Her fancy ran riot with bitter misunderstandings, purifications by fire, snow-white souls, and death in the cruel cold of a Christmas night. When she found that nothing would induce Philip to share the same room with her, when he spoke to her about it with a tone in his voice she had never heard before, she suddenly realised that he did not want her. She was astounded. She remembered all he had said in the past and how desperately he had loved her. She felt humiliated and angry, but she had a sort of native insolence which carried her through. He needn't think she was in love with him, because she wasn't. She hated him sometimes, and she longed to humble him; but she found herself singularly powerless; she did not know which way to handle him. She began to be a little nervous with him. Once or twice she cried. Once or twice she set herself to be particularly nice to him; but when she took his arm while they walked along the front at night he made some excuse in a while to release himself, as though it were unpleasant for him to be touched by her. She could not make it out. The only hold she had over him was through the baby, of whom he seemed to grow fonder and fonder: she could make him white with anger by giving the child a slap or a push; and the only time the old, tender smile came back into his eyes was when she stood with the baby in her arms.

She brooded over it all, and she thought to herself angrily that she would make him pay for all this some day. She could not reconcile herself to the fact that he no longer cared for her. She would make him. She suffered from pique, and sometimes in a curious fashion she desired Philip. He was so cold now that it exasperated her. She thought of him in that way incessantly. She thought that he was treating her very badly, and she did not know what she had done to deserve it. She kept on saying to herself that it was unnatural they should live like that. Then she thought that if things were different and she were going to have a baby, he would be sure to marry her. He was funny, but he was a gentleman in every sense of the word, no one could deny that. At last it became an obsession with her, and she made up her mind to force a change in their relations. He never even kissed her now, and she wanted him to: she remembered how ardently he had been used to press her lips. It gave her a curious feeling to think of it. She often looked at his mouth.

One evening, at the beginning of February, Philip told
her that he was dining with Lawson, who was giving a
party in his studio to celebrate his birthday; and he would
not be in till late; Lawson had bought a couple of bottles of
the punch they favoured from the tavern in Beak Street, and
they proposed to have a merry evening. Mildred asked if
there were going to be women there, but Philip told
her there were not; only men had been invited; and they
were just going to sit and talk and smoke: Mildred did not
think it sounded very amusing; if she were a painter
she would have half a dozen models about. She went to bed,
but could not sleep, and presently an idea struck her; she
got up and fixed the catch on the wicket at the landing, so
that Philip could not get in. He came back about one, and
she heard him curse when he found that the wicket was
closed. She got out of bed and opened.

"Why on earth did you shut yourself in? I'm sorry I've
dragged you out of bed."

"I left it open on purpose, I can't think how it came to
be shut."

"Hurry up and get back to bed, or you'll catch cold."

He walked into the sitting-room and turned up the gas.
She followed him in. She went up to the fire.

"I want to warm my feet a bit. They're like ice."

He sat down and began to take off his boots. His eyes
were shining and his cheeks were flushed. She thought he
had been drinking.

"Have you been enjoying yourself?" she asked, with a
smile.

"Yes, I've had a ripping time."

Philip was quite sober, but he had been talking and
laughing, and he was excited still. An evening of that sort
reminded him of the old days in Paris. He was in high
spirits. He took his pipe out of his pocket and filled it.

"Aren't you going to bed?" she asked.

"Not yet, I'm not a bit sleepy. Lawson was in great

form. He talked sixteen to the dozen from the moment I got there till the moment I left."

"What did you talk about?"

"Heaven knows! Of every subject under the sun. You should have seen us all shouting at the tops of our voices and nobody listening."

Philip laughed with pleasure at the recollection, and Mildred laughed too. She was pretty sure he had drunk more than was good for him. That was exactly what she had expected. She knew men.

"Can I sit down?" she said.

Before he could answer she settled herself on his knees.

"If you're not going to bed you'd better go and put on a dressing-gown."

"Oh, I'm all right as I am." Then putting her arms round his neck, she placed her face against his and said: "Why are you so horrid to me, Phil?"

He tried to get up, but she would not let him.

"I do love you, Philip," she said.

"Don't talk damned rot."

"It isn't, it's true. I can't live without you. I want you."

He released himself from her arms.

"Please get up. You're making a fool of yourself and you're making me feel a perfect idiot."

"I love you, Philip. I want to make up for all the harm I did you. I can't go on like this, it's not in human nature."

He slipped out of the chair and left her in it.

"I'm very sorry, but it's too late."

She gave a heart-rending sob.

"But why? How can you be so cruel?"

"I suppose it's because I loved you too much. I wore the passion out. The thought of anything of that sort horrifies me. I can't look at you now without thinking of Emil and Griffiths. One can't help those things, I suppose it's just nerves."

She seized his hand and covered it with kisses.

"Don't," he cried.

She sank back into the chair.

"I can't go on like this. If you won't love me, I'd rather go away."

"Don't be foolish, you haven't anywhere to go. You can stay here as long as you like, but it must be on the definite understanding that we're friends and nothing more."

Then she dropped suddenly the vehemence of passion and gave a soft, insinuating laugh. She sidled up to Philip and put her arms round him. She made her voice low and wheedling.

"Don't be such an old silly. I believe you're nervous. You don't know how nice I can be."

She put her face against his and rubbed his cheek with hers. To Philip her smile was an abominable leer, and the suggestive glitter of her eyes filled him with horror. He drew back instinctively.

"I won't," he said.

But she would not let him go. She sought his mouth with her lips. He took her hands and tore them roughly apart and pushed her away.

"You disgust me," he said.

"Me?"

She steadied herself with one hand on the chimney-piece. She looked at him for an instant, and two red spots suddenly appeared on her cheeks. She gave a shrill, angry laugh.

"I disgust *you*."

She paused and drew in her breath sharply. Then she burst into a furious torrent of abuse. She shouted at the top of her voice. She called him every foul name she could think of. She used language so obscene that Philip was astounded; she was always so anxious to be refined, so shocked by coarseness, that it had never occurred to him that she knew the words she used now. She came up to him and thrust her face in his. It was distorted with passion, and in her tumultuous speech the spittle dribbled over her lips.

"I never cared for you, not once, I was making a fool of you always, you bored me, you bored me stiff, and I hated you, I would never have let you touch me only for the money, and it used to make me sick when I had to let you kiss me. We laughed at you, Griffiths and me, we laughed because you was such a mug. A mug! A mug!"

Then she burst again into abominable invective. She accused him of every mean fault; she said he was stingy, she said he was dull, she said he was vain, selfish; she cast virulent ridicule on everything upon which he was most sensitive. And at last she turned to go. She kept on, with hysterical violence, shouting at him an opprobrious, filthy epithet. She seized the handle of the door and flung it open. Then she turned round and hurled at him the injury which she knew was the only one that really touched him. She threw into the word all the malice and all the venom of which she was capable. She flung it at him as though it were a blow.

"Cripple!"

Philip awoke with a start next morning, conscious that it was late, and looking at his watch found it was nine o'clock. He jumped out of bed and went into the kitchen to get himself some hot water to shave with. There was no sign of Mildred, and the things which she had used for her supper the night before still lay in the sink unwashed. He knocked at her door.

"Wake up, Mildred. It's awfully late."

She did not answer, even after a second louder knocking, and he concluded that she was sulking. He was in too great a hurry to bother about that. He put some water on to boil and jumped into his bath which was always poured out the night before in order to take the chill off. He presumed that Mildred would cook his breakfast while he was dressing and leave it in the sitting-room. She had done that two or three times when she was out of temper. But he heard no sound of her moving, and realised that if he wanted anything to eat he would have to get it himself. He was irritated that she should play him such a trick on a morning when he had over-slept himself. There was still no sign of her when he was ready, but he heard her moving about her room. She was evidently getting up. He made himself some tea and cut himself a couple of pieces of bread and butter, which he ate while he was putting on his boots, then bolted downstairs and along the street into the main road to catch his tram. While his eyes sought out the newspaper shops to see the war news on the placards, he thought of the scene of the night before: now that it was over and he had slept on it, he could not help thinking it grotesque; he supposed he had been ridiculous, but he was not master of his feelings; at the time they had been overwhelming. He was angry with Mildred because she had forced him into that absurd position, and then with renewed astonishment he thought of her outburst and the filthy language she had used. He could not help flushing when he remembered her final jibe; but he shrugged his shoulders contemptuously. He had long known that when his fellows were angry with him they never failed to taunt him with his deformity. He had seen men at the hospital imitate his walk, not before him as they used at school, but when they thought he was not looking. He knew now that they did it from no wilful unkindness, but because man is naturally an imitative animal, and because it was an easy way to make people laugh: he knew it, but he could never resign himself to it.

He was glad to throw himself into his work. The ward seemed pleasant and friendly when he entered it. The sister greeted him with a quick, business-like smile.

"You're very late, Mr. Carey."

"I was out on the loose last night."

"You look it."

"Thank you."

Laughing, he went to the first of his cases, a boy with tuberculous ulcers, and removed his bandages. The boy was pleased to see him, and Philip chaffed him as he put a clean dressing on the wound. Philip was a favourite with the patients; he treated them good-humouredly; and he had gentle, sensitive hands which did not hurt them: some of the dressers were a little rough and happy-go-lucky in their methods. He lunched with his friends in the club-room, a frugal meal consisting of a scone and butter, with a cup of cocoa, and they talked of the war. Several men were going out, but the authorities were particular and refused everyone who had not had a hospital appointment. Some-one suggested that, if the war went on, in a while they would be glad to take anyone who was qualified; but the general opinion was that it would be over in a month. Now that Roberts was there things would get all right in no time. This was Macalister's opinion too, and he had told Philip that they must watch their chance and buy just be-fore peace was declared. There would be a boom then, and they might all make a bit of money. Philip had left with Macalister instructions to buy him stock whenever the op-portunity presented itself. His appetite had been whetted by the thirty pounds he had made in the summer, and he wanted now to make a couple of hundred.

He finished his day's work and got on a tram to go back to Kennington. He wondered how Mildred would behave that evening. It was a nuisance to think that she would probably be surly and refuse to answer his questions. It was a warm evening for the time of year, and even in those gray streets of South London there was the languor of February; nature is restless then after the long winter months, growing things awake from their sleep, and there is a rustle in the earth, a forerunner of spring, as it resumes its eternal activities. Philip would have liked to drive on further, it was distasteful to him to go back to his rooms,

and he wanted the air; but the desire to see the child
clutched suddenly at his heart-strings, and he smiled to
himself as he thought of her toddling towards him with a
crow of delight. He was surprised, when he reached the
house and looked up mechanically at the windows, to see
that there was no light. He went upstairs and knocked, but
got no answer. When Mildred went out she left the key
under the mat and he found it there now. He let himself
in and going into the sitting-room struck a match. Something had happened, he did not at once know what; he
turned the gas on full and lit it; the room was suddenly
filled with the glare and he looked round. He gasped.
The whole place was wrecked. Everything in it had been
wilfully destroyed. Anger seized him, and he rushed into
Mildred's room. It was dark and empty. When he had got
a light he saw that she had taken away all her things and
the baby's; (he had noticed on entering that the go-cart was
not in its usual place on the landing, but thought Mildred
had taken the baby out;) and all the things on the washing-
stand had been broken, a knife had been drawn cross-ways
through the seats of the two chairs, the pillow had been slit
open, there were large gashes in the sheets and the counter-
pane, the looking-glass appeared to have been broken
with a hammer. Philip was bewildered. He went into his
own room, and here too everything was in confusion. The
basin and the ewer had been smashed, the looking-glass
was in fragments, and the sheets were in ribands. Mildred
had made a slit large enough to put her hand into the pillow and had scattered the feathers about the room. She had
jabbed a knife into the blankets. On the dressing-table were
photographs of Philip's mother, the frames had been
smashed and the glass shivered. Philip went into the tiny
kitchen. Everything that was breakable was broken, glasses,
pudding-basins, plates, dishes.

It took Philip's breath away. Mildred had left no letter,
nothing but this ruin to mark her anger, and he could

imagine the set face with which she had gone about her work. He went back into the sitting-room and looked about him. He was so astonished that he no longer felt angry. He looked curiously at the kitchen-knife and the coal-hammer, which were lying on the table where she had left them. Then his eye caught a large carving-knife in the fireplace which had been broken. It must have taken her a long time to do so much damage. Lawson's portrait of him had been cut cross-ways and gaped hideously. His own drawings had been ripped in pieces; and the photographs, Manet's *Olympia* and the *Odalisque* of Ingres, the portrait of Philip IV, had been smashed with great blows of the coal-hammer. There were gashes in the table-cloth and in the curtains and in the two arm-chairs. They were quite ruined.

Philip had two or three blue and white plates, of no value, but he had bought them one by one for very small sums and liked them for their associations. They littered the floor in fragments. There were long gashes on the backs of his books, and she had taken the trouble to tear pages out of the unbound French ones. The little ornaments on the chimney-piece lay on the hearth in bits. Everything that it had been possible to destroy with a knife or a hammer was destroyed.

The whole of Philip's belongings would not have sold for thirty pounds, but most of them were old friends, and he was a domestic creature, attached to all those odds and ends because they were his; he had been proud of his little home, and on so little money had made it pretty and characteristic. He sank down now in despair. He asked himself how she could have been so cruel. A sudden fear got him on his feet again and into the passage, where stood a cupboard in which he kept his clothes. He opened it and gave a sigh of relief. She had apparently forgotten it and none of his things was touched.

He went back into the sitting-room and, surveying the scene, wondered what to do; he had not the heart to begin trying to set things straight; besides there was no food in the house, and he was hungry. He went out and got himself something to eat. When he came in he was cooler. A little pang seized him as he thought of the child, and he wondered whether she would miss him, at first perhaps, but in a week she would have forgotten him; and he was thankful to be rid of Mildred. He did not think of her with wrath, but with an overwhelming sense of boredom.

"I hope to God I never see her again," he said aloud.

The only thing now was to leave the rooms, and he made up his mind to give notice the next morning. He could not afford to make good the damage done, and he had so little money left that he must find cheaper lodgings still. He would be glad to get out of them. The expense had worried him, and now the recollection of Mildred would be in them always. Philip was impatient and could never rest till he had put in action the plan which he had in mind; so on the following afternoon he got in a dealer in second-hand furniture who offered him three pounds for all his goods damaged and undamaged; and two days later he moved into the house opposite the hospital in which he had had rooms when first he became a medical student. The landlady was a very decent woman. He took a bedroom at the top, which she let him have for six shillings a week; it was small and shabby and looked on the yard of the house that backed on to it, but he had nothing now except his clothes and a box of books, and he was glad to lodge so cheaply.

And now it happened that the fortunes of Philip Carey, of no consequence to any but himself, were affected by the events through which his country was passing. History was being made, and the process was so significant that it seemed absurd it should touch the life of an obscure medical student. Battle after battle, Magersfontein, Colenso, Spion Kop, lost on the playing fields of Eton, had humiliated the nation and dealt the death-blow to the prestige of the aristocracy

and gentry who till then had found no one seriously to
oppose their assertion that they possessed a natural instinct
of government. The old order was being swept away: history was being made indeed. Then the colossus put forth
his strength, and, blundering again, at last blundered into
the semblance of victory. Cronje surrendered at Paardeberg,
Ladysmith was relieved, and at the beginning of March
Lord Roberts marched into Bloemfontein.

It was two or three days after the news of this reached
London that Macalister came into the tavern in Beak Street
and announced joyfully that things were looking brighter
on the Stock Exchange. Peace was in sight, Roberts would
march into Pretoria within a few weeks, and shares were
going up already. There was bound to be a boom.

"Now's the time to come in," he told Philip. "It's no
good waiting till the public gets on to it. It's now or never."

He had inside information. The manager of a mine in
South Africa had cabled to the senior partner of his firm
that the plant was uninjured. They would start working
again as soon as possible. It wasn't a speculation, it was an
investment. To show how good a thing the senior partner
thought it Macalister told Philip that he had bought five
hundred shares for both his sisters: he never put them into
anything that wasn't as safe as the Bank of England.

"I'm going to put my shirt on it myself," he said.

The shares were two and an eighth to a quarter. He advised Philip not to be greedy, but to be satisfied with a ten-
shilling rise. He was buying three hundred for himself and
suggested that Philip should do the same. He would hold
them and sell when he thought fit. Philip had great faith
in him, partly because he was a Scotsman and therefore by
nature cautious, and partly because he had been right before.
He jumped at the suggestion.

"I daresay we shall be able to sell before the account,"
said Macalister, "but if not, I'll arrange to carry them over
for you."

It seemed a capital system to Philip. You held on till you got your profit, and you never even had to put your hand in your pocket. He began to watch the Stock Exchange columns of the paper with new interest. Next day everything was up a little, and Macalister wrote to say that he had had to pay two and a quarter for the shares. He said that the market was firm. But in a day or two there was a set-back. The news that came from South Africa was less reassuring, and Philip with anxiety saw that his shares had fallen to two; but Macalister was optimistic, the Boers couldn't hold out much longer, and he was willing to bet a top-hat that Roberts would march into Johannesburg before the middle of April. At the account Philip had to pay out nearly forty pounds. It worried him considerably, but he felt that the only course was to hold on: in his circumstances the loss was too great for him to pocket. For two or three weeks nothing happened; the Boers would not understand that they were beaten and nothing remained for them but to surrender: in fact they had one or two small successes, and Philip's shares fell half a crown more. It became evident that the war was not finished. There was a lot of selling. When Macalister saw Philip he was pessimistic.

"I'm not sure if the best thing wouldn't be to cut the loss. I've been paying out about as much as I want to in differences."

Philip was sick with anxiety. He could not sleep at night; he bolted his breakfast, reduced now to tea and bread and butter, in order to get over to the club reading-room and see the paper; sometimes the news was bad, and sometimes there was no news at all, but when the shares moved it was to go down. He did not know what to do. If he sold now he would lose altogether hard on three hundred and fifty pounds; and that would leave him only eight pounds to go on with. He wished with all his heart that he had never been such a fool as to dabble on the Stock Exchange, but the only thing was to hold on; something decisive might happen any day and the shares would go up; he did not hope now for a profit, but he wanted to make good his loss. It was his only chance of finishing his course at the hospital. The summer session was beginning in May, and at the end of it he meant to take the examination in midwifery. Then he would only have a year more; he reckoned it out carefully and came to the conclusion that he could manage it, fees and all, on a hundred and fifty pounds; but that was the least it could possibly be done on.

Early in April he went to the tavern in Beak Street anxious to see Macalister. It eased him a little to discuss the situation with him; and to realise that numerous people beside himself were suffering from loss of money made his own trouble a little less intolerable. But when Philip arrived no one was there but Hayward, and no sooner had Philip seated himself than he said:

"I'm sailing for the Cape on Sunday."

"Are you!" exclaimed Philip.

Hayward was the last person he would have expected to do anything of the kind. At the hospital men were going out now in numbers; the Government was glad to get anyone who was qualified; and others, going out as troopers, wrote home that they had been put on hospital work as soon as it was learned that they were medical students. A wave of patriotic feeling had swept over the country, and volunteers were coming from all ranks of society.

"What are you going as?" asked Philip.

"Oh, in the Dorset Yeomanry. I'm going as a trooper."

Philip had known Hayward for eight years. The youthful intimacy which had come from Philip's enthusiastic admiration for the man who could tell him of art and literature had long since vanished; but habit had taken its place; and when Hayward was in London they saw one another once or twice a week. He still talked about books with a delicate appreciation. Philip was not yet tolerant, and sometimes Hayward's conversation irritated him. He no longer believed implicitly that nothing in the world was of consequence but art. He resented Hayward's contempt for action and success. Philip, stirring his punch, thought of his early friendship and his ardent expectation that Hayward would do great things; it was long since he had lost all such illusions, and he knew now that Hayward would never do anything but talk. He found his three hundred a year more difficult to live on now that he was thirty-five than he had when he was a young man; and his clothes, though still made by a good tailor, were worn a good deal longer than at one time he would have thought possible. He was too stout, and no artful arrangement of his fair hair could conceal the fact that he was bald. His blue eyes were dull and pale. It was not hard to guess that he drank too much.

"What on earth made you think of going out to the Cape?" asked Philip.

"Oh, I don't know, I thought I ought to."

Philip was silent. He felt rather silly. He understood that Hayward was being driven by an uneasiness in his soul which he could not account for. Some power within him made it seem necessary to go and fight for his country. It was strange, since he considered patriotism no more than a prejudice, and, flattering himself on his cosmopolitanism, he had looked upon England as a place of exile. His countrymen in the mass wounded his susceptibilities. Philip wondered what it was that made people do things which were so contrary to all their theories of life. It would have been reasonable for Hayward to stand aside and watch with a smile while the barbarians slaughtered one another. It looked as though men were puppets in the hands of an unknown force, which drove them to do this and that; and sometimes they used their reason to justify their actions; and when this was impossible they did the actions in despite of reason.

"People are very extraordinary," said Philip. "I should never have expected you to go out as a trooper."

Hayward smiled, slightly embarrassed, and said nothing.

"I was examined yesterday," he remarked at last. "It was worth while undergoing the *gêne* of it to know that one was perfectly fit."

Philip noticed that he still used a French word in an affected way when an English one would have served. But just then Macalister came in.

"I wanted to see you, Carey," he said. "My people don't feel inclined to hold those shares any more, the market's in such an awful state, and they want you to take them up."

Philip's heart sank. He knew that was impossible. It meant that he must accept the loss. His pride made him answer calmly.

"I don't know that I think that's worth while. You'd better sell them."

"It's all very fine to say that, I'm not sure if I can. The market's stagnant, there are no buyers."

"But they're marked down at one and an eighth."

"Oh yes, but that doesn't mean anything. You can't get that for them."

Philip did not say anything for a moment. He was trying to collect himself.

"D'you mean to say they're worth nothing at all?"

"Oh, I don't say that. Of course they're worth something, but you see, nobody's buying them now."

"Then you must just sell them for what you can get."

Macalister looked at Philip narrowly. He wondered whether he was very hard hit.

"I'm awfully sorry, old man, but we're all in the same boat. No one thought the war was going to hang on this way. I put you into them, but I was in myself too."

"It doesn't matter at all," said Philip. "One has to take one's chance."

He moved back to the table from which he had got up

to talk to Macalister. He was dumbfounded; his head suddenly began to ache furiously; but he did not want them to think him unmanly. He sat on for an hour. He laughed feverishly at everything they said. At last he got up to go.

"You take it pretty coolly," said Macalister, shaking hands with him. "I don't suppose anyone likes losing between three and four hundred pounds."

When Philip got back to his shabby little room he flung himself on his bed, and gave himself over to his despair. He kept on regretting his folly bitterly; and though he told himself that it was absurd to regret, for what had happened was inevitable just because it had happened, he could not help himself. He was utterly miserable. He could not sleep. He remembered all the ways he had wasted money during the last few years. His head ached dreadfully.

The following evening there came by the last post the statement of his account. He examined his pass-book. He found that when he had paid everything he would have seven pounds left. Seven pounds! He was thankful he had been able to pay. It would have been horrible to be obliged to confess to Macalister that he had not the money. He was dressing in the eye-department during the summer session, and he had bought an ophthalmoscope off a student who had one to sell. He had not paid for this, but he lacked the courage to tell the student that he wanted to go back on his bargain. Also he had to buy certain books. He had about five pounds to go on with. It lasted him six weeks; then he wrote to his uncle a letter which he thought very business-like; he said that owing to the war he had had grave losses and could not go on with his studies unless his uncle came to his help. He suggested that the Vicar should lend him a hundred and fifty pounds paid over the next eighteen months in monthly instalments; he would pay interest on this and promised to refund the capital by degrees when he began to earn money. He would be qualified in a year and a half at the latest, and he could be pretty

sure then of getting an assistantship at three pounds a week.
His uncle wrote back that he could do nothing. It was not
fair to ask him to sell out when everything was at its worst,
and the little he had he felt that his duty to himself made it
necessary for him to keep in case of illness. He ended the
letter with a little homily. He had warned Philip time after
time, and Philip had never paid any attention to him; he
could not honestly say he was surprised; he had long
expected that this would be the end of Philip's extravagance
and want of balance. Philip grew hot and cold when he read
this. It had never occurred to him that his uncle would refuse, and he burst into furious anger; but this was succeeded
by utter blankness: if his uncle would not help him he could
not go on at the hospital. Panic seized him and, putting
aside his pride, he wrote again to the Vicar of Blackstable,
placing the case before him more urgently; but perhaps he
did not explain himself properly and his uncle did not
realise in what desperate straits he was, for he answered
that he could not change his mind; Philip was twenty-five
and really ought to be earning his living. When he died
Philip would come into a little, but till then he refused to
give him a penny. Philip felt in the letter the satisfaction of
a man who for many years had disapproved of his courses
and now saw himself justified.

Philip began to pawn his clothes. He reduced his expenses by eating only one meal a day beside his breakfast; and he ate it, bread and butter and cocoa, at four so
that it should last him till next morning. He was so hungry
by nine o'clock that he had to go to bed. He thought of
borrowing money from Lawson, but the fear of a refusal
held him back; at last he asked him for five pounds. Lawson
lent it with pleasure, but, as he did so, said:

"You'll let me have it back in a week or so, won't you?
I've got to pay my framer, and I'm awfully broke just now."

Philip knew he would not be able to return it, and the thought of what Lawson would think made him so ashamed that in a couple of days he took the money back untouched. Lawson was just going out to luncheon and asked Philip to come too. Philip could hardly eat, he was so glad to get some solid food. On Sunday he was sure of a good dinner from Athelny. He hesitated to tell the Athelnys what had happened to him: they had always looked upon him as comparatively well-to-do, and he had a dread that they would think less well of him if they knew he was penniless.

Though he had always been poor, the possibility of not having enough to eat had never occurred to him; it was not the sort of thing that happened to the people among whom he lived; and he was as ashamed as if he had some disgraceful disease. The situation in which he found himself was quite outside the range of his experience. He was so taken aback that he did not know what else to do than to go on at the hospital; he had a vague hope that something would turn up; he could not quite believe that what was happening to him was true; and he remembered how during his first term at school he had often thought his life was a dream from which he would awake to find himself once more at home. But very soon he foresaw that in a week or so he would have no money at all. He must set about trying to earn something at once. If he had been qualified, even with a club-foot, he could have gone out to the Cape, since the demand for medical men was now great. Except for his deformity he might have enlisted in one of the yeomanry regiments which were constantly being sent out. He went to the secretary of the Medical School and asked if he could give him the coaching of some backward student; but the secretary held out no hope of getting him anything of the sort. Philip read the advertisement columns of the medical papers, and he applied for the post of unqualified assistant to a man who had a dispensary in the Fulham

Road. When he went to see him, he saw the doctor glance at his club-foot; and on hearing that Philip was only in his fourth year at the hospital he said at once that his experience was insufficient: Philip understood that this was only an excuse; the man would not have an assistant who might not be as active as he wanted. Philip turned his attention to other means of earning money. He knew French and German and thought there might be some chance of finding a job as correspondence clerk; it made his heart sink, but he set his teeth; there was nothing else to do. Though too shy to answer the advertisements which demanded a personal application, he replied to those which asked for letters; but he had no experience to state and no recommendations: he was conscious that neither his German nor his French was commercial; he was ignorant of the terms used in business; he knew neither shorthand nor typewriting. He could not help recognising that his case was hopeless. He thought of writing to the solicitor who had been his father's executor, but he could not bring himself to, for it was contrary to his express advice that he had sold the mortgages in which his money had been invested. He knew from his uncle that Mr. Nixon thoroughly disapproved of him. He had gathered from Philip's year in the accountant's office that he was idle and incompetent.

"I'd sooner starve," Philip muttered to himself.

Once or twice the possibility of suicide presented itself to him: it would be easy to get something from the hospital dispensary, and it was a comfort to think that if the worst came to the worst he had at hand means of making a painless end of himself; but it was not a course that he considered seriously. When Mildred had left him to go with Griffiths his anguish had been so great that he wanted to die in order to get rid of the pain. He did not feel like that now. He wished only that he could talk his worries over with somebody, but he could not bring himself to confess them. He was ashamed. He went on looking for work. He

left his rent unpaid for three weeks, explaining to his landlady that he would get money at the end of the month; she
did not say anything, but pursed her lips and looked grim.
When the end of the month came and she asked if it would
be convenient for him to pay something on account, it made
him feel very sick to say that he could not; he told her he
would write to his uncle and was sure to be able to settle
his bill on the following Saturday.

"Well, I 'ope you will, Mr. Carey, because I 'ave my rent
to pay, and I can't afford to let accounts run on." She did
not speak with anger, but with determination that was
rather frightening. She paused for a moment and then said:
"If you don't pay next Saturday, I shall 'ave to complain to
the secretary of the 'ospital."

"Oh yes, that'll be all right."

She looked at him for a little and glanced round the bare
room. When she spoke it was without any emphasis, as
thought it were quite a natural thing to say.

"I've got a nice 'ot joint downstairs, and if you like to
come down to the kitchen you're welcome to a bit of dinner."

Philip felt himself redden to the soles of his feet, and a sob
caught at his throat.

"Thank you very much, Mrs. Higgins, but I'm not at all
hungry."

"Very good, sir."

When she left the room Philip threw himself on his bed.
He had to clench his fists in order to prevent himself from
crying.

Saturday. It was the day on which he had promised to
pay his landlady. He had been expecting something to turn
up all through the week. He had found no work. He had
never been driven to extremities before, and he was so dazed
that he did not know what to do. He had at the back of
his mind a feeling that the whole thing was a preposterous

joke. He had no more than a few coppers left, he had sold all the clothes he could do without; he had some books and one or two odds and ends upon which he might have got a shilling or two, but the landlady was keeping an eye on his comings and goings: he was afraid she would stop him if he took anything more from his room. The only thing was to tell her that he could not pay his bill. He had not the courage. It was the middle of June. The night was fine and warm. He made up his mind to stay out. He walked slowly along the Chelsea Embankment, because the river was restful and quiet, till he was tired, and then sat on a bench and dozed. He did not know how long he slept; he awoke with a start, dreaming that he was being shaken by a policeman and told to move on; but when he opened his eyes he found himself alone. He walked on, he did not know why, and at last came to Chiswick, where he slept again. Presently the hardness of the bench roused him. The night seemed very long. He shivered. He was seized with a sense of misery; and he did not know what on earth to do: he was ashamed at having slept on the Embankment; it seemed peculiarly humiliating, and he felt his cheeks flush in the darkness. He remembered stories he had heard of those who did and how among them were officers, clergymen, and men who had been to universities: he wondered if he would become one of them, standing in a line to get soup from a charitable institution. It would be much better to commit suicide. He could not go on like that: Lawson would help him when he knew what straits he was in; it was absurd to let his pride prevent him from asking for assistance. He wondered why he had come such a cropper. He had always tried to do what he thought best, and everything had gone wrong. He had helped people when he could, he did not think he had been more selfish than anyone else, it seemed horribly unjust that he should be reduced to such a pass.

He thought of his uncle, who had told him that he would leave him at his death the little he had; Philip did not in the least know how much this was: it could not be more than a few hundred pounds. He wondered whether he could raise money on the reversion. Not without the old man's consent, and that he would never give.

"The only thing I can do is to hang on somehow till he dies."

He went on in this way for several days. He had very little food and began to feel weak and ill, so that he had hardly enough energy to go on looking for the work which seemed so desperately hard to find. He was growing used now to the long waiting at the back of a shop on the chance that he would be taken on, and the curt dismissal. He walked to all parts of London in answer to the advertisments, and he came to know by sight men who applied as fruitlessly as himself. One or two tried to make friends with him, but he was too tired and too wretched to accept their advances. He did not go any more to Lawson, because he owed him five shillings. He began to be too dazed to think clearly and ceased very much to care what would happen to him. He cried a good deal. At first he was very angry with himself for this and ashamed, but he found it relieved him, and somehow made him feel less hungry. In the very early morning he suffered a good deal from cold. One night he went into his room to change his linen; he slipped in about three, when he was quite sure everyone would be asleep, and out again at five; he lay on the bed and its softness was enchanting; all his bones ached, and as he lay he revelled in the pleasure of it; it was so delicious that he did not want to go to sleep. He was growing used to want of food and did not feel very hungry, but only weak. Constantly now at the back of his mind was the thought of doing away with himself, but he used all the strength he had not to dwell on it, because he was afraid the temptation would get hold of him so that he would not be able to help himself. He kept on saying to himself that it would be absurd to commit suicide, since something must happen soon; he could not get over the impression that his situation was too preposterous to be taken quite seriously; it was like an illness which must be endured but from which he was bound to recover. Every night he swore that nothing would induce him to put up with such another and determined next morning to write to his uncle, or to Mr. Nixon, the solicitor, or to Lawson; but when the time came he could not bring himself to make the humiliating confession of his utter failure. He did not know how Lawson would take it. In their friendship Lawson had been scatterbrained and he had prided himself on his common sense. He would have to tell the whole history of his folly. He had an uneasy feeling that Lawson, after helping him, would turn the cold shoulder on him. His uncle and the solicitor would of course do something for him, but he dreaded their reproaches. He did not want anyone to reproach him: he clenched his teeth and repeated that what had happened was inevitable just because it had happened. Regret was absurd.

The days were unending. Philip longed for Sunday to come so that he could go to Athelny's. He did not know what prevented him from going there sooner, except perhaps that he wanted so badly to get through on his own; for Athelny, who had been in straits as desperate, was the only person who could do anything for him. Perhaps after dinner he could bring himself to tell Athelny that he was in difficulties. Philip repeated to himself over and over again what he should say to him. He was dreadfully afraid that Athelny would put him off with airy phrases: that would be so horrible that he wanted to delay as long as possible the putting of him to the test. Philip had lost all confidence in his fellows.

Saturday night was cold and raw. Philip suffered horribly. From mid-day on Saturday till he dragged himself wearily to Athelny's house he ate nothing. He spent his last twopence on Sunday morning on a wash and a brush up in the lavatory at Charing Cross.

When Philip rang a head was put out of the window, and in a minute he heard a noisy clatter on the stairs as the children ran down to let him in. It was a pale, anxious, thin face that he bent down for them to kiss. He was so moved by their exuberant affection that, to give himself time to recover, he made excuses to linger on the stairs. He was in a hysterical state and almost anything was enough to make him cry. They asked him why he had not come on the previous Sunday, and he told them he had been ill; they wanted to know what was the matter with him; and Philip, to amuse them, suggested a mysterious ailment, the name of which, double-barrelled and barbarous with its mixture of Greek and Latin (medical nomenclature bristled with such), made them shriek with delight. They dragged Philip into the parlour and made him repeat it for their father's edification. Athelny got up and shook hands with him. He stared at Philip, but with his round, bulging eyes he always seemed to stare, Philip did not know why on this occasion it made him self-conscious.

"We missed you last Sunday," he said.

Philip could never tell lies without embarrassment, and he was scarlet when he finished his explanation for not coming. Then Mrs. Athelny entered and shook hands with him.

"I hope you're better, Mr. Carey," she said.

He did not know why she imagined that anything had been the matter with him, for the kitchen door was closed when he came up with the children, and they had not left him.

"Dinner won't be ready for another ten minutes," she said, in her slow drawl. "Won't you have an egg beaten up in a glass of milk while you're waiting?"

There was a look of concern on her face which made Philip uncomfortable. He forced a laugh and answered that he was not at all hungry. Sally came in to lay the table, and Philip began to chaff her. It was the family joke that she would be as fat as an aunt of Mrs. Athelny, called Aunt Elizabeth, whom the children had never seen but regarded as the type of obscene corpulence.

"I say, what *has* happened since I saw you last, Sally?" Philip began.

"Nothing that I know of."

"I believe you've been putting on weight."

"I'm sure you haven't," she retorted. "You're a perfect skeleton."

Philip reddened.

"That's a *tu quoque,* Sally," cried her father. "You will be fined one golden hair of your head. Jane, fetch the shears."

"Well, he is thin, father," remonstrated Sally. "He's just skin and bone."

"That's not the question, child. He is at perfect liberty to be thin, but your obesity is contrary to decorum."

As he spoke he put his arm proudly round her waist and looked at her with admiring eyes.

"Let me get on with the table, father. If I am comfortable there are some who don't seem to mind it."

"The hussy!" cried Athelny, with a dramatic wave of the hand. "She taunts me with the notorious fact that Joseph, a son of Levi who sells jewels in Holborn, has made her an offer of marriage."

"Have you accepted him, Sally?" asked Philip.

"Don't you know father better than that by this time? There's not a word of truth in it."

"Well, if he hasn't made you an offer of marriage," cried Athelny, "by Saint George and Merry England, I will seize him by the nose and demand of him immediately what are his intentions."

"Sit down, father, dinner's ready. Now then, you children, get along with you and wash your hands all of you, and don't shirk it, because I mean to look at them before you have a scrap of dinner, so there."

Philip thought he was ravenous till he began to eat, but then discovered that his stomach turned against food, and he could eat hardly at all. His brain was weary; and he did not notice that Athelny, contrary to his habit, spoke very little. Philip was relieved to be sitting in a comfortable house, but every now and then he could not prevent himself from glancing out of the window. The day was tempestuous. The fine weather had broken; and it was cold, and there was a bitter wind; now and again gusts of rain drove against the window. Philip wondered what he should do that night. The Athelnys went to bed early, and he could not stay where he was after ten o'clock. His heart sank at the thought of going out into the bleak darkness. It seemed more terrible now that he was with his friends than when he was outside and alone. He kept on saying to himself that there were plenty more who would be spending the night out of doors. He strove to distract his mind by talking, but in the middle of his words a spatter of rain against the window would make him start.

"It's like March weather," said Athelny. "Not the sort of day one would like to be crossing the Channel."

Presently they finished, and Sally came in and cleared away.

"Would you like a twopenny stinker?" said Athelny, handing him a cigar.

Philip took it and inhaled the smoke with delight. It soothed him extraordinarily. When Sally had finished Athelny told her to shut the door after her.

"Now we shan't be disturbed," he said, turning to Philip. "I've arranged with Betty not to let the children come in till I call them."

Philip gave him a startled look, but before he could take in the meaning of his words, Athelny, fixing his glasses on his nose with the gesture habitual to him, went on.

"I wrote to you last Sunday to ask if anything was the

matter with you, and as you didn't answer I went to your rooms on Wednesday."

Philip turned his head away and did not answer. His heart began to beat violently. Athelny did not speak, and presently the silence seemed intolerable to Philip. He could not think of a single word to say.

"Your landlady told me you hadn't been in since Saturday night, and she said you owed her for the last month. Where have you been sleeping all this week?"

It made Philip sick to answer. He stared out of the window.

"Nowhere."

"I tried to find you."

"Why?" asked Philip.

"Betty and I have been just as broke in our day, only we had babies to look after. Why didn't you come here?"

"I couldn't."

Philip was afraid he was going to cry. He felt very weak. He shut his eyes and frowned, trying to control himself. He felt a sudden flash of anger with Athelny because he would not leave him alone; but he was broken; and presently, his eyes still closed, slowly in order to keep his voice steady, he told him the story of his adventures during the last few weeks. As he spoke it seemed to him that he had behaved inanely, and it made it still harder to tell. He felt that Athelny would think him an utter fool.

"Now you're coming to live with us till you find something to do," said Athelny, when he had finished.

Philip flushed, he knew not why.

"Oh, it's awfully kind of you, but I don't think I'll do that."

"Why not?"

Philip did not answer. He had refused instinctively from fear that he would be a bother, and he had a natural bashfulness of accepting favours. He knew besides that the Athelnys lived from hand to mouth, and with their large family had neither space nor money to entertain a stranger.

"Of course you must come here," said Athelny. "Thorpe will tuck in with one of his brothers and you can sleep in his bed. You don't suppose your food's going to make any difference to us."

Philip was afraid to speak, and Athelny, going to the door, called his wife.

"Betty," he said, when she came in, "Mr. Carey's coming to live with us."

"Oh, that is nice," she said. "I'll go and get the bed ready."

She spoke in such a hearty, friendly tone, taking everything for granted, that Philip was deeply touched. He never expected people to be kind to him, and when they were it surprised and moved him. Now he could not prevent two large tears from rolling down his cheeks. The Athelnys discussed the arrangements and pretended not to notice to what a state his weakness had brought him. When Mrs. Athelny left them Philip leaned back in his chair, and looking out of the window laughed a little.

"It's not a very nice night to be out, is it?"

Athelny told Philip that he could easily get him something to do in the large firm of linendrapers in which himself worked. Several of the assistants had gone to the war, and Lynn and Sedley with patriotic zeal had promised to keep their places open for them. They put the work of the heroes on those who remained, and since they did not increase the wages of these were able at once to exhibit public spirit and effect an economy; but the war continued and trade was less depressed; the holidays were coming, when numbers of the staff went away for a fortnight at a time: they were bound to engage more assistants. Philip's experience had made him doubtful whether even then they would engage him; but Athelny, representing himself as a person of consequence in the firm, insisted that the manager could refuse him nothing. Philip, with his training in Paris, would be very

useful; it was only a matter of waiting a little and he was
bound to get a well-paid job to design costumes and draw
posters. Philip made a poster for the summer sale and
Athelny took it away. Two days later he brought it back,
saying that the manager admired it very much and regretted
with all his heart that there was no vacancy just then in that
department. Philip asked whether there was nothing else
he could do.

"I'm afraid not."

"Are you quite sure?"

"Well, the fact is they're advertising for a shop-walker tomorrow," said Athelny, looking at him doubtfully through
his glasses.

"D'you think I stand any chance of getting it?"

Athelny was a little confused; he had led Philip to expect something much more splendid; on the other hand
he was too poor to go on providing him indefinitely with
board and lodging.

"You might take it while you wait for something better.
You always stand a better chance if you're engaged by the
firm already."

"I'm not proud, you know," smiled Philip.

"If you decide on that you must be there at a quarter to
nine tomorrow morning."

Notwithstanding the war there was evidently much difficulty in finding work, for when Philip went to the shop
many men were waiting already. He recognised some whom
he had seen in his own searching, and there was one whom
he had noticed lying about the park in the afternoon. To
Philip now that suggested that he was as homeless as himself and passed the night out of doors. The men were of all
sorts, old and young, tall and short; but every one had
tried to make himself smart for the interview with the manager: they had carefully brushed hair and scrupulously clean
hands. They waited in a passage which Philip learnt afterwards led up to the dining-hall and the work rooms; it was

broken every few yards by five or six steps. Though there was electric light in the shop here was only gas, with wire cages over it for protection, and it flared noisily. Philip arrived punctually, but it was nearly ten o'clock when he was admitted into the office. It was three-cornered, like a cut of cheese lying on its side: on the walls were pictures of women in corsets, and two poster-proofs, one of a man in pyjamas, green and white in large stripes, and the other of a ship in full sail ploughing an azure sea: on the sail was printed in large letters 'great white sale.' The widest side of the office was the back of one of the shop-windows, which was being dressed at the time, and an assistant went to and fro during the interview. The manager was reading a letter. He was a florid man, with sandy hair and a large sandy moustache; from the middle of his watch-chain hung a bunch of football medals. He sat in his shirt-sleeves at a large desk with a telephone by his side; before him were the day's advertisements, Athelny's work, and cuttings from newspapers pasted on a card. He gave Philip a glance but did not speak to him; he dictated a letter to the typist, a girl who sat at a small table in one corner; then he asked Philip his name, age, and what experience he had had. He spoke with a cockney twang in a high, metallic voice which he seemed not able always to control; Philip noticed that his upper teeth were large and protruding; they gave you the impression that they were loose and would come out if you gave them a sharp tug.

"I think Mr. Athelny has spoken to you about me," said Philip.

"Oh, you are the young feller who did that poster?"

"Yes, sir."

"No good to us, you know, not a bit of good."

He looked Philip up and down. He seemed to notice that Philip was in some way different from the men who had preceded him.

"You'd 'ave to get a frock coat, you know. I suppose you

'aven't got one. You seem a respectable young feller. I suppose you found art didn't pay."

Philip could not tell whether he meant to engage him or not. He threw remarks at him in a hostile way.

"Where's your home?"

"My father and mother died when I was a child."

"I like to give young fellers a chance. Many's the one I've given their chance to and they're managers of departments now. And they're grateful to me, I'll say that for them. They know what I done for them. Start at the bottom of the ladder, that's the only way to learn the business, and then if you stick to it there's no knowing what it can lead to. If you suit, one of these days you may find yourself in a position like what mine is. Bear that in mind, young feller."

"I'm very anxious to do my best, sir," said Philip.

He knew that he must put in the sir whenever he could, but it sounded odd to him, and he was afraid of overdoing it. The manager liked talking. It gave him a happy consciousness of his own importance, and he did not give Philip his decision till he had used a great many words.

"Well, I daresay you'll do," he said at last, in a pompous way. "Anyhow I don't mind giving you a trial."

"Thank you very much, sir."

"You can start at once. I'll give you six shillings a week and your keep. Everything found, you know; the six shillings is only pocket money, to do what you like with, paid monthly. Start on Monday. I suppose you've got no cause of complaint with that."

"No, sir."

"Harrington Street, d'you know where that is, Shaftesbury Avenue. That's where you sleep. Number ten, it is. You can sleep there on Sunday night, if you like; that's just as you please, or you can send your box there on Monday." The manager nodded: "Good-morning."

Mrs. Athelny lent Philip money to pay his landlady enough of her bill to let him take his things away. For five shillings and the pawn-ticket on a suit he was able to get from a pawnbroker a frock coat which fitted him fairly well. He redeemed the rest of his clothes. He sent his box to Harrington Street by Carter Patterson and on Monday morning went with Athelny to the shop. Athelny introduced him to the buyer of the costumes and left him. The buyer was a pleasant, fussy little man of thirty, named Sampson; he shook hands with Philip, and, in order to show his own accomplishment of which he was very proud, asked him if he spoke French. He was surprised when Philip told him he did.

"Any other language?"

"I speak German."

"Oh! I go over to Paris myself occasionally. *Parlez-vous français?* Ever been to Maxim's?"

Philip was stationed at the top of the stairs in the 'costumes.' His work consisted in directing people to the various departments. There seemed a great many of them as Mr. Sampson tripped them off his tongue. Suddenly he noticed that Philip limped.

"What's the matter with your leg?" he asked.

"I've got a club-foot," said Philip. "But it doesn't prevent my walking or anything like that."

The buyer looked at it for a moment doubtfully, and Philip surmised that he was wondering why the manager had engaged him. Philip knew that he had not noticed there was anything the matter with him.

"I don't expect you to get them all correct the first day. If you're in any doubt all you've got to do is to ask one of the young ladies."

Mr. Sampson turned away; and Philip, trying to remember where this or the other department was, watched anxiously for the customer in search of information. Philip was glad to get back into the department. He was beginning to

315

remember where each one was, and had less often to ask
one of the assistants, when somebody wanted to know the
way.

"First to the right. Second on the left, madam."

One or two of the girls spoke to him, just a word when
things were slack, and he felt they were taking his measure. At five he was sent up again to the dining-room for tea.
He was glad to sit down. There were large slices of bread
heavily spread with butter; and many had pots of jam,
which were kept in the 'store' and had their names written
on.

Philip was exhausted when work stopped at half past
six. Harris, the man he had sat next to at dinner, offered to
take him over to Harrington Street to show him where he
was to sleep. He told Philip there was a spare bed in his
room, and, as the other rooms were full, he expected Philip
would be put there. The house in Harrington Street had
been a bootmaker's; and the shop was used as a bed-room;
but it was very dark, since the window had been boarded
three parts up, and as this did not open the only ventilation
came from a small skylight at the far end. There was a
musty smell, and Philip was thankful that he would not
have to sleep there. Harris took him up to the sitting-room,
which was on the first floor; it had an old piano in it with
a keyboard that looked like a row of decayed teeth; and on
the table in a cigar-box without a lid was a set of dominoes;
old numbers of *The Strand Magazine* and of *The Graphic*
were lying about. The other rooms were used as bed-rooms.
That in which Philip was to sleep was at the top of the
house. There were six beds in it, and a trunk or a box stood
by the side of each. The only furniture was a chest of drawers: it had four large drawers and two small ones, and Philip
as the new-comer had one of these; there were keys to them,
but as they were all alike they were not of much use, and
Harris advised him to keep his valuables in his trunk. There
was a looking-glass on the chimney-piece. Harris showed

Philip the lavatory, which was a fairly large room with eight basins in a row, and here all the inmates did their washing. It led into another room in which were two baths, discoloured, the woodwork stained with soap; and in them were dark rings at various intervals which indicated the water marks of different baths.

Philip went to sleep. He was awaked at seven by the loud ringing of a bell, and by a quarter to eight they were all dressed and hurrying downstairs in their stockinged feet to pick out their boots. They laced them as they ran along to the shop in Oxford Street for breakfast. If they were a minute later than eight they got none, nor, once in, were they allowed out to get themselves anything to eat. Sometimes, if they knew they could not get into the building in time, they stopped at the little shop near their quarters and bought a couple of buns; but this cost money, and most went without food till dinner. Philip ate some bread and butter, drank a cup of tea, and at half past eight began his day's work again.

"First to the right. Second on the left, madam."

Soon he began to answer the questions quite mechanically. The work was monotonous and very tiring. After a few days his feet hurt him so that he could hardly stand: the thick soft carpets made them burn, and at night his socks were painful to remove. It was a common complaint, and his fellow 'floormen' told him that socks and boots just rotted away from the continual sweating. All the men in his room suffered in the same fashion, and they relieved the pain by sleeping with their feet outside the bed-clothes. At first Philip could not walk at all and was obliged to spend a good many of his evenings in the sitting-room at Harrington Street with his feet in a pail of cold water.

The wages were paid once a month by the secretary. On pay-day each batch of assistants, coming down from tea, went into the passage and joined the long line of people waiting orderly like the audience in a queue outside a gallery door. One by one they entered the office. The secretary sat at a desk with wooden bowls of money in front of him, and he asked the employé's name; he referred to a book, quickly, after a suspicious glance at the assistant, said aloud the sum due, and taking money out of the bowl counted it into his hand.

"Thank you," he said. "Next."

"Thank you," was the reply.

Philip found himself with eighteen shillings left out of his month's pay. It was the first money he had ever earned in his life. It gave him none of the pride which might have been expected, but merely a feeling of dismay. The smallness of the sum emphasised the hopelessness of his position. He took fifteen shillings to Mrs. Athelny to pay back part of what he owed her, but she would not take more than half a sovereign.

"D'you know, at that rate it'll take me eight months to settle up with you."

"As long as Athelny's in work I can afford to wait, and who knows, p'raps they'll give you a rise."

At first Philip, in order not to forget what he had learned, tried to go on reading his medical books, but he found it useless; he could not fix his attention on them after the exhausting work of the day; and it seemed hopeless to continue working when he did not know in how long he would be able to go back to the hospital. He dreamed constantly that he was in the wards. The awakening was painful. The sensation of other people sleeping in the room was inexpressibly irksome to him; he had been used to solitude, and to be with others always, never to be by himself for an instant, was at these moments horrible to him. It was then that he found it most difficult to combat his despair. He saw himself going on with that life, first to the right, second on the left, madam, indefinitely; and having to be thankful if he was not sent away: the men who had gone to the war would be coming home soon, the firm had guaranteed to take them back, and this must mean that others would be sacked; he would have to stir himself even to keep the wretched post he had.

There was only one thing to free him and that was the death of his uncle. He would get a few hundred pounds then, and on this he could finish his course at the hospital. Philip began to wish with all his might for the old man's death. He reckoned out how long he could possibly live: he was well over seventy, Philip did not know his exact age, but he must be at least seventy-five; he suffered from chronic bronchitis and every winter had a bad cough. Though he knew them by heart Philip read over and over again the details in his text-book of medicine of chronic bronchitis in the old. A severe winter might be too much for the old man. With all his heart Philip longed for cold and rain. He thought of it constantly, so that it became a monomania. Uncle William was affected by the great heat too, and in August they had three weeks of sweltering weather. Philip imagined to himself that one day perhaps a telegram would come saying that the Vicar had died suddenly, and he pictured to himself his unutterable relief. As he stood at the top of the stairs and directed people to the departments they wanted, he occupied his mind with thinking incessantly what he would do with the money. He did not know how much it would be, perhaps no more than five hundred pounds, but even that would be enough. He would leave the shop at once, he would not bother to give notice, he would pack his box and go without saying a word to anybody; and then he would return to the hospital. That was the first thing. Would he have forgotten much? In six months he could get it all back, and then he would take his three examinations as soon as he could, midwifery first, then medicine and surgery. The awful fear seized him that his uncle, notwithstanding his promises, might leave everything he had to the parish or the church. The thought made

Philip sick. He could not be so cruel. But if that happened Philip was quite determined what to do, he would not go on in that way indefinitely; his life was only tolerable because he could look forward to something better. If he had no hope he would have no fear. The only brave thing to do then would be to commit suicide, and, thinking this over too, Philip decided minutely what painless drug he would take and how he would get hold of it. It encouraged him to think that, if things became unendurable, he had at all events a way out.

"Second to the right, madam, and down the stairs. First on the left and straight through. Mr. Philips, forward please."

Philip avoided the places he had known in happier times. The little gatherings at the tavern in Beak Street were broken up: Macalister, having let down his friends, no longer went there, and Hayward was at the Cape. Only Lawson remained; and Philip, feeling that now the painter and he had nothing in common, did not wish to see him; but one Saturday afternoon, after dinner, having changed his clothes he walked down Regent Street to go to the free library in St. Martin's Lane, meaning to spend the afternoon there, and suddenly found himself face to face with him. His first instinct was to pass on without a word, but Lawson did not give him the opportunity.

"I say, won't you come to the studio and have a talk?"

"No," said Philip.

"Why not?"

"There's nothing to talk about."

He saw the pain come into Lawson's eyes, he could not help it, he was sorry, but he had to think of himself; he could not bear the thought of discussing his situation, he could endure it only by determining resolutely not to think about it. He was afraid of his weakness if once he began to open his heart. Moreover, he took irresistible dislikes to the places where he had been miserable: he remembered the humiliation he had endured when he had waited in that studio, ravenous with hunger, for Lawson to offer him a meal, and the last occasion when he taken the five shillings off him. He hated the sight of Lawson, because he recalled those days of utter abasement.

"Then look here, come and dine with me one night. Choose your own evening."

Philip was touched with the painter's kindness. All sorts of people were strangely kind to him, he thought.

"It's awfully good of you, old man, but I'd rather not." He held out his hand. "Good-bye."

Lawson, troubled by a behaviour which seemed inexplicable, took his hand, and Philip quickly limped away. His heart was heavy; and, as was usual with him, he began to reproach himself for what he had done: he did not know what madness of pride had made him refuse the offered friendship. But he heard someone running behind him and presently Lawson's voice calling him; he stopped and suddenly the feeling of hostility got the better of him; he presented to Lawson a cold, set face.

"What is it?"

"I suppose you heard about Hayward, didn't you?"

"I know he went to the Cape."

"He died, you know, soon after landing."

For a moment Philip did not answer. He could hardly believe his ears.

"How?" he asked.

"Oh, enteric. Hard luck, wasn't it? I thought you mightn't know. Gave me a bit of a turn when I heard it."

Lawson nodded quickly and walked away. Philip felt a shiver pass through his heart. He had never before lost a friend of his own age. The news gave him a peculiar shock. It reminded him of his own mortality, for like everyone else Philip, knowing perfectly that all men must die, had no intimate feeling that the same must apply to himself; and

Hayward's death, though he had long ceased to have any warm feeling for him, affected him deeply. He remembered on a sudden all the good talks they had had, and it pained him to think that they would never talk with one another again; he remembered their first meeting and the pleasant months they had spent together in Heidelberg. Philip's heart sank as he thought of the lost years.

He thought of Hayward and his eager admiration for him when first they met, and how disillusion had come and then indifference, till nothing held them together but habit and old memories. It was one of the queer things of life that you saw a person every day for months and were so intimate with him that you could not imagine existence without him; then separation came, and everything went on in the same way, and the companion who had seemed essential proved unnecessary. Your life proceeded and you did not even miss him. Philip thought of those early days in Heidelberg when Hayward, capable of great things, had been full of enthusiasm for the future, and how, little by little, achieving nothing, he had resigned himself to failure. Now he was dead. His death had been as futile as his life. He died ingloriously, of a stupid disease, failing once more, even at the end, to accomplish anything. It was just the same now as if he had never lived.

The autumn passed into winter. Philip had left his address with Mrs. Foster, his uncle's housekeeper, so that she might communicate with him, but still went once a week to the hospital on the chance of there being a letter. One evening he saw his name on an envelope in a handwriting he had hoped never to see again. It gave him a queer feeling. For a little while he could not bring himself to take it. It brought back a host of hateful memories. But at length, impatient with himself, he ripped open the envelope.

> 7 William Street,
> Fitzroy Square.

Dear Phil,
   Can I see you for a minute or two as soon as possible. I am
in awful trouble and don't know what to do. It's not money.
> Yours truly,
> Mildred.

He tore the letter into little bits and going out into the
street scattered them in the darkness.

"I'll see her damned," he muttered.

A feeling of disgust surged up in him at the thought of
seeing her again. He did not care if she was in distress, it
served her right whatever it was, he thought of her with
hatred, and the love he had had for her aroused his loathing.
His recollections filled him with nausea, and as he walked
across the Thames he drew himself aside in an instinctive
withdrawal from his thought of her. He went to bed, but he
could not sleep; he wondered what was the matter with her,
and he could not get out of his head the fear that she was ill
and hungry; she would not have written to him unless she
were desperate. He was angry with himself for his weakness,
but he knew that he would have no peace unless he saw her.
Next morning he wrote a letter-card and posted it on his
way to the shop. He made it as stiff as he could and said
merely that he was sorry she was in difficulties and would
come to the address she had given at seven o'clock that evening.

It was that of a shabby lodging-house in a sordid street;
and when, sick at the thought of seeing her, he asked
whether she was in, a wild hope seized him that she had left.
It looked the sort of place people moved in and out of frequently. He had not thought of looking at the postmark on
her letter and did not know how many days it had lain in
the rack. The woman who answered the bell did not reply to

his inquiry, but silently preceded him along the passage and knocked on a door at the back.

"Mrs. Miller, a gentleman to see you," she called.

The door was slightly opened, and Mildred looked out suspiciously.

"Oh, it's you," she said. "Come in."

He walked in and she closed the door. It was a very small bed-room, untidy as was every place she lived in; there was a pair of shoes on the floor, lying apart from one another and uncleaned; a hat was on the chest of drawers, with false curls beside it; and there was a blouse on the table. Philip looked for somewhere to put his hat. The hooks behind the door were laden with skirts, and he noticed that they were muddy at the hem.

"Sit down, won't you?" she said. Then she gave a little awkward laugh. "I suppose you were surprised to hear from me again."

"You're awfully hoarse," he answered. "Have you got a sore throat?"

"Yes, I have had for some time."

He did not say anything. He waited for her to explain why she wanted to see him. The look of the room told him clearly enough that she had gone back to the life from which he had taken her. He wondered what had happened to the baby; there was a photograph of it on the chimney-piece, but no sign in the room that a child was ever there. Mildred was holding her handkerchief. She made it into a little ball, and passed it from hand to hand. He saw that she was very nervous. She was staring at the fire, and he could look at her without meeting her eyes. She was much thinner than when she had left him; and the skin, yellow and dryish, was drawn more tightly over her cheek-bones. She had dyed her hair and it was now flaxen: it altered her a good deal, and made her look more vulgar.

"I was relieved to get your letter, I can tell you," she said at last. "I thought p'raps you weren't at the 'ospital any more."

Philip did not speak.

"I suppose you're qualified by now, aren't you?"

"No."

"How's that?"

"I'm no longer at the hospital. I had to give it up eighteen months ago."

"You are changeable. You don't seem as if you could stick to anything."

Philip was silent for another moment, and when he went on it was with coldness.

"I lost the little money I had in an unlucky speculation and I couldn't afford to go on with the medical. I had to earn my living as best I could."

"What are you doing then?"

"I'm in a shop."

"Oh!"

She gave him a quick glance and turned her eyes away at once. He thought that she reddened. She dabbed her palms nervously with the handkerchief.

"You've not forgotten all your doctoring, have you?" She jerked the words out quite oddly.

"Not entirely."

"Because that's why I wanted to see you." Her voice sank to a hoarse whisper. "I don't know what's the matter with me."

"Why don't you go to a hospital?"

"I don't like to do that, and have all the stoodents staring at me, and I'm afraid they'd want to keep me."

"What are you complaining of?" asked Philip coldly, with the stereotyped phrase used in the out-patients' room.

"Well, I've come out in a rash, and I can't get rid of it."

Philip felt a twinge of horror in his heart. Sweat broke out on his forehead.

"Let me look at your throat?"

He took her over to the window and made such examination as he could. Suddenly he caught sight of her eyes. There
was deadly fear in them. It was horrible to see. She was terrified. She wanted him to reassure her; she looked at him
pleadingly, not daring to ask for words of comfort but with
all her nerves astrung to receive them: he had none to offer
her.

"I'm afraid you're very ill indeed," he said.

"What d'you think it is?"

When he told her she grew deathly pale, and her lips even
turned yellow; she began to cry, hopelessly, quietly at first
and then with choking sobs.

"I'm awfully sorry," he said at last. "But I had to tell you."

"I may just as well kill myself and have done with it."

He took no notice of the threat.

"Have you got any money?" he asked.

"Six or seven pounds."

"You must give up this life, you know. Don't you think
you could find some work to do? I'm afraid I can't help
you much. I only get twelve bob a week."

"What is there I can do now?" she cried impatiently.

"Damn it all, you *must* try to get something."

He spoke to her very gravely, telling her of her own danger and the danger to which she exposed others, and she
listened sullenly. He tried to console her. At last he brought
her to a sulky acquiescence in which she promised to do all
he advised. He wrote a prescription, which he said he would
leave at the nearest chemist's, and he impressed upon her
the necessity of taking her medicine with the utmost regu-
larity. Getting up to go, he held out his hand.

"Don't be downhearted, you'll soon get over your throat."

But as he went her face became suddenly distorted, and
she caught hold of his coat.

"Oh, don't leave me," she cried hoarsely. "I'm so afraid,
don't leave me alone yet. Phil, please. There's no one else I
can go to, you're the only friend I've ever had."

He felt the terror of her soul. Philip looked down. Twice that woman had come into his life and made him wretched; she had no claim upon him; and yet, he knew not why, deep in his heart was a strange aching; it was that which, when he received her letter, had left him no peace till he obeyed her summons.

"I suppose I shall never really quite get over it," he said to himself.

What perplexed him was that he felt a curious physical distaste, which made it uncomfortable for him to be near her.

"What do you want me to do?" he asked.

"Let's go out and dine together. I'll pay."

He hesitated. He felt that she was creeping back again into his life when he thought she was gone out of it for ever. She watched him with sickening anxiety.

"Oh, I know I've treated you shocking, but don't leave me alone now. You've had your revenge. If you leave me by myself now I don't know what I shall do."

"All right, I don't mind," he said, "but we shall have to do it on the cheap, I haven't got money to throw away these days."

She sat down and put her shoes on, then changed her skirt and put on a hat; and they walked out together till they found a restaurant in the Tottenham Court Road. Philip had got out of the habit of eating at those hours, and Mildred's throat was so sore that she could not swallow. They had a little cold ham and Philip drank a glass of beer. They sat opposite one another, as they had so often sat before; he wondered if she remembered; they had nothing to say to one another and would have sat in silence if Philip had not forced himself to talk. In the bright light of the restaurant, with its vulgar looking-glasses that reflected in an endless series, she looked old and haggard. Philip was anxious to know about the child, but he had not the courage to ask. At last she said:

"You know baby died last summer."

"Oh!" he said.

"You might say you're sorry."

"I'm not," he answered, "I'm very glad."

She glanced at him and, understanding what he meant, looked away.

"You were rare stuck on it at one time, weren't you? I always thought it funny like how you could see so much in another man's child."

When they had finished eating they called at the chemist's for the medicine Philip had ordered, and going back to the shabby room he made her take a dose. Then they sat together till it was time for Philip to go back to Harrington Street. He was hideously bored.

Philip went to see her every day. She took the medicine he had prescribed and followed his directions, and soon the results were so apparent that she gained the greatest confidence in Philip's skill. As she grew better she grew less despondent. She talked more freely.

"As soon as I can get a job I shall be all right," she said. "I've had my lesson now and I mean to profit by it. No more racketing about for yours truly."

Each time he saw her, Philip asked whether she had found work. She told him not to worry, she would find something to do as soon as she wanted it; she had several strings to her bow; it was all the better not to do anything for a week or two. He could not deny this, but at the end of that time he became more insistent. She laughed at him, she was much more cheerful now, and said he was a fussy old thing. She told him long stories of the manageresses she interviewed, for her idea was to get work at some eating-house; what they said and what she answered. Nothing definite was fixed, but she was sure to settle something at the beginning of the following week: there was no use hurrying, and it would be a mistake to take something unsuitable.

"It's absurd to talk like that," he said impatiently. "You

must take anything you can get. I can't help you, and your money won't last for ever."

"Oh, well, I've not come to the end of it yet and chance it."

He looked at her sharply. It was three weeks since his first visit, and she had then less than seven pounds. Suspicion seized him. He remembered some of the things she had said. He put two and two together. He wondered whether she had made any attempt to find work. Perhaps she had been lying to him all the time. It was very strange that her money should have lasted so long.

"What is your rent here?"

"Oh, the landlady's very nice, different from what some of them are; she's quite willing to wait till it's convenient for me to pay."

He was silent. What he suspected was so horrible that he hesitated. It was no use to ask her, she would deny everything; if he wanted to know he must find out for himself. He was in the habit of leaving her every evening at eight, and when the clock struck he got up; but instead of going back to Harrington Street he stationed himself at the corner of Fitzroy Square so that he could see anyone who came along William Street. It seemed to him that he waited an interminable time, and he was on the point of going away, thinking his surmise had been mistaken, when the door of No. 7 opened and Mildred came out. He fell back into the darkness and watched her walk towards him. She had on the hat with a quantity of feathers on it which he had seen in her room, and she wore a dress he recognized, too showy for the street and unsuitable to the time of year. He followed her slowly till she came into the Tottenham Court Road, where she slackened her pace; at the corner of Oxford Street she stopped, looked round, and crossed over to a music-hall. He went up to her and touched her on the arm. He saw that she had rouged her cheeks and painted her lips.

"Where are you going, Mildred?"

She started at the sound of his voice and reddened as she

always did when she was caught in a lie; then the flash of
anger which he knew so well came into her eyes as she instinctively sought to defend herself by abuse. But she did not
say the words which were on the tip of her tongue.

"Oh, I was only going to see the show. It gives me the
hump sitting every night by myself."

He did not pretend to believe her.

"You mustn't. Good heavens, I've told you fifty times
how dangerous it is. You must stop this sort of thing at
once."

"Oh, hold your jaw," she cried roughly. "How d'you
suppose I'm going to live?"

He took hold of her arm and without thinking what he
was doing tried to drag her away.

"For God's sake come along. Let me take you home. You
don't know what you're doing. It's criminal."

"What do I care? Let them take their chance. Men haven't
been so good to me that I need bother my head about them."

She pushed him away and walking up to the box-office put
down her money. Philip had threepence in his pocket. He
could not follow. He turned away and walked slowly down
Oxford Street.

"I can't do anything more," he said to himself.

That was the end. He did not see her again.

The weeks passed into months. The winter wore away,
and in the parks the trees burst into bud and into leaf. A terrible lassitude settled upon Philip. Time was passing, though
it went with such heavy feet, and he thought that his youth
was going and soon he would have lost it and nothing would
have been accomplished.

When at last the news came that the Vicar was dying
Philip, who had been thinking of other things, was taken by
surprise. It was in July, and in another fortnight he was to
have gone for his holiday. He received a letter from Mrs.
Foster to say the doctor did not give Mr. Carey many days

to live, and if Philip wished to see him again he must come
at once. Philip went to the buyer and told him he wanted to
leave. Mr. Sampson was a decent fellow, and when he knew
the circumstances made no difficulties. Philip said good-bye
to the people in his department; the reason of his leaving
had spread among them in an exaggerated form, and they
thought he had come into a fortune.

It was strange, but he was actually sorry to leave these
people whom he thought he had loathed, and when he
drove away from the house in Harrington Street it was with
no exultation. He had so anticipated the emotions he would
experience on this occasion that now he felt nothing: he was
as unconcerned as though he were going for a few days'
holiday.

"I've got a rotten nature," he said to himself. "I look forward to things awfully, and then when they come I'm always disappointed."

He reached Blackstable early in the afternoon. Mrs. Foster met him at the door, and her face told him that his
uncle was not yet dead.

"He's a little better today," she said. "He's got a wonderful constitution."

She led him into the bed-room where Mr. Carey lay on his
back. He gave Philip a slight smile, in which was a trace of
satisfied cunning at having circumvented his enemy once
more.

"I thought it was all up with me yesterday," he said, in
an exhausted voice. "They'd all given me up, hadn't you,
Mrs. Foster?"

"You've got a wonderful constitution, there's no denying
that."

"There's life in the old dog yet."

Mrs. Foster said that the Vicar must not talk, it would
tire him; she treated him like a child, with kindly despotism;
and there was something childish in the old man's satisfaction at having cheated all their expectations. It struck

him at once that Philip had been sent for, and he was
amused that he had been brought on a fool's errand. If he
could only avoid another of his heart attacks he would get
well enough in a week or two; and he had had the attacks
several times before; he always felt as if he were going to
die, but he never did. They all talked of his constitution, but
they none of them knew how strong it was.

"Are you going to stay a day or two?" he asked Philip,
pretending to believe he had come down for a holiday.

"I was thinking of it," Philip answered cheerfully.

"A breath of sea-air will do you good."

Presently Dr. Wigram came, and after he had seen the
Vicar talked with Philip. He adopted an appropriate manner.

"I'm afraid it is the end this time, Philip," he said. "It'll
be a great loss to all of us. I've known him for five-and-
thirty years."

"He seems well enough now," said Philip.

"I'm keeping him alive on drugs, but it can't last. It was
dreadful these last two days, I thought he was dead half a
dozen times."

The doctor was silent for a minute or two, but at the gate
he said suddenly to Philip:

"Has Mrs. Foster said anything to you?"

"What d'you mean?"

"They're very superstitious, these people: she's got hold of
an idea that he's got something on his mind, and he can't
die till he gets rid of it; and he can't bring himself to confess
it."

Philip did not answer, and the doctor went on.

"Of course it's nonsense. He's led a very good life, he's
done his duty, he's been a good parish priest, and I'm sure
we shall all miss him; he can't have anything to reproach
himself with. I very much doubt whether the next vicar
will suit us half so well."

For several days Mr. Carey continued without change.

His appetite which had been excellent left him, and he could eat little. Dr. Wigram did not hesitate now to still the pain of the neuritis which tormented him; and that, with the constant shaking of his palsied limbs, was gradually exhausting him. His mind remained clear. Philip and Mrs. Foster nursed him between them. She was so tired by the many months during which she had been attentive to all his wants that Philip insisted on sitting up with the patient so that she might have her night's rest. He passed the long hours in an arm-chair so that he should not sleep soundly, and read by the light of shaded candles *The Thousand and One Nights*. He had not read them since he was a little boy, and they brought back his childhood to him. Sometimes he sat and listened to the silence of the night. When the effects of the opiate wore off Mr. Carey grew restless and kept him constantly busy.

At last, early one morning, when the birds were chattering noisily in the trees, he heard his name called. He went up to the bed. Mr. Carey was lying on his back, with his eyes looking at the ceiling; he did not turn them on Philip. Philip saw that sweat was on his forehead, and he took a towel and wiped it.

"Is that you, Philip?" the old man asked.

Philip was startled because the voice was suddenly changed. It was hoarse and low. So would a man speak if he was cold with fear.

"Yes, d'you want anything?"

There was a pause, and still the unseeing eyes stared at the ceiling. Then a twitch passed over the face.

"I think I'm going to die," he said.

"Oh, what nonsense!" cried Philip. "You're not going to die for years."

Two tears were wrung from the old man's eyes. They moved Philip horribly. His uncle had never betrayed any particular emotion in the affairs of life; and it was dreadful to see them now, for they signified a terror that was un-speakable.

"Send for Mr. Simmonds," he said. "I want to take the Communion."

Mr. Simmonds was the curate.

"Now?" asked Philip.

"Soon, or else it'll be too late."

Philip went to awake Mrs. Foster, but it was later than he thought and she was up already. He told her to send the gardener with a message, and he went back to his uncle's room.

"Have you sent for Mr. Simmonds?"

"Yes."

There was a silence. Philip sat by the bed-side, and occasionally wiped the sweating forehead.

"Let me hold your hand, Philip," the old man said at last.

Philip gave him his hand and he clung to it as to life, for comfort in his extremity. Perhaps he had never really loved anyone in all his days, but now he turned instinctively to a human being. His hand was wet and cold. It grasped Philip's with feeble, despairing energy. The old man was fighting with the fear of death. And Philip thought that all must go through that. Oh, how monstrous it was, and they could believe in a God that allowed his creatures to suffer such a cruel torture! He had never cared for his uncle, and for two years he had longed every day for his death; but now he could not overcome the compassion that filled his heart. What a price it was to pay for being other than the beasts!

They remained in silence broken only once by a low inquiry from Mr. Carey.

"Hasn't he come yet?"

At last the housekeeper came in softly to say that Mr. Simmonds was there. He carried a bag in which were his surplice and his hood. Mrs. Foster brought the communion plate. Mr. Simmonds shook hands silently with Philip, and then with professional gravity went to the sick man's side. Philip and the maid went out of the room.

Philip walked round the garden all fresh and dewy in the morning. The birds were singing gaily. The sky was blue, but the air, salt-laden, was sweet and cool. The roses were in full bloom. The green of the trees, the green of the lawns, was eager and brilliant. Philip walked, and as he walked he thought of the mystery which was proceeding in that bedroom. It gave him a peculiar emotion. Presently Mrs. Foster came out to him and said that his uncle wished to see him. The curate was putting his things back into the black bag. The sick man turned his head a little and greeted him with a smile. Philip was astonished, for there was a change in him, an extraordinary change; his eyes had no longer the terror-stricken look, and the pinching of his face had gone: he looked happy and serene.

"I'm quite prepared now," he said, and his voice had a different tone in it. "When the Lord sees fit to call me I am ready to give my soul into his hands."

Philip did not speak. He could see that his uncle was sincere. It was almost a miracle. He had taken the body and blood of his Saviour, and they had given him strength so that he no longer feared the inevitable passage into the night. He knew he was going to die: he was resigned. He only said one thing more:

"I shall rejoin my dear wife."

It startled Philip. He remembered with what a callous selfishness his uncle had treated her, how obtuse he had been to her humble, devoted love. The curate, deeply moved, went away and Mrs. Foster, weeping, accompanied him to the door. Mr. Carey, exhausted by his effort, fell into a light doze, and Philip sat down by the bed and waited for the end. The morning wore on, and the old man's breathing grew stertorous. The doctor came and said he was dying. He was unconscious and he pecked feebly at the sheets; he was restless and he cried out. Dr. Wigram gave him a hypodermic injection.

"It can't do any good now, he may die at any moment."

The doctor looked at his watch and then at the patient. Philip saw that it one o'clock. Dr. Wigram was thinking of his dinner.

"It's no use your waiting," he said.

"There's nothing I can do," said the doctor.

Philip watched curiously the process of death. There was nothing human now in the unconscious being that struggled feebly. Sometimes a muttered ejaculation issued from the loose mouth. The sun beat down hotly from a cloudless sky, but the trees in the garden were pleasant and cool. It was a lovely day. A bluebottle buzzed against the windowpane. Suddenly there was a loud rattle, it made Philip start, it was horribly frightening; a movement passed through the limbs and the old man was dead. The machine had run down. The bluebottle buzzed, buzzed noisily against the window-pane.

Josiah Graves in his masterful way made arrangements, becoming but economical, for the funeral; and when it was over came back to the vicarage with Philip. The will was in his charge, and with a due sense of the fitness of things he read it to Philip over an early cup of tea. It was written on half a sheet of paper and left everything Mr. Carey had to his nephew. There was the furniture, about eighty pounds at the bank, twenty shares in the A. B. C. company, a few in Allsop's brewery, some in the Oxford music-hall, and a few more in a London restaurant. They had been bought under Mr. Graves' direction, and he told Philip with satisfaction:

"You see, people must eat, they will drink, and they want amusement. You're always safe if you put your money in what the public thinks necessities."

His words showed a nice discrimination between the grossness of the vulgar, which he deplored but accepted, and the finer taste of the elect. Altogether in investments there was about five hundred pounds; and to that must be added the balance at the bank and what the furniture would fetch. It was riches to Philip. He was not happy but infinitely relieved.

A few days later he went up to London, and for the first time for two years entered by day the hall of St. Luke's Hospital. He went to see the secretary of the Medical School; he was surprised to see him and asked Philip curiously what he had been doing. Philip's experiences had given him a certain confidence in himself and a different outlook upon many things: such a question would have embarrassed him before; but now he answered coolly, with a deliberate vagueness which prevented further inquiry, that private affairs had obliged him to make a break in the curriculum; he was now anxious to qualify as soon as possible. The first examination he could take was in Midwifery and the Diseases of Women, and he put his name down to be a clerk in the ward devoted to feminine ailments; since it was holiday time there happened to be no difficulty in getting a post as obstetric clerk; he arranged to undertake that duty during the last week of August and the first two of September. After this interview Philip walked through the Medical School, more or less deserted, for the examinations at the end of the summer session were all over; and he wandered along the terrace by the river-side. His heart was full. He thought that now he could begin a new life, and he would put behind him all the errors, follies, and miseries of the past. The flowing river suggested that everything passed, was passing always, and nothing mattered; the future was before him rich with possibilities.

Philip spent the few weeks that remained before the beginning of the winter session in the out-patients' department, and in October settled down to regular work. He had been away from the hospital for so long that he found himself very largely among new people; the men of different years had little to do with one another, and his contemporaries were now mostly qualified: some had left to take up assistantships or posts in country hospitals and infirmaries, and some held appointments at St. Luke's. The two years during which his mind had lain fallow had refreshed him, he fancied, and he was able now to work with energy.

The Athelnys were delighted with his change of fortune. He had kept aside a few things from the sale of his uncle's effects and gave them all presents. He gave Sally a gold chain that had belonged to his aunt. She was now grown up. She was apprenticed to a dressmaker and set out every morning at eight to work all day in a shop in Regent Street. Sally had frank blue eyes, a broad brow, and plentiful shining hair; she was buxom, with broad hips and full breasts; and her father, who was fond of discussing her appearance, warned her constantly that she must not grow fat. She attracted because she was healthy, animal, and feminine. She had many admirers, but they left her unmoved; she gave one the impression that she looked upon love-making as nonsense; and it was easy to imagine that young men found her unapproachable. Sally was old for her years: she had been used to help her mother in the household work and in the care of the children, so that she had acquired a managing air, which made her mother say that Sally was a bit too fond of having things her own way. She did not speak very much, but as she grew older she seemed to be acquiring a quiet sense of humour, and sometimes uttered a remark which suggested that beneath her impassive exterior she was quietly bubbling with amusement at her fellow-creatures. Philip found that with her he never got on the terms of affectionate intimacy upon which he was with the rest of Athelny's huge family. Now and then her indifference slightly irritated him. There was something enigmatic in her.

When Philip gave her the necklace Athelny in his boisterous way insisted that she must kiss him; but Sally reddened and drew back.

"No, I'm not going to," she said.

"Ungrateful hussy!" cried Athelny. "Why not?"

"I don't like being kissed by men," she said.

Philip saw her embarrassment, and, amused, turned Athelny's attention to something else. That was never a very difficult thing to do. But evidently her mother spoke of the matter later, for next time Philip came she took the opportunity when they were alone for a couple of minutes to refer to it.

"You didn't think it disagreeable of me last week when I wouldn't kiss you?"

"Not a bit," he laughed.

"It's not because I wasn't grateful." She blushed a little as she uttered the formal phrase which she had prepared. "I shall always value the necklace, and it was very kind of you to give it me."

Philip found it always a little difficult to talk to her. She did all that she had to do very competently, but seemed to feel no need of conversation; yet there was nothing unsociable in her. One Sunday afternoon when Athelny and his wife had gone out together, and Philip, treated as one of the family, sat reading in the parlour, Sally came in and sat by the window to sew. The girls' clothes were made at home and Sally could not afford to spend Sundays in idleness. Philip thought she wished to talk and put down his book.

"Go on reading," she said. "I only thought as you were alone I'd come and sit with you."

"You're the most silent person I've ever struck," said Philip.

"We don't want another one who's talkative in this house," she said.

There was no irony in her tone: she was merely stating a fact. But it suggested to Philip that she measured her father, alas, no longer the hero he was to her childhood, and in her mind joined together his entertaining conversation and the thriftlessness which often brought difficulties into their life; she compared his rhetoric with her mother's practical common sense; and though the liveliness of her father amused her she was perhaps sometimes a little impatient with it. Philip looked at her as she bent over her work; she was healthy, strong, and normal; it must be odd to see her among the other girls in the shop with their flat chests and anæmic faces. Mildred suffered from anæmia.

After a time it appeared that Sally had a suitor. She went out occasionally with friends she had made in the workroom, and had met a young man, an electrical engineer in a very good way of business, who was a most eligible person. One day she told her mother that he had asked her to marry him.

"What did you say?" said her mother.

"Oh, I told him I wasn't over-anxious to marry anyone just yet awhile." She paused a little as was her habit between observations. "He took on so that I said he might come to tea on Sunday."

It was an occasion that thoroughly appealed to Athelny. He rehearsed all the afternoon how he should play the heavy father for the young man's edification till he reduced his children to helpless giggling. Just before he was due Athelny routed out an Egyptian tarboosh and insisted on putting it on.

"Go on with you, Athelny," said his wife, who was in her best, which was of black velvet, and, since she was growing stouter every year, very tight for her. "You'll spoil the girl's chances."

She tried to pull it off, but the little man skipped nimbly out of her way.

"Unhand me, woman. Nothing will induce me to take it off. This young man must be shown at once that it is no ordinary family he is preparing to enter."

"Let him keep it on, mother," said Sally, in her even,

indifferent fashion. "If Mr. Donaldson doesn't take it the way it's meant he can take himself off, and good riddance."

Philip thought it was a severe ordeal that the young man was being exposed to, since Athelny, in his brown velvet jacket, flowing black tie, and red tarboosh, was a startling spectacle for an innocent electrical engineer. When he came he was greeted by his host with the proud courtesy of a Spanish grandee and by Mrs. Athelny in an altogether homely and natural fashion. They sat down at the old ironing-table in the high-backed monkish chairs, and Mrs. Athelny poured tea out of a lustre teapot which gave a note of England and the country-side to the festivity. She had made little cakes with her own hand, and on the table was home-made jam. It was a farm-house tea, and to Philip very quaint and charming in that Jacobean house. Athelny for some fantastic reason took it into his head to discourse upon Byzantine history; he had been reading the later volumes of the *Decline and Fall;* and, his forefinger dramatically extended, he poured into the astonished ears of the suitor scandalous stories about Theodora and Irene. He addressed himself directly to his guest with a torrent of rhodomontade; and the young man, reduced to helpless silence and shy, nodded his head at intervals to show that he took an intelligent interest. Mrs. Athelny paid no attention to Thorpe's conversation, but interrupted now and then to offer the young man more tea or to press upon him cake and jam. Philip watched Sally; she sat with downcast eyes, calm, silent, and observant; and her long eye-lashes cast a pretty shadow on her cheek. You could not tell whether she was amused at the scene or if she cared for the young man. She was inscrutable. But one thing was certain: the electrical engineer was good-looking, fair and clean-shaven, with pleasant, regular features, and an honest face; he was tall and well-made. Philip could not help thinking he would make an excellent mate for her, and he felt a pang of envy for the happiness which he fancied was in store for them.

Presently the suitor said he thought it was about time he was getting along. Sally rose to her feet without a word and accompanied him to the door. When she came back her father burst out:

"Well, Sally, we think your young man very nice. We are prepared to welcome him into our family. Let the banns be called and I will compose a nuptial song."

Sally set about clearing away the tea-things. She did not answer. Suddenly she shot a swift glance at Philip.

"What did you think of him, Mr. Philip?"

She had always refused to call him Uncle Phil as the other children did, and would not call him Philip.

"I think you'd make an awfully handsome pair."

She looked at him quickly once more, and then with a slight blush went on with her business.

"I thought him a very nice civil-spoken young fellow," said Mrs. Athelny, "and I think he's just the sort to make any girl happy."

Sally did not reply for a minute or two, and Philip looked at her curiously: it might be thought that she was meditating upon what her mother had said, and on the other hand she might be thinking of the man in the moon.

"Why don't you answer when you're spoken to, Sally?" remarked her mother, a little irritably.

"I thought he was a silly."

"Aren't you going to have him then?"

"No, I'm not."

At the beginning of August Philip passed his Surgery, his last examination, and received his diploma. It was seven years since he had entered St. Luke's Hospital. He was nearly thirty. He walked down the stairs of the Royal College of Surgeons with the roll in his hand which qualified him to practice, and his heart beat with satisfaction.

"Now I'm really going to begin life," he thought.

Next day he went to the secretary's office to put his name down for one of the hospital appointments. The secretary was a pleasant little man with a black beard, whom Philip had always found very affable. He congratulated him on his success, and then said:

"I suppose you wouldn't like to do a locum for a month on the South coast? Three guineas a week with board and lodging."

"I wouldn't mind," said Philip.

"It's at Farnley, in Dorsetshire. Doctor South. You'd have to go down at once; his assistant has developed mumps. I believe it's a very pleasant place."

There was something in the secretary's manner that puzzled Philip. It was a little doubtful.

"What's the crab in it?" he asked.

The secretary hesitated a moment and laughed in a conciliating fashion.

"Well, the fact is, I understand he's rather a crusty, funny old fellow. The agencies won't send him anyone any more. He speaks his mind very openly, and men don't like it."

"But d'you think he'll be satisfied with a man who's only just qualified? After all I have no experience."

"He ought to be glad to get you," said the secretary diplomatically.

Philip thought for a moment. He had nothing to do for the next few weeks, and he was glad of the chance to earn a bit of money. He could put it aside for the holiday in Spain which he had promised himself when he had finished his appointment at St. Luke's or, if they would not give him anything there, at some other hospital.

"All right. I'll go."

"The only thing is, you must go this afternoon. Will that suit you? If so, I'll send a wire at once."

Philip would have liked a few days to himself; but he had seen the Athelnys the night before (he had gone at once to take them his good news) and there was really no reason

why he should not start immediately. He had little luggage
to pack. Soon after seven that evening he got out of the
station at Farnley and took a cab to Doctor South's. It was
a broad low stucco house, with a Virginia creeper growing
over it. He was shown into the consulting-room. An old
man was writing at a desk. He looked up as the maid ush-
ered Philip in. He did not get up, and he did not speak; he
merely stared at Philip. Philip was taken aback.

"I think you're expecting me," he said. "The secretary of
St. Luke's wired to you this morning."

"I kept dinner back for half an hour. D'you want to
wash?"

"I do," said Philip.

Doctor South amused him by his odd manner. He got up
now, and Philip saw that he was a man of middle height,
thin, with white hair cut very short and a long mouth
closed so tightly that he seemed to have no lips at all; he
was clean-shaven but for small white whiskers, and they
increased the squareness of face which his firm jaw gave
him. He wore a brown tweed suit and a white stock. His
clothes hung loosely about him as though they had been
made for a much larger man. He looked like a respectable
farmer of the middle of the nineteenth century. He opened
the door.

"There is the dining-room," he said, pointing to the door
opposite. "Your bed-room is the first door you come to
when you get on the landing. Come downstairs when
you're ready."

During dinner Philip knew that Doctor South was exam-
ining him, but he spoke little, and Philip felt that he did
not want to hear his assistant talk.

"When were you qualified?" he asked suddenly.

"Yesterday."

"Were you at a university?"

"No."

"Last year when my assistant took a holiday they sent

me a 'Varsity man. I told 'em not to do it again. Too damned gentlemanly for me."

There was another pause. The dinner was very simple and very good. Philip preserved a sedate exterior, but in his heart he was bubbling over with excitement. He was immensely elated at being engaged as a locum; it made him feel extremely grown up; he had an insane desire to laugh at nothing in particular; and the more he thought of his professional dignity the more he was inclined to chuckle.

But Doctor South broke suddenly into his thoughts.

"How old are you?"

"Getting on for thirty."

"How is it you're only just qualified?"

"I didn't go in for the medical till I was nearly twenty-three, and I had to give it up for two years in the middle."

"Why?"

"Poverty."

Doctor South gave him an odd look and relapsed into silence. At the end of dinner he got up from the table.

"D'you know what sort of a practice this is?"

"No," answered Philip.

"Mostly fishermen and their families. I have the Union and the Seamen's Hospital. I used to be alone here, but since they tried to make this into a fashionable sea-side resort a man has set up on the cliff, and the well-to-do people go to him. I only have those who can't afford to pay for a doctor at all."

Philip saw that the rivalry was a sore point with the old man.

"You know that I have no experience," said Philip.

"You none of you know anything."

For two or three days Doctor South watched Philip closely, ready to fall on him with acid sarcasm if he gave him the opportunity; and Philip, aware of this, went about his work with a quiet sense of amusement. He was pleased with the change of occupation. He liked the feeling of independence and of responsibility. All sorts of people came to the consulting-room. He was gratified because he seemed able to inspire his patients with confidence; and it was entertaining to watch the process of cure which at a hospital necessarily could be watched only at distant intervals. His rounds took him into low-roofed cottages in which were fishing tackle and sails and here and there mementoes of deep-sea travelling, a lacquer box from Japan, spears and oars from Melanesia, or daggers from the bazaars of Stamboul; there was an air of romance in the stuffy little rooms, and the salt of the sea gave them a bitter freshness. Philip liked to talk to the sailor-men, and when they found that he was not supercilious they told him long yarns of the distant journeys of their youth.

Once or twice he made a mistake in diagnosis: (he had never seen a case of measles before, and when he was confronted with the rash took it for an obscure disease of the skin;) and once or twice his ideas of treatment differed from Doctor South's. The first time this happened Doctor South attacked him with savage irony; but Philip took it with good humour; he had some gift for repartee, and he made one or two answers which caused Doctor South to stop and look at him curiously. Philip's face was grave, but his eyes were twinkling. The old gentleman could not avoid the impression that Philip was chaffing him. He was used to being disliked and feared by his assistants, and this was a new experience. He had half a mind to fly into a passion and pack Philip off by the next train, he had done that before with his assistants; but he had an uneasy feeling that Philip then would simply laugh at him outright; and suddenly he felt amused. His mouth formed itself into a smile against his will, and he turned away. In a little while he grew conscious that Philip was amusing himself systematically at his expense. He was taken aback at first and then diverted.

"Damn his impudence," he chucked to himself. "Damn his impudence."

Philip had written to Athelny to tell him that he was doing a locum in Dorsetshire and in due course received an answer from him. It was written in the formal manner he affected, studded with pompous epithets as a Persian diadem was studded with precious stones; and in the beautiful hand, like black letter and as difficult to read, upon which he prided himself. He suggested that Philip should join him and his family in the Kentish hop-field to which he went every year; and to persuade him said various beautiful and complicated things about Philip's soul and the winding tendrils of the hops. Philip replied at once that he would come on the first day he was free.

The four weeks of his engagement at Farnley passed quickly.

One evening, when Philip had reached his last week with Doctor South, a child came to the surgery door while the old doctor and Philip were making up prescriptions. It was a little ragged girl with a dirty face and bare feet. Philip opened the door.

"Please, sir, will you come to Mrs. Fletcher's in Ivy Lane at once?"

"What's the matter with Mrs. Fletcher?" called out Doctor South in his rasping voice.

The child took no notice of him, but addressed herself again to Philip.

"Please, sir, her little boy's had an accident and will you come at once?"

"Tell Mrs. Fletcher I'm coming," called out Doctor South.

The little girl hesitated for a moment, and putting a dirty finger in a dirty mouth stood still and looked at Philip.

"What's the matter, Kid?" said Philip, smiling.

"Please, sir, Mrs. Fletcher says, will the new doctor come?"

There was a sound in the dispensary and Doctor South came out into the passage.

"Isn't Mrs. Fletcher satisfied with me?" he barked. "I've

attended Mrs. Fletcher since she was born. Why aren't I good enough to attend her filthy brat?"

The little girl looked for a moment as though she were going to cry, then she thought better of it; she put out her tongue deliberately at Doctor South, and, before he could recover from his astonishment, bolted off as fast as she could run. Philip saw that the old gentleman was annoyed.

"You look rather fagged, and it's a goodish way to Ivy Lane," he said, by way of giving him an excuse not to go himself.

Doctor South gave a low snarl.

"It's a damned sight nearer for a man who's got the use of both legs than for a man who's only got one and a half."

Philip reddened and stood silent for a while.

"Do you wish me to go or will you go yourself?" he said at last frigidly.

"What's the good of my going? They want you."

Philip took up his hat and went to see the patient. It was hard upon eight o'clock when he came back. Doctor South was standing in the dining-room with his back to the fire-place.

"You've been a long time," he said.

"I'm sorry. Why didn't you start dinner?"

"Because I chose to wait. Have you been all this while at Mrs. Fletcher's?"

"No, I'm afraid I haven't. I stopped to look at the sunset on my way back, and I didn't think of the time."

Doctor South did not reply, and the servant brought in some grilled sprats. Philip ate them with an excellent appetite. Suddenly Doctor South shot a question at him.

"Why did you look at the sunset?"

Philip answered with his mouth full.

"Because I was happy."

Doctor South gave him an odd look, and the shadow of a smile flickered across his old, tired face. They ate the rest of the dinner in silence; but when the maid had given them the port and left the room, the old man leaned back and fixed his sharp eyes on Philip.

"It stung you up a bit when I spoke of your game leg, young fellow?" he said.

"People always do, directly or indirectly, when they get angry with me."

"I suppose they know it's your weak point."

Philip faced him and looked at him steadily.

"Are you very glad to have discovered it?"

The doctor did not answer, but he gave a chuckle of bitter mirth. They sat for a while staring at one another. Then Doctor South surprised Philip extremely.

"Why don't you stay here and I'll get rid of that damned fool with his mumps?"

"It's very kind of you, but I hope to get an appointment at the hospital in the autumn. It'll help me so much in getting other work later."

"I'm offering you a partnership," said Doctor South grumpily.

"Why?" asked Philip, with surprise.

"They seem to like you down here."

"I didn't think that was a fact which altogether met with your approval," Philip said drily.

"D'you suppose that after forty years' practice I care a two-penny damn whether people prefer my assistant to me? No, my friend. There's no sentiment between my patients and me. I don't expect gratitude from them, I expect them to pay my fees. Well, what d'you say to it?"

Philip made no reply, not because he was thinking over the proposal, but because he was astonished. It was evidently very unusual for someone to offer a partnership to a newly qualified man; and he realised with wonder that, although nothing would induce him to say so, Doctor South had taken a fancy to him. He thought how amused the secretary at St. Luke's would be when he told him.

"The practice brings in about seven hundred a year. We

can reckon out how much your share would be worth, and
you can pay me off by degrees. And when I die you can
succeed me. I think that's better than knocking about hospitals for two or three years, and then taking assistantships until you can afford to set up for yourself."

Philip knew it was a chance that most people in his profession would jump at; the profession was over-crowded,
and half the men he knew would be thankful to accept the
certainty of even so modest a competence as that.

"I'm awfully sorry, but I can't," he said. "It means giving
up everything I've aimed at for years. In one way and another I've had a roughish time, but I always had that one
hope before me, to get qualified so that I might travel; and
now, when I wake in the morning, my bones simply ache
to get off, I don't mind where particularly, but just away,
to places I've never been to."

Now the goal seemed very near. He would have finished his appointment at St. Luke's by the middle of the
following year, and then he would go to Spain; he could
afford to spend several months there, rambling up and down
the land which stood to him for romance; after that he
would get a ship and go to the East. Life was before him
and time of no account. He could wander, for years if he
chose, in unfrequented places, amid strange peoples, where
life was led in strange ways. He did not know what he
sought or what his journeys would bring him; but he had
a feeling that he would learn something new about life.
And even if he found nothing he would allay the unrest
which gnawed at his heart. But Doctor South was showing
him a great kindess, and it seemed ungrateful to refuse his
offer for no adequate reason; so in his shy way, trying to
appear as matter of fact as possible, he made some attempt
to explain why it was so important to him to carry out the
plans he had cherished so passionately.

Doctor South listened quietly, and a gentle look came into
his shrewd old eyes. It seemed to Philip an added kindness

that he did not press him to accept his offer. Benevolence is often very peremptory. He appeared to look upon Philip's reasons as sound. There was something in Philip that attracted him, and he found himself smiling at him he knew not why. Philip did not bore him. Once or twice he put his hand on his shoulder. When the time came for Philip to go Doctor South accompanied him to the station: he found himself unaccountably depressed.

"I've had a ripping time here," said Philip. "You've been awfully kind to me."

"I suppose you're very glad to go?"

"I've enjoyed myself here."

"But you want to get out into the world? Ah, you have youth." He hesitated a moment. "I want you to remember that if you change your mind my offer still stands."

"That's awfully kind of you."

Philip shook hands with him out of the carriage window, and the train steamed out of the station. Philip thought of the fortnight he was going to spend in the hop-field: he was happy at the idea of seeing his friends again, and he rejoiced because the day was fine. But Doctor South walked slowly back to his empty house. He felt very old and very lonely.

It was late in the evening when Philip arrived at Ferne. It was Mrs. Athelny's native village, and she had been accustomed from her childhood to pick in the hop-field to which with her husband and her children she still went every year. Like many Kentish folk her family had gone out regularly, glad to earn a little money, but especially regarding the annual outing, looked forward to for months, as the best of holidays. The work was not hard, it was done in common, in the open air, and for the children it was a long, delightful picnic. In the old days the hoppers slept in barns, but ten years ago a row of huts had been erected at the side of a meadow; and the Athelnys, like many others, had the same hut every year.

Athelny met Philip at the station in a cart he had borrowed from the public-house at which he had got a room for Philip. It was a quarter of a mile from the hop-field. They left his bag there and walked over to the meadow in which were the huts. They were nothing more than a long, low shed, divided into little rooms about twelve feet square. In front of each was a fire of sticks, round which a family was grouped, eagerly watching the cooking of supper. The sea-air and the sun had browned already the faces of Athelny's children. Mrs. Athelny seemed a different woman in her sun-bonnet: you felt that the long years in the city had made no real difference to her; she was the country woman born and bred, and you could see how much at home she found herself in the country. She was frying bacon and at the same time keeping an eye on the younger children, but she had a hearty handshake and a jolly smile for Philip. Athelny was enthusiastic over the delights of a rural existence.

"Come and eat your supper, children," said Mrs. Athelny. "Where's Sally?"

"Here I am, mother."

She stepped out of their little hut, and the flames of the wood fire leaped up and cast sharp colour upon her face. Of late Philip had only seen her in the trim frocks she had taken to since she was at the dressmaker's, and there was something very charming in the print dress she wore now, loose and easy to work in; the sleeves were tucked up and showed her strong, round arms. She too had a sun-bonnet.

"You look like a milkmaid in a fairy story," said Philip, as he shook hands with her.

Sally sat in silence, but she attended to Philip's wants in a thoughtful fashion that charmed him. It was pleasant to have her beside him, and now and then he glanced at her sunburned, healthy face. Once he caught her eyes, and she smiled quietly.

Before he went Mrs. Athelny said to him:

"We breakfast about a quarter to six, but I daresay you won't want to get up as early as that. You see, we have to set to work at six."

"Of course he must get up early," cried Athelny, "and he must work like the rest of us. He's got to earn his board. No work, no dinner, my lad."

"The children go down to bathe before breakfast, and they can give you a call on their way back. They pass The Jolly Sailor."

"If they'll wake me I'll come and bathe with them," said Philip.

Jane and Harold and Edward shouted with delight at the prospect, and next morning Philip was awakened out of a sound sleep by their bursting into his room. The boys jumped on his bed, and he had to chase them out with his slippers. He put on a coat and a pair of trousers and went down. The day had only just broken, and there was a nip in the air; but the sky was cloudless, and the sun was shining yellow. Sally, holding Connie's hand, was standing in the middle of the road, with a towel and a bathing-dress over her arm. He saw now that her sun-bonnet was of the colour of lavender, and against it her face, red and brown, was like an apple. She greeted him with her slow, sweet smile, and he noticed suddenly that her teeth were small and regular and very white. He wondered why they had never caught his attention before.

"I was for letting you sleep on," she said, "but they would go up and wake you. I said you didn't really want to come."

"Oh, yes, I did."

They walked down the road and then cut across the marshes. That way it was under a mile to the sea. The water looked cold and gray, and Philip shivered at the sight of it; but the others tore off their clothes and ran in shouting. Sally did everything a little slowly, and she did not come into the water till all the rest were splashing round Philip. Swimming was his only accomplishment; he felt at home in the water; and soon he had them all imitating him as he played at being a porpoise, and a drowning man, and a fat lady afraid of wetting her hair. The bathe was uproarious, and it was necessary for Sally to be very severe to induce them all to come out.

"You're as bad as any of them," she said to Philip, in her grave, maternal way, which was at once comic and touching. "They're not anything like so naughty when you're not here."

They walked back, Sally with her bright hair streaming over one shoulder and her sun-bonnet in her hand, but when they got to the huts Mrs. Athelny had already started for the hop-garden. Athelny, in a pair of the oldest trousers anyone had ever worn, his jacket buttoned up to show he had no shirt on, and in a wide-brimmed soft hat, was frying kippers over a fire of sticks. He was delighted with himself: he looked every inch a brigand. As soon as he saw the party he began to shout the witches' chorus from *Macbeth* over the odorous kippers.

"You mustn't dawdle over your breakfast or mother will be angry," he said, when they came up.

And in a few minutes, Harold and Jane with pieces of bread and butter in their hands, they sauntered through the meadow into the hop-field. They were the last to leave. A hop-garden was one of the sights connected with Philip's boyhood and the oast-houses to him the most typical feature of the Kentish scene. It was with no sense of strangeness, but as though he were at home, that Philip followed Sally through the long lines of the hops. The sun was bright now and cast a sharp shadow. Philip feasted his eyes on the richness of the green leaves. The hops were yellowing, and to him they had the beauty and the passion which poets in Sicily have found in the purple grape. As they walked along

Philip felt himself overwhelmed by the rich luxuriance. A sweet scent arose from the fat Kentish soil, and the fitful September breeze was heavy with the goodly perfume of the hops.

Philip had not a basket of his own, but sat with Sally. Jane thought it monstrous that he should help her elder sister rather than herself, and he had to promise to pick for her when Sally's basket was full. Sally was almost as quick as her mother.

"Won't it hurt your hands for sewing?" asked Philip.

"Oh, no, it wants soft hands. That's why women pick better than men. If your hands are hard and your fingers all stiff with a lot of rough work you can't pick near so well."

He liked to see her deft movements, and she watched him too now and then with that maternal spirit of hers which was so amusing and yet so charming. He was clumsy at first, and she laughed at him. When she bent over and showed him how best to deal with a whole line their hands met. He was surprised to see her blush. He could not persuade himself that she was a woman; because he had known her as a flapper, he could not help looking upon her as a child still; yet the number of her admirers showed that she was a child no longer; and though they had only been down a few days one of Sally's cousins was already so attentive that she had to endure a lot of chaffing. His name was Peter Gann, and he was the son of Mrs. Athelny's sister, who had married a farmer near Ferne. Everyone knew why he found it necessary to walk through the hop-field every day.

Calling-off time depended on the state of the oast-house. Sometimes it was filled early, and as many hops had been picked by three or four as could be dried during the night. Then work was stopped. But generally the last measuring of the day began at five. As each company had its bin measured it gathered up its things and, chatting again now that work was over, sauntered out of the garden. The women went back to the huts to clean up and prepare the supper, while a good many of the men strolled down the road to the public-house. A glass of beer was very pleasant after the day's work.

"I expect you'll be ready for your bed," said Mrs. Athelny to Philip. "You're not used to getting up at five and staying in the open air all day."

"You're coming to bathe with us, Uncle Phil, aren't you?" the boys cried.

"Rather."

He was tired and happy. After supper, balancing himself against the wall of the hut on a chair without a back, he smoked his pipe and looked at the night. Sally was busy. She passed in and out of the hut, and he lazily watched her methodical actions. Her walk attracted his notice; it was not particularly graceful, but it was easy and assured; she swung her legs from the hips, and her feet seemed to tread the earth with decision. Athelny had gone off to gossip with one of the neighbours, and presently Philip heard his wife address the world in general.

"There now, I'm out of tea and I wanted Athelny to go down to Mrs. Black's and get some." A pause, and then her voice raised: "Sally, just run down to Mrs. Black's and get me half a pound of tea, will you? I've run quite out of it."

"All right, mother."

Mrs. Black had a cottage about half a mile along the road, and she combined the office of postmistress with that of universal provider. Sally came out of the hut, turning down her sleeves.

"Shall I come with you, Sally?" asked Philip.

"Don't you trouble. I'm not afraid to go alone."

"I didn't think you were; but it's getting near my bed-time, and I was just thinking I'd like to stretch my legs."

Sally did not answer, and they set out together. The road

was white and silent. There was not a sound in the summer night. They did not speak much.

"It's quite hot even now, isn't it?" said Philip.

"I think it's wonderful for the time of year."

But their silence did not seem awkward. They found it was pleasant to walk side by side and felt no need of words. Suddenly at a stile in the hedgerow they heard a low murmur of voices, and in the darkness they saw the outline of two people. They were sitting very close to one another and did not move as Philip and Sally passed.

"I wonder who that was," said Sally.

"They looked happy enough, didn't they?"

"I expect they took us for lovers too."

They saw the light of the cottage in front of them, and in a minute went into the little shop. The glare dazzled them for a moment.

"You are late," said Mrs. Black. "I was just going to shut up." She looked at the clock. "Getting on for nine."

Sally asked for her half pound of tea, (Mrs. Athelny could never bring herself to buy more than half a pound at a time,) and they set off up the road again. Now and then some beast of the night made a short, sharp sound, but it seemed only to make the silence more marked.

"I believe if you stood still you could hear the sea," said Sally.

They strained their ears, and their fancy presented them with a faint sound of little waves lapping up against the shingle. When they passed the stile again the lovers were still there, but now they were not speaking; they were in one another's arms, and the man's lips were pressed against the girl's.

"They seem busy," said Sally.

They turned a corner, and a breath of warm wind beat for a moment against their faces. The earth gave forth its freshness. There was something strange in the tremulous night, and something, you knew not what, seemed to be waiting; the silence was on a sudden pregnant with meaning. Philip had a queer feeling in his heart, it seemed very full, it seemed to melt, (the hackneyed phrases expressed precisely the curious sensation,) he felt happy and anxious and expectant. To his memory came back those lines in which Jessica and Lorenzo murmur melodious words to one another, capping each other's utterance; but passion shines bright and clear through the conceits that amuse them. He did not know what there was in the air that made his senses so strangely alert; it seemed to him that he was pure soul to enjoy the scents and the sounds and the savours of the earth. He had never felt such an exquisite capacity for beauty. He was afraid that Sally by speaking would break the spell, but she said never a word, and he wanted to hear the sound of her voice. Its low richness was the voice of the country night itself.

They arrived at the field through which she had to walk to get back to the huts. Philip went in to hold the gate open for her.

"Well, here I think I'll say good-night."

"Thank you for coming all that way with me."

She gave him her hand, and as he took it, he said:

"If you were very nice you'd kiss me good-night like the rest of the family."

"I don't mind," she said.

Philip had spoken in jest. He merely wanted to kiss her, because he was happy and he liked her and the night was so lovely.

"Good-night then," he said, with a little laugh, drawing her towards him.

She gave him her lips; they were warm and full and soft; he lingered a little, they were like a flower; then, he knew not how, without meaning it, he flung his arms round her. She yielded quite silently. Her body was firm and strong. He felt her heart beat against his. Then he lost his head.

His senses overwhelmed him like a flood of rushing waters. He drew her into the darker shadow of the hedge.

Philip slept like a log and awoke with a start to find Harold tickling his face with a feather. There was a shout of delight when he opened his eyes. He was drunken with sleep.

"Come on, lazy bones," said Jane. "Sally says she won't wait for you unless you hurry up."

Then he remembered what had happened. His heart sank, and, half out of bed already, he stopped; he did not know how he was going to face her; he was overwhelmed with a sudden rush of self-reproach, and bitterly, bitterly, he regretted what he had done. What would she say to him that morning? He dreaded meeting her, and he asked himself how he could have been such a fool. But the children gave him no time; Edward took his bathing-drawers and his towel, Athelstan tore the bed-clothes away; and in three minutes they all clattered down into the road. Sally gave him a smile. It was as sweet and innocent as it had ever been.

"You do take a time to dress yourself," she said. "I thought you was never coming."

There was not a particle of difference in her manner. He had expected some change, subtle or abrupt; he fancied that there would be shame in the way she treated him, or anger, or perhaps some increase of familiarity; but there was nothing. She was exactly the same as before. They walked towards the sea all together, talking and laughing; and Sally was quiet, but she was always that, reserved, but he had never seen her otherwise, and gentle. She neither sought conversation with him nor avoided it. Philip was astounded. He had expected the incident of the night before to have caused some revolution in her, but it was just as though nothing had happened; it might have been a dream; and as he walked along, a little girl holding on to one hand and a little boy to the other, while he chatted as unconcernedly as he could, he sought for an explanation. He wondered whether Sally meant the affair to be forgotten. Perhaps her senses had run away with her just as his had, and, treating what had occurred as an accident due to unusual circumstances, it might be that she had decided to put the matter out of her mind. It was ascribing to her a power of thought and a mature wisdom which fitted neither with her age nor with her character. But he realised that he knew nothing of her. There had been in her always something enigmatic.

They played leap-frog in the water, and the bathe was as uproarious as on the previous day. Sally mothered them all, keeping a watchful eye on them, and calling to them when they went out too far. She swam staidly backwards and forwards while the others got up to their larks, and now and then turned on her back to float. Presently she went out and began drying herself; she called to the others more or less peremptorily, and at last only Philip was left in the water. He took the opportunity to have a good hard swim. He was more used to the cold water this second morning, and he revelled in its salt freshness; it rejoiced him to use his limbs freely, and he covered the water with long, firm strokes. But Sally, with a towel round her, went down to the water's edge.

"You're to come out this minute, Philip," she called, as though he were a small boy under her charge.

And when, smiling with amusement at her authoritative way, he came towards her, she upbraided him.

"It is naughty of you to stay in so long. Your lips are quite blue, and just look at your teeth, they're chattering."

"All right. I'll come out."

She had never talked to him in that manner before. It was as though what had happened gave her a sort of right over him, and she looked upon him as a child to be cared for. In a few minutes they were dressed, and they started to walk back. Sally noticed his hands.

"Just look, they're quite blue."

"Oh, that's all right. It's only the circulation. I shall get the blood back in a minute."

"Give them to me."

She took his hands in hers and rubbed them, first one and then the other, till the colour returned. Philip, touched and puzzled, watched her. He could not say anything to her on account of the children, and he did not meet her eyes; but he was sure they did not avoid his purposely, it just happened that they did not meet. And during the day there was nothing in her behaviour to suggest a consciousness in her that anything had passed between them. Perhaps she was a little more talkative than usual. When they were all sitting again in the hop-field she told her mother how naughty Philip had been in not coming out of the water till he was blue with cold. It was incredible, and yet it seemed that the only effect of the incident of the night before was to arouse in her a feeling of protection towards him: she had the same instinctive desire to mother him as she had with regard to her brothers and sisters.

It was not till the evening that he found himself alone with her. She was cooking the supper, and Philip was sitting on the grass by the side of the fire. Mrs. Athelny had gone down to the village to do some shopping, and the children were scattered in various pursuits of their own. Philip hesitated to speak. He was very nervous. Sally attended to her business with serene competence and she accepted placidly the silence which to him was so embarrassing. He did not know how to begin. Sally seldom spoke unless she was spoken to or had something particular to say. At last he could not bear it any longer.

"You're not angry with me, Sally?" he blurted out suddenly.

She raised her eyes quietly and looked at him without emotion. "Me? No. Why should I be?"

He was taken aback and did not reply. She took the lid off the pot, stirred the contents, and put it on again. A savoury smell spread over the air. She looked at him once more, with a quiet smile which barely separated her lips; it was more a smile of the eyes.

"I always liked you," she said.

His heart gave a great thump against his ribs, and he felt the blood rushing to his cheeks. He forced a faint laugh.

"I didn't know that."

"That's because you're a silly."

"I don't know why you liked me."

"I don't either." She put a little more wood on the fire. "I knew I liked you that day you came when you'd been sleeping out and hadn't had anything to eat, d'you remember? And me and mother, we got Thorpy's bed ready for you."

He flushed again, for he did not know that she was aware of that incident. He remembered it himself with horror and shame.

"That's why I wouldn't have anything to do with the others. You remember that young fellow mother wanted me to have? I let him come to tea because he bothered so, but I knew I'd say no."

Philip was so surprised that he found nothing to say. There was a queer feeling in his heart; he did not know what it was, unless it was happiness. Sally stirred the pot once more.

"I wish those children would make haste and come. I don't know where they've got to. Supper's ready now."

"Shall I go and see if I can find them?" said Philip.

It was a relief to talk about practical things.

"Well, it wouldn't be a bad idea, I must say. . . . There's mother coming." Then, as he got up, she looked at him without embarrassment.

"Shall I come for a walk with you tonight when I've put the children to bed?"

"Yes."

"Well, you wait for me down by the stile, and I'll come when I'm ready."

He waited under the stars, sitting on the stile, and the hedges with their ripening blackberries were high on each side of him. From the earth rose rich scents of the night, and the air was soft and still. His heart was beating madly. He could not understand anything of what happened to him. He associated passion with cries and tears and vehemence, and there was nothing of this in Sally; but he did not know what else but passion could have caused her to give herself. But passion for him? He would not have been surprised if she had fallen to her cousin, Peter Gann, tall, spare, and straight, with his sunburned face and long, easy stride. Philip wondered what she saw in him. He did not know if she loved him as he reckoned love. And yet? He was convinced of her purity. He had a vague inkling that many things had combined, things that she felt though was unconscious of, the intoxication of the air and the hops and the night, the healthy instincts of the natural woman, a tenderness that overflowed, and an affection that had in it something maternal and something sisterly; and she gave all she had to give because her heart was full of charity.

He heard a step on the road, and a figure came out of the darkness. "Sally," he murmured.

She stopped and came to the stile, and with her came sweet, clean odours of the country-side. She seemed to carry with her scents of the new-mown hay, and the savour of ripe hops, and the freshness of young grass. Her lips were soft and full against his, and her lovely, strong body was firm within his arms.

"Milk and honey," he said. "You're like milk and honey."

He made her close her eyes and kissed her eyelids, first one and then the other. Her arm, strong and muscular, was bare to the elbow; he passed his hand over it and wondered at its beauty; it gleamed in the darkness; she had the skin that Rubens painted, astonishingly fair and transparent, and on one side were little golden hairs. It was the arm of a Saxon goddess; but no immortal had that exquisite, homely naturalness; and Philip thought of a cottage garden with the dear flowers which bloom in all men's hearts, of the hollyhock and the red and white rose which is called York and Lancaster, and of love-in-a-mist and Sweet William, and honeysuckle, larkspur, and London Pride.

"How can you care for me?" he said. "I'm insignificant and crippled and ordinary and ugly."

She took his face in both her hands and kissed his lips.

"You're an old silly, that's what you are," she said.

When the hops were picked, Philip with the news in his pocket that he had got the appointment as assistant housephysician at St. Luke's, accompanied the Athelnys back to London. He took modest rooms in Westminster and at the beginning of October entered upon his duties. The work was interesting and varied; every day he learned something new; he felt himself of some consequence; and he saw a good deal of Sally. He found life uncommonly pleasant. He was free about six, except on the days on which he had outpatients, and then he went to the shop at which Sally worked to meet her when she came out. There were several young men, who hung about opposite the "trade entrance" or a little further along, at the first corner; and the girls, coming out two and two or in little groups, nudged one another and giggled as they recognised them. Sally in her plain black dress looked very different from the country lass who had picked hops side by side with him. She walked away from the shop quickly, but she slackened her pace when they met, and greeted him with her quiet smile. They walked together through the busy street. He talked to her of his work at the hospital, and she told him what she had been doing in the shop that day. He came to know the names of the girls she worked with. He found that Sally had a restrained, but keen, sense of the ridiculous, and she made remarks about the girls or the men who were set over them which amused him by their unexpected drollery. She had a way of saying a thing which was very characteristic, quite gravely, as though there were nothing funny in it at all, and yet it was so sharp-sighted that Philip broke into delighted laughter. Then she would give him a little glance in which the smiling eyes showed she was not unaware of her own humour. They met with a handshake and parted as formally. Once Philip asked her to come and have tea with him in his rooms, but she refused.

"No, I won't do that. It would look funny."

Never a word of love passed between them. She seemed not to desire anything more than the companionship of those walks. Yet Philip was positive that she was glad to be with him. She puzzled him as much as she had done at the beginning. He did not begin to understand her conduct; but the more he knew her the fonder he grew of her; she was competent and self-controlled, and there was a charming honesty in her: you felt that you could rely upon her in every circumstance.

"You are an awfully good sort," he said to her once à propos of nothing at all.

"I expect I'm just the same as everyone else," she answered.

He knew that he did not love her. It was a great affection that he felt for her, and he liked her company; it was curiously soothing; and he had a feeling for her which seemed to him ridiculous to entertain towards a shop-girl of nineteen: he respected her. And he admired her magnificent healthiness. She was a splendid animal, without defect; and physical perfection filled him always with admiring awe. She made him feel unworthy.

Then, one day, about three weeks after they had come back to London as they walked together, he noticed that she was unusually silent. The serenity of her expression was altered by a slight line between the eyebrows: it was the beginning of a frown. "What's the matter, Sally?" he asked. She did not look at him, but straight in front of her, and her colour darkened. "I don't know."

He understood at once what she meant. His heart gave a sudden, quick beat, and he felt the colour leave his cheeks.

"What d'you mean? Are you afraid that. . . ?"

He stopped. He could not go on. The possibility that anything of the sort could happen had never crossed his mind. Then he saw that her lips were trembling, and she was trying not to cry.

"I'm not certain yet. Perhaps it'll be all right."

They walked on in silence till they came to the corner of Chancery Lane, where he always left her. She held out her hand and smiled.

"Don't worry about it yet. Let's hope for the best."

He walked away with a tumult of thoughts in his head. What a fool he had been! That was the first thing that struck him, an abject, miserable fool, and he repeated it to himself a dozen times in a rush of angry feeling. He despised himself. How could he have got into such a mess? But at the same time, for his thoughts chased one another through his brain and yet seemed to stand together, in a hopeless confusion, like the pieces of a jig-saw puzzle seen in a nightmare, he asked himself what he was going to do. Everything was so clear before him, all he had aimed at so long within reach at last, and now his inconceivable stupidity had erected this new obstacle. Philip had never been able to surmount what he acknowledged was a defect in his resolute desire for a well-ordered life, and that was his passion for living in the future; and no sooner was he settled in his work at the hospital than he had busied himself with arrangements for his travels. In the past he had often tried not to think too circumstantially of his plans for the future, it was only discouraging; but now that his goal was so near he saw no harm in giving away to a longing that was so difficult to resist. First of all he meant to go to Spain. That was the land of his heart; and by now he was imbued with its spirit, its romance and colour and history and grandeur; he felt that it had a message for him in particular which no other country could give. He knew the fine old cities already as though he had trodden their tortuous streets from childhood. Cordova, Seville, Toledo, Leon, Tarragona, Burgos. The great painters of Spain were the painters of his soul, and his pulse beat quickly as he pictured his ecstasy on standing face to face with those works which were more significant than any others to his own tortured, restless heart. He had read the great poets, more characteristic of their race than the poets of other lands; for they seemed to have drawn their inspiration not at all from the general currents of the world's literature but directly from the torrid, scented plains and the bleak mountains of their country. A few short months now, and he would hear with his own ears all around him the language which seemed most apt for grandeur of soul and passion. His fine taste had given him an inkling that Andalusia was too soft and sensuous, a little vulgar even, to satisfy his ardour; and his imagination dwelt more willingly among the wind-swept distances of Castile and the rugged magnificence of Aragon and Leon. He did not know quite what those unknown contacts would give him, but he felt that he would gather from them a strength and a purpose which would make him more capable of affronting and comprehending the manifold wonders of places more distant and more strange.

For this was only a beginning. He had got into communication with the various companies which took surgeons out on their ships, and knew exactly what were their routes, and from men who had been on them what were the advantages and disadvantages of each line. He put aside the Orient and the P. & O. It was difficult to get a berth with them; and besides their passenger traffic allowed the medical officer little freedom; but there were other services which sent large tramps on leisurely expeditions to the East, stopping at all sorts of ports for various periods, from a day or two to a fortnight, so that you had plenty of time, and it was often possible to make a trip inland. The pay was poor and the food no more than adequate, so that there was not much demand for the posts, and a man with a London degree was pretty sure to get one if he applied. Since there were no passengers other than a casual man or so, shipping on business from some out-of-the-way port to another, the life on board was friendly and pleasant. Philip knew by heart the list of places at which they touched; and each one called up in him visions of tropical sunshine, and magic colour, and of a teeming, mysterious, intense life. Life! That was what he wanted. At last he would come to close quarters with life. And perhaps, from Tokio or Shanghai it would be possible to tranship into some other line and drift down to the islands of the South Pacific. A doctor was useful anywhere. There might be an opportunity to go up country in Burmah, and what rich jungles in Sumatra or Borneo might he not visit? He was young still and time was no object to him. He had no ties in England, no friends; he could go up and down the world for years, learning the beauty and the wonder and the variedness of life.

Now this thing had come. He put aside the possibility that Sally was mistaken; he felt strangely certain that she was right; after all, it was so likely; anyone could see that Nature had built her to be the mother of children. He knew what he ought to do. He ought not to let the incident divert him a hair's breadth from his path. He thought of Griffiths; he could easily imagine with what indifference that young man would have received such a piece of news; he would have thought it an awful nuisance and would at once have taken to his heels, like a wise fellow; he would have left the girl to deal with her troubles as best she could. Philip told himself that if this had happened it was because it was inevitable. He was no more to blame than Sally; she was a girl who knew the world and the facts of life, and she had taken the risk with her eyes open. It would be madness to allow such an accident to disturb the whole pattern of his life. He was one of the few people who was acutely conscious of the transitoriness of life, and how necessary it was to make the most of it. He would do what he could for Sally; he could afford to give her a sufficient sum of money. A strong man would never allow himself to be turned from his purpose.

Philip said all this to himself, but he knew he could not do it. He simply could not. He knew himself.

"I'm so damned weak," he muttered despairingly.

She had trusted him and been kind to him. He simply could not do a thing which, notwithstanding all his reason, he felt was horrible. He knew he would have no peace on his travels if he had the thought constantly with him that she was wretched. Besides, there were her father and mother: they had always treated him well; it was not possible to repay them with ingratitude. The only thing was to marry Sally as quickly as possible. He would write to Doctor South, tell him he was going to be married at once, and say that if his offer still held he was willing to accept it. That sort of practice, among poor people, was the only one possible for him; there his deformity did not matter, and they would not sneer at the simple manners of his wife. It was curious to think of her as his wife, it gave him a queer, soft feeling; and a wave of emotion spread over him as he thought of the child which was his. He had little doubt that Doctor South would be glad to have him, and he pictured to himself the life he would lead with Sally in the fishing village. They would have a little house within sight of the sea, and he would watch the mighty ships passing to the lands he would never know. Perhaps that was the wisest thing.

His wedding present to his wife would be all his high hopes. Self-sacrifice! Philip was uplifted by its beauty, and all through the evening he thought of it. He was so excited that he could not read. He seemed to be driven out of his rooms into the streets, and he walked up and down Birdcage Walk, his heart throbbing with joy. He could hardly bear his impatience. He wanted to see Sally's happiness when he made her his offer, and if it had not been so late he would have gone to her there and then. He pictured to himself the long evenings he would spend with Sally in the cosy sitting-room, the blinds undrawn so that they could watch the sea; he with his books, while she bent over her work, and the shaded lamp made her sweet face more fair. They would talk over the growing child, and when she turned her eyes to his there was in them the light of love. And the fishermen and their wives who were his patients would come to feel a great affection for them, and they in their turn would enter into the pleasures and pains of those simple lives. But his thoughts returned to the son who would be his and hers. Already he felt in himself a passionate devotion to it. He thought of passing his hands over his little perfect limbs, he knew he would be beautiful; and he would make over to him all his dreams of a rich and varied life.

He had arranged to meet Sally on Saturday in the National Gallery. She was to come there as soon as she was released from the shop and had agreed to lunch with him. Two days had passed since he had seen her, and his exultation had not left him for a moment. It was because he rejoiced in the feeling that he had not attempted to see her. He had repeated to himself exactly what he would say to her and how he should say it. Now his impatience was unbearable. He had written to Doctor South and had in his pocket a telegram from him received that morning: *"Sacking the mumpish fool. When will you come?"*

He thought of Sally, with her kind blue eyes; and his lips unconsciously formed themselves into a smile. He walked up the steps of the National Gallery and sat down in the first room, so that he should see her the moment she came in. It always comforted him to get among pictures. He looked at none in particular, but allowed the magnificence of their colour, the beauty of their lines, to work upon his soul. His imagination was busy with Sally. It would be pleasant to take her away from that London in which she seemed an unusual figure, like a cornflower in a shop among orchids and azaleas; he had learned in the Kentish hop-field that she did not belong to the town; and he was sure that she would blossom under the soft skies of Dorset to a rarer beauty. She came in, and he got up to meet her. She was in black, with white cuffs at her wrists and a lawn collar round her neck. They shook hands.

"Have you been waiting long?"

"No. Ten minutes. Are you hungry?"

"Not very."

"Let's sit here for a bit, shall we?"

"If you like."

They sat quietly, side by side, without speaking. Philip enjoyed having her near him. He was warmed by her radiant health. A glow of life seemed like an aureole to shine about her.

"Well, how have you been?" he said at last, with a little smile.

"Oh, it's all right. It was a false alarm."

"Was it?"

"Aren't you glad?"

An extraordinary sensation filled him. He had felt certain that Sally's suspicion was well-founded; it had never occurred to him for an instant that there was a possibility of error. All his plans were suddenly overthrown, and the existence, so elaborately pictured, was no more than a dream which would never be realised. He was free once more. Free! He need give up none of his projects, and life still was in his hands for him to do what he liked with. He felt no exhilaration, but only dismay. His heart sank. The future stretched out before him in desolate emptiness. It was as though he had sailed for many years over a great waste of waters, with peril and privation, and at last had come upon a fair haven, but as he was about to enter, some contrary wind had arisen and drove him out again into the open sea; and because he had let his mind dwell on these soft meads and pleasant woods of the land, the vast deserts of the ocean filled him with anguish. He could not confront again the loneliness and the tempest. Sally looked at him with her clear eyes.

"Aren't you glad?" she asked again. "I thought you'd be as pleased as Punch."

He met her gaze haggardly. "I'm not sure," he muttered.

"You are funny. Most men would."

He realised that he had deceived himself; it was no self-sacrifice that had driven him to think of marrying, but the desire for a wife and a home and love; and now that it all seemed to slip through his fingers he was seized with despair. He wanted all that more than anything in the world. What did he care for Spain and its cities, Cordova, Toledo, Leon; what to him were the pagodas of Burmah and the lagoons of South Sea Islands? America was here and now. It seemed to him that all his life he had followed the ideals that other people, by their words or their writings, had instilled into him, and never the desires of his own heart. Always his course had been swayed by what he thought he should do and never by what he wanted with his whole soul to do. He put all that aside now with a gesture of impatience. He had lived always in the future, and the present always, always had slipped through his fingers. His ideals? He thought of his desire to make a design, intricate and beautiful, out of the myriad, meaningless facts of life: had he not seen also that the simplest pattern, that in which a man was born, worked, married, had children, and died, was likewise the most perfect? It might be that to surrender to happiness was to accept defeat, but it was a defeat better than many victories. He glanced quickly at Sally, he wondered what she was thinking, and then looked away again.

"I was going to ask you to marry me," he said.

"I thought p'raps you might, but I shouldn't have liked to stand in your way."

"You wouldn't have done that."

"How about your travels, Spain and all that?"

"How d'you know I want to travel?"

"I ought to know something about it. I've heard you and Dad talk about it till you were blue in the face."

"I don't care a damn about all that." He paused for an instant and then spoke in a low, hoarse whisper. "I don't want to leave you! I can't leave you."

She did not answer. He could not tell what she thought.

"I wonder if you'll marry me, Sally."

She did not move and there was no flicker of emotion on her face, but she did not look at him when she answered.

"If you like."

"Don't you want to?"

"Oh, of course I'd like to have a house of my own, and it's about time I was settling down."

He smiled a little. He knew her pretty well by now, and her manner did not surprise him.

"But don't you want to marry *me*?"

"There's no one else I would marry."

"Then that settles it."

"Mother and Dad will be surprised, won't they?"

"I'm so happy."

"I want my lunch," she said.

"Dear!"

He smiled and took her hand and pressed it. They got up and walked out of the gallery. They stood for a moment at the balustrade and looked at Trafalgar Square. Cabs and omnibuses hurried to and fro, and crowds passed, hastening in every direction, and the sun was shining.

THESE SYMBOLS GUARANTEE
THE BEST IN READING

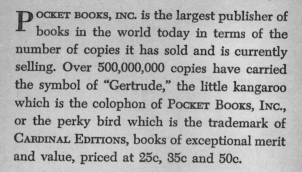

POCKET BOOKS, INC. is the largest publisher of books in the world today in terms of the number of copies it has sold and is currently selling. Over 500,000,000 copies have carried the symbol of "Gertrude," the little kangaroo which is the colophon of POCKET BOOKS, INC., or the perky bird which is the trademark of CARDINAL EDITIONS, books of exceptional merit and value, priced at 25c, 35c and 50c.

Only genuine POCKET BOOK and CARDINAL editions carry these symbols. The titles are carefully chosen from the lists of all leading publishers and present the most distinguished and most widely diversified group offered today by any publisher of paper-bound books. Watch for these symbols. They are your guarantee of the best in reading at the lowest possible price.